He's taking their first date to new heights. . . .

"Do you want to fly her?" Finn asked.

She did, desperately. She hadn't flown a plane since her last stint in an F-14. But that wasn't the role she was playing. She shook her head. "I better not," she said. "I wouldn't know what to do."

"Nothing to it. It's dual control. Your control stick is attached to mine, and I won't let you do anything that would scare me."

"Well, with an offer like that, how could I say no?"

She started to take control, then remembered that she was supposed to be clueless. "Um, so what do I do?"

"Just take a hold of the stick," he said. "I know you can handle that."

She grinned. "Right you are."

"You want her to respond to the lightest of touch. Don't force it. Just take it gentle."

"We're still talking about flying, right?"

"For now," he said. "But hold that thought."

Praise for bestselling author
Julie Kenner
and
NOBODY BUT YOU

More praise for Julie Kenner!

"Julie Kenner does it again! Hilarious and amazing . . . Excellent reading!"

—*Romantic Times*

"Funny, witty, and unbelievably erotic."

—*Affaire de Coeur*

"Julie Kenner's books [are] an autobuy for me."

—All About Romance

"Marvelous antics and sparkling dialogue."

—Cindy Penn, WordWeaving

"Just plain wonderful, a non-stop roller-coaster ride full of humor, emotion, action, and endearing characters."

—Lauren Michaels, Heart Rate Reviews

"Julie Kenner's imagination is to be applauded."

—Road to Romance

"Deserves a place on any keeper's shelf."

—WordWeaving

Also by Julie Kenner

NOBODY BUT YOU

Available from Pocket Books

The Spy Who Loves Me

JULIE KENNER

POCKET BOOKS
New York   London   Toronto   Sydney

This book is a work of fiction. Names, characters, places and incidents are products of the author's imagination or are used fictitiously. Any resemblance to actual events or locales or persons, living or dead, is entirely coincidental.

An *Original* Publication of POCKET BOOKS

POCKET BOOKS, a division of Simon & Schuster, Inc.
1230 Avenue of the Americas, New York, NY 10020

Copyright © 2004 by Julie Kenner

ISBN: 0-7434-4605-4

First Pocket Books printing June 2004

10   9   8   7   6   5   4   3   2   1

POCKET and colophon are registered trademarks of Simon & Schuster, Inc.

Cover design by Anna Dorfman
Illustration by Jane Hallman
Interior book design by Davina Mock

Manufactured in the United States of America

For information regarding special discounts for bulk purchases, please contact Simon & Schuster Special Sales at 1-800-456-6798 or business@simonandschuster.com.

Acknowledgments

Once again, the Internet has proven to be my friend. It's truly amazing what you can find out there in cyberspace (and just a little scary). More tangibly, I'd like to acknowledge the invaluable assistance of Ken Pruitt, for sharing his knowledge of helicopters, and Kate and Tom at Barnstorming Adventures Ltd., who so graciously provided me with information not only on the physical details of biplanes but on the joy that comes with flying in one. The help was much appreciated, and any errors or omissions are purely my own.

To some of the adventurous men I've known over the years: My dad, for actually letting me "fly" the plane at the ripe old age of ten; Rick Sullivan, who has had some amazing adventures lately; David Cohen, for sharing adventures in screenwriting (when *are* we going to sell that screenplay?); Steve Carver, for a lifetime of adventures; Sam Bernstein, for an assortment of memories and adventures in both New York and Los Angeles; and, of course, to Don, for all the adventures, including parenting—the biggest adventure of all.

Prologue

The tiny lightbulbs on the console winked, flickering like starlight in the dimly lit room. Drake allowed himself a tiny smile as the children's tune danced through his mind—*"When you wish upon a star..."*

He'd wished all right. Wished and planned and plotted. Over two years of tracking down information, making alliances, paying off informants. All to ensure that his plan was absolutely foolproof. And soon it would all be over.

He paced in front of the console, his fingers folding the paper without conscious thought. Instead, all his attention was riveted to this one moment. A pivotal, almost sad moment. In fact, all that stood between him and a full-fledged bout of melancholy was the promise of revenge and several billion dollars wired to his Swiss bank account.

Oh, yes. Revenge was sweet. Even more so when it was profitable.

Diana moved closer, and he looked at his hands, realizing he'd crafted a swan. He gently placed it on the top of the console between the origami dragon and the nautilus shell, then he slid his arm around Diana's waist and nuzzled her hair.

"Are we ready for a test run?" she asked, regarding him over the tortoiseshell glasses she wore when she worked. Right now, she was the consummate professional, her perfect body clad in a tailored suit he'd purchased for her during their last trip to Milan. The woman had a Ph.D. in nuclear physics and a libido to match his own. No wonder he loved her.

"We are," he said, squeezing her hand. "What's our target?"

She turned to face him, one eyebrow raised. "You don't have something already picked out?"

He stroked her cheek. "Don't be silly, my sweet. This moment is as much yours as mine."

She kissed his fingertips, then turned back to the console, her face full of concentration.

He stayed silent, even though a dozen perfect test locations filled his head, any one of them satisfying in both impact and simplicity. No, he would wait and have the satisfaction of having picked the final demonstration target. *That* was a moment worth savoring. His very own big bang, all packaged up with a nice pretty bow and ready to cajole the highest bidder.

Dollar signs flashed in his eyes, and he pictured Diana in diamonds and silks, lounging on a yacht anchored off Bali. He wondered just how many billions he needed to keep them in style.

He smiled in anticipation. In a plot straight from the comic books of his youth, he intended to hijack one of the government's top secret weapons. Oh, yes. Drake was going to fund his retirement with a great big laser beam from space.

"Something unobtrusive," Diana was saying, apparently running through a mental catalog of test sites. "Like this." She leaned forward and punched a few buttons on the console. The projection screen in front of them crackled to life, displaying a satellite photo of the western United States.

"I think taking out a state might be a bit more than we need for a test run," Drake said.

She cast a sidelong look, but otherwise ignored him, punching buttons until the image zoomed in. She made a few minor adjustments, scanning the image while she focused and refocused until, finally, she honed in on a lone vehicle on an abandoned highway. "That," she said. "It's perfect."

Indeed it was. Out of the way. Miles from any signs of life. And as an added bonus, it was an SUV. He hated the way the gas-guzzling vehicles wreaked havoc on the environment. He met her eyes. "You may fire when ready."

"I bet you say that to all the girls." She laughed, then started to punch a set of numbers into the keypad. "Okay. That gives us our targeting data. Now all we need to do is take control of the satellite."

As she moved efficiently down the console to another keypad, Drake fisted his hand. Moment of truth time. He'd taken a risk bringing in a partner. Now he'd find out if the risk had paid off.

Her eyes met his. He drew in a breath, then nodded.

She licked her lips, her finger poised above a flashing red button. "Once I take control, they'll know. Do you want to show our hand so early? The demonstration is almost two weeks away. If they find a way to lock us out once we're in—"

"My darling," he said, raising her fingers to his lips, "you have so little faith." He glanced at the digital clock mounted on the far wall. Their timing was perfect. "I assure you, our little experiment will go quite unnoticed." He tapped the end of her nose. "Trust me. They'll never know."

She kissed him. "You say the sweetest things." Their eyes met, then hers darted down to the console. She took a deep breath and pushed the button.

He picked up the swan, cupping it in his palm as his gaze shifted to the projection screen. Any second now the surgically precise beam of deadly light would shoot from space and atomize the car.

Any time now . . .

But there was nothing. *Zip. Nyet. Jamais. Nada.*

No surgically precise laser, no giant pulsing beam of light, not even a pathetic little fizzle and spurt. Just . . . *nothing.*

"Shit." Diana's voice, barely a whisper, reached his ears. "They changed the code."

In front of her, the readout flashed red, the liquid crystal display mocking him—*Access Denied. Access Denied.*

The veins in his neck tightened, and he felt the thrum of adrenaline rushing through his body. *Double-cross!*

Diana turned to him, fear in her eyes. "Are we compromised?"

He ran the pad of his thumb over the swan's perfectly formed head. "I don't know."

Resolutely, he pushed the doubt away. He needed to have a little talk with his so-called partner. That much was certain. But in the end, Drake would prevail. This was a setback, true, but he'd overcome challenges before. This was merely an obstacle, not a barrier. And in the end, his ultimate victory would be that much sweeter.

"Drake?" she prompted, her voice tentative.

"Two weeks," he said. "We have two weeks to get that code." He closed his fist, crushing the swan in his hand. "And I swear I'll lobotomize anyone—*anyone*—who gets in my way."

One

lmost two weeks later . . .

With a practiced hand, agent Phineus
Teague—code-named Python—adjusted the
bow tie of his midnight blue Briani tuxedo,
aiming the miniature camera toward the
statuesque blonde seated at the baccarat
table on the far side of the casino. Static
hissed in his ear, then, "We got picture.
You're good to go."

Finn tipped his head, letting his partner
know he'd copied the message. But he didn't
move. Not yet. The timing needed to be perfect. This mission was just too damn important.

"Le Grande," said the croupier. "Madam
wins."

The woman nodded, her face impassive. She slid a hundred Euro chip across the table, a tip for the dealer. Then she stood, her shimmering evening gown clinging to her extravagant curves. At least he knew she was unarmed; there was no place to hide a gun under that dress.

As she gathered her chips, her gaze met his. Her lips curved into a seductive smile, but it was her eyes that caught Finn's attention—ice blue and treacherous. Tatiana Nicasse. A double agent, only she'd gone bad. Very bad.

There was no hint of recognition in her eyes, just a pure, sexual heat. Good. He needed information, and he was happy to extract it by whatever means necessary.

He stepped away from the wall, moving toward her, ignoring the appreciative glances from the other women in the room. A waiter passed, and Finn took two flutes of champagne, holding one out to Tatiana. She took it, then held the glass up in a silent toast before taking a sip, her lipstick leaving an imprint on the glass.

"You know the way to a woman's heart," she said, her accent alluring.

Her gaze drifted down, then back up again, and his body fired in response. She might be the enemy, but he wasn't dead. Far from it.

"What else do you know about women?" she asked, the invitation in her voice unmistakable.

"I think it's fair to say I'm an expert." He
drifted closer, brushing his fingers over her
bare shoulder and down her arm. The woman
was pure danger, all wrapped up in a silky
black dress.

"And modest, too." She raised one deli-
cately shaped eyebrow. *"I like that in a man.
Perhaps we can determine the extent of your
expertise, no?"*

She reached between her breasts, extract-
ing a thin, gold-plated case. She clicked it
open and pulled out a cigarette, clearly
expecting him to light it. He didn't disap-
point, and her hand curved around his as he
held the burning match. The tobacco glowed
red, and she leaned back, exhaling toward the
ceiling. *"Merci, Mr. . . . ?"*

"Teague," he said. *"Phineus Teague."*

Finn rubbed his palms vigorously over his face,
pulling himself out of his fantasy and trying instead
to concentrate on the pile of work stacked up on his
kitchen table. It wasn't easy. The work was deathly
dull, the blonde across the courtyard so much more
intriguing.

He didn't know one damn thing about her, but
in the single week he'd been watching her, she'd
sparked his imagination. She rarely closed her curtains, and her patio door was right across from his
kitchen window. Fair game. Especially since he
enjoyed watching her move a hell of a lot more than
he enjoyed answering interrogatories.

The woman was spectacular. Tall, like a model,
but not stick thin and flat chested like so many of

the magazines liked to hawk these days. The kind of woman a man could get his hands around.

He imagined she knew her appeal, too, and used it to her advantage. Probably smuggling something into the country, using her feminine wiles to bribe customs agents, kissing them with poisoned lipstick if other means didn't prevail.

Not that he had any real reason to think that. From what he could tell, her life never veered from the normal. She worked out every night in a skintight black leotard, then popped a movie into the VCR. Every once in a while, she'd practice some kicks—like she thought she was Buffy or something. Once in a while she dressed up, and Finn could only assume she had a date. If so, she met him somewhere, because lover boy never came to her door.

Overall, pretty standard stuff. Compared to him, though, her life was a mile-a-minute thrill ride. His was a slow ride on a kiddie train.

Law school. What the hell had he been thinking? He'd fantasized about pacing a courtroom, a modern day Perry Mason, and winning the day for truth, justice, and all the rest of it. Not hardly. Instead he was pulling seventeen-hour days trapped in a tiny office researching bullshit procedural points, answering discovery, and summarizing depositions.

Damn it all, he should have just been a bartender.

When he was younger, he'd have simply packed his bags, moved to Florida, and worked a few weeks as a scuba instructor. Or headed up to Silicon Valley and signed on with a couple of his buddies to design computer games. Or set out cross-country in his car, stopping to flip burgers for minimum wage whenever his cash ran short. But none of those options appealed anymore. Or, more honestly, they appealed, but they just weren't practical.

He was thirty-seven years old, and it was time to buckle down and have a life. The trouble was, he still didn't know what he wanted to be when he grew up.

He frowned. That wasn't exactly true. He knew. But it was too late to do anything about it now. He'd made a choice, and from what he could tell, he'd made the wrong one. But he was stuck, trapped by three years invested in a career he didn't want, and thousands of dollars in student loans he needed to pay down. Until his weekly attempts to play the lottery paid off, he had no choice but to follow a paycheck. And that, frankly, was his own damn fault.

He snorted, disgusted with himself, and got up to inspect the contents of his refrigerator. Nothing except a bottle of Gatorade, a three-day-old burrito from Taco Bell, and a jar of dill pickles. Not exactly appetizing.

He grabbed his keys off the microwave, mentally debating between a full-blown grocery run and another trip to Taco Bell. Then he headed for the door, yanking it open with more force than he intended.

The woman on the walkway jumped, turning to press her back against the shrubbery that lined the sidewalk. "Oh!" she said. "You startled me."

"Sorry." He stepped outside, squinting against the bright light of day. "Amy, right?"

"Amber," she said. "Amber Robinson." She was decked out in sweatpants and a T-shirt topped with a hooded jacket. A backpack hung casually from one shoulder. She wore no makeup, and her long brown hair was pulled back from her face, a few tendrils, damp with sweat, curling around her hairline.

She'd lived next door to him for five days now, and he'd never seen her in anything but baggy jeans or sweatpants, her hair always pulled into a ponytail, her face usually shadowed by a baseball cap. She could probably be pretty, but she didn't seem like the type who cared.

"Going out?" she asked. Her voice held a sensual undertone that seemed out of place in such a laidback woman. He wanted to say something clever, something that would provoke a response, just so he could hear those soft tones once again.

"Grocery run," he said instead. Neither clever nor provoking, but it was the first thing he thought of. He considered asking her to join him for a coffee, but ruled it out. He had no time for socializing. And, he reminded himself, this woman wasn't his type. Instead, he gestured toward his front door. "I'm working at home," he said, as if his lack of invitation required an explanation.

Her entire face lit up when she smiled. "You lawyers," she teased. "They grind you into the ground."

"No kidding," he said, wondering when he'd told her his profession. Maybe in the laundry room . . . ?

She aimed a thumb at her doorway, facing him as she walked backward in that direction. "I should be getting inside. Good to see you." Her hand closed around her doorknob, and she turned just enough to insert the key. She leaned in as the door opened, then disappeared from his view.

Something akin to disappointment settled in

Finn's chest, and he frowned. Clearly, he was working too much, not getting enough quality interaction with the opposite sex. Amber Robinson wasn't on his radar. Not even close.

No, if he was stuck in a boring job, he wanted excitement in the rest of his life, and particularly in his bed. An adventurous woman. One who could keep him on his toes, both in and out of the bedroom.

The woman in the window, maybe.

Amber Robinson?

Definitely not.

Amber clicked the door shut and locked it, the precaution automatic. She reached behind her to the waistband of her sweats, her fingers closing around the molded butt of her Walther PPK.

She slipped the gun free as she walked into her living room, tossing it onto the couch as a vivid curse slipped from her lips. She'd been careless out there, stupidly adjusting the gun when Finn had opened his door. Dumb and dangerous. She wasn't usually so sloppy—hell, she'd developed a reputation within Unit 7 as being dead-on perfect—and her lapse pissed her off.

"Temper, temper," a voice chastised.

She whipped around, muscles tight, the knife she'd sheathed under her sleeve pulled out and ready.

From her bathroom doorway, Brandon Kline held up his hands, his eyes dancing with mirth. "Shit, Robinson, it's just me."

"Dammit, Brandon." She pitched the knife next to the gun. "Haven't I asked you nicely to please not break in? Someone might see."

"Not to worry," he said, moving to sit on one of her barstools. "I'm good."

She frowned but didn't argue. He *was* good. They'd been recruited together—rescued by Providence from the hell of juvie hall—and had trained hard to become top operatives in Unit 7, a shadowy government organization that did everything from hostage rescue to out-and-out espionage. She'd known him for sixteen years, and she'd trusted Brandon to watch her back on more than one occasion. Significant stuff, especially considering there weren't many people in the world Amber would trust with her phone number, much less her life.

"So what's got your panties in a wad?" he asked, striding into the room.

"I just did a stupid thing, and it's irritating me." She kicked off her running shoes, careful not to damage the camera hidden in the toe, then unzipped her warm-up jacket and threw it over the back of a chair. The T-shirt followed, then the sweatpants—each layer revealing more of the short, flirty red dress she'd worn to the U.N.–sponsored luncheon Brandon had sent her to.

Brandon raked an appreciative gaze over her. "You know, kid, there are times when I think maybe we should just get it on," he said, a tease in his voice.

"Not a chance," she answered, deadpan. "What if we fell in love? Neither one of us could live with the consequences."

"Bullshit, babe. We already know where your loyalty lies. Mine too, for that matter. Hell, if we weren't so loyal we'd be out there freelancing."

Amber frowned, avoiding Brandon's eyes as she reached under her skirt to tug her panty hose down. Everything he said was true. They'd joked about striking out on their own a number of times. Joining the ranks of freelance mercenaries around the globe. But neither had seriously considered it. For one thing, if she was on her own, she'd lose access to the Unit's seemingly endless resources. Amber wasn't stupid. She knew a good deal when she saw one. And the jets, disguises, and weaponry currently at her fingertips cost a pretty penny.

Not that there weren't other well-funded organizations that would be interested in acquiring her particular talents. But it wasn't just about the Unit's resources. The Unit was her life, her family. She'd never give it up. Not for anyone; not for anything.

"Besides," Brandon said, his tone light as he picked up the conversation's thread, "me? Fall in love with you? Never happen."

"Nonsense," she said, shaking off the unwelcome bout of melancholy. "I'm irresistible."

He laughed, and she stepped out of the damn constricting garment and tossed the panty hose across the room.

"I hate these things," she muttered.

"But they do such nice things to the curve of your ass."

Her mouth twitched, and she fought hard to hold back a smile. "See, this is why we can't have a relationship. No respect."

"Who wants a relationship? I just want to get laid."

At that, she laughed outright. She certainly couldn't argue with that. It had been months since she'd had sex. But she wasn't about to use Brandon to scratch that itch, and they both knew it.

"So how'd it go?" he said, the tone of his voice letting her know the teasing was over. Back to work.

"Smooth as silk. Everything's in place." Translation, she'd tagged their target with the homing device.

"Good girl. Sorry for such a mundane assignment. And sorry you had to work with Bedichek to do it. I know you prefer to work alone."

"No problem," she said, crossing to her back patio and opening the door a crack. "I play well with others," she said, "so long as I don't have to play with them for very long. And besides, the assignment brought back memories." She'd been fifteen when the Unit had trusted her with her first solo mission. A diplomatic party in Prague, posing as a senator's daughter. She'd planted a bug on a foreign prime minister, never asking why. It hadn't mattered. Nothing had mattered back then. Nothing except doing the job right so that they wouldn't send her back to the center. Or, worse, back home.

"That's what I mean," Brandon said. "Kid's play. I think you're a little overtrained for the job." He shrugged. "But there was no one else available."

"Don't worry about it." Blackie, the ancient stray cat she'd pseudo-adopted, wandered in, whiskers twitching. Amber reached down and gave it a good scratch behind the ears. "Your job was the highlight of my week." *That* was an understatement. Eight days ago she'd been in Chechnya, deep undercover on one of James Monahan's pet projects. She frowned. "He's going to raise hell when he learns I'm back in the States."

Brandon grimaced. "Probably," he said, clearly knowing exactly who Amber meant. "But there's no way he could have known that you'd met Eli before. The moment he saw you, the deal would have collapsed."

"True enough," Amber said. Her mission had been to go undercover as a photojournalist and use her manufactured press credentials to get close to a suspected gunrunner. Pretty standard stuff, until Amber learned that Eli Janovich, ex-CIA, had stepped in as head of security for her mark. Considering she and Eli went way back, she'd aborted the mission and called Roderick Schnell, Unit 7's head honcho. Technically, she reported to James, the second-in-command. But he'd been unavailable, and she'd needed reassignment.

"I left James a message," she said, tamping down on a niggle of guilt. James had recruited both her and Brandon. No, that wasn't quite right. He'd recruited her, yes. But considering the course of her life back then, he'd also saved her from sure hell. She'd been thirteen, a smart-mouthed kid, scared out of her mind and facing a felony murder charge and a district attorney determined to try her as an adult.

James had pulled strings, gotten the charges dropped, and sent her to the Unit's training facility in Montana. More than that, though, he'd given her a sense of self-worth, and in doing that, he'd given her the world. Going over his head felt disloyal, even when her safety was at issue. It was a crazy business, with loyalties lost and won over coffee or a beer. And with James on the verge of retiring, she didn't want him to think that she'd already moved on.

"He'll understand," Brandon said, reading her mind as usual.

"I hope so," she said. "But he's going to be pissed. Too bad, too. If I'm going to incur James's wrath, I wish I were at least making some headway." Schnell had ordered her to Los Angeles to keep an eye on Diana Traynor, a known associate of Drake Mackenzie, a former Navy SEAL and Black Ops commander. Mackenzie had even served with Schnell years ago. But while Schnell still worked for God and country, Drake had left the military for more profitable pursuits and had landed on the watch list of every intelligence organization in the free world.

Diana kept a Los Angeles apartment, but rarely used it. So when she'd returned a week ago, the Unit took notice. And then, when she started hanging out with a low-level programmer at Zermatt Aeronautical Engineering Labs, Unit 7 had gone on alert.

A defense contractor, ZAEL was currently working on a prototype of Prometheus, a space-based weapon system that had been commissioned by the Unit. All very hush hush; Amber doubted if the president even knew about the satellite. For that matter, only a few highly placed Unit members had knowledge, and then only on a need-to-know basis.

Amber was not one who needed to know—not everything, anyway. But the whisper was that the satellite controlled a laser with unheard of precision, so focused and accurate it could melt a dime on a sidewalk. That was only a rumor, of course. Amber had no way of knowing what the thing actually did, much less if it was finished. Still, she knew enough to do her job, and that was all that was necessary.

The information she *did* have was sketchy. According to the dossier she'd reviewed before it had self-destructed, security had been compromised and the access code leaked. The operator who'd revealed the code had shot himself rather than undergo interrogation, and the Unit had no way of knowing with whom he'd been working.

ZAEL had changed the access code immediately, of course, but one thing was clear—someone unauthorized knew about Prometheus . . . and wanted it for himself.

So when Diana had appeared in L.A. and started dating a data processor at ZAEL, it had seemed prudent to put a tail on her. But so far, nothing remotely incriminating had turned up. For seven days, the woman had done aerobics, visited spas, and had an endless stream of manicures.

"I don't know, Brandon," Amber said. "Mackenzie might be plotting the end of civilization as we know it, but his girlfriend just wants to look good for the final party. I've been watching the woman do nothing but primp and fluff and flirt for days." She sighed. "I know I shouldn't complain, but this assignment is a dead end." Like any business, the prime assignments went to the best players. She could have shined in the Chechnya mission. This one, though . . . Amber feared this one was going to spiral into nothingness and she'd end up facing years of surveillance work before she could wrangle another primo job. Not a pleasant possibility.

"Maybe that's why you got sloppy in the hallway,"

Brandon said, heading for the kitchen. "Too dull too keep you on your toes." Blackie followed, probably hoping Brandon would accidentally dump an entire can of tuna on the floor.

Amber frowned, considering the theory. The idea that she'd been sloppy because she'd been bored didn't sit well at all. She loved her life—loved the rush of adrenaline she got just waking up in the morning. But she knew as well as the next agent that the excitement was countered by days of waiting and watching. That was the job, too. Part of both good and bad assignments. And she kicked herself for letting her professionalism slip, even if only for an instant.

Even worse, she'd been sloppy in front of Phineus Teague. And the mysterious Mr. Teague was a living, breathing question mark. Losing her cool around him wasn't smart.

She'd first run across Finn when she'd been assigned to track down Albert Alcott and the diamonds he'd stolen. Gemstone quality stones, they were originally intended for use as bait in a smuggling sting operation. When the diamonds had been stolen from Unit 7's undercover operative, that had been a serious setback. It had only gotten worse when Alcott had spirited them out of the country.

Amber had been assigned to locate Alcott, and in doing so she realized she wasn't the only one looking for him. A woman had hired a private investigator to find the man, and Finn had apparently come along for the ride.

So while Finn didn't know about Amber, *she* knew about *him*. And in her line of work, she didn't tend to run across the same civilian twice. The moment she realized he was also watching Diana Traynor, she'd run a full background check. The man had held every job imaginable and had ended up a lawyer in a firm that represented ZAEL.

A coincidence? Amber didn't think so. Finn was watching Traynor too closely. With most men, she'd simply assume that the interest was borne of testosterone. With Finn, though . . .

With Finn there were too many coincidences, and his persistent proximity was unnerving. She didn't know what he was up to, if anything. But she damn sure intended to find out.

Brandon headed back from the kitchen, a beer in each hand. "Anything new on your neighbor?"

"I was just thinking about him," she admitted. "There's more to Phineus Teague than meets the eye."

"I'll buy that," Brandon said. He tossed her a beer, and she caught it one-handed. "But who does he work for? Chances are, we'd know if he was a Company man. N.S.C.?"

Amber shrugged. "Maybe. Could be a freelancer. That would explain the odd array of jobs."

"Odd is right," Brandon said. "Everything from ski bum to short-order cook to computer hacker."

"The hacking put him on the FBI's watch list," Amber said. But that had been years ago. All the computer stuff Finn had done recently was apparently legit—programming, game design, stuff like that. "Think he's a plant?" she asked. They'd run across that before—an operative with a manufactured background planted so deep even Unit 7's resources couldn't break the agent's cover.

"Could be," Brandon said. "Or maybe he's just a

computer-hacking, downhill-skiing civilian with a severe case of lust."

Amber laughed. "In that case, he's in over his head."

"Hell," Brandon said, "even if he is an operative, he's in over his head. The man's green. It took you what, less than a day to make him?"

"About that."

"Chances are Diana's made him, too."

"I know," she said. "If he's not careful, he's going to end up as fish food." A shame, actually. The man was exceptionally good-looking. She might have forsworn relationships, but that didn't mean she couldn't appreciate a well-built man—and she certainly knew what to do with one.

"There are too many questions out there," she continued, thinking aloud. "Teague's law firm represents ZAEL. Diana Traynor's been hanging around one of ZAEL's data processors. Finn moved in across the courtyard from Traynor. And when he's home, he keeps a pretty close eye on her." She popped the top on her beer. "That must add up to something."

The corner of Brandon's mouth twitched. "Seems like you know an awful lot about Mr. Teague's habits."

"The man's got his eye on my quarry. Damn straight I'm going to watch him." Was it her fault the view was nice? "As a matter of fact, I'm planning on doing a bit more than watch."

Brandon's eyebrows raised. "Oh?"

"Teague's an unknown quantity, and I don't like unknowns. Too messy. Is he friend or enemy? We need to know whom he works for. Hell, we need to know if he works for anyone at all."

"And how do you propose to find that out?" Brandon asked, amusement lacing his voice. "Hidden cameras? Listening devices? A hypodermic filled with truth serum?"

"Last resorts," she said, meeting his smile. "First, I'm going to simply get close to Mr. Phineus Teague."

Two

mber paused outside the briefing room for Unit 7's Los Angeles field office. The steel door was closed tight, as usual, and she stepped automatically to the left, taking off her sunglasses as she moved.

"Identify." A computer-modulated command.

"Robinson, Amber," she said, stepping closer for the retinal scan.

A burst of light, and then the voice again: "Accepted." The heavy door slid open with a gentle whoosh, and she stepped through, waiting in the anteroom while Brandon completed the same process behind her. After a few seconds, the door whooshed open again, and he entered. Amber fought a grin. "They let anybody in this place these days."

"Riff-raff," Brandon agreed. "A tragic commentary on our times." He cocked his head forward. "Come on. He's waiting."

Another door—this one heavy oak, not steel—and then they were in the main briefing room. Thirteen chairs surrounded an oblong mahogany table, each empty except for one. Roderick Schnell sat at the head of the table, a file folder open in front of him. A lean man with salt and pepper hair, Schnell gave the appearance of a corporate executive about to head up a board meeting. Only Schnell was no corporate schmo. The man had dissident leaders killed before the *Washington Post* even knew they existed, and he organized coups with more style and flair than Martha Stewart ever dreamed of.

Amber stood, Brandon beside her, while Schnell finished reading. He looked up, and after he nodded toward the chairs, they sat.

"So there's a fly in our ointment," Schnell said, without preamble.

"Could be," Amber said. "We've done a preliminary background check and he seems to be civilian, but—"

"But he's watching Ms. Traynor." Schnell's hands rested on the file folder, his fingers steepled. "That certainly raises questions."

"I want authorization to move in closer," she said. "Find out what this guy's up to."

"We can't compromise the surveillance of Traynor."

"No, sir," Amber agreed. "That's why I'd like to request reassignment for Brandon. Have him help me out."

Schnell had already turned to Brandon, clearly having anticipated the request. "Kline?"

"I have no problem with reassignment." He flashed a smile that was uniquely Brandon. "I even emailed Linus. A new assignment requires new equipment."

Amber hid her own grin. Linus Klondike's gadgets were famous within the intelligence community, and Brandon never missed a chance to check out the latest fruits of Klondike's tinkerings.

"Very well," Schnell said, his tone even. He closed the file folder as he looked from Amber to Brandon. "Authorization granted."

Amber stood, then paused.

Her hesitation wasn't lost on Schnell. "Is there something else?"

She drew in a breath, considering. Final authority for all the Unit's missions came from Schnell, so it wasn't as if she needed James's approval. But, even so . . . "I still haven't been able to contact James. Has he been informed of my reassignment?"

"The message has been dispatched," Schnell said, which wasn't really an answer, but Amber knew it was as much as she was going to get. Oh well. If James was pissed that he'd been kept out of the loop, she'd deal with that later. In the meantime, she trusted that Schnell knew what he was doing.

"Is there something else?" Schnell asked.

"No, sir."

Schnell's smile was dismissive. "Then I'll let you two get back to work."

"Yes, sir."

The Unit was located in one of Los Angeles's many high rises, purportedly doing business as a legitimate publishing company. Brandon went out the back, but Amber exited toward the front, stepping out into the main offices.

The floor was lined with windowed offices, the interior filled with cubicles housing men and women hunched over computers. They all received paychecks from the publisher; they all worked for the Unit. She waved at a few of the clerks she recognized, her eyes scanning the cubicles for a particular person. She found him four cubicles down, centrally located under the watchful eye of the Unit's security cameras.

"Hello, Al."

Albert Alcott looked up from the computer, his eyes blank at first, then brightening as he recognized her. "Amber," he said, climbing to his feet. "Wow. It's good to . . . I mean, why are you here?" He frowned, concern flashing across his features. "I'm not going to be—"

"Of course not," Amber said. "As far as I know, the Unit's perfectly happy with you. Your job is safe."

Amber almost laughed at the wave of relief that swept across Al's face. Spending all day in front of a computer would bore her to tears, but from Al's perspective, she supposed it was a dream job. After she'd tracked him down, she'd cut a deal with him. Instead of serving jail time for grand larceny, now Alcott was working for the Unit.

Not a bad deal for a guy like Alcott.

And, she had to admit, not a bad deal for her, either. Alcott had learned the ropes quickly. And on more than one occasion he'd been able to ferret out information when she'd needed it.

"I brought you something," she said, digging into

her day pack for the dog-eared novel. She passed it to him. "You liked the Ludlum that I lent you last month, so I thought you might like this one, too."

"Thanks," Al said, riffling the book's pages. "You're on that Traynor assignment, right?"

She nodded. "Anything new for me?"

"Nothing. I'll keep my eyes open."

"Thanks." She cocked her head toward the door. "I'm out of here. See you around."

"Thank you," Al said, lifting the book. "And, Amber . . ."

She turned, an eyebrow raised in question.

"Watch your back."

By the time he'd read the entire Sunday *Los Angeles Times*, showered, dressed, downed two cups of coffee, and watched *Meet the Press*, Finn knew he had no other options—it was time to get back to work.

He levered himself up and off the couch, then headed toward the table, eyeing the little stacks he'd left last night like a big game hunter might eye his prey. A yellow highlighter, a copy of the *California Code of Civil Procedure*, a brand new bag of Cheetos, two yellow pads covered with notes, and the dreaded pleadings and depositions that had been giving him grief all weekend. Everything was in order; he had no excuses anymore. It was time to rock 'n' roll.

He frowned, not thrilled by the prospect. Particularly when his imagination was so much more enticing.

With a sigh, Finn drummed his fingers on the tabletop. Too bad he couldn't really be his fantasy alter ego. After all, Agent Python wouldn't be cooped up reading depositions. No, if Python were locked up in this apartment, it would be because the mission required it.

Finn grinned, letting his imagination run wild. As a top government agent, it was Agent Python's job to bring down the key players in Superior Criminals United for Mayhem, a notorious group of international bad guys bent on world domination. But rather than engage in a risky helo drop into the New Mexico desert that surrounded the S.C.U.M. headquarters, Python was using this seemingly dull Los Angeles safe house to keep an eye on S.C.U.M.'s exotic blonde agent, Tatiana.

At the moment, Tatiana was holed up in her apartment, so Python would use the time to poke around in S.C.U.M.'s files. If he couldn't go there in person, he'd go there virtually.

In that regard, Python's undercover identity as a mild-mannered attorney actually helped quite a bit. The law firm represented ZAEL, a defense contractor that Agent Python knew had been infiltrated by S.C.U.M. agents. With a chuckle, Finn fired up his laptop. As Agent Python, Finn hadn't really spent week after boring week reviewing endless boxes of documents as part of a pretrial review; instead, he'd been gleaning information crucial to his super-secret mission.

The truth was, during those dull weeks of document production, Finn probably *had* gleaned enough to hack past ZAEL's security. Which meant that all he needed to do now was plug in some basic company information and the decryption software he'd developed two years ago would do the rest. . . .

His fingers flew over the keys. Then he pressed

enter, and the computer hummed and whirred, the software doing its thing. A few electronic beeps and gurgles, and then *voila* . . . he was past the first level of security.

Was he the man, or what?

Now to poke around and figure out what S.C.U.M. had in mind for ZAEL. Just hack a little further in, and then—

No!

With a frustrated groan, Finn killed the power to his computer and pushed back from his desk. What kind of an idiot was he? ZAEL was a *client*, for Christ's sake. There was no plot, no evil scheme. Just highly classified information he had no business accessing. Hell, if anyone found out he'd hacked into the system, his ass would be grass. And nobody would believe he'd done it on a whim while he was engaged in a bit of fantasy. No, that would not only get him fired, it would get him an appointment with the company shrink.

Irritated with himself for letting his imagination run so far astray, he headed across the room and back to the kitchen table. He picked up his highlighter, opened the first deposition, and started reading.

He was all the way to page three when a blast sounded from the courtyard, so loud his patio door shook. *The twins!* Finn was on his feet and through the door in seconds, worrying that one of his young neighbors had managed to blow off a body part.

But no, both Elijah and Callie were perfectly whole, thank goodness, smiling up at him like the little hellions they were. The exploded remains of a bottle rocket lay on the charred grass between them, smoke still rising from the debris.

Finn grimaced. The kids had moved with their parents from Idaho two months ago, and he'd met them, bored and lonely, in the laundry room. The twins had looked like they needed entertaining, and so he'd wasted half a Saturday building a bubbling volcano out of Play-Doh and household chemicals. Apparently, he'd created a monster. Or two.

"Are you kids insane? You could get yourselves killed!"

Callie looked at Elijah, who shrugged. "We were careful," she said.

Finn raised an eyebrow, trying for a stern parental look and probably not succeeding. "Then why the large explosion?"

"An accident?" Callie said, turning what should have been a statement into a question.

"No kidding."

"It wasn't *that* big an explosion," Elijah added, looking toward his sister for confirmation.

Finn ignored him. "Your mother's going to have a cow if she sees you two out here." And considering Finn had piqued their interest in things that go boom, he really didn't want to incur Mrs. Jacoby's wrath. "Especially if—" He clamped his mouth shut. He'd noticed something in his peripheral vision, and now he locked on target. *Blasting caps?* "Where the devil did you get those?"

"We found them," Callie said. "Last month at our grandpa's farm. There were a whole bunch in an old trunk in the attic."

"These," Finn said, "are dangerous." He bent over and grabbed up the one remaining cap.

"Oh, please," Callie said, "couldn't you just show us a trick with it? A rocket or something, like you did last week."

"And the green goo smoke bomb," Elijah added, looking up at Finn with puppy dog eyes. "That was really cool."

Finn felt his resolve weaken and he steeled himself. "No. I don't want you getting hurt."

"But, Finn," Callie said, drawing his name out into a full-fledged whine. "You'll be here. It'll be safe."

"I mean it," he said, shoving the cap deep into the front pocket of his jeans. "Enough explosions for the day. Go home. Watch television. Read *Harry Potter.* Clean your rooms."

"But—"

"No buts." He was getting the hang of this paternal thing. "And give me those matches."

Elijah rolled his eyes but complied, placing the book of matches into Finn's outstretched hand.

"Now go," Finn said, pocketing the matches.

And amazingly enough, the kids went. Finn watched them slump their way up the stairs, duly impressed by his newly acquired preadolescent negotiating skills.

Of course, as soon as they disappeared from view, he realized the implications of sending them away—now he had to go back to work.

Well, hell.

With an appalling lack of enthusiasm, he parked himself at the table again, and was finally about to settle down for a scintillating few hours lost in legalese, when a movement across the courtyard caught his eye. Tatiana's curtains had been closed, but they were wide open now . . . and Finn turned just in time to see her slip through her front door.

She was going out.

Interesting. Because while Finn might need to work, Agent Python had a patriotic duty to follow her.

And, really, who was he to argue with patriotism?

"They're on the move," Brandon said. He pulled back from the window and turned to face Amber. Dressed head to toe in black leather, she looked like a cross between Lara Croft and Emma Peel. The only thing marring the kick-ass persona was the paperback novel she held in her lap and the scraggly black cat curled up beside her. And, frankly, neither one marred the image much.

Yesterday, he'd suggested sleeping together in jest, but he had to admit the idea had a certain appeal. Amber would be anything but boring in bed. He wasn't, however, inclined to mess up a perfectly good friendship by bringing sex into it.

"Let's roll," she said, giving the cat one final pet as she tossed the book on the floor. "I've got Finn covered. You take Traynor."

"Absolutely," he said. "Of course, I only intend to observe my prey. But you . . ." He trailed off with a grin. "Do you think we need to devise a code? If you tie a red handkerchief to your doorknob, I'll know you're *entertaining.*"

She aimed her eyes heavenward and gave a little shake of the head. "Why?" she asked. "Why couldn't I do this job with someone who isn't an asshole?"

"The last woman I had to seduce for a job smelled

like wet leather and had the personality of a pit bull," Brandon said. "Some people have all the luck."

She flashed him a brilliant smile. "Clean living," she said. She tossed her hair, and he watched her head toward the door, the leather pants managing to destroy any illusion of innocence.

"Maybe I'll try that someday," he said, following. He wouldn't, of course. Clean living was boring. And right now, his life was just too damn interesting.

What the hell was he doing? The thought spun round and round in Finn's mind, so persistent that he almost pulled over to the side of the road. After all, the question was a good one—what the hell *was* he doing?

Not working, that was for sure. Already past noon on Sunday and so far he'd eaten breakfast, screwed around, and prevented two kids from blowing up the courtyard. All in all, not a bad way to pass a Sunday morning . . . unless you had an eight A.M. meeting with the senior partner to go over the stack of still-unfinished interrogatories on your kitchen table. The very same partner who signed his paychecks.

The same paychecks Finn needed to pay off his staggering student loans.

So you'd think he'd be a little more into the whole work thing.

He wasn't.

Instead, he was cruising down Santa Monica Boulevard in his primer-paint-gray Mustang convertible tailing a blonde who probably wouldn't be caught dead with a guy who drove anything less exciting than a Lamborghini.

Of course, she didn't know about all the hidden little extras that had been installed in his classic car. The '67 Mustang might look like a heap, but it was loaded. Missile launch behind the headlights complete with a state-of-the-art targeting system. A buoyancy control device and rudder system in case a land chase veered onto the sea. Oh, yeah. He was set. Sometimes looks could be very, very deceiving.

The car was an integral part of his work. It allowed him to get close. To move in unobserved. To fade into the background. Which made it very useful for a mission like the one he was on today—trailing S.C.U.M. über-agent Tatiana Nicasse.

Of course, Tatiana's tastes tended more toward elegance, and he knew he wouldn't impress her in his junk-heap-looking car. But that wasn't a problem. The agency provided everything he needed, including a fabulous Type-E Jaguar—a two-seater, with a hood as long as Tatiana's legs. Once he was done observing, he'd dry-clean his tux, rev up the Jaguar, and move in. Close. Very close . . .

Finn ran his hand over the steering wheel, imagining the smooth skin of her thigh under his touch, his gaze locked on the taillights of her red Dodge Viper. She was half a block ahead of him and moving fast, while he was stuck at a light behind a brand-new Lexus and a battered Honda Accord.

The light changed to green, and he laid on the horn, but the noise didn't inspire any forward motion in the two cars blocking his path. After a seemingly interminable pause, they finally pulled forward, and he took advantage of the gap to whip around them into the left-hand lane. He ran through the gears, shifting like a maniac, until he was cruising along at a nice clip, his eyes scanning the road for any hint of the Viper.

There. About three blocks ahead, zipping dangerously between a couple of fast-moving SUV's. Traffic was piling up fast, but that wasn't any obstacle to the Python. He whipped around a station wagon, waving an apology when the old man raised a fist in what was probably a colorful curse.

More cars blocked his path, and he glanced to his right, eyeing Little Santa Monica wistfully. The smaller street ran parallel to the main thoroughfare, and if he was over there—just a few yards to the right—he'd have smooth sailing. Heck, from his current vantage point he could even see a black Buick LeSabre cruising down that wide-open street. That's the kind of car Finn needed. A blend-into-the-background kind of car. Perfect for undertaking a little espionage on the lunch hour.

He squinted at the Buick, watching as the driver hit each light perfectly, his good fortune speeding him toward Tatiana and away from Finn. *Probably a lover heading for a secret rendezvous. Or a counteragent out to get the jump on Python.*

Or not.

He rolled his eyes at himself, realizing that his imagination had once again got the better of him. He was just about to hit the brakes, turn around, and hightail it away from such foolishness when he saw the Viper just two cars ahead. She'd gotten hung up behind a bus.

There was no way he could lose her now.

Determined, he zipped up close in the parallel lane. When traffic started moving again, he darted over, ending up right behind her. He laughed, almost giddy from the success, even though he knew that was stupid. After all, he wasn't on a real mission, and she wasn't out to avoid him. He was just a guy wasting time on a Sunday. But what the hell? This was the most fun he'd had in months.

They were moving now, and her brake lights flashed briefly as they approached an intersection. He didn't have any reason to think she knew he was back there, but still he slowed, planning to pull back a bit and follow at more of a distance. No sense getting caught. Especially since he didn't have a sane-sounding reason for tailing her in the first place.

Just then, the light changed to yellow, and she slammed on the brakes instead of gunning it through the light. The action caught Finn by surprise, and he had to react quickly, hitting his own brakes to keep from hitting her. Tires squealed and the scent of rubber burning against asphalt assaulted him.

In front of him, she adjusted her rearview mirror, then reapplied her lipstick. Then she twisted around in her seat, looked him straight in the eye, and blew him a kiss.

Finn just sat there clutching the steering wheel, his stomach knotting as he told himself that couldn't possibly be right. He turned to look at the cars in the two lanes sandwiching him. Both women. He checked his rearview mirror. Also a woman.

Tatiana had blown *him* a kiss?

Surely not. Surely he was mistaken. His eyes playing tricks or something.

He was still trying to convince himself that he was hallucinating when his cell phone rang. He picked it up, expecting to hear his boss's booming voice.

"Do you like what you see, Mr. Teague?" The feminine voice seemed to ooze over him like warm honey, but not in a good way. Instead it seemed sticky. Like a trap. Like she was the spider and he was the fly.

Busted.

Somehow, she'd gotten his cell phone number. How? He didn't know, but that little mystery was nothing compared to the tidal wave of complete and utter mortification that washed over him, its power so strong it almost knocked him over. Never once had his imagination crossed over into the real world, so why did it have to start with this woman?

The light was still red, but she hit the accelerator, racing through the intersection and barely missing a black BMW. The driver slammed on his brakes and cursed, then shook a fist at Tatiana. But she was gone, a red dot disappearing into the afternoon traffic. Well, damn.

He half-considered racing through the light after her, if for no other reason than to apologize and explain. But no explanation would sound sane, so he nixed that idea. In truth, he didn't mind losing her. After all, he didn't even know her.

She'd sparked his imagination, all right, but he knew she wasn't really smuggling microfiche in her cosmetic case or bringing down double agents with poisoned lipstick kisses. That was just a fantasy.

Now, though, she'd crossed from fantasy into reality. And he wanted nothing more than to get the hell out of there. And while Tatiana disappeared into a distant red dot, Finn downshifted, made a tight—and illegal—U-turn, and headed away from Beverly Hills. If he was lucky, a tidal wave was brewing off the California coast.

That, at least, would get his mind off his troubles.

"She made him," Amber reported, the incredulity in her voice echoing back through the tiny earpiece. What kind of a spy-guy couldn't even manage a simple tail on Diana Traynor's oh-so-obvious blood red car?

A guy who's not a spy at all.

All the evidence suggested that Finn really was just your average guy. The thought depressed her more than it should. After all, what did she care who Finn was? He was just a subject, and she was just doing her job. And that job involved peeking behind the curtain of Phineus Teague's life to see the wizard behind. If he turned out to be an uninvolved civilian, she could wash her hands of him. And if it turned out he was in the game . . . well, she'd deal with that development later.

Grimacing, she revved the BMW bike, leaning sideways into a tight turn as she spun around to follow Finn. Loose asphalt kicked up in her wake, punctuating her mood. "I can't believe it. She practically stepped out of her car and gave him a big sloppy kiss."

"No sweat." Brandon's voice came back without even a hint of static. "Chances are she won't even consider the possibility that she still has a tail. But what Harriet doesn't know is that I've got her in my sights."

Amber grinned. She'd come up with the code name of Harriet for Diana after one of her favorite children's books, *Harriet the Spy*. "She's all yours," Amber said. "I'm going to catch up with our boy."

"Roger that."

Satisfied that Brandon would keep up the tail on Diana, Amber turned back to the business at hand, following Finn as he headed back toward the beach. The wind whipped around her as she leaned over the handlebars, her black helmet and outfit all the disguise she needed. The bike vibrated beneath her, the purr of the engine working on her like some sort of erotic caress.

The truth was, she was wired tight and hadn't had sex for months. Before she'd left for Chechnya, she'd burned off some nervous energy by hanging out at a funky Irish pub on Wilshire and going home with the lead singer from the band that played there Wednesday nights.

But that had just been a quick roll, nothing earth shattering, and certainly nothing to sustain her through the long months on assignment. Now that she was back, the thought of simple sex—wild and hot and satisfying—was undeniably appealing. Unfortunately, she was fresh out of lead singers, bass players, or any of the usual suspects. And while she'd toyed with the idea of taking Brandon up on his offer, she knew better. Sex was a tool, and no matter what, it inevitably changed things.

No, Brandon was out of the question. Which meant she'd simply just have to find some other man.

And, lucky for her, Phineus Teague was up at bat.

* * *

A day spa? Brandon blinked and took another look at the sign. Beverly Glen Spa. No doubt about it. He'd just spent half an hour tailing a woman who'd been racing through Los Angeles on her way to get a facial peel.

Talk about a waste of time.

"Rebecca, do you copy?" He spoke normally, knowing the microphone in the dental cap he'd put on before leaving Amber's apartment would adjust to the appropriate volume. No answer. Not even a hint of static in his earpiece. "Rebecca, come in, Rebecca," he said, trying again.

She'd picked the handle herself, something about Ken Follett and a cipher and spies and some book she'd read years ago. Brandon's handle was Han. He rarely had time for books, but he'd seen *Star Wars* and felt a kinship with the smuggler.

Still no answer. She'd either tailed Finn out of range or the hills were blocking the signal.

Frustrated, he tightened his grip on the steering wheel. Diana's destination had strengthened his suspicions that he and Amber were on a wild goose chase, and he was tempted to turn around and head back toward the beach.

From what Amber had told him about Diana's habits over the last few days, their target's primary occupation in Los Angeles seemed to involve the application and reapplication of makeup. Not exactly incriminating, or even interesting. And, frankly, the situation pissed him off. Amber was one of the Unit's best agents, and Schnell damn well knew it. So the thought of her wasting her time learning nothing more scintillating than a few new makeup tricks was more than Brandon could stomach.

And now Brandon was in the mix, too. He slammed his palm against the steering wheel, the action doing little to quell his irritation. But he owed everything to the Unit, so if Schnell thought monitoring Traynor was useful, then by God, that's what he'd do.

For that matter, he'd never once seen Schnell do anything without a purpose. And so he held fast to his faith, silently praying that they weren't chasing a decoy while Mackenzie went off and did something heinous like blow up Disneyland.

That would be very bad indeed.

He released a bitter sigh, contemplating his next move. He needed to get inside. She might be going in for Botox injections and a mineral bath, but she could also be planning an information drop. He needed to find out, and he needed to do it without Diana noticing him.

He frowned, considering the problem. At the moment, he was idling two cars behind her Viper in the valet zone, watching the view as her well-defined leg slipped out of the tight bucket seat. The entire woman followed, her short skirt and summer sweater clinging like a wet T-shirt.

She took the ticket from the valet, then bent back down to retrieve her purse from inside the car. The skirt pulled tight against her ass, and Brandon noticed the valet ogling her with appreciation. Brandon understood completely and even allowed himself a tiny smile. The woman might be boffing a terrorist, but she was still one hell of a looker.

For her part, Diana didn't notice the valet any more than she noticed the Cypress trees that lined the walk to the spa's front door. To her, the uniformed employee was simply part of the scenery, there for her convenience, but certainly no one she needed to pay attention to.

Pampered rich girls and their holier-than-thou ways rubbed Brandon the wrong way. But this time, her elitism had sparked a plan. And if everything went as he expected, her attitude just might be her downfall.

Three

 asadena.

Amber scowled at the tree-lined streets and perfectly manicured lawns to which Finn had led her. Swing sets and families and paper routes. Everyone going about their daily lives, never scratching beneath the surface. Amber had spent her childhood in a similar neighborhood, but she'd gotten her fingernails dirty. As a kid, she'd clawed down to the muck underneath, and it had sucked her in and never let her go.

She might have started life in a Pasadena-like place, but she could never go back. Her mistakes and then her work had changed her. Normally, that didn't bother her. Her life was her life. She loved it, and she didn't believe in having regrets. But every once in a while that other life snuck up, like something in her peripheral vision.

When James had stepped into her room at the tri-county juvenile detention center, he'd saved her life. Amber knew that. But still she wondered. . . .

If James hadn't come along, would she have eventually saved herself? And if she had, would this have been her destiny? Gladiolas and neighbors and children playing kickball on the lawn?

Her nose wrinkled in distaste, and the thought didn't linger. She'd never been big on what-ifs.

The motorcycle purred beneath her as she maneuvered the streets, keeping a decent distance from Finn in case he got curious about the black-clad biker who'd been on his tail all morning. But he seemed oblivious, which both heartened and pissed her off. In her line of work, agents who were oblivious tended to end up dead. Which meant Finn probably wasn't an agent. Or, if he was, he was a downright bad one.

At the end of the block, Finn turned into the driveway of a familiar house hosting a huge yard sale. Amber watched with a smile, realizing she'd correctly guessed his destination. Back when she'd first encountered Finn, he'd been searching for Albert Alcott with the help of a local P.I. who lived on this very street. As soon as Finn had turned away from the beach and headed up the freeway toward Pasadena, Amber had guessed that he was going to visit his buddy. Turned out she was right, and she gave herself a couple of Brownie points.

She slowed to a stop, idling across the street from a lawn party, complete with a smoking grill and a piñata for the kids. A dozen pairs of eyes regarded her with curiosity, and Amber grimaced with sudden realization—she was in the heart of suburbia, and she didn't have a thing to wear. Black leather simply wasn't the fashion statement she wanted to make.

"Han," she said. "Do you read me?" No answer. Probably out of range. Which meant that her plan to have Brandon deliver her something fun and flirty and sure to catch Finn's attention was out the window. Unless . . .

She shifted into gear and headed forward, finding a nice, normal-looking station wagon to park behind. She killed the engine, then bent over and pulled her helmet off, welcoming the cool rush of air as her hair tumbled loose. She lowered the kickstand, tossed her leg over the bike, and dismounted. Then she twisted the latch and lifted the seat to reveal the storage compartment underneath. *Thank you, Linus.*

The compartment was bigger than it looked from the outside, and it was filled with a variety of clear vacuum-packed bags, each with a purple label bearing a photo of the enclosed clothing item, along with the bisected compass logo that identified Unit 7 property.

Despite the fact that Linus Klondike had been with the Unit since the Paleolithic Age, he'd managed to pull together several fashionable and versatile male and female wardrobes. One bag contained what appeared from the photo to be a full-length evening dress complete with a sequined bodice. Another held a cute little silk outfit with walking shorts, a blouse, a jacket, and matching sandals. Not bad. Amber pulled that one out and continued to rummage.

At the very bottom, behind a black unitard accessorized with a red scarf, she found the perfect Sexy Girl Next-Door outfit. Ignoring the passing cars and other signs of neighborhood life, she went to work behind the station wagon. Less than two minutes later she was completely transformed. A blue and white sweater hugged her chest, the V-style neckline showing sufficient cleavage aided by a handy little bra that lifted and smooshed. Her midriff was bare, the ankle-length blue pants hugging her hips and staying in place with a two-inch wide belt that looked like something out of the Mod Squad but was, she knew, back in fashion. A tiny purse and low-heeled sandals completed the outfit.

She took one last look around to confirm that no one had noticed her little costume change, and then rolled up her leather outfit and locked it in the seat compartment. Her gun was too big for the tiny handbag, so she locked that up, too. Her Montblanc pen, she kept, moving it from the inside pocket of her leather jacket to the purse. The thing was simply too handy to leave behind.

Finally ready, she stood up straight, tossed her shoulders back . . . and headed off to catch herself a man.

Finn sat in his car until the last strains of Paul Simon's "Kodachrome" died out and the DJ finished his spiel about the song. Finn told himself that he was simply enjoying a favorite tune, but that was a load of bull. Instead, he was putting off the inevitable confession to his best friend that he'd behaved like a complete and utter ass.

"You Light Up My Life" started up next, a song that grated on Finn's nerves. He took that as a sign to get out of the car. The yard sale was going strong, clusters of people milling about, inspecting each and every item as if it might be fodder for the next episode of *Antiques Roadshow*.

Finn scanned the small crowd, locating Jacey and Millie on the wraparound porch. Someone had lugged a television outside, and Finn could see that the women were engrossed. Neither of the women noticed him, but he caught a line from the movie they were watching—*I'm too old for this shit*. Finn smiled. He should have known they'd be watching *Lethal Weapon*.

He crossed the lawn, cutting catty-corner in front of the house from the driveway to the area where David had set up the yard sale. As Finn approached, David was making change for a tall woman in an oversized flannel shirt who'd filled a basket with an odd assortment of coffee cups, empty Danish cookie tins, and rag dolls. As the woman left, apparently thrilled with her haul, David turned, his face breaking into a wide grin the second he saw Finn.

"Finn, buddy. Long time no see. Put on your sales cap and give me a hand with some customers."

Finn raised an eyebrow. "I haven't been over here in two months, and all you can do is pass out work assignments? How come I get roped in and your wife is relaxing on the porch?"

David laughed. "One word—Millie." He nodded toward the porch. "She said Jacey needed to get off her feet, and then she dragged my wife to the porch." He shrugged, a *what can you do* gesture, but Finn could tell David didn't really mind. For that matter, he was grinning from ear to ear.

"What am I missing?" Finn asked, his suspicion piqued.

"Not a thing," David said, but the corner of his mouth twitched. "I just need help making change." He nodded toward the porch. "My wife's lost in a sea of Mel Gibson. It's scary the way she and Millie have bonded."

Finn laughed. David's Aunt Millie was, as she liked to say, on the youthful side of ninety. But her mind was still sharp and, if her fascination with Mel Gibson was any indication, her libido wasn't in bad shape either.

"I'll help," Finn said, "but I came for food."

David cocked his head, regarding Finn carefully. "Female troubles." It was a statement, not a question.

"Something like that," Finn admitted.

"Maybe you should follow Millie's advice and just get married," David said. "I hate to admit it, but she was right about me."

Finn laughed. "Yeah, but you already married Jacey. All the good ones are taken."

"True," David said solemnly. "I guess you're screwed."

Finn rolled his eyes, his mood already lifting. Maybe he'd made a huge ass out of himself where Tatiana was concerned, but even if he had, so what? He'd made a huge ass out of himself before, and the odds were good he'd do it again, too.

David glanced at his watch, then scanned the yard. Finn followed his friend's gaze, counting six people still dotting the makeshift sales floor. The two old men he'd seen as he drove up were arguing over a bin of vinyl LPs. David's next-door neighbor's

son was taking a long, hard look at the skateboard
that had been Finn's doom so many years ago. Two
teenage girls squatted in front of a box of old magazines, flipping the pages and giggling like fiends.
And a brunette Finn hadn't seen earlier was standing under the oak tree, her back to Finn, as her finger traced down the side of David's ten-year-old
snow skis.

"How long are you keeping the store open?" he
asked.

"The signs say five, but I'll break it down before
then if all the stuff is sold." David grinned. "Don't
worry. Right now I just need you to help make
change. Manual labor won't be involved for at least
a few more hours."

"Well, then I'm your man," he said. "I can't
believe you're selling the skateboard," he said. His
eyes drifted toward the brunette. "Or the skis."

"The skateboard should have gone long ago,
although you're welcome to it if you want it for sentimental reasons."

Finn faked a shudder. "My collarbone would
never forgive me," he said. "The skis, though, I
might take you up on. Put on some new bindings,
and they'll be good as new."

"Take them," David said. "And anything else you
want."

"Thanks. I might just take—" He broke off,
squinting at something familiar laid out on the
middle of the card table. "Is that the watch I bought
you last Christmas?"

David had the good grace to look sheepish.
"Sorry," he said. "I should have asked if you wanted it
back. But the band's broken, and I don't exactly have

a need for a watch with a global positioning system."

Finn just stared at him. "Are you kidding? Who knows when something like that might come in handy?"

"In one of *your* fantasies, maybe."

Finn grunted in response, then pocketed the watch. He wasn't really ticked off—it *had* been a stupid gift for David. But when Casio had first come out with the affordable watch, Finn had wanted one for himself, but he couldn't really justify the purchase. And so he'd lived vicariously through his buddy's Christmas present. "The next time you're stranded in the desert, you're going to wish you had this thing, you know."

"I'll take my chances," David deadpanned.

One of the teenage girls rushed over to David, waving a stack of ancient *Mad* magazines. While David haggled over price, Finn glanced toward the tree. The woman had switched her attention to a pair of ski boots at the base, her back still toward him. The skis, red Rossignols, leaned against the tree, their waxy sheen shimmering in the late-afternoon sun.

He studied the woman—her rich brown hair, the curve of her ass—as he slid into fantasy. Agent Python knew her, of course. *Angelique Roquefort.* Tatiana's nemesis. She must be trying to intercept the information, just as Agent Python was doing. And while he and Angelique weren't technically allies, where Tatiana was concerned, they both realized the utility of cozying up to your enemy.

She stood next to the lone tree at the mountaintop, and Agent Python stood behind her. They each knew the other was there, but neither could acknowledge it. Their intermediaries had planned the rendezvous. Trail 6, at the fork. The left path by the bent pine. There, under cover of the dense fir trees and the sparsely populated black trail, they would make the exchange.

Without even a glance back, she took off, heading down the mountain with a speed and power that seemed to mock her petite size. He snapped his heel down, locking the boot into place, and pushed off after her.

He'd learned to ski during his time at a Swiss boarding school, and he'd developed a love for the sport. Now he swooped and swished, careful to stay a good distance behind her, the view of her rear as her body undulated down the mountain as invigorating as the icy wind on his face.

She slid to a perfect stop right beside the tree, then waited for him to halt beside her. "I've longed for this moment, Mr. Teague," she said, then pressed her lips, already warm with passion, against his. "You are," she said, "so very hard to resist."

The fantasy was just getting good when David laughed, the sound pulling Finn out of his reverie. "You're as bad as I am," David said. A writer, David had the habit of slipping into his scenes at the oddest of moments.

"I'm worse," Finn said, then told David about his run-in with Tatiana.

To David's credit, he only laughed hysterically for

a minute or two. "Well, I would say you should just ask her out. But chances are she thinks you're a nutcase and would run for the hills." His grin spread wide. "Either that, or she'd say yes, and I'm not sure what that would say about her."

Finn crossed his arms and scowled, trying hard not to laugh himself.

"Of course, just because you need to avoid her doesn't mean you need to avoid all females. Maybe you just need to get laid."

"David!" The surprisingly strong voice came from Millie, and Finn turned to see her and Jacey walking past a card table stacked with old T-shirts, and well within earshot. "Such talk. The boy needs to find a wife, not a warm body. Isn't that right, Finn?"

Finn turned to face the older woman, realizing he'd just been saddled with a *When did you quit beating your wife?* question. If he said no, then he sounded like he just wanted to boff any female who wandered by. If he said yes, he was giving Millie license to search out eligible females.

"Absolutely," he finally said. It was, after all, the only reasonable reply, since Millie would commence a scorched earth campaign to find him a wife no matter how he answered.

"Good boy." She pointed a finger at David. "You behave."

David managed to look both amused and sheepish at the same time. "Yes, ma'am."

Finn threw an arm around the older woman's shoulder. "I thought you and Jacey were watching Mel."

Jacey shook her head, her red hair dappled with

sunlight. "Apparently, you rank. Millie actually turned the television off and said we had to come say hi."

"Really?" Finn stood straighter and puffed out his chest, then pretended to buff his fingernails on his T-shirt.

"Now don't go getting a big head," Millie said. "It was a videotape, and I can start it up again right where I left off. If it had been HBO, I might not be down here talking to you."

At that, Finn and Jacey exchanged a glance, then both laughed. David moved up from behind Finn and put an arm around Jacey, who snuggled against his side. It was a nice, comfortable gesture, and Finn felt a pang of something akin to jealousy.

"I take it you haven't got a girl yet?" Millie continued, in typical Millie fashion.

"Not yet," he admitted.

"He's working on it, though," David put in. "There's one he's following around just like a puppy dog. If he's pathetic enough, maybe she'll adopt him."

Finn shot his friend a scathing look; David just smiled.

Millie ignored her nephew. "We need to find you a wife." She tapped a finger against her chin, then perked up. "Have you met Doreen?" Doreen cleaned the house twice a week. Before David had met Jacey, Millie had tried to set him up with the girl.

"Millie," David said, a note of warning in his voice.

Her eyes went wide, the picture of innocence. "What? I just want to see both my boys settled down."

"I think Doreen's married," Finn said.

Millie's face fell. "You mean she found a young man nicer than you?"

"Hard to believe, I know," Finn said.

"Well, there must be someone else." The finger was tapping again, and Finn imagined her flipping through the cards in a mental Rolodex. "*She* looks nice," Millie said, nodding somewhere behind Finn. His stomach sank. Surely the attractive brunette hadn't overheard this bizarre conversation. *Had she?*

He turned slowly, relieved to see that she was too far away to actually hear their conversation. Besides, she seemed engrossed in checking out David's old paperback novels.

"Now that's a woman who looks bright," Millie said. "Very sweet. Clearly intelligent. A good match." She gave him a tiny shove in the lower back, egging him toward her.

He glanced back, frowning. "And you can tell this how? By the keen way she's inspecting David's old dime novels?"

"She has clever eyes," Millie said, her chin going up.

"You can't even see her eyes from your angle," David said.

Millie just pursed her lips. "I better go talk to her," she said. "She might have questions about those books."

She started stepping in that direction, but David managed to catch her by the elbow.

Finn nodded toward the house. "I'm going to go inside and raid the refrigerator," he said. "And Millie's coming with me."

"But—" she started.

"Because I'm not interested," Finn finished. "Not at all."

But right then, the brunette turned, and Finn realized he had to eat his words. The woman standing there—the sexy creature wearing tight navy blue pants and sporting a bare midriff—was none other than Amber Robinson.

And, truth be told, Finn was very interested indeed.

Four

With a glorious sigh, Diana sank down in the mud, letting the warm goo ease over her breasts. *Heaven.* Beside her, a uniformed attendant bent down to adjust the temperature knobs on the tub.

"Comfortable?" he asked. "Can I get you anything?"

She nailed him with a regal stare. Really, would the man never leave? He'd been puttering around for at least ten minutes.

"The lady is fine," Drake said from the tub beside her. Like her, he was almost completely submerged. "Or she *will* be fine once we have some privacy."

The attendant shot Drake a venomous look, and Diana bit back a sigh of exasperation. She adored Drake, but he needed to learn how to address the little people. What kind of service would they get if he irritated their attendant?

"We're fine," she said, hoping to appease the boy. "Perhaps you could come back and check on us in twenty minutes?"

The attendant looked from her to Drake, then gave a curt, subservient nod. He crossed over the redwood decking to the door back into the facility, leaving her and Drake alone in their tubs, a stunning view of the Los Angeles basin looming before them.

"So what the fuck does he want?" Drake said as the door swung shut. He wasn't referring to the attendant.

Diana knew exactly whom he was talking about—Phineus Teague. Unfortunately, she didn't know the answer to Drake's question, and that irritated her. Diana hated being unprepared.

Drake smiled, that sexy, smoldering grin she knew so well. Then he pushed himself all the way out of the tub, the muscles in his arms flexing with the effort to lift the rest of his body. He stood there naked, gleaming and hard despite the muck and mire stuck to him. And then he casually stepped out of the tub, crossed the two paces to her mud bath, and climbed in to join her.

His foot grazed the inside of her thigh. "It's okay, babe. Just tell me what you do know," he said, the touch both relaxing and stimulating.

She eased lower into the mud. "I don't know much. He's my neighbor, and he's following me. Or he was until I lost him. *After* I had a little fun with him." She reached for the Perrier, then took a long swallow of water. "I've started gathering information, but right now all I really know is his name, his phone numbers, and his employer."

"A lawyer, you said," Drake noted.

"Basic commercial business litigation." She shrugged. "Beyond that, your guess is as good as mine."

Drake closed his eyes, his fingers intertwined beneath his chin. Diana took another sip of her water and studied his face. It was a strong face, the tiny wrinkles around his eyes and mouth adding character to the hard planes. It was also a recognizable face, and he'd taken a risk coming to the spa. Still, it was a risk he took at least monthly, saying he needed the relaxation. She didn't doubt it. Drake was as attractive as ever, but his eyes were tired and his skin was sallow. He was pushing himself to exhaustion, and she worried about him.

After this gig, he'd promised they would retire. But she doubted it. He already had more money than God, so she didn't believe he'd simply stop when his offshore accounts topped ten billion. And it wasn't really about revenge, even though Drake said it was. He probably even believed it. But Diana knew better. It was the chase that thrilled Drake. The hunt. The euphoria of sneaking a cookie out of the cookie jar.

She understood. She'd had more than her share of cookies, too, and she was still coming back for more.

Drake had pushed the envelope all his life, and his reward had been misunderstanding and misapprehension. He should never have ended up a criminal, but the government fools hadn't understood his particular brilliance. So now he had to move in shadows, cast in disguises. The theatrics of it suited him well.

But despite the shadows and the disguise, there was no escaping Drake's dark good looks. The man emitted some compelling force. Diana had counted five women as they'd passed through the spa to their private room, and each of the five had turned to watch Drake pass, their perky little breasts practically saluting.

But they couldn't have him. Drake was all hers. She was the one his eyes burned for at night, and no matter what, she intended to be the only woman who ever graced his bed.

"I don't want to speculate," he said, his eyes still closed. "I want to *know* who this wild card is." His eyes opened, dark and demanding. "It's your job to find out."

Diana pulled back, away from the persistent brush of his foot against her thigh. Her body tensed, anger flaring. But she tamped it down. He was right. Drake had trusted her with this mission, and that included dealing with her damn nosy neighbor. Still, justified or not, she didn't like it when Drake was mad.

"Maybe he's just a guy," she said, her voice even. She traced her fingertips down her neck and between her breasts. "Maybe he thinks I'm hot." She added a little pout to her voice, just for effect. It worked.

A chuckle erupted, starting from somewhere low in his chest. "Di, you're right. I'm an asshole."

Victorious, she leaned back, sliding her foot up to nestle at his crotch. "I just want you to remember what's important."

"You know I'd never forget." He closed his hand over her foot, pressing his fingertips into the tender arch and sending a flurry of activity racing through her blood. There were a lot of reasons why she was with Drake Mackenzie; the fact that together they could turn a bed to cinders was only one.

He rubbed her foot against him, and she pressed down with her toes. She wanted to feel him harden beneath her, to know she'd won, but already he was back in control. One slight concession to her ego, and then he'd replaced his blood with ice. It was the trait she most admired in him. And most despised.

"What else?" he asked, pure business once again.

She licked her lips, tempted to turn the charm up, to try once more to win their little game. But she didn't. It wouldn't work, anyway. "The truth is, I can't figure out what he's up to. It's driving me nuts." Diana didn't like things messy, and her neighbor had the potential to create a very big mess.

Drake nodded, rubbing his chin. "Well, you'll just have to keep trying, won't you, babe?"

"I'll do what I can," she replied tersely. "I seem to recall being assigned a very tight schedule."

"One we need to keep. Our bidders have already RSVP'd for the demonstration. Any more mistakes and we'll not only lose face, we'll lose billions." He squeezed her foot. "And our Oscar-worthy performance will be nothing more than a dim figment of your imagination instead of a pyrotechnical reality."

Her heart went pitty-pat. How many men would threaten to blow up the Hollywood sign? Not many. But Drake was doing just that for her. Well, not *only* for her. But that's what made them so good together. The way their goals intertwined. His for money and revenge, and hers for, well, money and revenge. "I love you."

"I know," he said.

She frowned. "But surely this guy isn't a serious threat. You said we were under the radar on this one." Of course, he'd said that before their test run, too, and that had been a fiasco.

"I'm not a miracle worker," he said with a scowl. "We've already had one screwup. I'm not going to risk another."

She nodded. The failure of the access code had been a huge setback. Once he'd calmed down, Drake had contacted his silent partner and was assured that the changed code had been the result of an underling's unfortunate attack of conscience. Drake's identity and plan remained unknown to the agency. Diana had her doubts, but Drake seemed convinced, citing old alliances and shared secrets. More, he'd refused to move back the demonstration, meaning they had to obtain the new access code.

In that regard, Diana's talents had proved useful. She cracked the code and, she thought, all was well. It wasn't. ZAEL implemented a changing code, reprogramming the access information every three hours. A smart move on ZAEL's part, but it put Diana in an impossible position. The software she'd developed took days, not hours, to ferret out access information.

Which meant they had only one choice, and that was to go in through a back door. Drake's invisible partner had pointed them to the man with the key to that door, and Drake had again turned to Diana, citing the need for her *other* talents.

His brow furrowed. "We *will* have control of the system in time, won't we?"

"Of course," she snapped, irritated at the hint of accusation. After all, she wasn't the one who set the presentation so soon. Only two more days, and he expected miracles. Defiant, she met his eyes. "It's all arranged. I'm meeting with Poindexter, and tonight's the night. Don't worry. I know exactly what we need." She slicked her hair back from her face, her distaste palpable. The job was too unpleasant by half.

"Good," he said. He squeezed her foot again, and she felt him harden under her touch.

She shivered slightly. "I don't want to sleep with him."

"But if you have to, you will."

"Of course." But she'd close her eyes and think of Drake.

"As for the neighbor," he said, "give me the name, and I'll see what I can find out."

"Phineus Teague," she said.

"Phineus? What the hell kind of name is that?"

"His, apparently."

Drake snorted. "Well, Mister Phineus Teague," he said, "I hope you're just angling for a quick roll with my lady. Because if you're up to anything else, your ass is toast."

Five

mber?"

Amber twisted around, clutching a battered copy of Ian Fleming's *On Her Majesty's Secret Service* as she feigned surprise. "Finn?" She blinked and took a tentative step toward him. "What on earth are you doing in Pasadena?"

"This is my best friend's house," he said, nodding at the small group gathered behind him. "What are *you* doing here?"

The question was a reasonable one, and said without any hint of suspicion. Amber mentally applauded her dramatic talent, and flashed her most innocent smile. "A friend and I decided to haunt garage sales today, but she got called away, and I told her I'd find my own way home."

"Called away?"

"She's a surgeon," she said, the lie tripping easily

off her tongue. "Got paged." She shrugged. "Happens all the time. I always carry taxi fare when I'm with her."

"Exciting life," he said, a hint of something close to wistfulness lacing his voice.

"For her," Amber said with a shrug. She twisted a strand of hair around her finger, her eyes locking onto his. "My life's about as dull as they come."

"Join the club," he said.

Her eyes narrowed, wondering if he meant it, or if they were both telling the same lie.

"You two know each other?" Millie came over and put her hand on Finn's back.

"Millie . . ." David's voice drifted over from a few yards away, the warning clear.

"I'm just making conversation," the older woman said.

"I'm Amber," she said, putting on her broadest smile. She stepped forward, hand outstretched, as she pretended she'd never seen Millie before, much less had her, David, and Jacey investigated. "Finn's my next-door neighbor."

"Isn't that nice, dear." The older woman took her hand off Finn's back so she could swing her entire arm around his shoulders. "Did I hear you say you're taking a taxi home?"

Amber nodded. "My friend drove us here. Well, a few blocks away, actually. I was just walking when I stumbled on your yard sale." Now *there* was a doozy. No one walked in Los Angeles if they could help it.

"Nonsense," Millie said, and for a moment Amber thought she'd been caught in a lie. "I wouldn't dream of you taking a taxi. Finn can drive you home, can't you, Finn?"

Amber smiled at Finn. "That's a very sweet offer, but I wouldn't want to put you out," she said, though that's exactly what she wanted to do. More than that, even. Finn hardly seemed like the type to play hard to get. So if everything went as planned, she'd have run through her basic flirting repertoire by dinner and be in his bed by midnight. Barring unforeseen circumstances, she should have a better handle on who Finn was, where he came from, and who he was working for before the morning paper landed on his doorstep.

Surprisingly, the thought made her a little sad.

"It actually wasn't *my* offer," Finn said. "But I'm happy to drive you home. We're going to the same place, after all."

"Right," she said. She met his eyes, saw amusement reflected there, and this time the smile that touched her lips was genuine. She liked this guy, which worked out well considering she was probably going to end up sleeping with him. She'd do what was necessary to get the job done, but if the guy wasn't a dud, that made it so much more palatable.

And Phineus Teague was definitely no dud. The man intrigued her. She might not be interested in a relationship, but she wasn't about to pass up a good time. Especially not one that was sanctioned by her job.

She'd watched Finn long enough to know the way his hips moved under his jeans, and the way his eyes crinkled when he smiled. He was quick to laugh, had an easygoing grin, and seemed to ooze testosterone. Unless she missed her bet, Phineus Teague knew his way around a woman, and Amber was looking forward to letting him practice his navigation skills.

Oh, yes. If she had to pull Mata Hari duty, she certainly could have done worse. As it was, she intended to thoroughly enjoy this project.

"You don't have to leave right now, do you?" Millie asked, closing a warm hand over Amber's wrist.

"I hope not," David said. "I just roped Finn into helping with the sale." He slipped his arm around Jacey's waist. "Since you've appropriated my help, I've been running this show alone."

Millie sniffed. "If recollection serves, this sale was your idea in the first place." She took a step backward and clasped Jacey's hand. "And Jacey needs her rest."

Amber's gaze swept over the group—Millie's protective stance, Jacey's tinted cheeks, David's proud eyes . . . and Finn's clueless stare. "Congratulations," she said to Jacey.

Jacey's face lit up. "Thanks. Obvious?"

Amber shook her head. "I'm just a good guesser."

Finn's brow furrowed and he swiveled his head, shifting his gaze from Amber to Jacey and back again. "What am I missing?"

Jacey leaned over and gave him a quick kiss on the cheek. "Not a thing. We haven't told anyone except Millie. I guess Amber really *is* a good guesser."

"You're—" Finn started.

"Mmm-hmm," Jacey said, practically glowing. "Ten weeks now."

At the news, Finn grabbed Jacey under the arms and started to swing her around. But he stopped abruptly, depositing her back on the ground and stepping back as if she were made of china. Millie and Jacey laughed, and Amber joined in. It was a thoroughly domestic scene, the kind she'd always thought would make her gag with the sickly sweetness of it all. But she wasn't gagging. And the delighted look on David's face, the way he watched Jacey with such emotion shining in his eyes, fascinated her.

Finn caught David in one of those overwhelming guy bear hugs, then backed off and slapped his buddy on the back. "Congratulations. You'll name the kid after me, of course."

"Boy or girl," David said with a grin. "No doubt about it. Little Phineus will be your namesake."

Jacey smiled sweetly. "Don't bet on it."

"At any rate," Finn said, "this calls for a celebration." He turned to Amber. "Are you in a hurry to get home?"

She shook her head. "Not at all." Now that she was in character, she intended to play it for all it was worth.

"Good." He turned to David. "You guys have dinner plans?"

David's eyebrows raised in not-so-subtle amusement. "If I remember correctly, you came here looking for food. Something about certain troubles."

Finn waved the remark away. "That's getting better all the time. Seriously, dinner? My treat. I'll put the meal together, you provide dessert." He glanced around the yard. "You didn't sell the grill, did you?"

David just rolled his eyes, not bothering to answer.

"Need anything from the store?" Finn asked.

"Some nonalcoholic champagne," Jacey said.

"And some alcoholic champagne," Millie added.

"Maybe we should send the girls," David said. "After all, you're my hired help."

"Indentured servitude," Finn said. "And nobody picks out my steaks but me."

"Besides," Millie added, "Finn and Amber should go together."

"Millie!" Jacey said, pure embarrassment lacing her voice.

"What?" Millie's face was the picture of innocence.

"It's okay," Finn said, turning to Amber. "It looks like we're being fixed up. At least for the evening. That okay with you?"

She laughed, the sound bubbling out in a way that surprised her. "As a matter of fact," she said, "it is."

Diana was on the move again, and Brandon had her in his sights. She'd spent less than two hours at the spa, and Brandon had been privy to their conversation on the deck, courtesy of the miniature microphone he'd hidden on the control panel of Diana's mudbath. He'd donned the uniform of an attendant, and the ruse had paid off.

When Diana departed, Drake remained, cooking in a hot tub while she dressed and headed out. Brandon's first instinct had been to stay in the spa and confront Drake, to surprise him and push his head under the bubbling water until the life drained out of him. But that wasn't a good idea, no matter how satisfying. For one, Drake "Maddog" Mackenzie was as well-trained—if not better—as Brandon. And while Brandon would clearly have the advantage over a half-naked man in a hot tub, he was astute enough to know that the advantage wasn't *that* great.

From a more practical standpoint, they didn't know how much of Mackenzie's plan had already been set in motion. Even if they took the leader out, the shit might still hit the fan. And they wouldn't be any closer to knowing when, where, or how.

So Mackenzie lived. For now, anyway.

And now while Mackenzie relaxed at the spa, Brandon was sticking close to Diana. At first, he'd vacillated over which one to follow, but in the end, the decision was easy. Drake was calling the shots, which meant he wasn't going to get his hands dirty.

So Brandon had made a call to the Unit's Los Angeles field office and ordered two new guys to tail Drake.

Diana was the go-to gal—the one to follow—and right now she was going to try to wrangle some information out of a contact.

Poindexter. Who the hell was this Poindexter she was going to meet? Brandon had already checked, and no one with that name worked at ZAEL.

Amber had been watching Diana for days now, and the only person she'd been spending any significant time around was Bernie Waterman, a Level I data processor who didn't even have access to classified information. So what was up with that?

The only thing Brandon could surmise was that Diana intended to use Bernie to get close to someone else . . . but whom?

Brandon had no idea, but he intended to keep the tail on Diana until he found out.

"Rebecca. You copy?" He waited, listening in his earpiece. Nothing.

He cruised for a while, following Diana up the 405 and then onto the 101. He tried again. "Rebecca. Do you read?"

A slight burst of static encouraged him. He was coming into range.

The static increased, and he heard the faint echo of her voice. What she was saying didn't make any sense—*maybe corn to go with the rib eye?*—but that really wasn't his concern.

"Rebecca," he tried again. "If you read, acknowledge."

"Oh, yes," she said. "Clear."

"I'm sorry." A male voice, presumably Finn's. "What's clear?"

Amber cleared her throat. "These," she said, and Brandon heard a plastic-sounding crinkle. "I hate these clear packages. Makes the food much too tempting."

"Pretzels are tempting?" Finn asked.

"Love them," Amber said, a little too enthusiastically. "And great for picnics."

"Do you want to get some?" Finn asked.

"I take it you can't talk," Brandon said.

"Absolutely," Amber said.

"Then I will," Brandon said.

"Throw them in the cart," Finn said.

"Great," Amber said.

"It's something big, all right," Brandon said. "But I still don't know what." He gave her a rundown of Drake's conversation with Diana. "You copy?"

"Mmm-hmm." He heard a muffled noise, probably Finn talking while Amber's mouth was closed, and then, "I'm just going to run over there and grab the champagne."

"You trust me on the steaks?"

"Implicitly," she said.

"Steak and champagne," Brandon said. "I knew you moved fast, but this is pretty amazing."

"Cut the crap, Brandon," she said.

"Any ideas?" he asked.

"He called it an Oscar-caliber show?" Amber said, repeating what Brandon had reported. "Think that's important?"

"Probably just talk," Brandon said. "Drake's always been a political guy. What would he care about celebrities or movie premiers or any of that?"

"Beats me," she said. "And the Academy Awards aren't until next year, anyway. He probably just means something large and flashy. You didn't get any sense of what they're cooking up?"

"Nada," he said. "But she's on her way to meet with this Poindexter right now. I'm on it."

"I just don't get it," she said.

"Neither do I," he admitted. "I get the impression something went wrong with their plan, and now they're scrambling to have all the pieces in place for checkmate."

"And we're playing blindfolded," she said.

"But we've got a lead with this mysterious Poindexter, so hopefully I'll know more later."

"What about Bernie? Has Schnell authorized you to interview him? See what's up with him and Diana?" Amber had put in a request days ago, but Schnell thought that making the contact would be tipping their hand. Brandon didn't agree, but what could you do?

"Negative," he said. "I put in a call, but still no authority."

"Shit."

"Well, if we're lucky, you'll find out something from Finn. He's been watching Diana, too. He may already have this figured out."

"Maybe," she said, dubious. "Either way, we wait and we watch."

"At least you'll be occupied during the wait." He chuckled. "Are you really having steak? Or is that a euphemism I haven't heard before."

"Ah, ah," she said with a laugh. "Don't you know a lady never tells?"

"Never tells what?"

Finn's voice.

Amber closed her eyes. Took one deep breath to help her drown out the sound of Brandon's laughter in her ear, and then turned around. "Never tells a gorgeous man what's on her mind," she said. "It destroys the mystery."

His warm grin was wide and genuine, and for the first time in her life, she felt a little guilty for playing a part. She told herself that was stupid—after all, for all she knew, he was playing a part, too. But none of that changed the fact that this was a man who—for whatever reason—got under her skin.

Dangerous.

"I guess that would be a problem," he said. "If there were any gorgeous men around. And if you had any secrets . . ."

"Oh, I've got secrets," she said. One true statement in a day that promised to be chock full of lies.

"Really?" He moved closer, and she caught the scent of mint mixed with soap. He seemed to loom over her, and Amber wasn't short. His dossier had said six foot three, but he seemed larger. All sinew and muscle and pent-up power. Truly, the man was spectacular. With narrow hips and broad shoulders, and a torso that screamed to have a woman's fingers caress those washboard abs.

"Come on," he teased. "You can tell me."

"I'm not sure that I can," she said. "You fall into that gorgeous category I mentioned earlier."

"Good going, girl," Brandon said, ribbing her. "Don't ever tell me you don't know how to flirt."

Amber felt her cheeks warm, an odd sensation considering she rarely blushed. She'd played this game dozens of times with Brandon listening in. So why did she suddenly find herself craving privacy?

"I'm flattered," Finn said. He leaned against the shelving, the motion bringing him infinitesimally closer, and her pulse began to race. "But I think that's just an excuse not to tell me those secrets," he said.

"Aw, shit," Brandon said.

"What?" Amber answered aloud, then mentally kicked herself.

"What?" Finn repeated. "Your secrets. Remember? You said you had plenty."

"Oh," Amber said. "Right."

"She's heading back into the canyons," Brandon said. "I'm going to lose you. Listen quick. Diana's on to Finn. And Drake's pissed."

Amber drew in a breath, the world seeming to shift slightly under her feet, and this time not because of the proximity of the man in front of her. She still needed to investigate Finn, needed to figure out his game. That much hadn't changed.

Now, though, she also needed to protect him.

So much for her plan to be done with the man by morning. Apparently, she was going to be sticking to him like glue. His own private, very personal, bodyguard.

Not an unwelcome proposition, really. She took a long look at him and stifled a sigh. There was just something about a man with a strong jaw and broad shoulders. . . .

With a scowl, she shook her head, trying to dissolve the fantasy. She didn't usually react so strongly to men, and it unnerved her. She needed to stay focused.

He brushed a strand of hair behind her ear. "Lost in thought? Or avoiding my question?"

"You want my secrets?" she murmured, pulling herself back into her role. "I can do that."

After all, there was no better time than the present to start her get-close plan with gusto. And so in one quick motion, she lifted herself onto her toes and swung her arms around his neck.

His mouth opened as if in surprise, but before any sound escaped, she pressed her lips against his. If she'd caught him off guard, he covered well. His mouth was hot and firm beneath hers, and his tongue demanded entrance, as if this kiss had been his idea all along.

She opened her mouth in response, her body trembling as she explored his deep, delicious mouth. He tasted of want and need, of infinite possibilities and untamed passion. Part of her wanted to simply give in, to meld against him and let him take the kiss where he would. But this was her kiss, she'd begun it, and she wasn't about to lose control.

She pulled back, her teeth grazing his lower lips, before she moved in, insistent, her hands pressed to the side of his face as she held him in place, his head tilted at just the right angle. He foiled her, though, cupping her butt as she moved and urging her closer until she was pressed hard against him. Amber heard a low moan of satisfaction and realized it was coming from her.

Slightly dazed, she broke off, holding on to the beer case for balance. She took a deep breath, gathering control and focusing on her plan. Her body hummed with passion that wasn't fading despite the few inches of air she'd placed between them.

Her reaction to this man had startled her, and she needed to regain the upper hand. She tilted her chin up just slightly, her eyes meeting his even as she let a slow, sultry smile ease across her face. "My secret, Mr. Phineus Teague, is that I followed you to Pasadena." She cocked her head, hoping she looked both sexy and beguiling. "I guess you could say I've got a little bit of a crush on you."

She'd expected him to register some surprise, but he didn't. Instead he just took a half step backward and regarded her with curiosity mixed with something else. Interest? Passion? She wasn't certain, and he was giving her no clues.

He said nothing, and his silence unnerved her. The man was too cool.

"I see you're speechless," she said, widening her eyes for maximum effect. "Was I too bold?"

Two seconds ticked by, the weight of the time almost unbearable. But then a lazy grin crossed his face and his eyes flashed, dark and dangerous. "Hell no," he said.

That was an answer she'd expected. He was, after all, a guy.

He moved toward her then, every male inch of him, until he was looking down at her from his five-inch vantage point. He hooked a finger under her chin, and she trembled slightly, annoyed with herself for allowing the unbidden reaction.

"Actually," he said, "I think you're just what the doctor ordered."

She wanted to ask what he meant, but he tilted her face up, his lips closing over hers before she could voice the question.

His response to her initial kiss might have been enthusiastic, but in comparison to *this* kiss, it had been a peck. This was more than just a kiss. Finn was making love to her with his mouth. His tongue dipped and teased, exploring and tasting. Demanding, and yet giving. Sensual, and yet flirtatious.

Her knees weakened, and she sagged a bit, but there was nowhere to go. Finn held her tight against him, the undeniable evidence of his interest pressed insistently against her thigh. Her body warmed, her veins filling with a liquid heat that seemed to pool between her legs, instigating a persistent throbbing that she itched to satisfy.

The man worked on her like a chemical reaction. Apart, she could remain inert, pretending he didn't affect her. But once they touched, she sizzled and sparked and there was no going back.

In her line of work, that was a dangerous reaction to have to a man. Especially a man she needed to bed.

Where Finn was concerned, Amber was going to have to be very, very careful.

He pulled away, his lips brushing her cheek. "Your kiss opened a door, babe. And I'll tell you just once, because I'm a gentleman—if you want to close that door, do it fast and do it now. Otherwise, we're going all the way inside."

She met his gaze. "The door stays open," she said. That was her mission, after all. And all she could do was hope that when they walked over the threshold, she'd be able to handle whatever lay on the far side of Finn's door.

Six

Finn's body tightened, the press of Amber's curves against him intoxicating. He barely knew this woman. Knew only, in fact, that in the space of twenty-four hours she'd done a complete one-eighty in looks and personality. Whereas yesterday she'd seemed quiet and shy, today she was aggressive and flirty. Yesterday she'd practically cleaved to her wardrobe of T-shirts and sweatpants, but today, she looked like she'd be perfectly comfortable in the middle of a fashion shoot for *Vogue*.

He had no idea what had brought about the change, but he did know that he was at the center of it—that she was deliberately trying to catch his attention.

And caught it she had. So much so that his whole body was standing at attention.

In a thoroughly dull week where most of his

excitement had been manufactured in his head, this was about the most interesting thing that had happened to him.

Right now, he intended to just go with the flow. He could worry about her motivations later.

Now he moved them backward, until her shoulders were pressed against the chilled cartons of beer in the open refrigerated case. She shivered slightly in his arms, pulling herself closer.

"Cold?" he asked.

"Hot," she said. "Very, very hot."

Footsteps sounded behind them, pausing slightly, and then Finn heard someone subtly clearing his throat. He had to smile; the last time he'd been caught in such a compromising position he'd been under the bleachers with Melissa Jane Hutchinson during halftime.

Drawing on every ounce of strength in his body, he managed to pull away, to put enough space between them for, as his grandma used to say, his guardian angel.

Amber's faint murmur of protest suggested that she wasn't too thrilled he'd invited the angel to the party. She pressed closer, brushing her lips against his. "No fair," she said. "Don't stop."

"Got to," he said. "People are starting to stare."

"I don't care," she said. She pulled back, her head tilted just enough to look him in the eyes. "Do you?" He saw amusement there, and a touch of defiance. And for an instant, Finn was absolutely positive that the woman would have no qualms about dropping down to the vinyl-tiled floor and making love next to the Chilean reds.

There was definitely more to Amber Robinson

than he'd seen before. And he intended to explore every single facet.

"If we keep this up, people will think we're advertising one of the wines. And then the vintner will come in and sign us for some big ad campaign. Suddenly we'll be on the road all the time, personal appearances, talk shows." He shook his head. "Too much, too soon. The stress. We couldn't handle it. And our relationship would crumble before it even got started."

He kept his eyes on her face, wondering if he'd just scared her off with his ramblings. If the twitch at the corner of her mouth was any indication, though, she was amused, not scared.

She licked her lips, the simple gesture desperately erotic under the circumstances. "Relationship, huh?" She cocked an eyebrow. "Is that what we have?"

He laughed. "Babe, a day ago you were my slightly shy, very reclusive neighbor. Today you're seducing me under fluorescent lights. Honestly, I don't know what's between us."

"Sex," she said, her eyes twinkling.

He couldn't argue with that, but her bold, straightforward announcement surprised him. "Oh?"

"Absolutely. Pheromones, chemistry. *Sex.*" She flashed a decadent smile. "We've got sex, Finn," she repeated, as if to clarify. "Or I hope we do." She trailed a finger down the front of his shirt. "If we end up in a relationship, great. But I thought we'd start with the sex and then go from there." She tilted her head slightly to the side, her eyes wide. "Assuming that's okay with you . . ."

"Oh, yeah," he said. "That's perfectly all right with me."

Hardly the typical first date, but he was fast learning that Amber wasn't the typical girl. Which was also perfectly okay with Finn. "So how do you feel about ditching?" he asked, his head bent close to her ear.

From her smile, Finn could tell that Amber knew exactly what he meant. "I'm willing to play hooky if you are." She cocked her head. "They won't mind?"

"Are you kidding? Millie would probably give me a stipend for the afternoon if I told her I was spending it with you."

"David and Jacey?"

"Nah, they're saving money for the baby. We won't get any cash from them."

Amber laughed. "I meant, will they care?"

"Not so long as we deliver the steaks first. You game?"

"I don't know," she said, the grin tugging at her mouth suggesting a different answer. "What do you have in mind?"

Something wild. What Finn had in mind was something wild and wicked and completely satisfying. Something that would make him forget his job and the projects scattered over his kitchen table. Something that would take him away.

He'd found that something in Amber, and now he wanted to make the moment perfect. For him, but especially for her. A mixture of sex and beauty and warmth and passion. And he knew just the place.

Fortunately, traffic was light, so it only took an hour for them to get to Corona del Mar. Finn had discovered the vacant lot with the cliff-side spiral staircase leading down to the sea on one of his diving trips to Laguna Beach, and he hoped that the property hadn't been sold or gated or otherwise closed off.

"Are we lost?" she asked from the passenger seat.

Finn shook his head. "Not yet."

She looked at him as if she didn't quite believe him. "Well, will you at least tell me where we're going?"

"Sorry, babe. I could tell you, but then I'd have to kill you. I guess you'll just have to wait and see."

"Hmmm." She leaned back in the bucket seat, her hand resting on his thigh. "A man who takes control. I like that."

He turned, genuinely surprised. "Funny, you struck me as a woman who preferred to take charge."

"Really? Why's that?"

She seemed so earnest that he couldn't help but laugh. "The way you came on to me in the grocery store leaps to mind."

"Fair enough," she said. "I'll concede the point. I do like being in charge." She lifted her hands up, her fingertips brushing the cloth roof as she arched her back, her sweater stretching tight against her breasts. "But sometimes it's nice to let go and let someone else drive." She turned and flashed him a smile, innocent with just a hint of mischief. "So long as he steers in my direction."

"Believe me, sweetheart," Finn said, finding the street he was looking for and turning onto it. "We've got the same destination in mind."

"Then why should I do anything but sit back and enjoy the ride?"

Her voice, low and sultry, seemed to wash over Finn, finally settling in his cock. Only with supreme effort did he keep the car on the road, overcoming the urge to simply stop right there and go at it like teenagers. Instead, he managed to maneuver the car into the cul-de-sac and steer it into the middle of the vacant lot overlooking the beach.

He put the car in park, killed the engine, and turned to her. The intensity of his desire was curious, though not at all unwelcome. He might be in charge at the moment, but she'd definitely set the wheels in motion, and the fact that she'd pursued him so single-mindedly was an undeniable turn-on.

But it was the *why* that perplexed him. Women had come on to him before, and he couldn't remember one instance where he'd turned a willing female down. But while he'd wanted those women, and while he'd enjoyed exploring their curves and sharing their beds, the hunger he felt for *this* woman was like nothing he'd ever felt before.

He knew that part of her allure had to stem from the inherent mystery—why had she suddenly turned her sights, and her sex appeal, on him? But knowing didn't lessen the lust one bit. He wanted her. Pure and simple. And Finn didn't intend to deny himself. Or her.

He reached out, his palm cupping the back of her neck as he turned his head. His lips met hers, his mouth swallowing up her little sigh of surprise. His tongue danced in her mouth, taking as much as he gave. His fingers twined in her hair, tilting her head to just the right angle.

She went limp in his arms, and he wondered if that was a gift. This woman who had called the shots—who craved control—giving him free rein to explore every inch of her body.

With his other hand, he cupped her breast, her nipple already tight and hard under her sweater and the thin material of her bra. Her breathing was fast and shallow, and her chest rose and fell. He massaged her breast, kneading her soft curves, then dipping his head to suckle her even through the thin, striped sweater.

She made a sound, something between an "oh" and a cry, and she raked her fingers through his hair, pulling him in tighter against her. Finn moaned, rock hard and ready.

He wanted her. More than he could remember wanting any woman. He wanted her fast and furious, and then slow and easy. All night, all day, all week.

"I'm not liking these bucket seats right now," he said.

"I can take care of that," Amber said, her voice a low murmur. "Slide your seat all the way back."

He complied without question, and she climbed over the gear shift to straddle him, her back to the steering wheel, her fingers threaded through his hair. Her mouth closed over his, her hand inching down to stroke his erection.

"Amber," he said, the word little more than a groan. "You're killing me."

"I should stop," she said. "You're no good to me dead."

"Don't you dare," he said. He cupped her ass in both hands, then slid his hand up to stroke her soft, warm back. With his other hand, he slipped her shirt up, exposing a flimsy lace bra. She arched her back, moaning as he closed his mouth over her hard nipple and the puckered, rosy areola.

He wasn't worried they'd be seen in the afternoon light. The cul-de-sac wasn't inhabited; just four large lots waiting for buyers to build fabulous houses with views. But even if they'd been in the middle of a downtown street, Finn doubted he would have cared, and he certainly couldn't have stopped.

He trailed his other hand down her back, then slid his fingertips under the waistband of her pants. A breathy moan escaped her lips, and her single word—*yes*—worked on him more than any aphrodisiac.

His hand crept lower, under the silk of her panties, cupping the smooth, warm skin of her rear. He was on a mission, one he wouldn't fail, to find the ultimate prize. And she helped him along the way, lifting up to give him better access, even as her fingers expertly worked at the buttons on his fly.

Her fingers slipped inside, stroking him through the thin cotton of his boxers. "Do you like that?" she whispered.

He struggled to breathe, his entire body stiffening under her touch. "Hell yes," he managed. She was working magic on his body, but for at least this moment, Finn intended to take control and keep it. In one bold movement, he found her core and slipped two fingers into her wet velvet heat.

Her cry of pleasure centered on his groin, and her muscles clenched around him. She hadn't reached the pinnacle yet, but he intended to take her there.

With his free hand, he covered hers, stilling her

expert ministrations on his cock. She whimpered a noise of protest, but he held fast. "Uh-uh, sweetheart. This is about you."

She opened her mouth again, but he took her in a kiss. Even as he did, he pulled his fingers out, delighted with the way her hips gyrated, silently begging him not to stop.

Her mouth was open to his, her hand now clutching his shirt front, twisting the material even as she writhed against him. He didn't intend to torment her—not for too long—and he slipped his fingers back inside, keeping his forefinger free to tease and stroke her clit.

She broke their kiss, a cry of "oh, yes," ripping from her throat as she arched her back. Her hips undulated as she pressed down on his hand, drawing him in deeper and harder as if she wanted to take all of him.

Finn smiled, knowing that, for the moment at least, Amber truly had lost control. And she'd lost it to him.

Amber couldn't think. Hell, she could barely breathe. Her entire body was lost to the sweet, decadent sensations that Finn was sending spinning through her.

His fingers were igniting a fire in her body, and it was burning wild. The sensations took hold, wresting control from her, so that all that mattered was his touch and the slow build to an inevitable explosion that she craved even as much as she wanted the climb to never, ever stop.

The pad of his finger stroked her clit, and she rolled her hips, helping and honing the sensations. With her hands she clutched her own breasts, the tight pressure on her nipples a delicious counter-point to the heat building between her thighs.

His finger slipped over her slick heat, his touch dead-on perfect, and a crest of pure pleasure washed over her. A low noise filled her ears, and she realized the moan came from her.

She'd never lost control like this. Never let down that barrier between what her body wanted and how far she let it go. But she'd dropped that barrier with Finn, and so easily, too.

And now there was no way back. Not, at least, until she'd come and could finally, maybe, think again. Until then, she was at his mercy, and frankly, she didn't much care.

His whispers, urging her to come for him, caressed her, and she latched onto the words, her entire body tensing as she climbed higher and higher toward the ultimate release. She held her breath as his finger moved faster and faster, the pressure perfectly placed. "Right there," she breathed. "Don't stop."

"I'm not stopping for anything," he said.

And as he spoke, her entire body seemed to explode. She held onto his shoulders, riding the crest of the orgasm, the pleasure so intense it bordered on pain.

When it passed, she collapsed against him, her body limp. He stroked her back as her mind started to clear.

"Thanks," he said.

She lifted her head just long enough to lift an eyebrow in question. "For what?" she said. "I'm the one who should be thanking you."

"For letting me drive," he said simply.

A knot of tension formed in Amber's stomach, and she pressed close to him again, afraid he'd read something in her face. She hadn't let him drive on purpose, but she'd been helpless against his onslaught.

No, that wasn't true. She could have kept a piece of herself tucked away. *She hadn't wanted to.* She'd wanted to lose herself to this man, and that was the most unsettling part of all.

The rush of adrenaline that Finn's touch sent through her body was rivaled only by the times she'd piloted an F-14 or rappelled down the side of Menara Petronas I in Kuala Lumpur. Each an all-consuming rush. The kind of thrill that kept her alive, that reminded her why she wanted to live in the first place.

To find that same thrill in a man's arms was both exhilarating and terrifying. Especially in the arms of *this* man, a dark, sensual enigma who made her blood burn with little more than a look.

And, even more, a man who still remained a mystery.

She'd let herself go, true. She'd lost herself in the moment, yes. But she wasn't about to indulge in useless recrimination. No, she'd simply take back the control, keep a tighter hold, and not let go—not like that—again.

"Amber?"

She didn't answer. Just leaned over and took the door handle and pushed it open.

A grin spread across Finn's face. "Need a little fresh air?"

Amber just cocked an eyebrow and slipped off his lap and into the outdoors. She kept hold of his hand and silently urged him to follow. "The view," she said.

In the distance, the sun reflected off the vibrant water of the Pacific. They couldn't see the beach, but they could hear the roar of the surf pounding against the rocks below. "It's beautiful," Finn said, his eyes focused not on the ocean but on her. "Are we searching for a scenic overlook?"

"Not exactly," Amber said. The lot sloped down toward the cliff, then flattened out again. She cast a glance over the ground, then led him to a smooth, grassy area. "I've seen views before," she said, turning to face him. "But there's something I haven't done yet."

His eyes were knowing. "I can't imagine what."

"Don't worry. No imagination required. This one's going to be pure reality." She nodded at the ground. "Sit."

"Yes, ma'am."

He sat, his legs out in front of him, his hands behind him for balance. Amber turned to face him, her legs planted on either side of his hips. "I don't want to seem ungrateful," she said. "But there's something I want."

"And you're just going to take it."

"Hell yes," she said. In one swift move she pressed the ball of her foot against his chest, pushing him back onto the grass.

"Am—"

"Oh, no," she said. "Not a word." She knelt over him, her knees firm against the ground, her inner thighs pressed against his jeans. The top two buttons of his fly were still open, and she made short work of the rest of them.

"Tell me," he said. "Tell me what it is you want."

She raised an eyebrow. "Darling, if you can't figure it out, I've got some serious doubts about your intelligence."

"Actually," he said, "I just might have an idea." He took her hand and tugged her down toward him.

Amber relaxed into the motion, letting him flip them over until he was straddling her. "Very good," she said with a laugh. "You're thinking along the right lines."

"Let's see if I can stay on track," he said. His hand stroked her face, his fingers tracing her lips. She licked the tip of his finger, taking the entire digit into her mouth, stroking and caressing it with her tongue.

Finn moaned, his eyes closing as she drew his finger in and out, in and out. An erotic rhythm that was starting with her lips and spreading like wildfire through her entire body.

When she stopped, he groaned in protest, but she only smiled, her eyes meeting his. "Lose the shirt," she said.

He didn't argue. Just shifted position so he could undo the row of buttons, then tugged it off. His chest was perfect, hard and ridged, with just a smattering of midnight black hair.

"Nice," she said.

"Glad you approve." He fingered the hem of her sweater. "I showed you mine, now you show me yours."

"Ah-ah," she said. "My rules, remember?"

"Maybe I'm not as intelligent as I thought," he retorted. "Because I don't think we can manage what I thought you wanted if you're still wearing that outfit."

"Trust me, Mr. Teague. We'll manage just fine." This time, she flipped him, kicking her leg up and using his body weight as leverage to get him under her on the grass. It was a nice move, one not many women probably knew, and from his expression, she could see he was suitably impressed.

"I was right," he said. "You do like to be in charge."

"I owned up to that," she said. "You don't have a problem with strong women, do you?"

"Only if they don't follow through," he said.

"Well, then," she said, "you've got nothing to worry about." She grabbed her sweater and tugged it over her head, tossing it on top of Finn's shirt. With Finn's eyes on her, she reached behind and unfastened her bra, adding it to the pile.

The sun was stil high in the sky, and the wind carried the faint hum of traffic from the Pacific Coast Highway. But other than that, only the crash of waves against the shore below filled the air.

She was straddling him, her sex right over his erection, so that he could feel every tiny move she made, and she could feel him harden beneath her. "Touch me," she demanded. And he did. His warm hands cupped her breasts as she tilted her head back, her eyes closed, letting the thrill of his touch zip through her like electricity. She might be taking control, but that damn sure didn't mean she couldn't enjoy herself.

His palms grazed her nipples, the touch so light as to be near torture. A million sparks shot down from her breasts to her clit. She'd been ready since he'd made her come, and now her sex throbbed, wanting him inside her with an intensity she didn't remember feeling for any other man. But not yet. Not that fast. She wanted to take this slow. Wanted to know that he was as desperate for her as she was for him. More, even.

In one fluid motion, she straightened, tracing her hand down her neck, then pushing his hand aside so she could snake a path between her breasts and down to the waistband of her pants.

"Watch," she whispered as she reached to her hip to pull down the side zipper, loosening the pants enough so that she could slide her fingers inside.

Finn's eyes met hers, and she saw desire burning there. "You're killing me," he said.

She just smiled, arching her back as she balanced one hand on his thigh, the other cupping and stroking her sex. She was wet, her panties drenched, her breath coming in little gasps as she slipped a finger inside, avoiding her all-too-sensitive clit. She didn't want to come, not yet. Not without Finn inside her.

Finn groaned, and she could feel him stiff and hard beneath her. "Do you like that?" she asked.

"If you're trying to torture me, you're doing a good job."

"Not torture," she said, sitting up and sliding both hands up his chest. "Anticipation."

"I don't know if I can survive much more anticipation."

She brushed her lips against his ear. "You don't have to."

She stood up, straddling his waist as she peeled the pants, adding them to the growing pile of their clothing. Then she lowered herself over him and slid backward down his body, her hands tugging his jeans and boxers down as he kicked off his shoes. His erection jutted free, and she licked the tip, just enough to tease, as he tugged his jeans the rest of the way off.

As soon as his clothes were tossed aside, she straddled him, still wearing her panties. Finn made a low growling noise, reaching between her legs to shove the crotch piece aside.

"No," she whispered. "Rip them off."

He did. And as the sound of the material ripping hung in the air, she plunged her body down, taking him deep inside her.

Her body tightened around him, and she rode him in slow, practiced movements, watching his face as the passion built. He hardened even more, his cock swelling to fill her, and she took his hand from her hip, pressing his fingers against her mound.

He didn't need any more encouragement, and his fingers found her clit, stroking and coaxing in soft, subtle movements even as she rode him hard. The combination of sensations, soft and wild, hard and gentle, whipped through her. The urge to let go overwhelmed her. But she fought it, willing to lose herself to the wild heat of sex, but not to lose herself completely.

The whirlwind built inside her, lifting her to the pinnacle but not quite taking her over the edge. Finn tensed beneath her, his face tightening and his body quivering. He was close, so close, and Amber let go, letting the storm inside her explode into a million pieces as Finn groaned beneath her, bursting with a storm of his own that both filled and satisfied her.

Sated, Amber sagged on top of him, then rolled to her side as he spooned against her.

"I think I approve of what you wanted," he said.

"I thought you might."

His arm tightened around her waist and she closed her eyes, satisfied. This time she'd kept control. *She'd won.* But as she pressed against him, exhausted but victorious, she couldn't help but wonder if, in winning, she'd lost a little bit, too.

It was a question she didn't examine closely, instead simply shutting her eyes and pressing tight against him, the heat of his body as intense as the heat from the afternoon sun.

"If we don't move," Finn finally said, "we're going to be sunburned in places I'd rather not be burned."

Amber pressed a kiss to his cheek. "I suppose putting our clothes back on is in order. And then what? Back home?"

Finn leaned over her, a world of playfulness in his eyes. "Actually, sweetheart, I had another idea. How about letting me show you a different kind of thrill?"

Seven

The little shit was tailing her!

Diana couldn't believe it, but somehow she'd managed to pick up a tail. She reached up, adjusting her rearview mirror and setting the magnification factor Drake had installed to four-hundred percent.

The driver was three cars back, but still she managed to focus in on his face. She squinted at the image now looming large in the mirror. She'd seen him before. But where . . . ?

And then she realized. The spa. The creep following her was their hunky spa attendant.

She tapped her fingers on the steering wheel even while her teeth worried at her lower lip. She wasn't concerned that he'd overheard her conversation with Drake. They'd been alone during their talk. But she certainly didn't need to risk the guy finding out her secrets by following her to Poindexter's house.

The odds were her tail was just a horny male who'd gotten a look at Diana's boobs slathered in mud. Now she had an admirer and he was insistent on following her to the ends of the earth. Easily dealt with. There wasn't a man on the planet—except Drake—that Diana couldn't intimidate the hell out of.

At the same time, though, she had to be smart about this. The guy was *probably* just an oversexed spa attendant, but she couldn't discount the possibility that he had other reasons for watching her. Like maybe someone was paying him off. And if that was the case, she needed to make absolutely certain that he didn't report back to whoever was pulling his strings.

Determined, she flipped on her blinker and crossed over two lanes of traffic to the access road. He followed, of course, and when she pulled into a nearby Ralph's grocery store, he parked one row away. *Perfect*.

She got out of the car, swung her purse over her shoulder, and headed inside. Rather convenient, really. After all, she really ought to show up at Poindexter's door bearing wine.

Brandon leaned against the ATM machine, watching Diana Traynor pick out a bottle of wine. Apparently that was a long, involved process, because it took her a good fifteen minutes to settle on a red wine from one of the shelves labeled FRANCE. He couldn't see the label, which was too bad. Brandon was always on the lookout for a good bottle of wine.

A uniformed security guard glanced at him, probably calculating the odds of Brandon trying to rob the ATM. Brandon flashed a smile, his eyes drifting casually over the rows of cash registers.

As soon as Diana stepped into the express checkout line, Brandon eased out the door, imagining the guard exhaling in relief as he passed. A few seconds later, the lady emerged behind, her eyes fixed on her car. Brandon slipped into the Buick and turned the key. The engine purred to life, and he gripped the steering wheel, keeping the car in gear while he waited to see what direction she took.

She exited onto Magnolia, and he shifted into reverse, planning on following. But a tapping at his window stopped him. He turned to face the security guard. Brandon closed his eyes, allowing himself one brief *oh shit* moment. Then he hit the button to roll down the window. "How can I help you, officer?"

"Would you step out of the car?"

Brandon flashed his *who me?* grin. "Is there a problem?" A stupid question. Of course there was a problem. And he knew exactly what it was—Diana had made his tail. And she'd set this little pit bull on him.

"Just shut off the engine and get out of the car, please."

Brandon considered gunning it and burning rubber on his way out of the parking lot. But he dismissed the idea. Officer Happy there had probably never fired his firearm, but he had the look of a man itching to do so. And the parking lot was bustling with civilians and children.

With a nod, he turned the key, killing the engine.

Then he stepped out of the car and faced the officer.

"Lady says you've been harassing her. Says you flashed her in the parking lot and then followed her inside. I saw you eyeing her myself." The officer stood up straighter, his hand on the butt of his gun and a sneer on his face. The victim of one too many bad cop films. "You're going down, buddy. The D.A.'s got a hard-line policy on indecent exposure."

Brandon had to hand it to Diana. The lady had spunk. Not only had she delayed him, but she'd ensured he'd get suckered into hours of procedural bullshit.

Eventually, he'd get out of this mess, of course. But by the time he did, Diana would be long gone.

And so would his only opportunity for discovering Poindexter's identity.

"You doing okay up there?" Amber heard Finn's voice filtering through the intercom; the man himself was in the cockpit behind her.

She tossed the headphone aside long enough to remove the leather helmet. Her hair streamed out behind her, caught in the prop wash, and she laughed, tossing her hands up above her head in pure joy. "Okay?" she repeated, donning the headphones again. "I'm fabulous!"

They were cruising at an altitude of about one thousand feet, and Amber couldn't have been happier. Finn's idea of a thrill suited her just fine.

"Yeah? Well, then you're going to love this. Hold on!"

The biplane started a climbing turn, transitioning nicely into a descending turn before climbing again. Amber had to grin. Finn was doing a lazy eight, a sexy maneuver, but hardly enough to appease her appetite.

"Not bad," she said, her voice laced with a tease. "But is that the best you can do?"

"You wound me, babe," he said, the suggestion clear in his voice. "I thought I already showed you just how much more I can do."

Amber laughed. "Yeah? Well, show me what you can do in the air."

Even as she spoke, the nose of the plane started to climb, and Amber clutched the smooth leather side of the cockpit, the shoulder harness keeping her firmly in place. Higher and higher, and as Finn aimed the nose back in the direction they'd come, Amber realized he was executing a loop. She let out a whoop for good measure, completely delighted with Finn's idea of showing her a good time. Sunlight glimmered on the fuselage, and as Finn completed the loop, the biplane passed through its own prop wash, shivering slightly as if she, too, found the maneuver exhilarating.

When Finn had suggested another thrill, Amber had expected a speedy return to Los Angeles and the hedonistic comfort of his bed. So when Finn had driven south to the private airstrip just outside San Diego, she'd been totally and completely blown away.

She'd known, of course, that he had a pilot's license. What she hadn't expected was that he'd use that skill as a dating tool. Even more, when Brandon had given her the rundown on Finn, he hadn't mentioned that her neighbor was proficient in biplanes—much less aerobatics.

All in all, a nice little surprise.

She'd known from the get-go that this assignment wouldn't be painful. Finn, after all, ranked up there on her eye candy chart, and the background check had revealed enough about his relationships to suggest that he knew his way around a woman, an assessment he'd confirmed that afternoon. But what the dossier hadn't conveyed was the rest of it. Like how he made her laugh, or how he kept surprising her.

Maybe she'd just been too long without a lay, but this mission couldn't have come at a better time. Or with a better man.

"Look to your left," he said.

She complied, and was rewarded with a stunning view of dolphins frolicking in the waves off the San Diego shoreline.

"Do you want to fly her?" he asked.

She did, desperately. She hadn't flown a plane since her last stint in an F-14. But that wasn't the role she was playing. She shook her head. "I better not," she said. "I wouldn't know what to do."

"Nothing to it. It's dual control. Your control stick is attached to mine, and I won't let you do anything that would scare me."

"Well, with an offer like that, how could I say no?"

She started to take control, then remembered that she was supposed to be clueless. "Um, so what do I do?"

"Just take a hold of the stick," he said. "I know you can handle that."

She grinned. "Right you are."

"You want her to respond to the lightest of touch. Don't force it. Just take it gentle."

"We're still talking about flying, right?"

"For now," he said. "But hold that thought."

An unintended bubble of laughter welled in her throat, and Amber sat up straighter, unable to remember when she'd had such a good time. God, she loved being behind the controls.

"You're doing great," he said.

Looking left, she banked slightly, gazing down to the Pacific below.

"Easy there," he said.

"Don't you trust me?"

"Only as far as I can throw you."

"Ye of little faith," she protested. She knew she was showing off, but she couldn't help it, and she pulled the plane into a tight turn, completing a three-sixty before she leveled out again.

"Whoo-hoo!" Finn yelled from behind her. "That was great. You sure you've never flown before?"

"Beginner's luck, I guess," Amber said, dodging the question. "I told you I like being in control."

"Uh-huh." He sounded more than a little dubious, and she couldn't blame him.

"Show me something else," she said, changing topics. Not particularly subtle, but it did the trick. Finn took control, finishing their aerial tour of the coastline with a flourish. All Amber had to do was sit and watch and think. A nice change, actually. She was so used to running and doing. To being the one in charge. And she would be again soon enough. So she might as well enjoy her fifteen minutes of freedom while she had them.

They roamed the skies, exploring San Diego Bay and doing twists and turns over Torrey Pines. All too quickly, Finn spoke again. "Ready to head on back?"

"No," she said. "But I suppose we should."

They landed about five minutes later, then taxied toward the hangar at the far side of the private landing strip. Finn got out first, stepping onto the wing walk before hopping down to the ground.

Amber climbed out next, standing up and brushing the tips of her fingers on the ribs and trailing edge of the top wing before climbing out onto the wing walk herself. She grasped a strut for balance, then took Finn's outstretched hand and jumped to the grass airstrip.

"That was great," she said. "Can we go again?"

"You kids have fun?" Tom, the biplane's owner, strode over.

"Fabulous," Amber said. "How old is she?"

"Built in twenty-seven," he said. "The same month Lindbergh crossed the Atlantic. Finn here has a logbook of hours in this wonderful old bird."

"So how do you two know each other?" Amber asked. The relationship was clearly a close one. Finn had simply driven up to the hangar, stuck his head in the door, and told the older man that he wanted to take the plane up. Tom hadn't even blinked.

"I've known that boy since he was in diapers," Tom said. "His daddy and I flew choppers in Korea together. We even bought a surplus Bell chopper and fixed it up for tourist flights, then decided biplanes had more cachet. This one we bought back in eighty-eight and got her completely restored by ninety-two. There's only about fifty Travel Airs still in any condition to fly, and she's one of them." He looked at Finn. "Your dad had three good years of flying her before the cancer got him."

Finn nodded. "And he loved every minute of it."

"I bought out Anthony's half when his medical bills started piling up," he said to Amber. He clapped Finn on the shoulder. "But this plane will come back to the Teague family. I don't have any kids of my own."

"Nonsense," Finn said. "You've got me. Even without the blood relation, I'm a handful, and you know it."

Tom laughed. "True enough." He turned to Amber. "How about you, young lady? Love it or hate it?"

"Love it," Amber said, trying to remember the last time anyone had called her a young lady.

"Well, then you're all right."

"Thanks," Amber said, realizing as she spoke that the sentiment was genuine. "That means a lot to me."

They spent another forty minutes with Tom shooting the breeze, and throughout the entire time, Finn paced in front of the battered gray desk. He was antsy and out of sorts, half of him wanting to get Amber alone, the other half wanting to show her off to this man who'd been like a father to him.

He'd known her for such a short time, but already the woman had bewitched him.

"Sun's gonna be settin' in half an hour," Tom said. "You two want to wait and take her up again?"

Finn shook his head. While the view of the sun slipping into the Pacific would be truly spectacular, he wanted more than just the view. He wanted Amber in his arms again, and that just wasn't possible if she was an entire cockpit in front of him, the turtledeck separating them as effectively as miles. "I thought we'd watch the sunset from the ground," he said. He took Amber's hand, delighted when she squeezed back. "That okay with you?"

Her smile, warm and genuine, did a little number on his insides. "Considering how impressed I've been with your dating itinerary so far," she said, "I don't think I'll second-guess your plans."

"You won't be disappointed," he said, earnestly hoping that was true.

They said good-bye, and fifteen minutes later they were heading back up the coast freeway. A comfortable silence settled between them, punctuated by the backdrop of Led Zeppelin streaming in from the classic rock station.

It was Amber who broke the silence, her finger tracing a long, thin slice in the Mustang's upholstery. "Let me guess," she said. "A knife fight with an enraged former lover . . . and the car lost."

"Could be," Finn said. "This car's seen its share of adventures."

"Considering the adventure you just took me on," she said, "I believe that." She reached forward, now running her finger over a crack in the dash. "And I think a few of those adventures have taken their toll."

Finn aimed a stern scowl her direction. "Don't mock my car," he said. "You'll hurt her feelings. She's a work in progress."

"Well, I certainly hope so." Amber raised an eyebrow. "I'd hate to think this is the look you were going for."

"Clearly, you have no artistic sensibilities. She's raw, unrefined, but with beauty hiding just beneath the surface."

"Kinda like some people, huh?" Amber quipped.

"Exactly," he said. He tapped the brakes as he

approached a car in the fast lane moving at a snail's pace. A can of motor oil rolled out from under the passenger seat and bumped against her ankles. He reached over, tossed it in the backseat, and gave her a sheepish grin. "I usually rent a car for dates."

"Really? But this is a great car."

"That it is," Finn agreed, his estimation of Amber rising even higher. "But sometimes a man has to face facts. And this just isn't a prime dating car." He aimed a smile her direction. "But you caught me by surprise."

"I have that effect on people," she said.

"That I believe."

"At any rate, I'm glad you don't have a rental. I want to know the real Finn. Not some facade."

At that, Finn almost laughed. He'd been wondering his whole life about who the real Finn was.

"What?" she asked.

He frowned, confused. "What, what?"

"I said I wanted to see the real Finn, and you got this distant look on your face." She lifted a single eyebrow. "What's the matter? Have you got a secret identity you're not allowed to share?"

"That's the first time I've been asked that." He had to admit, the question amused him. As if Agent Python was real, and Finn had to maintain a constant vigil lest his cover be broken.

She crossed her arms over her chest, her head cocked slightly to the left. "You haven't answered my question. . . ."

"Secret identity, you mean?" He wasn't entirely sure what game she was playing, but it was right up his alley. "I guess you're just going to have to get to know me better and find out."

"How convenient," she said. She pressed her hand against his thigh, then eased it slowly up toward his crotch. "As you may have noticed, that happens to be my plan."

"I noticed," he said. "Learned anything interesting?"

"As a matter of fact, I have." She leaned back in her seat, a teasing smile on her lips as she buffed her fingernails over her chest. "I think I know everything I need to know about you."

"Oh, really?" he asked. "What do you know?"

"You're a lawyer," she said. "And you're not too crazy about your job. But you're good at it. And you're good with kids."

"How the hell do you know that?"

She laughed. "I see you with the twins. The other day you helped them build kites and flew them in the courtyard." She cocked her head. "I told you. I've been watching you, Finn. And I like what I see."

"What else?"

She shrugged. "I learned a lot about you today. You like adventure. You respect your elders. You have an affinity for history, as well as a reverence for it. And you like natural beauty." She looked out the window at the stunning coastal view along PCH. "That's why we're taking the long way home, right? And it's why you took me to your scenic overlook earlier?"

"I guess you do know me," he conceded. "Of course, now I'm at a bit of a disadvantage. I think I need to get to know you better."

"Nothing to know," she said. "My life is an open book."

"Good," he said. "I love to read." He took his eyes

off the road long enough to face her. "Let's start on page one."

"To begin my life with the beginning of my life . . ."

"David Copperfield," he said.

"You're good."

"Nah," Finn said. "I've just seen *Gone With the Wind* one too many times."

"Never seen it," Amber said. "But I've read the book twice."

"You've never seen the movie? Melanie reads David Copperfield aloud when they're waiting to see if the men are safe."

Amber shrugged, then slipped out of her sandal and propped her bare foot on the dashboard. "Movies weren't exactly part of my childhood," she said. "And once I got older, I just never had the time."

"It's a long movie," Finn said, "but the book is longer."

"When I'm in a book, time doesn't really mean much."

Finn nodded. He got lost in his own fantasies for hours. Getting lost in someone else's sounded a hell of a lot more relaxing. "So you know what I do, but I don't know about you."

"You mean that you're a lawyer," she said.

"Right." He winked. "I'm not allowed to reveal my secret identity."

"Yeah," she said. "Those aliases are hell that way."

"Are you avoiding my question?"

"What? No. My job, you mean?" She twisted slightly in her seat, facing him more directly. "I'm a freelance editor for Machismo. Adventure books. Spies, intrigue. Stuff like that."

"No kidding? That's cool."

From her grin, Finn could tell she agreed 100 percent with that assessment. "Yeah, well, it's fun to get caught up in the fantasy." She faced him dead on, her eyes probing. "Doing something like that for real, though. Well, that has to be a dream come true."

"Something like what?"

She rolled one shoulder. "You know. Chasing down the bad guys. Fast cars, secret codes, the fate of the world hanging in the balance."

Finn just laughed.

"What?" she said. "Am I wrong? You don't think that would be a trip?"

"Yeah," he said. "I think that would be great." But a woman who thought like he did—*that* was even better.

"Oh, you poor baby," Diana crooned. She reached forward, sliding her hand through the crack in the doorway to press a hand to Poindexter's burning forehead. At the same time, she made a mental note to not call him that out loud.

Bernie. His name was *Bernie.*

She said the name over a few more times so she wouldn't forget. She was supposed to be all gooey with love for this guy. It simply wouldn't be prudent to spit out the wrong name in a moment of lust.

"I'm really sorry, Di," he said, his voice thick and raspy. "I don't think I'm up for coming out."

He started to push his front door closed, but she slid her foot neatly into the gap, her three-hundred-dollar pumps getting slightly marred in the process. "You poor, sweet baby," she said. She was repeating herself, but she didn't know what else to say. She didn't *want* to be with the sniffling, sneezing little dweeb, but she had to.

Bernie Waterman was the only one who could access the satellite through the back door. Without him, they couldn't fire the laser. And without the laser, they were out of business.

All of which meant that Diana was stuck with Bernie, at least until she got him to open the satellite's back door. And so she was going to suck it up, kick off her shoes, and open a can of chicken soup.

"I'm really not—"

"I want you to march right back into your bedroom and get under the covers."

His mouth hung agape, and she feared for drool. But then he blinked and took a step backward. She pressed the advantage, squeezing in through the half-open door. "Chicken soup, my pet." She brushed his hair off his forehead, resisting the urge to wipe her palm down her skirt. The man was a sweaty, oily mess. As far as Diana could tell, that was his usual state of being. The fever, however, exacerbated the problem.

"But—"

"No buts," she said, taking him by the shoulder and aiming him toward the bedroom. "You need your rest." She swatted him on the rump, congratulating herself for putting up such a convincing front. "Now off you go."

He turned, and from his expression she could tell he wanted to argue some more. Something in her eyes must have tied his tongue, however, because he pressed his lips together, nodded resignedly, and then padded toward the bedroom.

For the first time, Diana noticed his feet. Solid black socks, with a little sleeve for each individual toe.

Oh, please, God, don't make her have to sleep with this guy.

Standing a little straighter to fight distaste, she headed into the kitchen. The cupboard was mostly bare, but she found a can of tomato soup buried behind six cans of franks 'n' beans. She hoped the kitchen was in such pitiful shape because the man ate out often. Unfortunately, she doubted that was true.

The saucepan, at least, was clean. Sparkling, actually. And she noticed for the first time that the entire kitchen shined. Considering the man's own unkempt appearance, the pristine state of his apartment surprised her. If she'd cared one iota about him, she would have pondered the dichotomy. As it was, she simply filed the information away in case it later became useful.

The soup started bubbling around the edges, and she took it off the stove and poured it into one of the bowls in his cabinet. Heavy ceramic, hand painted with small yellow daisies. Another oddity. Another thing she wasn't going to worry about.

She found a yellow wicker tray in the shape of a fish behind the microwave and put the soup on it. Then she kicked off her shoes, picked up the tray, and headed to Bernie's bedroom in her stocking feet.

He was in the middle of the bed, a box of Kleenex in his lap, and crumpled, snotty tissues all around him. Diana wrinkled her nose and then eased up next to him, sliding the tray onto the bed. "Here you go, Pookie. You need to eat."

"I'm really not hungry."

"Nonsense." She ran her hand over his forehead, the oil from his skin clinging to her palm. "Poor baby," she said, then snaked her hand down the bedspread to his crotch, managing to wipe her palm in the process. "Isn't there anything I can do to make you feel better?"

"I don't—*Oh . . .*"

She'd pressed her hand down, rubbing him with a slow, methodical rhythm, and now she scooted closer, her breasts grazing his arm. "Anything at all?" she whispered, then flicked her tongue over his ear.

His face turned red and splotchy, and he closed his eyes, his head tilted back.

So easy. The man had been eyeing her like a dog in heat since the first day they'd met. She'd posed as a programmer at a competitor and struck up a conversation with him at the little diner where he grabbed a coffee and Danish in the morning.

Drake had wanted her to go in with both barrels blasting, but Diana knew better, and eventually she'd convinced Drake. Bernie wasn't the type of guy who had women falling all over him. Especially not women who looked like Diana. And so she'd kept her distance, talking to him about bits and bytes. She'd said all the right things about finding a man who liked her for her mind and not her tits. And when he'd moved on to chaos theory, she'd known he was flirting in his own little Bernie-like way.

The foundation was set. And Diana was certain that a little bout of the flu wasn't going to keep his libido in check. Not if she could help it.

"You just lay back and relax, honey," she said. "Diana will make you feel better."

Slowly, deliberately, she slid her hand up to grasp the bedspread. She tugged it down slowly, both for effect and because of her inherent distaste for this particular assignment. But it was important. Hell, it was probably the most important seduction she'd ever done.

She just hoped he gave up the information as easily as he got a hard-on.

Her cell phone rang, startling her. Bernie's eyes flew open. "Don't answer it."

"Oh, sweetie, you know I have to." *Please, please, let it be Drake. Let him have cracked the code.*

She checked the caller ID and exhaled with relief. It *was* Drake. She pressed the button to answer. "Yes."

"Plan B," he barked, and then hung up.

Diana took the phone away from her ear, stared mutely at it, and realized that she'd never loved Drake more than she did at that very moment.

Eight

Amber slipped off her second shoe and pressed both bare feet against the dashboard, settling in. Finn had put the top down on the convertible, and now the stars winked above them, watching as they winded their way back toward Los Angeles.

She'd pulled her hair back into the familiar ponytail, but a few strands had escaped and were tickling her face. She pushed them away as she twisted to look at him. "So are we heading for another thrill?"

"I hope so," he said. "But in a more traditional setting."

"Oh?"

"I'm heading home," he said. "Since we did so good on the grass, I thought we might try a bed."

She looked at him in mock horror. "A bed? How incredibly passé."

"I guess I'm just an old-fashioned guy."

She licked her lips. "Mmm. How did I manage to completely overlook that part of your personality?"

"Naughty, naughty."

She pointed a finger at herself. "Me?"

"Hell yes, babe." His smile was slow and sensual. "But, then again, that's what I like about you."

She laughed. Not only was she genuinely enjoying their easygoing banter, but their familiarity would hopefully pave the way for her to get some answers from him. The truth was, even though she'd had a thoroughly satisfying evening, it was time to get down to business.

"So long as we end up at *your* apartment," she said. "Nice girls don't invite men home on the first date." Of course, nice girls also didn't poke through a man's mail and private papers, either, like she planned to do. But she'd never said she was a nice girl.

"Oh, is *that* what nice girls don't do? Thanks for clearing that up for me."

"Any time," she said. She slipped her feet off the dash long enough to rummage on the floorboard for the bottle of water Tom had given her. She twisted the cap off, settled back in her seat, and took a sip. "So how did you get to be a lawyer," she asked. "Lifelong dream?"

"Not in the least," he said. "I sort of fell into it."

"Where'd you go to law school?" she asked, knowing the answer.

"Harvard," he said.

"That sounds like a pretty expensive fall."

He frowned. "No kidding. A fall I'm still paying for."

She nodded. The student loans had shown up on

his credit report. But that, unfortunately, wasn't helpful information. She didn't doubt that he'd gone to law school, and even if some agency was covering his loans, they'd still flow the payments through Finn for appearance's sake.

"I'd had a rather eclectic array of jobs," he said. "And then one day I woke up and realized I ought to do something serious with my life. That was where I landed."

"And now you're bored."

He turned to face her. "How do you know that?"

"I see you on your patio or on the sidewalk. You have that look." That was the literal truth. What she hadn't revealed was just how much time she'd spent watching him and Diana Traynor.

"Not bored so much as underwhelmed." He shrugged. "I guess I'd pictured *Perry Mason*, but I didn't even get a bad episode of *L.A. Law*." She wanted to ask another question, but he fired one toward her before she had the chance. "How about you? How'd you end up at a publisher like Machismo?"

"I guess I sort of fell into it, too," she said.

"How so?"

She pulled off the ponytail holder and shook out her hair while she considered how to answer. The Machismo cover story was solid; Unit 7 really did publish the popular books. Beyond that, though, she was inventing for Finn's benefit. But Amber had learned long ago to mix lies with as much truth as possible. In this case, that philosophy had two benefits. Not only were the lies easier to remember, but if she was right about Finn's status as an operative, the odds were good that his childhood had been as screwed up as hers. If she opened up, then maybe so would he.

"I had a rotten childhood," she admitted, measuring her words carefully. "Got mixed up with the wrong crowd." She shook her head. "I was in all sorts of trouble, believe me. And the first time I ended up in juvie court, my mom pretty much washed her hands of me."

His eyes reflected both shock and disapproval. "No way."

"Oh yeah," she said. "The charming woman beside you was a terror in her youth."

At that, he laughed. "*That* I believe. I meant your parents. Didn't they try to help you?"

She frowned, wondering about his own family. She had little experience with the concept of parents sticking by their kids. She and Brandon both had been orphaned young, even though their parents were very much alive. Maybe some of that was her own fault—she *had* been a terror. But her parents had never made any effort to pull her back, to rein her in. Hell, they barely even spoke to her.

"When I was seven, my sister died. My mom and dad split up about a year later, and I never saw him again. Hell, I hardly saw my mother. She threw herself into her work and hired a nanny. At the time, I thought she resented me for being the one who lived. Now, I don't know. Maybe it just hurt too much. Maybe she just thought it was supposed to be easy. Her motives didn't matter much. All I know is that she ignored me."

"So you started trying to get her attention."

"Yeah."

Finn shook his head. "I'm sorry."

She considered him. "I take it your childhood was rosier?"

"My childhood was great," he said. "My parents both worked full-time—no choice, we needed the money—and they stuck me in day care whenever my mom couldn't arrange a night shift. But I was the center of their universe when they were home."

She tried to imagine, but couldn't quite complete the mental picture. "Do you still see your mom?" She remembered what Tom had said about his father's cancer.

He shook his head. "She passed away last year. They were older—mom was forty-five and sure she'd never have kids when I showed up—so it wasn't entirely unexpected. But it still hurts."

She reached over and took his hand, clutching tight. "I'm sorry," she said. She meant it, too. Even though she couldn't truly empathize with the hollowness of losing a parent, she did understand the sadness and loss that seemed to cling to him like a blanket. About loss, Amber knew more than she cared to know.

"It's okay," he said. He took his hand away to shift gears. "But how did your rotten childhood land you in publishing?"

"A mentor program," she said. "My current boss, a guy named James Monahan, came to the detention center and did a presentation." She sat up a little straighter as she talked about it. From her perspective, James was a saint. Who but a saint could have pulled her from the fires of hell?

"What kind of presentation?"

Here, he skirted the truth. "One of those you're in charge of your destiny things. Only this one wasn't all touchy-feely. There was a job attached to it. It was tough. . . ." She paused, remembering just *how* tough. And the possibility of touchy-feely was laughable. The presentation had been an ultimatum—join us or take your chances being tried as an adult on a felony murder charge. She shook her head. "But I survived, and in the end we were trained."

"Trained?"

"In English and grammar and stuff like that," she said. Not exactly a lie. She'd taken extensive diction classes. Before the Unit, she'd had no clue how to speak proper English, much less French or Arabic. "I still share an office with one of the other kids, a guy named Brandon Kline."

"How old were you?" Finn asked.

"Thirteen."

"And you've been with the publisher ever since?"

She nodded. "I've been with James. He was with a magazine at the time, but later they spun off into publishing books."

"And your mom?"

She pressed her lips together, as always, surprised at how much the memory still hurt. "She filed papers," she said. "Terminating parental rights." She looked Finn in the eye. "Monahan became my legal guardian." Not that the legalities of it mattered to Amber. From the moment he'd taken her to Unit training, Amber had known the real truth. James cared for her more than her own parents. After a while, Amber quit wondering why. She loved and respected James and she hated her mother. And that was simply that.

"Shit," Finn whispered.

"Yeah, well . . ." There really wasn't anything else to say.

"But it sounds like you ended up with your real family."

Her brow furrowed. "How do you mean?"

"Mr. Monahan. And your friend. Brandon. It sounds like they've become your family."

Amber closed her eyes and allowed herself one deep breath. "You're very perceptive," she said. "They have." James, Brandon, all of Unit 7.

"Are you doing what you want to do?" he asked.

She blinked, not certain what he meant. "Want to do?"

"With your life, I mean. Did you have any dreams when you were a kid?"

"Only to get my mom back." She waved the words away before he could respond. "Sorry. Yes," she said. "I'm doing what I love more than anything in the world." She lifted her chin, recognizing the opening he'd handed her. "But you're not, are you? What was your childhood dream?"

"It's silly," he said.

"Dreams often are. Doesn't mean you shouldn't try."

"I guess I wanted the kind of life you read about in your job. Secret missions and beautiful women and all of that. Something important. Something that made a difference and kept my blood pumping all at the same time." He laughed. "Of course, first I wanted to be a vet, but when we had to put my dog to sleep when I was twelve, I decided I couldn't handle it."

"Animal doctor turned James Bond." She shrugged. "I dunno. Could be a character in one of my books."

"Secret messages smuggled in dog collars and kibble."

"And squeaky toys," she added, then laughed. If James had ever told her she needed to meet a contact named Rover, she would have keeled over right then. "But I thought you *did* become a secret agent," she said, watching his face even as she pressed her luck.

His expression was one of genuine surprise. But whether it was surprise that she'd make such an idiotic statement or surprise that he'd been discovered, she didn't know. "Why on earth would you say that?"

"You said it," she said. "Secret identity, remember?"

"Ah, yes," he said. "Right." He let go of the steering wheel long enough to hold up his hands. "You found me out. Phineus Teague, code-named Python. Licensed to kill." He turned to her, mirth dancing in his eyes. "But you'll keep my secret, right?"

"Of course," she said, her tone matching his mock solemnity even though she was fighting back laughter from the ridiculous code name.

"I did interview for the CIA," he said. "Turned down."

"Really? I would have thought you'd be just what they were looking for. Well-educated, well-spoken . . ." She slid her hand along his thigh. "Well-liked by the ladies."

"I guess they didn't know what they'd be missing."

"Well, I know," she said. She tucked her foot up under her. "And I consider myself very, very privileged."

He faced her again, passion flaring in his eyes. "So tell me, Ms. Robinson. Are you wearing panties?"

She raised an eyebrow. She wasn't, of course. His one bold tug had rendered the panties unwearable. "If you're that curious, I guess you'll just have to take a peek for yourself."

He stroked his palm over his beard stubble. "It's such a burning question, I'm tempted to pull over and answer it." He reached over, tracing a hand up the inseam of her pants.

She shivered, the extent of her desire for this man both exciting and unsettling. But the heat of desire in her veins was matched with the euphoria of victory. She'd needed to get close to Finn—so close he'd open up, either his mouth or his apartment. She'd take the information any way she could get it, whether he handed it to her or she stole it off his computer or from the papers in his desk.

His fingers continued their exploration, and she closed her hand over his, stopping him. Her plan had worked beautifully; he was taking her home. "Ah-ah," she said. "Wait until we get there." She wanted him, yes, but she didn't want any excuse for them to part ways once they reached the apartment. "Anticipation is good for you."

"Maybe," he said, "but I think *you're* bad for me."

"So's chocolate," she said. "But I bet you indulge."

"As a matter of fact, I do. Binges," he said. "Decadent, delicious binges."

"My kind of man," she said, her body warming merely from the thought of a decadent binge with Finn.

"Glad you approve," he said.

They drove in silence as he maneuvered the traffic near the exit for their apartment building. Just a few more blocks left if she wanted to scrounge for any more information before the next act in her evening of debauchery.

"What did you do when the CIA turned you down?" she asked. "There are other agencies."

He shrugged. "I figured anything intelligence related would give me the same response. I thought about the FBI, but in the end, I couldn't do it."

She squinted. "Why not?"

A wash of sadness colored his face. "My uncle was an agent," he said. "Died during a drug bust. It just about killed my mother."

She nodded, remembering that tidbit from the family history she'd pulled. "I'm sorry," she said. "What about after your mom died? You could have applied then."

He shook his head. "I didn't think about it in time. By the time I realized I could give it a shot, I was already thirty-seven. And that's their cutoff." He shrugged. "So I lost on all counts. Not with the bureau, not a spook. Just a litigator. Not my dream job, but it pays the bills."

"I guess so," Amber said, not sure where to go from there. An operative whose cover story was that he wanted to be an operative? That was a new one on her. And she had no idea whether Finn was spinning a cover or telling the truth. Her gut told her he wasn't really in the game, but she still didn't know for certain. And Brandon had said that Diana was on to him. All of which meant that Amber had no choice but to stick close to the man.

Damn, but she loved her job.

Nine

"This is it," Finn said, turning from the road into the parking lot. "Home sweet home."

He ran his hand along the edge of the steering wheel, then realized what he was doing and clutched it, willing his hands to steady. He'd brought countless dates to his apartment before, so why the hell was he suddenly having an attack of nerves? It wasn't as if he didn't already know he was going to get lucky.

Or maybe that was it after all. After Amber's story about her family, Finn wanted more than just to sleep with this woman. He wanted to hold her tight, pulling her close and sharing his strength. He wanted to let her know that not everyone was cold and absent like her parents.

He hoped she'd already learned that lesson, but he didn't think she had. When she'd spoken of James and Brandon, there was real admiration and respect in her eyes. Maybe even love. But he'd seen a shadow, too.

Stupid, probably, considering how little he really knew of her, but Finn wanted to be the one to bring light into her eyes.

He killed the engine, and she opened her door, the harsh glare of the overhead light wrenching him back to reality.

As Amber swung her legs out of the car, Finn got out, then circled the Mustang, meeting up with her in front of the trunk. She studied his face, her gaze penetrating.

"What?" he asked, knowing full well what she was about.

Her eyes widened, feigning innocence. "Nothing much," she said, moving closer to him. Just a step, but enough. She tilted her head back, and the moonlight caught the waves that framed her face. "I was just wondering if you were going to ask me in for coffee."

"Coffee?"

"Tea?" She let a slow, heated smile touch her lips. "Or me?"

He met her sultry grin with one of his own. Oh, yeah. He liked this woman. Liked the way she talked and teased, and liked even more the way she felt in his arms.

"You," he said, sliding his hand under her hair along the back of her neck. "I pick you."

She reached forward, pressing her hand against his neck, a perfect mirror of his own touch. "You'd better."

He slid his hand down her neck to cup her waist, then urged her closer, pressing her tight against him. She moaned as he feasted on her lips, tugging and teasing.

"Finn," she murmured as he broke off the kiss, pulling back just long enough to come up for air. "Don't stop."

He had no intention of stopping, but as he lowered his mouth to her lips one more time, the high-pitched squeal of tires rent the still night air. He pulled back, startled, and looked up just in time to see the glare of headlights bearing down.

"Shit!" No time to think, he could only react. He lurched sideways, twisting at the waist as he pushed off with his legs. The motion was quick, his balance awkward, but it worked, and he landed on top of Amber about two feet away—just far enough to put them safely out of the path of the oncoming limo.

"Son of a bitch," he muttered, as the taillights disappeared around the corner.

"No kidding," Amber said. She shifted, all sweet and soft beneath him, and Finn felt a surge of rage that the driver had been so careless. For Christ's sake, they could have been killed.

Amber rolled slightly to the left, then started to push herself up on her elbow. A flash of pain crossed her face, and she winced.

"Your shoulder?" Finn asked.

She nodded, her teeth digging into her lower lip. She craned her neck as she twisted around to look. "I can't see. How bad is it?"

He pushed himself up, then urged her slightly to the left until her back was illuminated by one of the spotlights the landlord had installed to keep the parking lot relatively safe. Not that the lights had helped tonight. The second he saw the wound, he exhaled.

"That bad, huh?"

"Sorry," he said. "It's not so bad, actually. I've seen worse." Not exactly true. The laceration was truly nasty. They'd landed on a rusty metal grating, and a raw edge had apparently caught her just below her left shoulder blade. They'd hit the ground first, then scooted, and the motion had torn her sweater and her flesh, leaving a long, deep wound surrounded by raw skin peppered with small bits of gravel and asphalt.

"Liar," she said. The blood had drained from her face, and she held her body unnaturally stiff. After a moment, she exhaled, the color returning to her cheeks. She met his eyes, and he saw a strength there that would have surprised him a day ago, but now just seemed like another of Amber's facets. "I'll be fine," she said. "But I should get it cleaned up."

"Right." He got to his feet, then stooped to pick up her purse. He shoved the scattered contents back in and handed the purse to her. Then he reached down and offered her a hand up.

She rose gracefully, as if she'd simply shut the pain away to deal with at some more convenient time. Even so, he slipped his arm around her waist and guided her to the rear of his car. She leaned against it, and twisted around again, still trying to see over her shoulder to assess the damage.

While she was occupied with her injury, Finn scanned the parking lot. Probably stupid, but he had the feeling they were being watched. That the limo hadn't come out of nowhere. That it had been waiting there for them. And that it would be back to finish the job.

Something glinted under the tire of the neighboring car, and he stooped to pick it up. A beat-up Montblanc pen, probably Amber's, and he pocketed it, intending to give it to her when they got back inside.

"Let's go," she said as he stood up. He nodded, taking her elbow and guiding her toward the front of the building.

The complex consisted of four buildings with eight apartments each, arranged to form a square around a courtyard. Amber and Finn lived in Building One, the furthest away from the parking lot. The easiest way in was to cut across the courtyard and go in through the patio door, but since it didn't have a keyed lock, Finn rarely used that entrance. The added convenience wasn't worth the risk of someone waltzing in and absconding with his DVD player and computer.

Which meant that they had to go around Building Two, meet up with the street, and follow the sidewalk all the way to Finn's apartment before they'd even be close to hydrogen peroxide or something else suitable for cleaning Amber's wound.

"I'm fine," she said, apparently reading his thoughts. "I've probably got some alcohol in my medicine cabinet."

"Well, I definitely have bandages and peroxide," he said. "And since it's my fault you're in the shape you're in, we'll go to my apartment and clean you up."

She paused, forcing him to slow his step and ultimately stop completely.

"Don't even think that," she snapped. "You probably saved my life. So I hardly think it's necessary to worry about one little scratch on my shoulder."

"I don't—"

She pressed her fingers to his mouth, effectively shutting him up. "Say, 'you're right, Amber.'"

"You're right, Amber." And he knew she was. He just wished that his first attempt at heroism could have gone over just a little bit better.

"Good." She flashed him a broad smile without any hint of pain. "Now that that's settled, we can head on in." She winked. "And your apartment is just fine."

Finn shook his head in mock bewilderment. The woman had almost been pulverized by a speeding limousine, and yet it sounded like she wanted to jump right back into their date at exactly the point where they left off. Well, on that score, Finn was more than happy to comply—*after* he got her shoulder fixed up. And then, very, very gently.

"By the way," she said, "I don't suppose you got the license plate number."

"Tried," he said. "Too dark."

"Damn."

They'd reached the corner, and now they cut across the grass, making a beeline for Finn's ground floor apartment. The neighborhood was normally quiet, but this evening the air seemed positively stagnant. No bass reverb from the teenager who lived in 3B. No muffled conversations drifting back from the courtyard. Just silence.

Amber squeezed his hand, her step quickening. "Come on," she said.

Finn wasn't sure if she felt as on edge as he did, or if she was just anxious to get inside, but he didn't argue. Just quickened his step to keep up.

As they reached the walkway that connected each of the apartments, a dark shadow moved across the ground in front of them. Finn turned—and saw a solid black limo backing out of the driveway of the building next door.

Amber saw it at the same moment he did. "Oh, shit," she said. And then she collapsed in a heap at his feet, a tiny dart protruding from the side of her neck.

Finn didn't even have time to react before the steely bite of a dart caught him, too, and the world turned inside out.

And his last thought before the blackness took him was that this was one hell of a way to end a first date.

Bernie closed his eyes as soon as Diana hung up her cell phone. He felt like shit—was certain he looked all puffy and pale—but Diana didn't seem to mind.

That's what he loved about her.

Women didn't tend to go for guys like him, the men who'd never quite figured out how to talk to girls. But Diana spoke his language. She knew stuff about mathematics and physics and computers. They'd toasted Nobel Prize winner Riccardo Giacconi and spent an entire dinner discussing his pioneering work with the Chandra telescope.

But it was when she'd recited a string of prime numbers in the same voice as someone might read Emily Dickinson that Bernie had known that it was love.

And now she was here with him, and she *wanted* him. Despite the fever. Despite the wheezing. Despite all of that, the woman was practically throwing herself on him.

Bernie wasn't about to question his good fortune.

"Bad news, sweetie?" he asked, letting his head fall back into the pillow.

Her voice drifted back to him, soft and sweet. "Nothing you need to worry your head about, precious." Her hand stroked his forehead, drifting down to cup his cheek. She trailed down his neck, over the stubble he wished he'd shaved, then her fingers played with the button on his pajama top.

Oh, sweet Jesus, this was really happening!

Her soft, warm fingertips traced circular patterns on his chest, and Bernie groaned from the pleasure of it all.

"Are you ready, baby?" she asked, her hand dipping lower, and then even lower still.

All the blood in his body rushed to his groin, and it was everything he could do to nod his head.

"Well, then here we go. . . ."

He took a deep breath, anticipating the pleasure of her touch. But instead of pleasure, a loud bang seared through his head, light flashing even past his closed eyelids. In a split second, he went from feeling warm and liquid to cold as ice, and he realized Diana was no longer straddling him.

His eyes flew open, and he found himself staring into the cold, dark eyes of a burly man with a chunk missing from his ear. The man grinned, then laughed, a raspy, fluid sound. "Getting yourself a little nookie, eh, buddy?"

"I . . . I . . . what?" was all Bernie could manage.

The thug just patted him on the face and stepped sideways. Behind him, Bernie saw a blond man with a two-day beard holding Diana around the waist, a gun to her beautiful head. She was silent, but the scream in her eyes broke his heart.

"You're coming with us, Bernie-boy," the thug said. "Unless you want the little lady to buy it here."

"No," Bernie said. "No, please."

The blond thug with squinty eyes nodded. "I told you he'd be reasonable. Our Mr. Waterman's a smart man. Aren't you, Bernie?"

"I, yes. I . . . Just don't hurt her." He had to pee. Was afraid he was going to pee right then, actually. But he didn't have long to worry about it. Because the thug smiled that hideous smile, reached out with his gun, and smacked Bernie across the head.

And the last thing Bernie saw was a tiny smile playing on Diana's fabulous red lips.

Diana stepped out of her shoes and curled her toes into the plush carpet. She'd picked it out herself, specifically because the carpet was thick and she hated to fly. Someone had told her to curl her toes during takeoff and landing, and the trick had worked. She'd picked the deep pile in honor of her toes.

Right now, though, the plane was still perched on the tarmac, awaiting take-off. Her toes weren't the problem. Phineus Teague was.

She traced her finger around the rim of her highball glass. The glass was filled with straight vodka, and this was her third one.

She'd been so happy when Drake had called, his two-word message letting her know she didn't have to get naked with the little worm. And then she found out the reason.

A spy. Phineus Teague was a goddamn spy!

She tossed back the last of the drink, letting the slow burn of alcohol seep through her veins. Then she crossed to the bar and poured herself another.

From the leather couch on the far side of the cabin, Prado, Drake's pilot and general kiss-ass boy, snorted.

She turned on him, itching for any reason to toss the ice-cold drink all over his perfectly groomed blond head. "Problem?"

He held up his hands in surrender. "Not me, baby."

Calm, Diana. She took three deep breaths. It wasn't as if this was unexpected; the man had been watching her for a week. Even so, the call she'd received from Drake had chilled her to the bone. The man had bounced from job to job, recently ending up at the very law firm that did most of the work for ZAEL.

Nobody changed jobs that much. Short order cook to ski instructor, maybe. But add in the fact that he'd spent two summers writing code for computer security systems, and that now he was supposedly an attorney at Baker and Crabb, and it was just too coincidental for comfort.

So Drake's boys had gone in and had a little look-see in Teague's apartment. The man had the component parts for various explosive devices under his kitchen sink and back issues of *Soldier of Fortune* in boxes under his bed. But the real kicker came when the boys had taken a little peek at his computer— and discovered that Teague had spent some time poking around uninvited in ZAEL's mainframe.

Son of a bitch.

The man was no attorney. He was a spy. And he'd set his sights on her.

Damn it all to hell.

Footsteps on the stairs pulled her out of her reverie. She turned, her eyes narrowed as she watched the door. Beltzer came in, a woman tossed over his beefy shoulder like so much dirty laundry.

Earlier that evening, when they'd loaded Bernie into the car, Diana had followed, squeezing in between the unconscious bodies of Phineus Teague and some tart he'd been planning to screw. Diana hadn't been happy about seeing the girl. She was, after all, just one more body to dispose of.

Now, Diana glared at Beltzer. She'd already chewed him out in the car, and she managed with effort to hold her tongue.

Beltzer stared at her impassively, fully aware of her displeasure. "Get over it, already. So you got two for the price of one. What's the big deal?"

Diana tossed back the rest of her drink. Clearly, it was going to be one of those days.

Prado got up, surrendering his seat to the unconscious woman. "It's not a big deal," he said. He looked Diana in the eye, and she could tell from his expression that he would broach no argument. "She might prove useful."

Diana held a hand up, signaling resignation even though she itched to slap the smarmy look right off his holier-than-thou little pig face. "Fine. But you deal with her."

Prado eyed the woman with a leer. "Now that, Diana my dear, is something we can definitely agree on."

A million tiny sledgehammers were going to town on her head, and steely knives of fire had embedded themselves in her shoulder blade. Even so, Amber stayed perfectly still. So long as they thought she was unconscious, she could buy herself some time.

The problem with that plan, of course, was that she didn't know if Finn was with her. Had they brought him, too? Were they on to her? Or were they on to Finn?

Fortunately, she'd taken her earpiece off after they'd left the grocery store. If they weren't already aware of her identity, at least the receiver wouldn't give her away. Of course, that also meant she was out of touch with Brandon. And considering she wasn't due to file another oral report with the Unit until oh-six-hundred, she hadn't called in to get updates as to the mission status. Which meant that although she had no doubt that Drake Mackenzie was at the heart of this new development, until she could get a handle on the entire situation, she'd be wise to just play possum.

Her mouth tasted stale and bitter, the lingering effects of the drug. Narcrylotine, unless she missed her guess. A bit surprising, actually. She'd spent two years building up a resistance to the little-known chemical compound. Considering how fast it had knocked her out, Mackenzie must have used a dangerously large dose or somehow refined the chemical properties of the drug.

A clammy hand closed over her wrist, the touch surprising Amber. Mentally, she started, but her body remained perfectly still. Not for the first time, Amber said a silent thank-you for Unit 7's insistence on intensive and prolonged training.

Her skills had saved her butt on more than one occasion.

"Well?" Diana's voice.

"Pulse is normal," a male voice said. "She'll survive. The cut on her shoulder's pretty nasty, though. Gonna get infected."

"Hardly my problem," Diana said.

"Whatever." He released her wrist, but Amber felt the couch on which they'd placed her give under his weight as he sat on the edge, so close that she could smell his breath. Acrid. Like old pickles. "Although she might be worth keeping healthy. Maybe I'll take her off Drake's hands once she outlives her usefulness."

"For God's sake, Beltzer, would you get your mind out of the gutter?" Diana again, but this time her voice was further away. The tinkle of ice hitting glass, then the splash of liquid.

"Better slow down." That was another male voice from even further away. Deeper, more refined. "I'd hate to have to search for a liquor store between here and the island."

Island? They weren't on a boat. At least not yet. A plane, maybe? She couldn't tell. She felt no motion, heard no engine. A safe house?

Wherever they were, they weren't staying put. And in the end, Diana was taking Amber to Drake's lair. Which was both good and bad. Good, in that Amber needed to confront the s.o.b., figure out what he was up to, and stop it. Bad, in that she had no way of communicating with the Unit. Which meant no Brandon, and certainly no backup.

"Prado," Diana said, "you're an ass." Then a pause, during which Amber could only assume that Diana had consumed the entire of whatever drink she'd poured.

Male laughter, and then— "Wait. Quiet."

Amber froze. Had she moved? Did they know she was awake?

A low groan cut through the still air.

"Well, well," Diana said. "Look who's rising and shining."

A wave of relief swept through her body. *Finn*. It had to be Finn.

"*Tat . . . i . . . ana . . .*"

Mentally, Amber blinked, trying to figure out what Finn had said. But nothing she came up with made sense.

"For God's sake, Beltzer. How many cc's did you inject? The man's delirious."

"He's fine," the one called Beltzer said. Footsteps, soft against a thick carpet. And then the resounding smack of flesh against flesh. Amber stifled a wince, sure that Finn's face was stinging with the hard bite of the slap.

"See?" Beltzer said. "He's coming to."

"You're a prick. You know that, right?"

The man laughed, an odd cackling sound. "That's why the big dog keeps me around. It sure as hell ain't for my looks."

"That," Diana said, "was never up for debate."

A strangled sound, like someone gulping for air, reached Amber's ears. She stiffened, fighting back a fear that Finn was choking, a common reaction to a Narcrylotine injection.

"What? What did you say?" Diana's voice was demanding yet gentle.

"Where am I?" The voice was weak but undeniably Finn's.

"The more relevant question, my dear, is *who are you*."

"Phineus Teague," he said. "The girl. Where's the girl."

Amber fought a smile, foolishly flattered that his first thought was of her.

"Sorry to have foiled your plans for a roll between the sheets. But she's fine. She's getting her beauty sleep."

"Where?"

"Beltzer," Diana commanded. The shuffle of feet, and Amber presumed they were helping Finn up so that he could see her over some obstruction.

"She's okay?"

"She's fine. Just more sensitive than you to our cocktail."

"I'm not sure this one's not sensitive, too." That was the other male voice. The one that still didn't have a name. "Look at his color. I don't want him going into cardiac arrest while we're in the air."

Fear raced through Amber.

"He's not coding," Beltzer said. "Jeez, Prado, you're such a fucking hypochondriac."

"Fuck you," Prado said.

"Oh, yeah, that's big talk," Beltzer retorted.

"Boys!" Diana's shrill yell silenced the men. "Is he or isn't he going to die on me?"

"Oh, for crying out . . ." Beltzer said. The rattle of metal on metal. "Give me a second to look him over." More rustling. "Pulse and BP are normal. The guy's healthy as a horse."

"Are you sure?" Diana asked.

"Positive," Beltzer said.

"Well, good. I need him healthy. At least until we get some answers."

"Depending on the questions," Finn cut in, his voice thin but strong, "you may not like the answers."

At that, Amber mentally applauded, relieved that Finn was not only healthy but sounded like he was on top of his game as well. She told herself that she was only concerned about the mission. But the truth was that she liked Phineus Teague. A lot. And, really, she'd rather not see him dead.

Finn couldn't believe he'd made such a smart-ass comment to a woman who'd drugged him and was holding both him and Amber hostage.

Amber. Thank God she was okay. At least, he hoped she was okay. Apparently the poor girl had been in the wrong place at the wrong time—namely, with him.

Finn had no specific explanation for why they found themselves drugged, handcuffed, and in the cabin of a plane, but did have an idea—he'd picked the wrong woman to spy on. In a perverse way, his fantasy had come true. Only now, interrogatories and depositions were looking better and better.

"Listen," he said, fighting to sit up straighter, his cuffed hands shoved behind his back. "You've made a mistake."

"No, Mr. Teague. I believe the mistake is yours."

"Look, Ta—" He broke off, realizing he had no inkling of her real name. "I'm not who you think I am."

"Is that a fact?" Her eyebrow lifted. "Let's just see, shall we? I think you're Phineus Teague. Am I right so far?"

He tightened his jaw, flexing the muscles in his

arm as he tried to determine how much control the drug had left him with. "So far," he admitted between gritted teeth.

"Oh, goody. One point for me."

"The game's not over yet," Finn said.

"Hmmm." She crossed to the bar. "Martini?"

"No, thank you," Finn said, although he desperately wanted something to cool his burning throat. Alcohol, however, wasn't the ticket. Not if he wanted to keep his wits about him.

"Of course," she said. "After all, you're on duty." She poured herself a drink. "Let's continue, shall we?"

He didn't bother to answer.

"You work for Baker and Crabb," she said.

He squinted at her, the fear in his gut rising. What the hell did his job have to do with this?

"No need to answer," she said. "One more point for me."

"I'm a lawyer. So what?"

"So you represent Zermatt Aeronautical Engineering Labs."

He nodded, pieces of the puzzle falling into place.

"Mmm-hmm." She came over to him then, sliding her hand around his neck, her fingers warm, her scent delicious. She perched herself in his lap, then nuzzled his ear. "But the question is, who do you *really* work for? And why were you poking around in ZAEL's operating system?"

A cold chill eased through Finn's body, like some living creature. Behind his back, he clenched his hands, fighting the urge to stand up and send her tumbling to the ground. Had he actually once thought she was attractive? Hell, yes. The woman was stunning. But it was a beauty tinged with ice, and Finn got no pleasure from the touch of her skin against his.

Automatically, his eyes drifted toward Amber. A table blocked his view, but he could see her foot. The woman was motionless, and he made a silent vow. No matter what, he'd get her out of this mess. Hell, he'd get them both out of it.

He just wasn't sure how.

"Don't worry," Tatiana said, whispering in his ear. "Your little minx is down for the count. I'm sure she won't mind if we have a little fun." She trailed a finger over his shirt, managing to unfasten the buttons with little more than a tiny flick of her fingers. Her fingertips found his chest, stroking and caressing with soft, seductive movements.

Finn stiffened, fighting a spurt of unwanted arousal. The woman whose touch he craved was on the other side of the plane, unconscious. But he'd watched Tatiana for too long, fantasized about her too many times for his body not to react to his imagination rather than the reality of the situation.

"I'll thank you to get your hands off me," he said. Considering the woman had drugged and kidnapped him, he probably should rethink the tough-guy response. But he'd responded out of instinct, and right now that was all he had to go on.

"Nonsense," she purred. "You'll thank me to continue. Believe me, men always do." She kept one hand on his chest and waved dismissively with the other. Like good little lap dogs, the two men moved forward into the cockpit, closing the door behind them. "How nice that we're now all alone."

"Nice isn't the word I would have chosen," he said.

She didn't respond in words. Instead, she trailed her hand down, pressing her palm against his crotch. A wave of revulsion washed over him, and any fear that his body would betray him—would spring to attention at this woman's touch—evaporated. He didn't know what she was up to, but he knew it was no good.

She pressed her lips against his neck. "Don't fight it, Mr. Teague. You know you want me. *I* know you want me." She pulled back, just enough to look into his eyes. Her lips pursed into a perfect, glossed kiss. "I've seen you watching me."

He said nothing, just turned his head away.

Her tongue flicked lightly over his ear. "Why do you watch, Mr. Teague?"

Play it cool, Finn. He took a deep breath. "Maybe I just like the view."

She laughed, the sound surprisingly sweet. "Of course you do. You're a man." Her lips brushed over his, and Finn stiffened, fighting the urge to jerk back away from her. "But that's not the only reason you watch, is it?" She took his bottom lip in her teeth and tugged, the pressure both gentle and insistent. Finn clenched his hands into fists. "Tell me who you work for," she murmured.

Now, Finn thought. Tell her the truth and then get the hell out of there.

But he didn't. As much as he wanted to believe he could simply tell Tatiana that this was all a big misunderstanding, he knew better. The woman believed he knew her secrets. And considering ZAEL had entered the picture, he could imagine just how sensitive her secrets might be. The company was renowned for its communications satellites, but lately it had expanded into space-based weapons systems. Both defensive and offensive.

The kind of technology any self-respecting terrorist would love to get his—or her—hands on.

If Finn told her the truth, one of three things would happen. She wouldn't believe him, and he'd be right back where he started. She'd believe him, and let him and Amber go, dropping them back off at the apartment and giving them a bottle of vodka in apology for all the trouble. Or she'd believe him, and then she'd have one of her two goons open the door while the plane was somewhere over the Pacific . . . and Finn and Amber would end up fish food.

Finn knew door number three was the most likely scenario.

And so he kept his mouth shut. So long as she thought he was a spy—so long as she believed he might have discovered some key bit of information and passed it along to his superiors—she'd keep him alive. If only for the purpose of torturing him until he spilled everything he knew.

Unfortunately for Finn, he didn't know a damn thing. And he wondered how long it would take for her to figure that out.

Her hand stroked his cheek, her touch light, like the caress of a lover. "Tell me," she crooned. She lowered her hand to stroke his inner thigh. "Tell me, and we can make this very, very pleasant." She nipped at his earlobe, the intensity of the bite making him wince. "Tell me, and we won't have to resort to more painful forms of persuasion."

He stared straight ahead, hopefully projecting the illusion of a superspy rather than a clueless civilian.

The cockpit door swung open and the gorilla with the missing earlobe stepped through. "Give it a rest, Diana. The guy's a professional. He ain't caving. From the look of it, even one of your famous blow jobs wouldn't suck the information out of him."

As she pressed her lips together, her eyes flashing, Finn said a silent thank-you. At least now he knew her name. Considering he supposedly had the goods on her, that was probably useful information.

For a moment Finn thought she was going to ignore the lug, but then she slid off his lap and returned to the bar. She downed two shots, then faced him, still ignoring her counterpart. "You should have talked," she said to Finn. "I would have put in a good word. As it is, now you have to face Drake alone, without any help from me. Or anyone."

The gorilla laughed. "Good luck with that," he said to Finn. "You'll need it." He turned to Diana. "What about the broad? Want me to relieve the plane of a little ballast?"

Finn tensed, not entirely sure what he was going to do if Diana said yes. Considering he was cuffed and still woozy from drugs, the opportunities for chivalry were severely lacking.

Diana shook her head. "No. We'll take her with us. Our Mr. Teague might be immune to my charms, but I doubt he's immune to an innocent woman's pain. If we need her, she'll be handy."

The gorilla lumbered toward Amber, and Finn

didn't like the leer that crossed his face. "And if we don't need her, well, maybe I can have a go."

Finn strained against his bonds, but Diana just laughed. She waved a hand toward the thug. "Go ask Prado what the holdup is. Why haven't we started to taxi?"

"That's what I came back here for. We're taking off."

As the gorilla returned to the cockpit, the plane started to move. Diana headed toward an empty chair, patting Finn lightly on the cheek as she passed by. "In the event of a water landing, darling, your seat cushion can be used as a floatation device." She strapped herself in, then pulled a copy of *Vogue* from a side pocket of the lush, leather seat. She opened the magazine, flipped the page, and utterly ignored him.

Finn blinked. The entire situation was surreal, and he wondered if he could somehow capture and bottle it. The FBI said he was too old, and the CIA had flat-out rejected his application. If he and Amber got out of this alive, could he resubmit and put this day down as work experience?

The engine hummed, the plane rushing forward. The force pressed him back against the seat, and he settled in for the ride.

If Finn couldn't go to espionage, espionage, it seemed, would come to Finn.

Ten

*S*o *he really was a spy.*

Amber resisted the urge to open her eyes and look at Finn. She had to give him credit. His cover story had fooled her. She'd been almost certain he was a civilian—not positive, but close.

And while she hated being wrong, she was happy to know she had a trained ally in this current predicament. If everything she'd heard about Drake Mackenzie was true, escaping from the maniac's grip wasn't going to be easy.

Fingers of pain shot through Amber's body, the unfortunate side effect of laying silently on the couch—her shoulder throbbing and her muscles cramping—for the duration of the flight.

No one expressed any surprise that the drug had kept her out of commission for so long, which only confirmed Amber's belief that not only had they

given her a large dose of Narc, but they also
assumed she wasn't worth worrying about, except
as a possible torture victim to entice Finn to spill
secrets. The torture thing aside, that wasn't a bad
position to be in. Being presumed a civilian meant
that she was practically invisible. And that could
result in a very tangible advantage.

For that matter, she'd be wise to keep her identity
secret from Finn as well. Just because they shared
an enemy didn't necessarily make them allies. And
at the moment, she was in the perfect position—
able to listen unobtrusively while Finn watched her
back.

The plane banked sharply, and Amber was lucky
she didn't tumble off the couch and onto the floor.
Time to wake up. She wanted a look at her cap-
tors—and at Finn—before they got off the plane
and, possibly, separated. With calculated movements, she stretched her legs, then wiggled her fingers. She raised herself slightly on her elbows and
conjured a low moan.

"She's coming around," Beltzer said.

Footsteps, and then someone grabbed her
roughly by the arm, pulling her into a sitting position. Amber blinked, peeling her eyes open to find
Diana peering right back at her. The other woman
let go, tossing Amber back like so much garbage.

"She's awake," Diana said, moving away. She gestured toward Beltzer. "Check her out."

"Wh-where am I?"

"Shut up," Beltzer said. He slapped a blood pressure cuff around her arm and pressed his finger to
her wrist.

"Finn?" she said. It was no work to keep her

voice hoarse. She'd been faking unconsciousness for hours. Her voice was raspy, and she would've traded state secrets for a glass of water. Well, not really. But she was pretty damn thirsty.

"I'm here," he said. She turned, widening her eyes in mock surprise when she saw him in the chair on the far side of the cabin.

The movement gave her the opportunity she needed to scope out the plane and its passengers. The cabin was lushly appointed, all leather, hardwoods, and crystal. The couch was framed by two small windows. A table, antique from the looks of it, was perched near the end of the couch, between her and the cabin door. Its mate was bolted to the floor between her and Finn. She let her gaze drift over both tables, searching for any knickknack that might be useful as a weapon, but the tabletops looked bare.

From what she could see, the rear of the cabin fed into a lavatory and, possibly, access to a cargo hold. If possible, she'd check it out before they began their descent. But escape wasn't her primary concern at the moment. After all, if what the pilot said was true, they were over water and there was nowhere to go. Besides, Diana was being kind enough to take her to Drake. It would be rude to skip out of the party.

"Well?" Diana asked.

"She's fine," Beltzer said. He caressed her face, curling a lock of hair around a finger as Amber fought back a gag. Mackenzie had done good recruiting this guy; Beltzer's breath alone could fell an army. "Hell," he added, "she's more than fine."

Amber jerked away, and Beltzer laughed.

"I'd advise you to leave the lady alone," Finn said.

Beltzer snorted. "You gonna make me?"

"I might."

"Yeah? You and what army?"

Diana held up a hand. "Just leave her alone," she said, but it was said without conviction.

"Please," Amber said, throwing herself into her role. "Tell me where I am."

"You're on a plane, sweetcakes," Beltzer said.

She licked her lips. "Why?"

"A fun-filled vacation package," Beltzer said. "Lucky you."

"Well, hell," Finn drawled. "And me without my suntan oil."

Amber fought a smile. Damn, but she liked that man's style.

Less than an hour later, they landed. In the meantime, Diana had permitted no more questions, instead demanding silence as she flipped the pages of *Cosmopolitan, Vanity Fair,* and *Maxim.*

Amber had wrangled an escort to the lavatory, but she'd learned nothing of import during the trek. For that matter, the only revelations during their entire time in the plane were that Finn was some sort of operative, and that whoever had decorated the plane had excellent—and expensive—taste.

The plane rolled down the tarmac and Amber peered out the window at paradise. Lush green hills peppered with palm trees sparkled in the dawn's light. And when she turned slightly, she saw that they were on a plateau, high above the island. Below them on one side, she could make out a crystal-clear lagoon. The plane turned again, and Amber realized that a large building covered most of the plateau not taken up by the airstrip, one side essentially forming an extension of the cliff. The view, of course, must have been amazing. On top of the building, Amber saw a helicopter. Probably Drake's primary form of transportation.

The plane continued to taxi for a few yards, then turned, shifting her view and revealing a smaller building she hadn't noticed before. This one was nestled against a hill on the far side of the tarmac. The building was topped with a satellite dish, eerily illuminated in the dawn's light. The plane came to a stop, and Amber turned from the window to face Finn. He met her gaze, his eyes serious. She knew what he was thinking—this was it. Time to enter the dragon's lair.

Diana stood, dusting her white slacks to remove nonexistent lint. The engine died, and the plane stilled, the low thrumming of the engine quieting. After a moment, the door to the cockpit opened and a tall blond man in an Italian suit stepped out. Prado, Amber presumed.

"Let's get these two into the truck," he said. "Wouldn't want them to be late for their appointment."

"Certainly not," Beltzer added. "That would be what they call a social fox paw."

"Faux pas," Diana said. "Take care of them, and then come back for our little package in the cargo hold."

Prado took Amber's left arm and yanked her to her feet. Fire radiated out from her shoulder, shooting all the way to her toes.

She stumbled slightly. She would have liked to say that she'd been playing a role, but the truth was that her muscles were sore and cramped, and with her hands cuffed behind her back, her sense of balance was even more compromised. Diana had led Finn toward the door, and now he was at her side. His smile was reassuring, and she returned it, trying to psychically let him know that whatever he had planned, he should count her in.

The cabin door was open, the fold-down kind that created a set of stairs leading to the tarmac, which reached out to touch the horizon. A truck painted in familiar green and brown camouflage loomed large before them.

Diana held what looked like a small stick in her hand, and as she stepped onto the stairs, she flicked her wrist, opening a small paper fan. As she descended, she waved the fan, creating her own personal cross-breeze.

Amber and Finn stayed put at the top of the stairs, Beltzer and Prado behind them. When she reached the ground, Diana looked back up at them, gesturing toward the truck as if she were Vanna White showing off one of the fabulous prizes. "Do hurry, you two. Your limo awaits."

As Beltzer jabbed his finger between her shoulder blades, Finn met her eyes. "Don't worry," he whispered. "I won't let anything happen to you."

Her skin flushed warm and Amber smiled. She was more than capable of taking care of herself. But for once, she had to admit, it felt nice to be on the receiving end of chivalry.

He was gonna die. Oh, god, he was gonna die.

Bernie shivered under a thin wool blanket. His nose was dripping, and he didn't have a tissue. He rubbed the blanket under his nose, but it was rough, and his upper lip was already cracked and split.

The room was made of cinder blocks, and had one heavy metal door with a tiny window blocked by three iron bars. The only furnishings were a cot and a chamber pot. Bernie eyed the second with distaste. Pretty soon he'd have to use it, and the thought made him gag.

He knew why he was there; he wasn't stupid. It was just his dumb luck that the one thing in the world he was good at was something terrorists and thugs wanted to get their hands on.

He'd always known his job was risky. But when the word came down that he was being reclassified to the lowest level and reassigned to data processing, he thought he'd be safe. Hiding in the open kind of thing.

Considering he was now stuck in a cell, that brilliant plan to keep him off the bad guys' radar screen apparently hadn't worked too well.

But he'd keep his mouth shut. Bernie Waterman wasn't a traitor. He wasn't talking. Not even if they ripped out his toenails. No sir, no how.

He shifted his bare feet under the blanket. Surely they wouldn't rip out his toenails. . . .

He snuffled, then blew his nose into the blanket. He let his head fall back and breathed through his mouth. He felt like shit.

But he had a feeling he was about to feel a whole lot worse.

Amber paced the room, noting its dimensions. Ten by ten, constructed of cinder blocks covered with plaster, with eight- . . . no, nine-foot ceilings. She glanced at her fingernails. Not in the best of shape now that she'd used them to scratch a section of plaster away, revealing the concrete blocks below.

But it had to be done. She needed to know how dire her situation was, and her meticulous inspection of the room had confirmed what she already knew—pretty damn dire.

The room was sparsely furnished with a cot and a stainless steel toilet with no seat or lid. Bummer. Not the best of weapons, but either one would do in a pinch.

As it was, there wasn't even enough water in the bowl to drown a man. And her wish for a mirror was sadly ungranted.

Too bad. Not only was she willing to trade seven years bad luck for a deadly shard of glass, she also wanted to get a look at her aching shoulder. Not gonna happen, though, and she pushed the wish, and the pain, out of her mind.

She dropped to the floor by the cot and scooted under on her back, tilting slightly to the right so her left shoulder didn't scrape the ground. She felt a bit like a mechanic taking a look at a car's suspension, only she didn't intend to repair anything. At the moment, she was deep in destruction mode.

Unfortunately, there wasn't anything to destroy. She'd hoped for a tensile spring. If nothing else, she could sharpen the end on the concrete and hide the makeshift knife in her cleavage. But Drake had thought of everything. The cot base was made from tightly pulled webbing. Not a spring to be found.

She considered busting off one of the metal legs,

but that was so obvious. Still, she hated being unarmed. . . .

She grabbed the edge of the cot and flipped it over, taking some satisfaction in the clatter as it bounced, then settled on the hard floor. She slammed her foot against the cot's leg. One, two, three times.

The metal bent, and she squatted for a closer look. Good. Just one more time.

She lifted her leg, ready to slam it down one last time and free the metal cylinder, but then the door burst open and Beltzer strode through.

"Getting cocky, there, princess?"

"You have no idea," Amber said, eyeing the open door behind him and making her decision in a split second. She twirled around, thrusting her leg out and up in a move that would have made her sensai proud. She caught him in the jaw, and his head flew back, knocking him off balance so that he fell to the ground with a satisfying thud.

Too easy.

She was at his side in an instant, going for the gun in his hand. In less than twenty seconds, she was armed and in the doorway, Beltzer groaning and half-conscious behind her.

She stepped into the hallway, allowing herself just the tiniest sigh of relief.

"Drop it." Prado's voice.

Amber closed her eyes, her relief short-lived. The cold barrel of a pistol pressed against her temple, and she knew she was out of options. For now.

She tossed the gun on the ground, grimacing when Prado kicked it out of range.

"You're out of your league, babycakes," he said.

Amber said nothing. He was wrong. About that, she was sure. But right now wasn't the time to prove it.

A nightmare.

This was a nightmare all done up in silks and satins and high-gloss paint.

Finn paced the room, more lush than a suite at the Plaza. He'd expected to be tossed in a cold, stone cell or tied to a cement slab with a buzz saw swinging like a pendulum over his chest. Instead, he'd been tossed into the lap of luxury.

Disconcerting, to say the least.

He sat down on the edge of the firm mattress and ran his palm over the silky bedspread, his mind going a million miles an hour. *He needed to get out.* Needed to find Amber. But he'd already been over every inch of the room. If there were any hidden passages or secret escape routes, he hadn't found them.

The bathroom was simply stocked, lacking anything from which he could fashion even the most remedial of explosives or weapons. He ran his fingers through his hair with a sigh. Probably just as well. If he blew the door out, he'd most likely end up with a bullet in his head. And he was no good to Amber dead.

They'd been separated as soon as the truck had pulled to a halt inside a concrete bunker, and he could only hope that her accommodations were as appealing. He had a suspicion, however, that her quarters were much more spartan. Diana thought that Finn had information, and apparently she was going to attempt to extract it with honey.

But Amber was just along for the ride. On the plane they'd made it perfectly clear that they had no need to keep her happy. Only to keep her alive—in case they needed to use her to get to him.

He closed his eyes and drew in a deep breath. He'd tell them whatever they wanted if it would keep her from being hurt. But it wouldn't do any good. Because at the end of the day, he didn't know a thing.

He pounded a fist against the bed, the gesture unsatisfying against the thick, downy covering.

"Now, now, sugar." The soft, feminine voice drifted to him from across the room. "What could possibly be troubling you?"

Finn opened his eyes and saw Diana standing in the now-open doorway. She wore only a silky negligee, transparent against the light of the hallway. She glided forward, every movement calculated to entice.

He ignored her question, staying perfectly silent as she moved toward him. A muscle in his cheek twitched, and he bit down on the inside of his mouth, stifling the overpowering urge to push himself up and off the bed. He'd never before wanted to hit a woman. But he wanted to now. And how.

When she reached him, she ran her fingertip along the line of his jaw, even as he turned away, trying to escape her caress.

"Now, sweetie, what kind of a reaction is that? I thought you'd be happy to see me." She took his knees and pushed his legs apart, then moved to stand in the V of his thighs. "I thought we could enjoy this time alone."

"Somehow," he said, "I sense an ulterior motive."

"Nonsense." She turned in a full circle, her peignoir swishing against the rough fabric of his jeans. "You can see I'm completely unarmed."

"I'm not sure that makes you any less deadly."

She tossed her head back and laughed, as if he'd skewered her with his rapier wit. Then she moved closer, pressing her hand on his shoulder and leaning forward. She smelled like strawberries, and Finn wondered if he'd ever be able to have short-cake again without suppressing a surge of rage.

She twisted slightly, then sat down, balancing on his thigh. She pressed close, her hand dangerously close to his crotch, as she whispered in his ear. "You know you want me, Mr. Teague."

"I'd appreciate it if I could have my leg back, Diana," he said. He met her eyes, his confidence tenuous but intact.

"Say please," she said, her breath tickling his ear.

"Please," Finn said.

"I don't think so." Her hand closed over his crotch, the unexpected touch sending waves of unwanted sensations coursing through his body.

"Oooh," she whispered. "You really do want me to stay."

Finn grimaced, at the moment hating his body, testosterone, and mostly, his cock. "Just being polite, ma'am."

"I love a man with manners." She slid off, once again standing in front of him. Finn breathed in and out, slowly and deliberately, willing control back into his body.

Her smile suggested she had his number, and he hoped to hell she was wrong. Then she reached up and pulled at the silken bow at her neck. The peignoir seemed to dissolve, like so much spun sugar touching water, and suddenly she was naked before him. A crest of lust crashed over him, smothered quickly by a wash of rage and self-loathing.

This wasn't the woman he wanted. Not now, not ever. She'd been a fantasy, nothing more.

"What's the matter, sugar? You want me. We're all alone. There's no reason why you can't have me." She slid her hands along his inner thighs, pressing, urging. "She's not here to see," Diana whispered. "And I promise, you won't regret it."

She took his hand, touching his palm to her breast. Her nipple tightened against his skin, and Finn's entire body tensed, blood pounding in his ears.

She leaned forward, her breast plump in his hand, and when the soft moan escaped her lips, Finn lost it. He jerked upright, grabbing her by the waist as he twisted around and tossed her back onto the bed. His hands clutched her neck, and he squeezed. Not hard enough to block her air passage, but hopefully enough to cool her down.

"Oh, baby." Her voice, low and raspy, held not even a hint of fear. Her hand reached out, grasping for his fly as she wrapped her legs around him, her ankles intertwined behind his knees. "You like it rough," she said. "So do I."

He pressed her down by the shoulders, ignoring her little sounds of pleasure. "Where is she?" he asked.

"I told you. She won't know. She'll never know." She spread her legs wider, revealing more of her perfect body. Her pubic hair glistened, and he realized she was genuinely turned on. Maybe she was trying to seduce the information out of him, but she was enjoying herself in the process.

For half a second, he imagined taking her right there, as if nailing her would prove some dubious point, or serve any purpose other than a release of this horrible, burning anger.

"Enough." In one swift movement, he flipped her over, pulling her off the bed and ending with her neck in the crook of his arm. "One wrong step, and I swear I'll break your neck."

"Darling," she whispered, "was it something I said?"

He turned, tugging her along with him, until they were facing the door. He half-walked, half-dragged her that way, stopping in front of the electronic pad that controlled ingress and egress. "Open it."

For a moment, he thought she was going to argue. And then she leaned forward. He tugged her back, wary.

"Do you want me to open the door or not? Let me at the goddamn pad."

He relaxed his grip ever so slightly, and she pressed her palm against the translucent pad. A horizontal bar of light moved up and down, like a photocopy machine storing an image. And the instant the light faded, the door slid open.

A man Finn had never seen before stood there, a pistol aimed at Finn's head. "Let her go, Mr. Teague."

Finn complied, raising his hands and taking a step backward as Diana walked into the hall and stood, naked, by the man.

"Who are you?" Finn asked.

"There'll be time enough for that later," the man

said. "In the meantime," he said, his hand stroking Diana's bare flesh, "I think I'll go take care of your unfinished business."

The door slid shut, trapping Finn once again. He collapsed against it, losing himself to a haze of anger and frustration.

After a moment, he straightened up, then pressed his hand against the electronic pad. *Nothing.*

Not that he'd really expected anything, but he had to try.

He turned back around to face the room, taking in its luxury, its careful appointments. A room for seduction, all right. And right then, damn him, he wanted release. *Amber.*

He wanted her. Craved her. So badly his body ached. He wanted to hold her, to touch her, and to lose himself in her.

But he had no way of finding her. Much less of knowing if he'd ever see her alive again.

Eleven

Drake swept his eyes over Diana's flushed body. Her nipples were tight and hard, her eyes warm and dreamy. "So glad to see you enjoyed your assignment," he said. He shrugged out of his uniform jacket, draping it over her bare shoulders.

A sultry smile touched her mouth. "I thought you wanted me to enjoy my work," she cooed. She moved closer, pressing her body against his, and he felt himself tighten with the contact. She slipped her hand between them, rubbing lightly at his crotch. "And this way, we can skip all that pesky foreplay."

He laughed. He couldn't stay mad at her. Hell, this whole operation was for her. For them. "He's a good-looking man. Are you sure you didn't want him just a little?"

"He's an ass," she said.

At that, Drake laughed harder. In Diana's world, there were two kinds of men. Those who succumbed to her charms, and those who didn't.

Diana might be more than willing to use Mr. Teague as a human vibrator, but she didn't want him. Not really.

Not any more than Teague wanted her.

No, Teague didn't want Diana, he wanted the brunette that Beltzer had snared. And Drake intended to let him have her. One night of prison passion, of bonding in fear and solitude, of jointly wondering what their fate would be . . . oh, yes. That would make Mr. Teague even more susceptible to persuasion when Drake began his interrogation.

All in all, Drake had nothing to worry about with Phineus Teague.

Diana pressed him against the wall, shifting his thoughts quite effectively from Teague to her soft, hot curves.

"Now," she said. "Right here. Right now."

He shook his head. "Later, my pet." He squeezed her nipple, twisting until she cried out in pain and pleasure. "Right now I have a different kind of foreplay in mind."

About five minutes after Diana left, the door opened again. Finn tensed, expecting a second try from Diana or an unpleasant visit from the man with the gun.

Instead he got Amber.

The wave of relief that washed over him was so palpable that seconds ticked by before what his eyes saw registered in his brain—she was utterly naked, her wrists bound behind her back. Even so, she held her head high, defiant.

"If it was up to me, I'd just take you myself," Beltzer said from behind her. A nasty bruise swelled on his cheek, and his lip was split, exacerbating his already snarlish appearance. "You'd like it, too."

"I wouldn't bet the ranch," Amber said, as Finn silently cheered her spunk.

"Bitch," Beltzer muttered.

Beltzer shoved her through the door, pressing the butt of his gun into the small of her back. She stumbled, landing on her knees as the door slid shut.

Finn was at her side in an instant, shrugging out of his shirt. The deep wound under her left shoulder blade was raw and angry, the skin around it swollen and brownish yellow in color. *Infection.* He traced a finger along the edge of it. "We need to take care of this."

"It'll be fine," she said, her quick smile going straight to his heart.

He knew better than to argue with her, but as he draped the shirt over her, he ran through a mental inventory of the contents of the bathroom. Nothing for First Aid, that was for sure.

"Nice accommodations," she said as she stood up. "They must have put me in one of the budget rooms."

"Did they hurt you?" he asked, turning her slightly and working on the ropes binding her wrists.

"I'm fine," she said. "Pissed, but fine."

He turned just long enough to study her face and decided he believed her. Good. Because if Beltzer or any of them had laid a hand on her, Finn was going to have to kill them. And at the moment he wasn't entirely certain how he would go about that.

One more tug and the ropes fell from her wrists. "Done," he said. Beltzer had used a simple slip-knot, and Finn made easy work of it. As soon as the rope fell away, Amber pulled her arms through the sleeves, then rubbed her red, raw wrists.

He wanted to talk to her, to reassure her that somehow, some way, he'd make this right. But the words wouldn't come.

Instead of speaking, he clutched her shoulders, pulling her to him. Primal emotion had pushed reason aside. All he knew was that he wanted her. Wanted to know she was safe. Wanted to erase the memory of Diana. Wanted to ease Amber's fears and hurts. Hell, he just wanted to find one good place inside this nightmare.

His lips met hers, and she opened her mouth, returning the kiss greedily, as if her hunger was as intense as his. She hadn't yet buttoned the shirt, and now he slid one hand inside, stroking her back as the other cupped her neck. He feasted on her lips, seeking satisfaction, but needing so much more.

He'd been craving her. And now, by God, he had to have her.

In one bold movement, he pressed her down, straddling her as she lay on the soft carpet. "I don't want to hurt you," he said, stroking her shoulder.

"If you *don't* touch me," she said, "*that* would be torture." She smiled, and he saw no hesitation in her eyes. Just an invitation. Hell, a demand.

That was all the encouragement he needed.

The shirt had fallen open, and her chest rose and fell with her quick breaths. He reached out to stroke her breasts, then bent over, flicking his tongue over her nipple. She moaned, her hips lifting slightly off the floor.

His hand went to his fly, and he eased out of his jeans and briefs. Then he hesitated, wanting to explain to her. To let her know that he didn't know why they were on this island, but that he'd do everything in his power to keep her safe. "Amb—"

She reached up, silencing him with a single finger as she spread her legs wider.

Already rock hard, that unspoken command just about killed him. He slid his hand down to cup her sex, slipping his finger inside, testing, wanting to be certain she was ready for him. He wasn't disappointed. She was ready. Hot and wet and slick. And with one determined thrust, he entered her.

She exhaled, a soft moan of pleasure, and her hips rose to meet him. Her hands cupped his ass, and she pulled him toward her, forcing him in harder and deeper. Amber closed her eyes, moaning as they ground together in pure, raw passion. But he kept his eyes open, memorizing the way her breasts tightened and puckered, the way her teeth grazed her lower lip, the way her stomach quivered as her passion built.

Her velvet heat pulled him in, and he wanted to curl up inside her and never let the moment end. At the same time, he wanted the explosion that was building inside him.

He thrust again and again, as if with each thrust he could replace some of the bad with pure, wonderful good.

And when she shuddered beneath him and cried out his name, Finn had to wonder if, despite the horror of the situation, he had somehow managed to touch heaven.

The orgasm washed over her, wave after wave of pleasure so intense she wasn't entirely sure she could survive the sensation.

He groaned, a deep, male sound, and she felt his entire body harden against her and then relax as he, too, found release.

"Finn." His name left her lips as naturally as breathing, and she pulled him to her, wanting the crush of his weight against her. He took her in his arms, and she could feel the tension drain from him as they lay together, their bodies still thrumming as if they'd touched a live wire.

She hadn't expected the burst of passion that had pulled her into his arms, but she wasn't going to reprimand herself for it. She'd wanted him. She wasn't about to deny it.

After a few moments, he shifted, raising himself on his elbow to look at her. His eyes were intense, filled with raw emotion—desire and something else. Something that left her feeling naked for the first time since she'd been tossed into the room. She scowled, then eased slightly out of his embrace.

"I wonder if I should apologize," he said.

"Why?" she asked, genuinely confused.

"We're doing exactly what they want."

"Ah." Understanding dawned, as she rolled the rest of the way away from him and sat up. "I thought we were doing exactly what *we* wanted." She closed his shirt over her and began to methodically button it.

Something had happened with Finn and Diana.

He hadn't made love to Amber so much as he'd worked something out. And while she'd enjoyed it intensely, now she actually felt shy. *Shy.* Her of all people.

She didn't know why and she wasn't inclined to examine her psyche. All she knew was that she wanted this man. Not for the mission, because she hardly needed to seduce him for his secrets anymore. And not because they'd been tossed into the Bridal Suite with the expectation that they'd do exactly what they were doing.

No, she wanted the man she'd come to know, even despite all the secrets between them. A man she liked more than she cared to admit. And, even more, she wanted him to want her more than he wanted to erase a bad memory.

Which was why it irked her that they hadn't been alone. Diana's ghost had been in the room with them.

Without thinking, she lifted her chin. "Did you work it out?" she asked, then immediately regretted the question. She'd wanted the sex as much as he had. What did she care about his motives so long as the package deal came complete with an orgasm? She was a big girl, after all. And she knew better than anyone that sex was a sharp-edged tool.

But she did care. Damn her, she did.

His smile was sad as he stroked her cheek. "Yeah," he said. "I think I did."

He held her by both shoulders, and she lifted her gaze to his eyes—then gasped at the emotion she saw burning there. Any doubt that she'd been only a warm body fizzled away. The man wanted *her,* and the knowledge thrilled her more than it should.

She reached out, stroking his cheek, now rough with stubble. "Finn—?"

"Shhh." He closed his eyes, then kissed her palm. A sweet, tender gesture that sent a rush of warmth through Amber's veins. But when he looked at her again, there was nothing sweet or tender in his gaze. Just raw emotion. Passion. Heat. *Need*.

And all of it directed at her.

"I shouldn't have—"

She hushed him with a kiss. She had no interest in looking backward. With Finn, she wanted only to move on. "It's okay," she whispered.

He looked at her, the intensity of his gaze almost frightening.

Intellectually, she knew she should back off. They needed to talk, and that meant they needed to get clear of the sexual mist surrounding them. After all, she needed to know what he'd learned, what he'd seen, and they had to figure out what Drake was up to.

She knew all of that. And yet she couldn't seem to move.

And when Finn pressed forward, capturing her mouth with his own, the last vestiges of reason left her, her thoughts boiling down to the simplest of equations. He wanted her. She wanted him. And they were trapped. Not exactly a hard sell.

His mouth closed over hers, and even those simplistic thoughts vanished as she surrendered to a crest of emotions and sensations that seemed to build in one syllable increments—yes, please, yes, *more*.

The room was plush, the bed looming just in front of them. But once again they never made it that far. Never made it any further than the spot they'd started in.

Finn's hands traced down her sides, sending shivers racing through her body. He pressed her back against the carpet, his need palpable and so very erotic.

Her shoulder ached, generating a heat all its own, but she hardly noticed. She was too lost in a haze of erotic sensations. He cupped her breasts in his hands and buried his face in her cleavage, giving her much more satisfying sensations to cling to.

His breath came hard and fast, matching hers, and his fingers caressed her breast as he closed his mouth over her nipple.

Amber moaned, losing herself in the riot of sensations ripping through her body. The throbbing between her legs increased, and she raised her hips, seeking his heat. His leg was between her thighs, and as she raised up, her body met the hard muscle of his thigh.

She ground against him, her body still warm and tingly from making love just minutes before. He sucked and teased her nipple, fueling the fire that was fast building into an inferno.

"Slow?" he said.

"*Now.*" Slow was nice in theory, but not now. Not when she needed to feel him inside her. Needed to know that it was her and only her that was taking him to the edge and back again.

With a low, guttural groan, he balanced himself over her; she felt him press against her, hot and insistent.

"Yes," she said, answering his unspoken question. He thrust against her, and her body opened to him, drawing him closer and tighter. She crossed her legs behind him, arching her back, and meeting his thrusts. He was deep inside her, and the pleasure washed over and through her.

Her shoulder rubbed against the carpet, the thin shirt little protection for the raw skin. But the pain was lost in the cacophony of sensations that grabbed hold of her body and danced across her nerve endings. Everything seemed to spiral in, and she knew that if this whirlwind of sensations collapsed in on itself, her body would explode into a million pieces.

And oh, how she craved that explosion.

They rocked together, and he whispered her name, encouraging her to come to him, to come with him. Her body answered his call, desire building and building until it reached a pinnacle that was impossible to climb, and the mountain of pleasure exploded around her in a fit of colors and stars.

He collapsed against her, his body slick with sweat. The press of his weight felt comfortable, not confining, and she lay there, idly stroking his back, as she sorted through her thoughts.

They stayed like that arm in arm for a few more moments, their steady breathing the only sound in the still, warm room. Amber continued to stroke her fingers idly up and down his back, the rhythmic motion calming and relaxing.

Soon enough, Drake would come for them, and she'd be wired, her body running on instinct and adrenaline. Amber intended to enjoy this moment while she could.

He rolled to the side, lifting his head until his eyes met hers. "That had to have been the best captive sex I've ever had."

Her mouth twitched. "You're a connoisseur, then?"

"Absolutely. I try to hit all the finer detention centers."

"I see. And how does this one compare?"

He glanced around the room, and she followed his gaze, taking in the lush carpet, fine linens, and etched teak headboard. Finally, Finn shrugged. "So-so," he said. "This doesn't quite top the Four Seasons Holding Facility," he said. "But I suppose it'll do." He traced a lazy circle on her stomach. "It's the personal touch that really makes this place stand out."

"Naked women as an amenity?" she asked.

"Something like that."

She closed her eyes, resting her head against the carpeting. "You're right, you know. We're just playing into his hands."

"His?"

She frowned, wondering if he was playing dumb or if he really didn't know about Drake Mackenzie. "Surely you don't believe that woman is doing all of this."

"No. She's someone else's pawn. And you're right—a man. Military, unless the uniform is bullshit. He was here earlier."

Amber perked up. So far, she'd seen no evidence of Drake on the island. But if the man was in uniform . . . "What kind of uniform? Do you know his name? What he wants?"

"Navy," Finn said. "And no, and no."

She pressed her lips together, then nodded, accepting the answer, but not at all certain she believed it.

Amber twisted to her left and sat up, grimacing as her shoulder bore the brunt of her weight.

Finn's brow furrowed. "Are you okay?"

She waved the question off. "I'm fine." She flashed what she hoped was a bright smile. In truth, her shoulder was burning, and she feared that Finn was right about an infection. "Just need to stretch."

Finn's eyes followed her as she headed to the bathroom. She'd hoped to find some alcohol or ointment, but the room was bare. Not even a toothbrush. Luxury, apparently, didn't extend so far as to include items that might be used as a weapon.

She shrugged out of Finn's shirt, then she craned her neck and tried to see just how bad the damage was. She couldn't see much, but what she could see told her enough. The wound itself was raw and oozing, and her entire shoulder blade seemed pink and hot. She cringed, the injury beginning to hurt more now that she was focusing on it.

"Amber?" Concern laced Finn's voice.

"Coming," she called. She took three deep breaths, willing her mind to ignore the sensation of pain shooting from her shoulder. The Unit's training had been thorough, and she closed her eyes, letting James's soft maxim—*there is no pain except in your mind*—flow through her. As she knew it would, the pain dulled to a low throb. She took two more deep breaths, then two more, until the wound was only a memory.

She didn't have time to worry about injuries or infection. She'd deal with it after they got the hell off the island.

When she stepped back into the bedroom, Finn was running his hands over the door.

"No luck?" she said.

He turned, then shrugged almost sheepishly.

"Just thought I'd try again. I've been over this room backward and forward. I know we're trapped, but I don't want to believe it."

"They'll come get us soon enough," she said, moving to sit on the bed.

"From one trap to another," he said.

A sheer pink negligee lay in a crumpled pile on the floor by the bed. She picked it up, dangling it from one finger. "I see the traps haven't been altogether unpleasant."

For the first time since Amber had entered the room, Finn's face hardened, hate filling his eyes. "She tried to seduce me."

Amber nodded. She'd expected as much. "I can't say I blame her," she said, wanting to lighten the moment.

A genuine smile touched his mouth. "Ah, but you're not trying to romance me for my secrets."

Amber stifled a wince. Twenty-four hours ago, that had been exactly her plan. "What secrets are those?" she asked, keeping her tone light. "Your secret identity?" She still had to find out. No matter what she felt for this man, she still had to find out whom he worked for. If he was an ally or an enemy.

He flashed an ironic smile. "That's the joke," he said. "I don't have any secrets. Not even a secret identity." He lifted an eyebrow. "Just like you, I'm an open book."

He spoke so earnestly she almost believed him. He was good. But in the end, she'd prove that she was better.

Twelve

The guy without an earlobe rolled a television into Bernie's cell, then left, pausing in the doorway just long enough to say, "Enjoy the show."

Bernie frowned, wondering if he'd crossed over into some sort of delirious state. His fever still raged, that much was sure. And they'd been stingy with the water and food. But even so, he didn't think he'd started hallucinating.

So why was he looking at a Sony television balanced on one of those black carts he hadn't seen since elementary school?

He didn't have time to ponder the problem, because the television sprang to life. And the image that popped onto the screen was enough to make him forget his own troubles.

Diana. Wearing only a flimsy lace bra and tiny bikini panties. Her wrists and ankles were shackled to a stone tablet tilted at the slightest of angles. She struggled, but the bindings held tight.

In his cell, Bernie clutched the tatty blanket, his knuckles turning white from gripping it so very hard. *He'd* done this to her. They were torturing her because of him, and he was powerless to do anything but watch.

Sound and picture popped on with a sharp, staticky hum, and Diana's high-pitched cries grabbed hold of his intestines and twisted.

"Bernie," she cried. "Why are they doing this? Bernie!"

"Diana!" He knew she couldn't hear him, but he had to do something. Had to go to her.

Had to help.

Tossing the blanket aside, he ran for the door, then threw himself against it, pounding with his fists on the cold metal.

"Shut up, bitch." The harsh voice came from the television, and Bernie raced back, his stomach twisting at the image on the screen—a leather whip cracking across Diana's beautiful belly.

Her scream seemed to shake his cell. He saw no tears, but she blinked, her chin quivering. "Bernie," she whispered, her voice low and weak. "Please, why?"

"Did I say you could talk?" Again, that cruel voice.

Bernie's eyes scanned the screen, but he could see no one. Only his darling Diana, and he was powerless to help her.

The camera pulled back, revealing a man dressed in a pressed white uniform, his back to the camera. He held a whip in one hand, and now he leaned over Diana, his mouth close to her ear. He traced the handle of the whip down, between her breasts and down to her belly button. Diana shut her eyes tight, but Bernie could see the way her entire body tightened with fear.

"Are you ready for another round, my pretty?" the man asked. He raised the whip then, dangling the tasseled end over Diana's firm, beautiful stomach. "Tell me what I need and I'll stop. Tell me," he crooned. "Tell me everything."

She struggled against the bonds. "I don't know anything. Please. I shouldn't be here."

"Well, aren't you the unfortunate one?" He raised his whip hand, and as he started to strike, Bernie cried out.

"No!" he yelled, even though it was futile. He didn't even know where Diana was, much less if anyone could hear him. But it didn't matter. He couldn't watch this. Couldn't let the monster hurt her. "No, don't! I'll tell you everything." In a spurt of anger, he threw himself against the television, and it crashed to the floor in a flurry of electronic sparks and beeps. "Everything!"

He collapsed in a heap on the floor. They were going to kill her. Diana, and then him. And there wasn't anything he could do about it. He was all alone.

All alone, and doomed.

The door slid open, and the uniformed man walked in. Bernie blinked, but the wash of relief was so overpowering that it erased all questions of how or where.

"Talk," he said. "Talk, and the girl lives."

And Bernie did.

* * *

Finn watched as Amber walked the room's perimeter, her eyes taking in every inch. She wore a black cocktail dress she'd found in the closet. Probably Drake's idea of a joke, but Finn appreciated it nonetheless. It was hard enough to focus when she was near him. It was even harder when she was near him and naked.

When she reached the touch pad, she swiped her hand over it. She'd done this twice before, and Finn had told her he'd done the same. As it had before, the door remained firmly closed and locked. "You're right," she said. "The only way out is through that touch pad."

"And our hands don't work."

After a moment, her shoulders sagged. She ran her fingers through her hair, an unreadable expression crossing her face. "At any rate," she said, "we're stuck." She moved to sit on the edge of the bed. "So why do you think they're doing this?"

He shook his head. "I don't know."

"Well, then *who* are they? I'd like to at least know who kidnapped me."

"Terrorists," he said simply. "Don't worry. I got you into this mess, and I'll get you out."

"Finn, for Christ's sake, I have a right to know what you know. Tell me."

He shook his head. "I honestly don't know. But I'll get us out of here."

She scowled, then gave a curt nod. "Okay. How?"

It was a reasonable question, but Finn didn't have a reasonable answer. Agent Python would have an answer. Hell, Python's Rolex would shoot a precise laser from the diamond above the twelve.

He'd cut an escape route through the door and pull the girl to safety.

Once in the passageway, he'd disarm a guard with a really keen martial arts move, take his AK-47, and race with the girl to the exit. Along the way, they'd plant enough C-4 to destroy the whole complex, then sprint to the tarmac, where they'd steal the plane and soar to safety, the island exploding into a pyrotechnical wonder below them.

The girl would throw her arms around Python's neck and cover him with kisses of gratitude. He'd put the plane on autopilot and they'd make love until they reached the mainland.

A nice fantasy, but not damn likely.

"Finn?" she said. "*How?* How are we going to get out?"

He sighed, shaking his head. "I'm sorry, babe. I really don't know."

She looked at him almost as if she didn't believe him, and he felt like the biggest failure on the planet.

After a moment, she stood up and started pacing the room. "What about weapons? If Beltzer or that bitch comes back, we can use one of their hands to open the door."

From the look on her face, Finn had the distinct impression that she'd happily detach either of their hands from their wrists.

"I've looked," he said. "There's not a thing here. There's not even a mirror in the bathroom." He stood up, moving to the doorway. "I could wait here," he said. "Attack as they enter. In the fray, you might be able to get out." What she'd do once out was a question he didn't raise.

She nodded. "It's a possibility. But now that we're both in here, they have to know we're planning. They won't come alone. And I don't know that I'm in any shape to take someone down." She rolled her shoulder slightly, and he saw the shadow of a wince touch her face.

He frowned, realizing he'd been an ass to forget her injury. Not that he'd let her do something so foolhardy even if she was all in one piece. He made a circular motion with his finger. "Turn."

She complied, and he unzipped the dress, then pushed the material aside. The wound was bright red, oozing yellow, and warm to the touch. "It's infected," he said.

"It will be fine."

He tugged at her right hand. "It will after I clean it."

"I've already looked in there," she protested as he led her toward the bathroom. But she didn't otherwise resist, and he gestured for her to sit on the side of the tub.

"You should have said something," he scolded. "My God, everything we did, every time I—"

"It hardly hurts at all," she said.

"Bullshit."

At that, she smiled. "It hurts some," she amended. "But it didn't hurt then." She licked her lips, cocking her head ever so provocatively. "I had other things on my mind to block out the pain."

He shook his head but didn't reply. Instead, he scoured the bathroom, looking for anything with which to clean the wound. He might not be able to get her off this island, or even out of this room, but he was damn sure going to clean up her shoulder.

"There's nothing here," she said.

Unfortunately, she was right. Nothing except a bar of French-milled soap sitting on the edge of the tub. Not even antibacterial, but it was the best he could do.

"Turn around," he instructed.

"Finn . . ."

"Just do it."

She rolled her eyes but complied. "I can take care of myself," she said.

"I'm sure you can." He soaked the bathroom's single washcloth with warm water, then rubbed the soap on it. Slowly, carefully, he washed the wound, working the soap into the ragged flesh, and then rinsing carefully with a plastic cup he'd found sitting by the sink.

Throughout the whole process, she never flinched or cried out. Hell, she barely even moved. And Finn wondered if maybe she'd been telling the truth. Maybe the wound wasn't that bad, and it really didn't hurt her.

"There," he said, rinsing the last of the soap away.

She tugged her sleeve back up, and he reached down to zip the dress. Except for, well, everything, the scene was utterly domestic. A couple getting ready to go out. Sharing the bathroom. Getting dressed.

He half-expected her to go to the mirror and primp. Except, of course, there was no mirror.

He shook his head, banishing the ridiculous thoughts.

"What?"

"Nothing," he said. "Just hoping your shoulder is okay."

"It's fine," she said, getting up and moving into the bedroom. "Don't worry about it."

He followed her, coming to a dead stop when he saw the man standing in their room. He put a hand on Amber's elbow, wanting her safely within his reach.

The man wore Navy whites, complete with a sidearm. Diana stood beside him, her arm linked through his. "We haven't been formally introduced," he said. "I'm Drake Mackenzie. Welcome to my humble home. I do hope you find the accommodations adequate."

"Astounding," Finn deadpanned.

"And how nice to see you two looking so . . . relaxed," Drake continued, not missing a beat.

"I do hope you enjoyed last night," Diana added, her eyes on Finn. "Despite my absence."

"I managed to muddle through," he said.

"A pity that the time for *muddling* is over," the man said. He lifted the gun. "Time to move on to other things." He motioned to Finn. "Get dressed."

Finn considered arguing but decided against it. He was already wearing his jeans, and now he shrugged into his shirt, buttoning it up, but leaving the shirttails out. Without taking his eyes off Diana or the man, he sat on the edge of the bed and put on his socks and shoes.

"As far as fashion goes," Diana says, "this is your lucky day. We even have accessories." She tossed a pair of handcuffs toward Finn. "Bracelets. One side for each of you."

He scowled, but didn't fight it. Just snapped the cuff onto his right wrist and Amber's left. If he was lucky, she was right-handed. And since he was a leftie, that would leave them both with their favored hand free.

As Drake gestured toward the door, Amber met Finn's eyes. "Like I said, don't bother worrying about my shoulder," she said. "We've got more important things to worry about."

"That," Diana said, "is a certainty."

"She's *gone?*" James Monahan paced the situation room in the Los Angeles field office, his near-black eyes cutting into Brandon like hot steel through butter. "What the hell was she doing in Los Angeles in the first place?"

"Working a lead," Schnell said. "Doing her job."

Brandon kept his mouth shut. Schnell and Monahan were the big dogs, and he wasn't about to piss in their puddle.

"I should have been told," Monahan said. "She was in Chechnya under *my* orders." The look he aimed at Schnell was pure ice. "I'm not retired yet."

"You weren't available," Schnell said. He moved behind the podium and punched a button, dimming the lights and dropping a projection screen. The intent was obvious—subject closed. Time to move on.

That was fine with Brandon. He'd give his right arm for James, but he'd give his life for Amber. And this petty power trip between Schnell and Monahan was wasting valuable time.

As it was, Brandon had already managed to waste enough time on his own.

It had taken a full hour and all of Brandon's energy to extricate himself from the overzealous security guard. His smart-ass comments probably hadn't helped, but the guy had decided to lecture Brandon on the ins and outs of polite society.

What a crock of shit.

By the time the guard sent Brandon on his merry way, Diana was truly lost. He'd expected that. What he hadn't anticipated was to find skid marks in the parking garage and the contents of Amber's purse on the walkway leading up to her building.

He'd done some asking around, and the little girl who lived above Finn had spotted a limo idling across the street. Not exactly par for the neighborhood.

Whoever had been driving that limo had taken his partner. And Brandon didn't know if they'd taken Finn as well, or if Finn was the one holding Amber.

And to make matters worse, Drake had managed to lose his tail. So they had absolutely no leads.

Too many questions and not enough answers.

"What equipment does she have on her?" James asked. His voice was tight and professional, but Brandon caught the hint of concern.

"Hard to say," he said. "She doesn't have her purse, but she's not out much there. Standard issue lipstick scanner and comb/knife. The strap doubles as a garrote."

"Useful tools," Schnell said.

"But not essential," Brandon said. "As for what she has on her, I don't know."

"Homing beacon?" James asked.

"Not that I'm aware of," Brandon said.

"Gun?" Schnell asked.

Brandon shook his head. "In the motorcycle. As far as we know, she's unarmed."

"And this fellow you think is with her," James added. "A Company man?"

"We don't know," Brandon said honestly. "Either way, he seems to be green."

"I've already put feelers out and got a negative all the way around," Schnell said. "C.I.A., N.S.A., F.B.I. All the agencies deny knowing anything about Phineus Teague."

"Shit," Brandon said. "I hope she wasn't snatched along with a civilian. If Mackenzie's holding her, she's got enough to worry about without having to babysit a civie, too."

"Either way," Schnell said, "you've got your work cut out for you." He met Brandon's eyes. "If Mackenzie's got a hold of Prometheus, we've got big problems. I need to know. And I want my agent back. That's your assignment, Agent Kline. Do us all a favor and ace this one."

Albert Alcott watched as Monahan, Schnell, and Kline paced the situation room. Something was going on. Something big.

The door burst open, and Brandon Kline walked out, his face marked in shadows. Albert saved his work and pushed back from the computer desk. Natalie, the woman who worked in the cubicle next to him, lifted an eyebrow, but Albert ignored her. In his position breaks were strictly scheduled, but he had a feeling this was about Amber Robinson and he wanted to know the story.

As Brandon pushed through the double doors that led into the lobby, Albert followed.

The phone rang, and the receptionist snatched it up. "Machismo," she said. "What kind of adventure can we take you on today?" After a pause, she spoke again, her tone only slightly altered. "Yes, sir. I'll transfer you now," she said, and Albert saw her press a button on the phone's third row, thereby securing the line between the agent and his contact in-house.

The elevator doors were sliding open when Al caught up to Brandon. "Kline," he said, gasping for breath.

Brandon turned, his expression blank.

"Was that about Amber?"

Brandon didn't say anything for what felt like a full minute, and Al began to wonder if the guy was just going to get on the elevator and head back out into the world. A world Al hadn't seen for well over a year now.

"You're Alcott," he finally said.

Al nodded. "I saw"—he waved his hand in a circle—"all of that. Is Amber okay?"

"What's it to you?"

Al shrugged. "I like her, is all." He could understand Brandon's hesitation. Amber had been the one who'd caught him. She'd single-handedly plucked a million bucks out of his fingers—figuratively, anyway. But Al didn't hold a grudge. Especially considering the other folks who'd been after him for the same money. Joey Malone would have just killed him. With Amber, he'd been able to strike a deal.

He might not have his freedom, but he had his life. And, he had to admit, the work was interesting, even if he did have to live in a tiny room in the basement.

After what seemed like forever, Brandon nodded, jerking his head sideways to indicate the conference room just off the lobby.

"What's your assignment, Alcott?" he asked, closing the door behind them.

Al wasn't supposed to share that information with anyone. "Data entry," he said. "Intelligence. The watch list."

"Mackenzie?" Brandon asked.

Al nodded, realizing they were getting to the meat of it.

"What about Prometheus?" Brandon asked.

Al frowned. "Never heard of it." The answer was the God's honest truth, but Brandon looked skeptical. And Al made a mental note to find out everything he could about something called Prometh— Promethi-*what?*

"I'm putting my ass on the line telling you this."

Al nodded, solemn. He didn't doubt that what Brandon said was true. But he wasn't too sympathetic. Al knew perfectly well that Brandon wasn't going to confide out of the goodness of his heart. He'd only share information if he thought Al might be useful.

"Amber was watching Diana Traynor," Brandon said.

Al nodded; that much he already knew.

"And now she's disappeared."

"She found something out?"

"Maybe," Brandon said. He paused again, taking a long, hard look at Al. Al stood up straighter. "Prometheus is a weapons system," Brandon finally said. "You work on the computer. Poke around. See if you can find anything about who designed it. And see if there's any connection to a fellow named Bernie Waterman or if there's anyone with a code name of Poindexter."

Al nodded, knowing better than to ask why Brandon wanted the information. "I'll give it a whirl." It was dangerous. If he got caught, the Unit could toss him out and he'd have to take his chances with the district attorney. Or, worse, Joey Malone. But for Amber's sake, he'd try.

Besides, he intended to be very, very careful.

They left the conference room, and Al headed back to the double doors while Brandon waited for the elevator. He tugged the door open, then stopped, turning back to Brandon.

"When you see her . . . I mean, when you find her, tell her I liked the book." Amber had lent him Clancy's *The Hunt for Red October*. He'd never read Clancy and already he was hooked. He met Brandon's eyes. "She promised I could borrow some more."

Something flickered in Brandon's eyes. "Don't worry, Alcott," he said. "I'll find her."

Thirteen

They were in a long expanse of hallway when an underling Amber hadn't seen before rushed forward, stopping in front of Drake and whipping off a tight salute.

"A communiqué, sir," he said. "Mr. Black requests that you contact him posthaste."

A muscle in Drake's cheek twitched, but he seemed otherwise unaffected by the news. He took a step forward, his hand held out to Diana. "Come along, my dear." He faced Amber and Finn in turn. "You'll pardon my leaving you for a moment, but I must run ahead and make a quick call to the mainland. I'll leave you in the capable hands of Mr. Beltzer."

"Oh, joy," said Amber.

Drake didn't reply, and Beltzer jabbed her in the lower back with the butt end of his gun. Clearly the man hadn't warmed to her.

He kept the gun at her back during the rest of their journey through the complex. Amber spent the time memorizing their path and wondering who in the hell Mr. Black was. A true alias? Or a twist on another name. Blackman, Blackstone . . . ? Useless. She had no clue, and running through names was a waste of time.

They'd reached a set of steel double doors, and Beltzer activated the panel to open them. Then he jammed the gun in Amber's back and shoved. She stumbled forward, Finn at her side, and found herself in a computer-filled room that appeared to be solid concrete, as if someone had turned the Hollywood Bowl upside down over Houston's mission control.

Banks of computers filled the room, running in arcs that mimicked the curve of the room. About every fifth terminal was manned by a young man wearing a white lab coat. Whether the coats were another of Drake's weird affectations or simply designed to hide a weapon, Amber didn't know. All she knew, in fact, was that the exits seemed quite well protected. And considering the number of people in the room, the odds of winning a fight were pretty damn slim.

She was still attached to Finn, and now he brushed her fingers. She looked up at him, and he smiled, his eyes reassuring. Despite the circumstances, she found herself smiling back.

"Mr. Teague, Miss Robinson. Glad you caught up. Come in, come in." Mackenzie stood up, appearing to materialize from behind a bank of computer consoles. He looked Amber in the eye. "Apparently I misjudged the caliber of my guests.

After the beating Mr. Beltzer took, I should have known whom I was dealing with."

Amber pressed her lips together, remaining silent.

"What the hell are you talking about?" Finn asked.

"Don't you know?" Drake asked. "I find that so very hard to believe." He stepped forward. "So tell me, just how long have you two been working together?"

"What—"

But Drake waved a hand, cutting off Finn's question. "It doesn't matter. At any rate, I'm delighted that you both can join me for this little demonstration."

"Damn," Amber said. "And here I thought we'd been invited to dinner."

Drake's smile never faltered. "I'm so sorry, but I don't eat during my heavy work weeks." He raised a glass filled with a thick, green liquid. "Reoxygenates the blood." He pressed a button on the console. "Diana, dear, our guests are famished."

"I'm sure we'll survive," Finn said, casting a sideways glance toward Amber. She just shrugged, too distracted by her attempts to figure a way out of this mess to bother with coming clean.

Drake flashed Finn a winning smile. "I wouldn't be so certain. But I assure you your death won't be the result of starvation." He clapped his hands. "Now, Prado, show our guests to their places of honor."

Amber almost rolled her eyes. Mackenzie was rumored to be a pompous ass. Now he was proving that the reports were right.

Prado came over from the far side of the room and steered them to two theater seats bolted to the ground in the center of the room.

"Oh, good," Finn said. "I hope it's something I haven't seen."

"I assure you," Drake said, "you've seen nothing like this before."

"Perhaps we should skip dinner and just have popcorn," Amber added.

Drake didn't respond, and Prado fastened their shared handcuff to their adjoining armrest with a heavy-duty lock. Then he pocketed the key. Amber frowned, wishing she had her purse. At least Finn hadn't been stripped naked. If she was lucky, his agency issued the same standard tools and he could pick the lock. Hell, even if he was a civilian, maybe he had a paper clip.

"Thanks," Amber said. "We'll just stay here awhile."

The metal door slid open, and Diana walked through, holding a large cardboard bucket filled with popcorn. The butter scent wafted toward them, and Amber's stomach growled.

Amber met Finn's eyes, and she saw her own amusement reflected there. Drake might be a murderous son of a bitch, but he definitely had a sense of humor.

"This is just to tide you over until what comes later," he said, as Diana handed them the popcorn.

"I can hardly wait," Finn said.

Drake cocked his head, an oily smile easing across his face. "Anticipation," he said. "One of life's true pleasures." He glanced at Finn as if expecting a snappy comeback, and when none was forthcoming, he continued on. "Actually, I owe you two an apology."

"After treating us so well?" Amber cut in. "I find that hard to believe."

Drake ignored her, continuing to address his remarks to Finn. "I had intended to spend today, shall we say, getting to know you better. Trading state secrets, as it were." He moved closer, stopping in front of Amber to stroke her cheek. She jerked her head away, both in defiance and revulsion at the icy chill of his palm.

Drake's smile was cold and cruel as he twisted a lock of Amber's hair around his finger. "Using a different kind of feminine persuasion if you weren't inclined to share."

He dropped her hair, his mood visibly shifting. "But, things change. I'm so sorry, but we won't be having our little meeting. Recent information has made it . . . unnecessary."

"Pity," said Finn.

"Yes, I knew you'd see it that way," Drake said. "But my compatriot was quite insistent that I skip such pleasantries and simply dispose of you. And with billions of dollars on the table, who am I to argue?"

"Darling," Diana said, tapping her watch, "it's time."

"Of course." Drake nodded to Amber, then Finn. "If you'll excuse me, I have a few matters to attend to before my other guests arrive."

"Witnesses at our execution?" Amber said.

At that, Drake actually laughed. "Oh, no, no, no, my dear. We'll do that in private. This, I'm afraid, is strictly business. You can consider yourselves lucky to get to sit in on the negotiations."

"We're honored, of course," Finn said.

Amber caught Finn's eyes, but despite his smooth response, she got the impression he was as clueless as she. Not good news in the saving-their-butts department, but at least she wasn't behind in the game.

Beside her, Finn reached into the tub and popped a handful of popcorn into his mouth. She raised an eyebrow.

Finn shrugged. "Somehow death by popcorn doesn't seem this guy's speed."

"You seem to know him rather well," she said, agreeing wholeheartedly with his assessment.

"I know the type," he said, grabbing some more popcorn. "When the end does come, it's going to be more dramatic than poison."

"Oh?" It was the best she could come up with. She'd been hoping for some clue as to how much Finn knew about Drake. Instead, she got common sense.

"I'm thinking shark food, actually." He drew in a deep breath. "Sorry about that."

Amber sank back against her chair. From Drake's little spiel, it seemed clear that he was on to Amber. Whether he'd discovered Finn's true identity was anybody's guess, but it appeared that he had, and Amber was willing to give him brownie points. He'd accomplished a hell of a lot more than she had on that score.

She frowned. This tiptoeing around the subject was driving her nuts. She opened her mouth to simply ask him who the hell he worked for, but right then the room dimmed, metal panels in the walls curving up to cover the light fixtures even while revealing flat panel monitors.

Six static-filled screens surrounded the large projection screen, three on each side. One by one, the static faded, replaced with a close-up of a face. Six faces, each of which Amber recognized. Her mark from Chechnya, General Orlov, was in the top left. Right below him was Libyan Colonel Buton, a known arms dealer with serious anger-management issues. The rest were of the same ilk. Terrorists and arms dealers the government had been watching for months. No one who'd yet made the cover of *Newsweek*, but unless Amber—and Finn—did their jobs, she had a feeling they were heading that way.

She curled her toes, the pressure a counterpoint to her rising frustration. What the hell was Drake up to, and how did it involve Project Prometheus?

She turned to face Finn, trying to read his expression. His brow was slightly furrowed, his eyes slightly narrowed. She had to hand it to the guy. Not only was he displaying not even a hint of recognition, but he looked positively confused.

Saudi Prince Mujabi was the first to speak. "Well?" he said, the Oxford-educated lilt in his voice remaining despite the shift in frequency. Drake, apparently, didn't want his six video guests to recognize the others. The voices were severely altered and, she assumed, they saw only Drake and not the other men that she and Finn could see.

"I arranged my schedule to accommodate this meeting," Mujabi continued. "Shall we get on with it, then? My time, Mr. Mackenzie, is valuable."

"Of course," Drake said. "Gentlemen, if you will

please direct your browsers to our secure site, then punch in the password oh, niner, seven, Q, five." Drake did the same as he spoke, and the projection screen came to life, displaying an image of Los Angeles.

"Gentlemen," Drake said, "the bidding starts at two billion."

Amber swallowed. She didn't know exactly what Drake was up to, but it had to be big.

General Lao from China laughed, the harsh sound reverbing off the stone walls. "I have heard from many sources that your sanity hangs by a thread, Mackenzie. Now, I see it is so."

Drake nodded. "It appears, then, that we have something in common. I've heard the same about you."

The man chuckled, not the least bit perturbed by Drake's response.

"The gentleman is right," said Anthony Cornwallis, an American expatriate operating as an arms dealer out of North Korea. "You've told us nothing about this so-called service you intend to provide. Only that it is remarkable. You piqued our curiosity and here we are. Now it's time to shit or get off the pot."

Drake spread his arms wide. "Gentlemen, you're absolutely right." He turned to Diana. "My darling, if you please."

Diana moved to the console and began to tap on the keyboard. As she did, the image of the Los Angeles skyline sharpened and clarified. The camera seemed to move forward until the famous Hollywood sign filled the screen.

Amber closed her eyes as the realization of

Drake's plan hit her—Prometheus was not only operational, but it lived up to its rumors. And somehow, Drake had actually managed to get his hands on it.

"Behold, our target." Drake's voice boomed.

"The Hollywood sign?" Finn whispered. "What the hell is this guy up to?"

Amber could only shake her head and silently pray that she was wrong.

Drake's six guests expressed much the same comment as Finn, each talking over the other, the clamor of their voices rising to fill the room.

"Gentlemen," Drake said, "please." He waited, drumming his fingers on the lectern until the voices died down. "I have picked the test site as a tribute. A demonstration, if you will, to the world that shunned a brilliant actress." He flashed a smile filled with genuine warmth toward Diana, whose cheeks bloomed pink. "Truly brilliant," he repeated. "In fact, my dear, you deserve an Oscar for your command performance last night for the benefit of our friend in the West Wing."

She blew him a kiss.

"Of course," he continued, "Hollywood's loss is science's gain. Ms. Traynor enrolled at MIT after certain shortsighted Hollywood producers failed to see her potential. I, of course, am forever grateful for their foolishness."

"Cut the crap, Mackenzie," Cornwallis said. "Just get on with it."

"I see you are all anxious to begin," Drake said, ignoring Cornwallis's outburst. "Diana, if you please . . ."

At Drake's command, Diana tapped at a keypad.

Finn's brow was furrowed in concentration, Amber's own in frustration. She tugged uselessly against her restraint, but Beltzer had fastened the cuffs securely to the seats and she wasn't going anywhere.

"We've taken access," Diana said.

"Excellent." Drake actually rubbed his hands together. "Paint the target."

On screen, the image shifted to infrared, a pinpoint of intense heat apparent in the image.

"As you can see, gentlemen," Drake said, "the technology requires two steps. First the target is painted, and then . . ."

"Voilà," Diana said.

As they watched, the sign exploded, shards of burning wood and metal littering the sky, and the screen filling with smoke.

Amber met Finn's eyes. This was definitely an *oh shit* moment if she'd ever seen one.

"I must apologize for the lack of pyrotechnics before the explosion," Drake said. "It would be so much more satisfying to actually see the laser racing down from space. But as my technical advisor, Ms. Traynor, tells me, the frequency of the beam from the satellite is invisible to the human eye."

"That's it?" Mujabi said. "We're supposed to pay you two billion because you blew up an icon of the Western world?"

"No," Drake said, infinitely patient. "Half is for the second demonstration. At a time and location designated by the high bidder. If you're pleased, upon receipt of the second half of the sum, I'll turn the technology over to you. And please recall, the bidding *starts* at two billion. For technology such as this, I expect much higher numbers."

"Ridiculous," Lao said. "There will be no second demonstration. The United States will destroy the satellite."

At that, Drake actually laughed. "Oh," he said, "I don't think so." He gestured for Diana, stepping aside to allow her to share space at the lectern.

"The weapon you've just seen fired is code-named Prometheus," she said. "As you've seen, it's part of a space-based weapons system. It is not, however, acknowledged by the Americans. It was created for one specific intelligence branch, presumably as a creative means for assassinations. We are not entirely sure if the president is even aware of its existence."

Amber licked her lips. Their information had to have come from Unit 7. But who was the mole?

"Then that organization will destroy it," Cornwallis said. "They'll do that rather than let it stay in your hands."

"Undoubtedly," Drake said. "But they don't know we have access."

He turned to look directly at Amber. "And there's no one alive who can tell them."

Fourteen

Brandon was going to talk to Bernie Waterman. Schnell might have forbidden such contact previously, but the commander had just given Brandon carte blanche to find Amber. To Brandon's mind, that gave him an open ticket to talk to anyone he damn well pleased.

That wasn't, however, an interpretation he intended to confirm. There were times, Brandon had learned, when it really was easier to ask forgiveness than to ask permission.

He headed first to ZAEL, expecting to find Bernie mindlessly entering data into the mainframe. Instead, he learned that the man hadn't shown up for work in a week.

"I think he's got the flu," the receptionist said. "I talked to him a few days ago, and he sounded terrible."

Brandon thanked her and headed back out, this time aiming his car in the direction of Bernie's apartment. Brandon hoped the guy was truly home sick and not just skipping out on work. Bernie was the only lead Brandon had. He needed to talk to the data processor now. Amber had been gone too long for comfort, and Brandon needed to find some answers.

But there was only silence when Brandon knocked, and he sagged against the door, trying to decide his next move. He could interview the neighbors, see if he could get some clue as to where Bernie might go if he was off playing hooky.

But he'd end up chasing from one end of Los Angeles to the other, and the odds of actually finding the man were slim. And even if he did find Bernie, he'd have wasted a hell of a lot of time looking for a man who wasn't even his ultimate goal.

No, Brandon needed Bernie only to get to Poindexter. And since there might be something in Bernie's apartment revealing the programmer's identity, that was the option Brandon chose.

He kept a set of lock picks in his car, and now he went and got them. Bernie hadn't locked his deadbolt, just the spring lock in the doorknob. Brandon *tsk-tsk'*ed. Really, Bernie should be more diligent.

The lock wasn't a challenge, and Brandon was inside in well under thirty seconds. No surprise there. What he encountered inside, however, *that* was a surprise.

The place had been completely ransacked. Brandon pulled his gun, not really expecting to find anyone there, but cautious nonetheless.

Apparently someone else had had the same

thought as Brandon—to use Bernie to lead them to
Poindexter.

Unless . . .

A crazy thought pushed its way into Brandon's
mind, but he shoved it aside. No way.

That couldn't be right.

But Brandon knew better than to ignore his
instincts. And as soon as he finished searching
Bernie's apartment, he was going to put Albert
Alcott on the trail of his newest theory.

On the projection screen, the Hollywood sign still
burned, fire trucks converging on it from all over
Los Angeles.

"Maybe this agency didn't know you had access,"
Mujabi continued, "but they'll bloody well know
someone fired the weapon."

"Actually," Drake said, "they won't."

"That," Diana said, "is the beauty of our method
of access. Prometheus is still a prototype, and as
such has a few, shall we say, glitches. In this case,
we utilized the programmer's back-door code.
Unless it's fired during a routine simulation test, the
weapon's firing won't even register on the organization's control panel. They will be as curious about
why the Hollywood sign exploded as everyone else
on the planet."

Finn sucked in a breath. He'd done enough programming to know that what Diana said was likely
true. It wasn't at all uncommon for a programmer
to put in a back door, especially while the equipment was still a prototype. And once in through a
back door, keeping a signal from the legitimate
controller wasn't difficult for someone who knew

what they were doing. Hell, he'd done the same thing in some of his game programs. Not to wreak havoc or anything. He just liked to keep his hand in things.

But this was no game. The Hollywood sign had exploded with a simple punch of a button, and the potential for destruction on a worldwide scale was glaringly obvious. Instinctively, he jerked forward, his efforts once again thwarted by the handcuffs.

Damn. He needed to get to the computer. If he could only manage that, maybe he could hack in and close the back door.

Maybe.

But since he was currently attached to both Amber and the chair, that plan wasn't exactly overflowing with potential. Even his new realization that Amber knew more about all of this than she let on was no help. Even if she had lied to him—even if she was an operative with the agency that had commissioned Prometheus—at the moment she was as tied up as Finn and no use whatsoever.

"And now," Drake said, "let's start the bidding." The screen changed from the view of the Hollywood sign to a graphic of a piggy bank over a bar graph showing six bars labeled A through F. "The process is simple. Enter your bids in the box on your browser and the computer will compile your information. You can see your bid and your competitors' bids. And, of course, feel free to increase your bid as frequently—and as generously—as you see fit." He held his arms wide. "Gentlemen, start your bidding."

Apparently the sales pitch worked, because almost immediately, the bids hit $5 billion. Drake slipped his arm around Diana's waist, an expression remarkably close to sexual on his face as he watched the bar graph climb.

Beside him, Amber brushed Finn's hand. "He's insane," she whispered.

Finn could only nod. He was insane, all right. But he was also well financed—and soon to be more so—as well as brilliant.

At $6.5 billion, the bidding slowed down, then stopped at an even $7 billion.

"That's it?" Drake asked. "That's all you'll pay for access to this technological marvel? A device that could not only launch a world war, but elevate the weapon's controller to superpower status?"

"Eight," the one with the Oxford accent said. "And that's my final offer."

Drake spread his arms wide. "Do I hear nine?" Silence. And then Drake nodded. "Very well. Eight it is."

He pressed a button on the lectern console and five of the surrounding screens went blank, leaving only the high bidder. "Congratulations, Prince Mujabi. You've bought yourself a war."

A war, Amber knew, was exactly what a man like Mujabi wanted. And when he named his target— the Al-Aqsa mosque in old Jerusalem—she knew her suspicions were right on.

"If you'll check your screen," Diana said, "you'll see a calendar showing potential firing dates and times—the limitations stem from the satellite's position as well as the scheduled simulations for the satellite."

Amber focused on the projection screen, committing the dates to memory.

"The twenty-first," Mujabi said. "That will give me time to lay my foundation."

"A delightful date," Drake said, pulling a small appointment book from his inner coat pocket. "Prometheus will be in range on that date at oh-two-hundred hours. As for the details, the funds must hit my accounts by no later than noon on the twentieth. Ms. Traynor is sending you wiring instructions right now."

"And access?" Mujabi asked.

"For the balance of the funds, it will be yours," Drake confirmed. "We'll expect those funds within twelve hours of the destruction of the mosque. Otherwise, the deal's off."

Mujabi nodded. "The instructions have arrived. Your funds will arrive in time." He bowed slightly. "Mr. Mackenzie, it has been a pleasure doing business with you."

"Likewise," Drake said, and signed off.

Four days. They had only four days to prevent a full-scale war in the Middle East that would likely escalate into World War III. First, of course, they had to get free.

She jerked against the cuffs, frustration building. Finn covered her hand with his, and she met his eyes. She saw the question there, and knew she had some explaining to do. "Four days," though, was all she said.

He nodded. "Any ideas on how we prevent the next step in Drake's agenda?"

She frowned. *They* were the next step, and she knew full well that Drake intended to kill them. After what they'd seen, he certainly couldn't let them live.

"Nothing," she said.

"What? No laser in your wristwatch to cut through the cuffs? No false hair that's actually a garrote. No secret decoder ring?"

"We'll talk about it later," she said, more harshly than she intended. But the truth had just hit her upside the head—this man wasn't an agent. He'd come to the attention of the wrong people for the same reason he'd come to the Unit's attention—he'd been watching Diana Traynor. And now Amber had to get both herself and a civilian out of this mess. She closed her eyes and sighed. She'd seduced a civilian, dammit. She'd wanted information and all she'd gotten was an orgasm. *Shit*.

"Later," Finn repeated. "Absolutely we'll talk later. *If* we live."

"We'll live," she said. "I promise."

But then a jolt of movement shot through Amber's body.

"I'm afraid," Drake said, "that it's time to say good-bye."

They were descending, their chairs moving them down into the floor on some type of hydraulic lift. And as they sank deeper and deeper, Amber had to admit that she had no idea how she'd go about keeping her promise to Finn.

Apparently the section of floor to which their chairs were bolted doubled as some sort of open elevator, because now Finn was eye level with the command center's stone floor.

"I'm not liking this development," he said, as the floor began to descend even faster.

"You and me both," Amber admitted. She jerked

forward, and pain seared against his wrist as the cuff caught on the chair.

"I don't think so, sweetie," Diana said. "I've been wanting to do this since the first moment I met you." She aimed a small flat device at Amber, then pressed a button and two wires shot out, catching her in the chest. A Tazer. Amber's body jolted and jerked, and she collapsed back into the seat.

"Amber?" Finn clutched her hand and she squeezed back, weak.

"She'll be fine," Diana said. "This Tazer is particularly weak. But it does the trick."

Amber aimed a puny smile at Finn. "I really don't like that woman."

They both looked up as they were lowered farther and farther into the floor. The passage through which they were descending was made out of smooth steel and exactly the same shape and size as the bit of floor to which the chairs were bolted. So even if they could have gotten their wrists free, there was nowhere to go.

They continued that way for at least a minute, and then the walls disappeared as they entered another chamber. Their pseudoelevator came to a halt with a thud. Finn twisted, trying to check out their new cell.

"I apologize for the accommodations," Drake said, his voice hollow as it filtered down the passage through which they'd traveled. "But I promise you won't have much time to bemoan the lack of amenities."

"You won't get away with this," Amber said, her voice already stronger.

"Big words, considering your current predicament."

"If not me," Amber said, "then someone else. But you are going down."

"I'm quaking in my boots," Drake said. "Actually, my dear, I was quite pleased to learn your true identity. I so hate to kill civilians."

Finn grimaced but didn't say anything. And then he noticed that his feet were damp.

Amber noticed at the same time. "Drowning?" she said. "Not very original."

"I don't have time to tie you over a cistern and wait for the rats to eat away the ropes, I'm afraid," Drake said. "This will have to do. As you can see, the room is filling with water."

That much was true. Water was beginning to seep in from tiny jets just inches off the floor.

"Don't even think about digging your way out. This island was designed as a weapons test site. It was never used, but the room you're in was originally intended as a bomb shelter. The walls are five feet thick. Take my word for it."

Amber frowned, her eyes darting around the room. "Thanks for the tip," she said.

"My pleasure." Drake cleared his throat. "I've made modifications, of course, one of which you're experiencing now. The water is seventy-eight, so I don't expect you'll be chilled while you die. In case you're wondering, at the current rate of entry, it will take thirty-two minutes for this chamber to fill. Not really enough time for you to compare your various agencies' retirement packages. But since you won't be retiring, I suppose that doesn't matter." He saluted, then disappeared, a stone tile sliding into place in the ceiling.

Trapped.

Around them the trickle of water from the walls seemed to increase in both volume and velocity. A trick of the eye, surely. Finn sincerely doubted that Drake wanted them to have the benefit of a fast death.

He tugged uselessly at the cuff, then looked over at Amber, who was visually scouring the walls. "See anything interesting?" he said.

She scowled. "I don't suppose you've got anything on you to pick the lock?"

"Fresh out of bobby pins," he said. "You?"

"Not a damn thing." She sighed. "Too bad I don't have my pen."

"Need to draft a codicil to your will?"

She raised an eyebrow. "Well, it doesn't double as a garrote," she mimicked, "but it would come in handy."

"I didn't—" He cut off the protest, remembering the pen he'd picked up after the limo had almost rammed them. "_This_ pen?" he asked, pulling the Montblanc from the back pocket of his jeans.

Her eyes widened and she brushed a kiss across his lips. "Phineus Teague," she said, "I think I love you."

As he watched, she uncapped the pen, bent the nib slightly, and then inserted the tip into the lock. "Lock pick," she said. "Standard issue."

"Who exactly do you work for?" he said.

"Unit 7." The lock sprang free and she looked up at him, her face triumphant. "Mean anything to you?"

"Not a thing," he admitted.

"We're the CIA's illegitimate stepchild," she said. "I know you've heard of the CIA."

He ignored the comment. "And this agency operates giant space lasers?"

She shrugged. "Not my area," she said. "I first heard about Prometheus when I started watching Diana."

Reality clicked into place like cogs in a gear. "And you saw me watching her," he said.

"Absolutely." His cuff snapped open, and she went to work on her own. "You want to tell me why?"

He didn't even bother to answer.

"Oh, come on," she said. "I know you're not an agent."

He blinked. "You know I'm not . . . ?" He trailed off, the elusive "why" settling in the pit of his stomach. He knew why she'd come on so hot and heavy. She'd assumed he was an operative and was trying to get information.

"So what's up?" she continued. "Fancy yourself James Bond?"

At that, Finn cringed. But he wasn't about to explain Agent Python. Not now. He released a long breath. "I was bored. She was hot. And she kept her curtains open. So I watched."

Amber just stared at him. "You have got to be kidding me. That's it?"

"Do I look like I'm kidding? I've had it up to here with the lies and the bullshit. Like you said, it's time to just lay everything out on the table."

For a moment, he thought she wasn't going to answer. Then she made a face like she'd tasted something sour and shook her head. "Great. This is just great," she said. "Not only am I in charge of our escape, but now I get to babysit, too."

Finn's temper flared. *"Babysit?* Look, sweetheart, you may have gone through Spying 101, but I've been holding my own here. And I'm not the one who confused a civilian with a CIA operative."

She just stared at him. "Finished?"

But he wasn't. "This has all been part of a mission. Me. Your little seduction routine. Everything."

"I hardly think that matters now," she said. "Maybe we could table this discussion until after we escape."

Shit. She was right, of course. "Got anything in mind?"

She turned in a circle, her eyes scouring the floors, the wall. And then she tilted her head back, and he saw just the hint of a smile creep across her mouth. "Yeah," she said, "as a matter of fact, I do."

Fifteen

Al's eyes shifted left to right, and then he slid a piece of paper across his desk toward Brandon.

Brandon picked it up, half-amused, half-irritated. *The men's room. Five minutes.* He looked at Al, wondering if the twerp was joking. But Al just made a shooing motion, insisting that Brandon walk away.

Brandon did, leaving the note on Al's desk. That was one guy who'd let working in espionage go to his head.

At exactly the five-minute mark, Brandon pushed through the door to the men's room. No Albert.

Brandon ran a hand through his hair, fighting irritation. If the little shit was going to play spy games, the least he could do would be stick to his own schedule. Frowning, Brandon glanced at his watch again and turned toward the door. Thirty more seconds, and he was heading out to find the man, Al's cloak and dagger routine be damned.

"*Pssst.*"

Brandon closed his eyes. Please, let that not be Al summoning him to the handicapped stall.

"Over here," came the stage whisper.

Stifling the urge to drag Al out by the scruff of his neck, Brandon went over, then joined Al in the stall. "Is this really necessary?"

"I've got news," Al whispered. "Big news."

"Yeah?" Brandon said, doubting Al could have found anything that big. "I'm sure it's fascinating. But here's what I need you to find out. Bernie Waterman. I think he may be—"

"Your Poindexter," Al said.

"Shit." The curse rolled off Brandon's tongue, and he poked his head out of the stall, checking to make sure they really were alone.

"I told you it was big," Al said.

"You're sure?"

Al nodded. "He was reclassified."

Brandon frowned. "By ZAEL?"

Al shook his head vigorously. "No. The order came down from within the Unit. They probably did it so someone on the outside wouldn't know how important he was."

"Or the inside," Brandon said. He clapped Al on the shoulder. "Good job."

"It helps?"

"Oh yeah," Brandon said, running the scenario through his head. The Unit had reclassified Bernie to keep his peculiar knowledge secret. And yet the secret immediately made it to Drake. That meant only one thing to Brandon—there was a mole in Unit 7. But Brandon had no idea who.

Which meant that at the moment, Brandon was sharing a toilet stall with the only person in the world he could trust.

"You're six three, right?" Amber asked.

"And a half," Finn said.

"Bend down," she said.

Finn complied without question, and Amber said a silent thank you. She didn't want to play one-up with him. And she sure as hell wasn't going to discuss her decisions in committee.

And, of course, at the moment, not talking was fine with Amber. They'd have *the* conversation eventually. Considering the hurt look in Finn's eyes, he'd realized her motives had been so very similar to Diana's; soon enough, he'd want to talk. But she didn't look forward to it. Because as much as she wanted to tell him she'd just been doing her duty and to get over it, that wasn't the truth. There had been something else there. Something indefinable between them.

Something she had no intention of analyzing too closely or ever letting happen again.

He was squatting on the floor, the water already hitting him midcalf, and she climbed onto his back. "Can you stand?"

"I think so." He balanced himself with the wall until he was upright, and then she did the same, holding herself steady as she climbed up his back. "Not that this isn't loads of fun," he said, "but do you mind telling me what you're doing?"

She was standing on his shoulders now, one hand against the wall to steady herself, the other reaching up to the metal grate covering the air vent. No luck.

She was at least a foot shy of her goal.

"Damn," she said, scooting down Finn's back and dismounting with a splash into the water.

"Damn?" he repeated. "Damn isn't good."

"No," she agreed, "it's not."

"Tell me," he said. His face was stern, and she could tell he was uninterested in platitudes.

"The grate," she said, tilting her head up. "If we could get up there, get it open, and get into the air passage, we might stand a chance. My guess is there are sensors in the roof and the water stops at the top without going into the duct."

"Is that all?" Finn asked. "Why didn't you say it was just a little matter of removing a welded metal grid and squeezing into a vertical metal shunt that probably leads straight into Drake's private office."

"You have a better idea?"

"Not a single one." He tilted his head back to look at the grate. "How were you figuring to get the grate off? Your magic pen?"

"As a matter of fact, yes," she said.

"Why the hell not," Finn said, the edge of sarcasm in his voice coming through loud and clear.

She ignored it. The water was up to her knees now, and Amber slipped the pen out of the tight bodice of the dress where she'd stored it.

She unscrewed it and pulled out the ink cartridges. Standard issue in the Unit, the first cartridge contained ink. The second was molded C-4. The stuff was intense, and she didn't want her and Finn to get caught in the blast, so she pulled a tiny bit off, rolling it between her fingers like she was making a tiny plastic ball.

"C-4?" Finn said. He raised an eyebrow. "I guess the pen really is mightier than the sword."

Amber rolled her eyes. "Don't worry. It won't explode until I tell it to."

He crossed his arms over his chest and leaned against the wall. "Cyclotrimethylene-trinitramine, commonly called RDX for 'research development explosive.' It's mixed with binders—disebacate, for example—to make it malleable. And until it's triggered by an energy source—a detonator—it's essentially harmless."

"A man who knows about things that go boom. I'm impressed." She kept her voice impassive, but in truth, she really *was* impressed.

"I also know we're going to get blown to smithereens if you do what I think you're going to do."

"You got a better idea?"

He sighed. "We're going to die anyway. Might as well go out with a bang."

"Not a whimper," she said.

He grinned. "Right. So what exactly do you have in mind?"

"Surviving," she said. "And this is how." She unscrewed the starred tip of the pen, ready to remove the lapel clip and extract the detonator cleverly hidden underneath. Except it wasn't there. *Shit.*

"What?"

"There's nothing here," she said. The water was above her knees now, and this was really not a good development.

"No detonator?"

"Damn it all to hell," she said. "It must have been knocked out in the parking lot. Damn, damn, *damn.*"

"Well, hell," Finn said, his voice little more than a whisper. Clearly she didn't need to explain to him the gravity of the situation.

A hell of a pickle, and she racked her brain, trying to think of some other way to generate the force necessary to get the C-4 to do its thing. But there just wasn't a way. Even if she had matches, that wouldn't do any good. The stuff burned like wood. She needed a baby explosion to fuel the bigger one, but she had no way to conjure one.

Finn stood there, in as much of a funk as she was. His eyes were closed and he jammed his hands deep into his pockets. "Shit," he whispered after a second. His eyes flew open.

"What?" she asked.

"Kiss me quick," he said, a smile tugging at his mouth. "Because I've got some news that's going to blow you away."

Finn was feeling absurdly pleased with himself, and even the fact that he'd been treading water for the last fifteen minutes with one hand high above his head hadn't lessened the glow.

The water had almost completely flooded the chamber, leaving only about two feet of air space above them. At the moment, Finn was holding Callie and Elijah's blasting cap and matches high while he kicked and used his other hand to stay afloat.

When he got out of this jam, he was taking the twins to McDonald's. Heck, he'd even take them to

Disneyland. Not only was their blasting cap going to save his and Amber's butts, but they'd made him look pretty damn good to Amber as well.

Beside him, Amber was also working to stay afloat as she held the marble-sized ball of C-4 above her head. She was paddling with her left arm, and every once in a while, her face twisted in pain. As soon as they got out of there— *if* they got out of there—he'd take another look at that shoulder.

"Almost there," Amber said. "Assuming this works, remind me to give you a big kiss."

"Don't worry," he said. "I'll remind you."

She met his eyes, and he knew she was getting off on this. Despite the possibility that the twin's cap was a dud or, worse, they'd be pulverized in the explosion, Amber was totally in her element. For that matter, so was Finn. He couldn't remember ever feeling so alive. Ironic, really, since he was so close to dying.

"I still can't believe you had a blasting cap on you."

"Boy Scout training," he said. "I like to be prepared."

"Hmm."

He just grinned. He was, after all, a man of mystery.

She tilted her head back. "Another minute," she said. "Maybe two."

"You're sure that's not too much C-4?"

She frowned. "Honestly? No. I don't tend to use it for detail work. But we only get one shot at this. We can't risk *not* blowing the grating open."

Finn nodded. He had to agree. The grating over the ventilation system was welded tight to the air shaft. As it was, they were going to blow one side and hope they could weaken the surrounding ceiling enough to pull the grate down. Ideally, they needed four marbles of C-4 and four detonators. Then they could take out the corners and make a clean break.

But they had to work with what they had.

His fingers brushed the ceiling.

"Okay," Amber said. She molded the explosive onto the grating, then held her hand out for the cap. He passed it. It was the fuse kind, much more common a few decades ago than now, but it would do the trick just fine. Assuming, that is, that the thing wasn't a dud. For all Finn knew, that's why grandpa had decided to hang onto it. A harmless souvenir.

He shoved the thought away. No sense manufacturing problems.

"Okay," she said. "Light it."

Finn nodded. This was the tricky part. One of his hands was necessarily wet, and he had to rip off a paper match, keep it dry, and light it—all while staying above water. As soon as the fuse was lit, he and Amber would dive down to crouch behind the theater seats.

If they were lucky, the water would absorb the intense shock of the explosion. If they were unlucky, they wouldn't much care.

His hands shook as he tore off the first match.

"Finn!"

He dropped it. "Damn it, Amber, shut up."

"Do you want me to do it?"

But he didn't. He could do this. And with her bum shoulder, he was afraid she couldn't hold her arm steady enough.

He struck again, and this time the match burst to life . . . then fizzled out.

"The vent," she said. "There's a draft." She eased around in front of him, then grabbed the grate with both hands, pulling herself up, the C-4 right in front of her. "There," she said. "Some air's getting in, but I should be blocking most of it."

Only about eight inches left. Finn was working with his head and hands in the air space. And if he missed this time, he'd have one more shot—with his hands above water and his head below.

Not exactly ideal working conditions.

Steady . . . steady . . .

Carefully, he ripped off a match. Then, trying to be forceful enough to spark the match and yet not so forceful he splashed water, he ran the head of the match over the striker.

Success.

He nodded to Amber as he cupped his free hand around the tiny flame. As he did, she sank quietly back into the water. He carefully eased up, maneuvering until the flame found the fuse . . . and it lit.

Their eyes met and, without a word, they dove in unison down, down, down to the bottom. Behind the theater chairs they crouched, holding the metal seats to keep them from floating back up. Finn grasped Amber's hand, noting with satisfaction that, not only did she not pull away, but she held on tight.

He looked up, his body tense, expecting the shock waves from the explosion to vibrate through the water at any moment.

Nothing.

His lungs started to burn. Had the fuse gone out? Was it just slow? Was the cap a dud?

He didn't know, and time was running out.

He looked up, but couldn't see anything through the murky water, much less the red glow of a fuse. He tapped Amber's shoulder and shook his head, then pushed off toward the surface. He wasn't certain what he intended to do—the last few matches were in his pocket, now soggy—but he had to do something.

She grabbed his shirttail to tug him back. And as she did, the cap did its job. Above them, the world exploded in a powerful blast. Even with the several feet of water as a buffer, they were both shoved across the room, landing against the far wall.

Finn gasped and swallowed water, panic rising as the need for air built in him. He tamped down on the fear, then started to head quickly but carefully toward the surface.

Amber was at his side, and when they got there, they still had one more problem to tackle. All the air was on the other side of the grate, and only one side of the grate had been ripped free.

Finn grabbed the steel bars of the grating and pulled. At first he felt nothing except his body's urge to inhale, needing oxygen to fuel the exertion.

He fought the urge, tugging again on the grate. This time, it gave ever so slightly.

He scooted over, holding one corner and gesturing for Amber to do the same. Then he kicked up, pressing his feet against the ceiling and using the leverage to propel the rest of his body—and the grate—down with him.

It worked.

Between him and Amber they got the grate open. She entered first, the skirt of the cocktail dress swirling around her legs as she swam into the air shaft, then climbed into the intersecting perpendicular shaft.

He joined her seconds later, laying prone inside the cold metal tube, gulping in gallons of glorious, wonderful air. "Hey," he said, the single word all he could manage.

"Hey yourself." She drew in three long, loud breaths. "Not bad work for a civilian," she added.

"Thanks," he said. "You're not so bad yourself."

She rolled toward him, still breathing hard, and brushed a kiss across his lips. And right then, Finn knew that his reality had finally caught up to his fantasies.

Agent Python, it seemed, had nothing on Phineus Teague.

Sixteen

Brandon located Linus in the basement. As Brandon knew Linus well, it was the first place he looked. The old man had been with the Unit since time began, and he showed no signs of slowing down. And although his lab was tucked away in a back corner of the D.C. office, Linus had insisted on having satellite facilities in all of the branch offices. Schnell's predecessor had readily complied. And now Linus spent his time in Los Angeles happily holed up in the subbasement.

The sign on the door read "janitorial services," but Brandon knew better. He pushed the door open, then moved with ease past the stacks of buckets and bins filled with every imaginable cleaning product. A rack of coveralls stretched across the back wall, and when he reached it, he shoved the clothing aside, revealing the gray wall. A portion of the paint had faded, worn thin by repeated touch. Brandon pressed his hand against the wall, waiting as the sensor read his palm print.

One click, and then the wall slid silently open, revealing a glassed-in antechamber. Brandon stepped inside, and the wall closed behind him. He was surrounded now by three sides of crystal-clear glass, through which he could see Linus's lab. A mannequin stood in the far corner, her left arm blown to smithereens and her head missing. A table to the left was covered with firearms ranging from cap guns to Uzi's. A dozen or so navy blue suits hung from a rack just to the left of Brandon.

Lots of gadgets, but no Linus.

"Brandon, my boy." Linus's voice filled the antechamber. "It's so good to see you."

Brandon frowned. "I'd say the same," he said, "except I *don't* see you." Squinting, he peered through the glass, wondering if the old man was down on his hands and knees doing God-knows-what experiments.

"Ah, but that's the beauty of it." Linus's voice rang out loud and strong, belying his seventy-eight years. "You see only what I want you to see."

And then he was right there, right in front of Brandon, just on the other side of the glass. First a shimmer, then a hint of a shape, and then a full-blown, albeit skinny, man. He held his arms wide at his side, his bony frame and wiry hair making him look like an Einstein effigy tacked to a scarecrow. "How about a round of applause for a brilliant old man?" he asked.

Brandon complied. Hell, the trick deserved applause. "Not bad," he said. "When did you become the invisible man?"

"Not invisible," Linus said. "*Hidden.*" He tapped on the glass that separated them. "A computer monitor is embedded in the glass, and the image you see is exactly what you expect. The computer just blots me out."

"Assassinations," Brandon said, zeroing in on the practical applications.

Linus tapped his nose. "Bingo. We install this glass in the home of some dissident leader"—he formed a gun with his thumb and forefinger—"and *ptoowey,* no more bad guy."

"Except for the little problem of installing the glass," Brandon said, "that's not a bad plan at all."

Linus opened the door from the antechamber to the lab, all the while brushing Brandon's comment away. "I only provide the tools," he said. "It's your job to figure out how to use them."

"That's why I'm here, actually."

"To assassinate someone? Who?"

Brandon laughed. "To see what new tools you have in your arsenal. Tools more portable than large panes of glass."

"Right-o." Linus took his glasses off and began to chew thoughtfully on the earpiece. "Let's see, I've improved on this laser pointer." He picked up a small metal pen, the kind that emitted a red light so that a presenter could help the audience follow along on a projection screen. Only this little red light zapped a hole right through the mannequin. "Sorry about that, Alice," Linus said. He looked at Brandon. "Poor girl takes one hell of a beating."

"Mmm." Brandon plucked the pointer from Linus's fingers and tucked it into his breast pocket. "What else have you got?"

"Not sexy enough for you? Well, you'll like this." He held up what looked to be a Lycra unitard.

Brandon raised an eyebrow. "I want to defeat the bad guys," he said. "Not dance ballet over them."

"Very funny, Agent Kline." Linus headed for the table and plucked a SIG Sauer from the lineup of weapons. He handed it to Brandon, then spread his arms wide. "Shoot me," he said, then tilted his head back, his eyes closed. A second later, his head bobbed back up, his eyes opening. "Only not in the head," he said. "A good gut shot."

Brandon just stood there, mildly amused, while Linus stood, arms akimbo, ready to be slayed.

"Well?" Linus prodded, his voice impatient.

"Not that I don't trust you," Brandon said, "but I'm not inclined to put myself through a Unit investigation because one of your gizmos went kablooey."

"You should have more faith, young man." He grabbed up the unitard and headed for Alice. "Help me dress her."

"My experience runs more toward undressing," he said.

"Yes," Linus said. "I bet it does." As soon as Alice was clad in the unitard, Linus nodded toward her. "Go ahead. One straight in the gut."

"Sorry, dear," Brandon said as he aimed the gun. "It's just not going to work out between us." He got off two shots, then looked at Linus. "Well?"

"Well?" the man repeated, clearly indignant. "Look closer."

Brandon did—and realized that the bullets hadn't penetrated the cloth. "What the hell is this stuff?"

"Marvelous, isn't it? Better than Kevlar."

"Long underwear that doubles as body armor." Brandon shook his head in amazement. "Not bad. Not bad at all."

"Take one," Linus said, passing him a garment wrapped in plastic. "Give it a test run."

Brandon eyed it dubiously. The stuff seemed to work great, true, but there was a certain bit of style-cramping that would necessarily follow from wearing stretchy Lycra. "I don't—"

"Don't be a prick, Kline." The curse rolled off the old man's tongue. "Just take it."

"Yes, sir." Brandon whipped off a salute. "What else have you got I can test out?"

Plenty, it turned out. And forty-five minutes later, Brandon walked away laden down with an abundance of gadgets, any of which might help rescue Amber, but none of which, unfortunately, could help him find her.

"Do you think he'll drain the chamber, then look for our bodies?" Finn asked. They were pressed tight together in the confined space of the vent, their combined body heat battling the chill of the metal. Amber took refuge in the comfort. Her shoulder ached and her eyes burned, a sure sign of a fever. All in all, she felt like shit, and for once in her life she allowed herself a moment of solace in Finn's arms. Soon enough, she'd have to battle past the pain. One brief moment didn't seem like too much to ask.

"Amber?" he prodded.

"I don't know," she said. She rolled over to face him, the movement putting unintended pressure on her shoulder. But as soon as she saw the emotion in his eyes, all thoughts of pain left her.

Amber knew well enough that a brush with death could spark an intense sexual reaction. She'd felt it herself plenty of times, her missions often ending in a frantic coupling that she could only chalk up to the afterglow of survival, a primal instinct to mate and make sure the species really *did* survive. Always hot. Sometimes tender. But never, ever personal.

But there was nothing impersonal in Finn's eyes. The man's dark gaze was meant only for her, and it sucked her in, taking her to a place she didn't want to go. Sex with Finn had been spectacular, but she'd gone into it as part of the job. She wouldn't—*couldn't*—make it personal. Couldn't make it more than the sex.

With great effort, she fought the urge to stay in the circle of his arms and let her battered body rest. But they had to move, and so she rolled over, crouching on her elbows.

"Come on," she said. "Drake has a hell of an ego, and he wants us dead. Even if he didn't hear the explosion, I wouldn't put it past him to drain the chamber. And when he realizes we're gone, he'll come looking for us."

Finn let her scoot past him. "If we can just get back into that control center—"

"We're getting off the island," Amber said.

"Are you nuts? He's going to blow up the mosque in four days. We've got to stop him."

She paused long enough to look over his shoulder. "No, really? I thought we'd just leave and go have tea. Of *course* we have to stop him. But we can't do it alone. We don't have any weapons, and there's just two of us." She wasn't about to mention how much pain she was in.

"But—"

"We do it my way, Finn," she said. "And my way is to get off this island and get backup." She wasn't about to argue with a civilian over how to handle a mission. And while Amber didn't shrink from dangerous missions, she also didn't dive headfirst into foolhardy ones. And barreling into Drake's command center without weapons would be beyond foolhardy.

"Besides," she said, "we're the only people on earth who know Drake's plan. Mujabi must be planning to blame the bombing on the Israelis, and we need to get the information out that it's a setup." She met Finn's eyes. "You can come with me, or take your chances here."

"I'm with you," he said.

She nodded, then turned back to face the shaft. "Try and keep your weight evenly distributed," she said. "These HVAC shafts are generally held in place by sheet metal straps."

"Slide if you can," Finn said.

She allowed herself a smile, glad to see he knew his stuff. "Right."

"Are we going the right way?"

"Hell if I know," she admitted.

"We should at least head south," he said. "We were brought in through an entrance on the south side of the island."

"True enough," Amber said, impressed that he'd bothered to notice the location of the entrance.

"Unfortunately, I'm not really in a position to navigate." Her watch had been shattered in the parking lot. An unfortunate accident considering the watch included a global positioning system, and she really needed to know the island's location.

"I am." He paused, and she turned to see him pulling a watch face out of his back pocket. Then he pointed behind them. "That way."

She raised an eyebrow.

"Casio," he said. "Pathfinder."

She crossed her arms over her chest. "Blasting caps and a G.P.S. watch. Anything else in your pockets you want to tell me about?"

"I used to carry Trojans," he said, fixing her with an unwavering stare. "But I don't have any on me at the moment."

"Pity," she said, then smiled.

He met her smile and she mentally shook her head, amused and enamored all at the same time. "Looks like you've been elected navigator," she said. "Lead the way. And," she said after a brief pause, "memorize our location. We'll need to find this island again."

She followed as he crawled through the vent, crossing over the vertical shaft through which they'd entered as they continued south. After five minutes of slithering, the shaft ended abruptly, with the only way out being back the way they came or straight down.

"Your call," Finn said.

Amber squeezed in next to him, her body brushing against his. She could only see a few feet down before the shaft curved and was lost in darkness. But considering most ventilation shafts terminated in basements or roofs, their best bet was to travel vertically, however uncomfortable that might be. "This way," she said.

She went first, slipping carefully into the shaft and keeping her back pressed against one side with her feet flat against the other. In that position, she inched downward—lowering one leg, then the other, then her back—until there was enough room for Finn to join her. "You okay?" she asked.

"Feeling rather like a sardine," he said. "But otherwise fine. How's your shoulder holding out?"

"Hurts like hell," she admitted. "But I can't do anything about it now."

He didn't argue with that, and they traveled in silence for some seemingly interminable amount of time. Finally, the shaft opened onto another horizontal vent, and they continued in a more or less southerly direction, again sliding forward on their bellies.

After five minutes of that, they reached the end of the line. A metal grate blocked their path, through which they could see some sort of utility tunnel.

Finn stuck his fingers through the grate and tugged. Nothing happened. He tugged again. Still nothing.

"Well, hell," he said, turning to face her. "Unless you've got some more C-4 hidden in that dress, it looks like we're stuck."

James was coming into the building just as Brandon was heading out. "Any luck?" the older man asked.

Brandon shook his head, automatically moving

toward the wall and out of earshot of anyone passing by. "I've got some feelers out," he said when they sat down. "But nothing concrete yet."

He wanted to tell James about the mole in the Unit, but he held his tongue. He wore his hesitancy uncomfortably, and for the first time since he'd met James, he felt antsy around the man. But Brandon knew he was doing the right thing. Whoever had reclassified Bernie had to have been highly placed; someone who not only had access to Prometheus's personnel records, but also knew the key players' roles and could manipulate the computer system at the highest level.

Schnell. Based on everything Brandon knew so far, the Unit chief was his prime suspect. In the past, Brandon had assumed that Schnell's history with Drake had given him unique insight into the man. Now he wondered if there wasn't more to the relationship.

But he kept his thoughts in check. Right now, Schnell was only a suspect, and Brandon wasn't about to sully the man's reputation with his subordinates by voicing his suspicions without confirmation.

"How can I help?" James asked. His face was newly etched with deep lines, and the dark bags under his eyes further evidenced his worry.

Brandon understood. James had been like a father to both him and Amber. Her disappearance and subsequent lack of contact had been eating at Brandon's gut. It was surely doing the same to James. "I don't know that you can," Brandon said. "But I'll find her. Schnell's orders, remember? And I've never disobeyed a direct order yet."

A hint of a smile touched James's lips. "Your word is good enough for me," he said. He shook his head. "Sometimes I wonder why I got into this business. I'm retiring in less than a month and instead of going home to spend the rest of my days with the little woman at my side, my children bringing the grandkids over for cookies and milk, I'm going to spend it alone." His eyes, sad and penetrating, turned on Brandon. "I don't want to enter retirement knowing that one of my agents faded into the void, never to return."

Brandon nodded, hearing the unspoken message—James loved Amber like his own daughter.

And he wanted her found, no matter what the cost.

Seventeen

ome here," Amber said, tugging on the waistband of his jeans.

"I hardly think this is the place," Finn retorted.

She grabbed hold of the top button of his 501's and yanked, plucking the button free. She held it up in triumph. "When you don't have a screwdriver . . ."

Finn had to give her credit. He'd gotten himself out of a lot of tricky situations—all in his head, of course—but never once had he used a button to loosen a screw.

It worked, too, which was fortunate, as they were otherwise out of options, and in under two minutes Amber had the grate off and they were lifting it quietly into the shaft. She slipped out first, hopping silently to the ground, then giving him the all's-clear signal. He followed, dropping from the shaft to the hard concrete floor and immediately assuming a crouch, just in case. But the room was silent except for a dull electric hum.

"Where are we?" he asked.

"Not sure," she admitted. "Some sort of utility room." Lockers lined the wall, and she opened one, revealing a pair of green coveralls. Janitor's garb.

"Drake's staff?" Finn asked.

Amber shook her head. "I'm guessing leftover. Drake said this was designed as a testing facility. I bet it was occupied for some period of time."

"Good luck for us, though," Finn said. His wet jeans were clinging tenaciously, constricting his movements and rubbing uncomfortably against his skin. Amber might be less constricted, but he doubted she was thrilled about escaping the island in a cocktail dress, no underwear, and bare feet.

Amber agreed, then started opening lockers. She pulled a faded green garment out, gave it a once over, then winked at Finn. "Not exactly haute couture."

"Nonsense. Janitorial chic is all the rage in Paris."

"Well, if you find a pair of matching strappy sandals, you just let me know."

Finn nodded, then started checking the bottoms of the lockers for work boots that would fit her.

Beside him, Amber unzipped her cocktail dress and let it fall to the ground. Finn turned to watch— he couldn't help himself—as she stood guilelessly in absolutely nothing, then stepped into the one-piece outfit. She zipped it up, then met his eyes with a saucy grin. "Sorry, guy. Showtime's over."

He let his gaze linger on her breasts, then traced

his gaze up to her face. "I figure this might be my last cheap thrill. I want to make it good."

"Too bad we need to get the hell out of here," she said, something low and intimate in her voice. "If it's just a cheap thrill you want, I think I could come through for you on that."

Finn's body tightened, and he turned away to continue his perusal of the lockers, finally finding a coverall that would fit his frame. He slipped out of his jeans and tossed his shirt, then stepped into the uniform.

The truth was, he wanted Amber more than he should, especially since he wasn't at all sure that he was anything more than a mission to her. She'd take sex, of that much he was certain. And so, for that matter, would he. But he wanted more. The whole package. Amber Robinson had snuck up on him, and now she was in his blood. On a certain level, he supposed he envied her. Hell, she was leading the life he wanted. But it was more than that. It was the woman underneath the steel that he'd fallen for, and hard. He thought they could be good together, and he wanted to give it a try.

Amber, he was certain, would not. She'd all but told him he'd been nothing more than Project Seduction.

But her withdrawal didn't faze him. In the grocery store, she'd told him they'd start with sex, and if they ended up in a relationship, great. It may have been a line, but Finn intended to run with it.

Assuming, of course, that he survived the day.

Drake sat in the dining room and surveyed the feast laid out across the table. Sea bass with an almondine sauce, pears drenched in liqueur, and potatoes twice baked with an assortment of cheeses. The presentation was excellent, of course, which pleased him.

He might be dining only on tofu and wheatgrass smoothies, but that didn't mean Diana had to suffer. She deserved the best.

All in all, his mood was exceptional. He'd resolved the little problem of Mr. Teague and Ms. Robinson. He'd proven his brilliance to the tune of several billion dollars, and in less than a week he'd be the richest man on the planet. Not that *Forbes* would ever identify him as such. No, unlike Mr. Gates, Drake's wealth was secret, divided between the Caymens and Switzerland, but certainly just as useful for acquiring the finer things in life.

He cast a glance toward Diana, and she smiled at him, holding her champagne flute up in a silent salute. She deserved the finer things. He'd build her a palace perhaps, overlooking the sea. A modern day Xanadu. Or, hell, maybe he'd just buy Xanadu.

He sipped his champagne. Altogether a truly extraordinary day.

The door burst open, and Beltzer stormed in. "They're gone, sir."

"Gone?" Drake repeated. His euphoria fizzled away, like so many bubbles in his wine, only to be replaced by a cold, hard knot of rage.

"We drained the chamber, sir. They're not there. It looks like they managed to blow part of the ceiling away."

Drake slammed his hand down, sending the silverware flying. "An explosion? Who the hell was the idiot who didn't strip-search them." He held up his hand to ward of Beltzer's response. "Never mind.

Just get Prado and scour this island. I want those two dead."

"Sir, Prado's doing the supply run. He took off hours ago."

Drake swiped his arm over the table, sending the china and stemware flying. "Do I look like I give a fuck where he is? If Prado's not available, then enlist someone else's help. Hell, enlist everyone's help. I want every inch of this island searched. I don't want any nook, cranny, or cubbyhole left uninvestigated. Do you understand me? I don't—"

The telephone buzzed, and Drake stabbed the speaker button with his finger. "Goddammit, what?"

"Prado, here, sir." He paused, and Drake heard the roar of the engine and the rush of the wind. "I think I may have a little problem."

Finn hadn't relaxed until the plane was airborne. Now, though, they'd been cruising for a while, and boredom was setting in.

Amber stood at the far side of the cabin, just outside the closed door to the cockpit. With one hand, she grasped the frame, keeping herself steady. Even from several feet away, he could see that she was hyperaware, ready to leap into action if Prado should emerge.

After they'd swiped the clothes from the utility room, they'd raced down the corridor, finally finding themselves under a grating through which sunlight streamed. They'd pushed the grating aside—this time needing neither a screwdriver nor a button—and peeked out carefully onto the airstrip. The main bunker was back over Finn's shoulder, and to his left across the tarmac was the small building topped with a huge satellite dish. A helicopter was perched at the far end of the tarmac, and a Gulfstream jet was refueling in front of them. Emerging as they were from the ground, they had to be conspicuous, and with no place to hide, they'd immediately raced for the nearest cover—a fuel truck parked next to the jet.

A squatty little man was fueling the plane and appeared entirely uninterested in the task. A lit cigarette dangled from his lips, and he leaned against the fuel truck, an old issue of *Playboy* open in front of him. Prado was walking the plane's perimeter, going over his preflight checklist.

And, best of all, the cabin door was open and the stairs were in place. A ladder was propped near the nose, and as soon as Prado climbed up, Finn gave Amber a nudge. "Go," he said.

He half-expected her to argue, to remind him that he didn't have a clue what he was doing and she was in charge. But she said nothing. Just took off for the stairs.

They were in the plane within seconds, crouching at the very back of the cabin behind a crate topped with a stack of moving blankets.

They stayed that way for a good twenty minutes, and the muscles in Finn's thighs were screaming in protest when they finally heard Prado's footsteps on the stairs. He entered the plane and headed straight for the cockpit without even a second glance in their direction.

They stayed behind the crate until they were airborne, still on high alert. Finn lowered his defenses somewhat, moving from a crouch to a kneel, but Amber stayed put, ready to spring in a moment's notice.

Only when the plane leveled off did Finn see her allow herself one deep breath of relief.

"That had to have been the easiest escape from island captivity I've ever been through," he'd said.

"Don't knock it," she'd answered, ignoring his irony. "Besides, we're not home free yet."

She'd stationed herself by the cockpit door, and Finn had followed, parking himself next to her. "There," she'd said, pointing across the cabin. "I really don't have the energy to nail Prado and keep you out of trouble."

"I can keep myself out of trouble." But he'd complied anyway. In the end, it wasn't worth picking a fight. Better to tend to his wounded pride once they were safely on the ground, not at several thousand feet.

Now Finn stood at alert at the far end of the cabin. Useless, really, since Prado was the only other human on board, but at least it gave Finn the illusion that he wasn't totally extraneous. If the design of the plane was any indication, Prado was en route on a regular supply run. The entire passenger space had been gutted. Instead of hardwood and leather, they were traveling in the midst of cold steel and canvas webbing. Judging from the hollow sound under his feet, a false floor had been put in as well. For smuggling, perhaps?

The visible space was lined with storage compartments built from what looked like chain-link fence, each individual cage secured by a web of slightly elastic netting. At the moment, the compartments were empty, the webbing hanging limp. Finn imagined that when the plane returned the compartments would be full of a wild conglomeration of food stuffs, electronic equipment, and biological weaponry. He didn't know the latter for a fact, but considering what he'd learned about Drake Mackenzie, he wouldn't put it past the man.

In the compartment under the false floor, Finn imagined Drake stored the necessary evils of his trade—pilfered electronic equipment, magnetic tape carrying secret codes, state of the art weapons and, quite possibly, a dead body or two.

A clatter sounded from behind the cockpit door, and Finn tensed. Prado might stay in the cockpit until they landed. Or he might decide to come back into the main cabin, if for no other reason than to hit the lavatory.

Amber's position shifted as well, and he knew she had the same thought. "Stay alert," she whispered, her words carrying little sound, only the exaggerated movement of her lips.

He nodded. "Don't worry. I w—"

An arm around his neck silenced him, and in that split second of time, Finn realized the one characteristic he'd overlooked about the compartment below the floor—as handy as it would be for smuggling goods, it could also hide the pilot and crew. And considering the choke hold around his neck, the crawl space extended from the cockpit all the way to the rear of the plane.

Not that he had time to ponder the plane's layout. Instead, he reacted instinctively, twisting so that his neck was in the crook of Prado's arm. At the same time, Finn leaned his head forward, then slammed it back, and was rewarded with the satisfying crunch of Prado's nose against Finn's skull. With the crunch still echoing in his ear, he lifted his foot and stomped down. Prado howled, and Finn twisted, freeing himself from the choke hold.

Breathless, he stumbled backward toward the interior of the cargo hold.

"Don't let him get back in the crawl space," Amber shouted. She'd raced to his side during the tussle, and now she stood next to Finn.

"You two are going down," Prado said.

"Don't count on it," Amber retorted.

But then Prado pulled a gun. Finn met Amber's steady gaze. "Chalk one up for the bad guys," he said.

"He won't use it in the cabin," she said, and Finn wasn't sure whether or not she was bluffing.

"The hell I won't," he said.

He stepped sideways, his hand clutching the cargo netting. Finn frowned, not sure what the other man was up to.

But then the plane shifted left, and Prado's plan became absolutely clear. Finn and Amber stumbled sideways as Prado struggled to the opposite side of the cabin toward the door.

He pulled the emergency lever, and the door blew free even as the plane leveled out. "Thought you two might enjoy some preprogrammed aerobatics," he said.

"I like to save my rides for Disneyland," Finn retorted.

"Well, this ride is definitely an e-ticket," he said. "Courtesy of Drake. He said I should be sure and entertain my guests."

The gun was still aimed at them, and Finn watched as Amber's eyes narrowed, her tongue wetting her lips. Finn glanced at the cockpit door, then back to Amber. She nodded, then rushed forward toward Prado as Finn raced to the cockpit.

It was a long shot, and Amber was risking a bullet in the gut as much as Finn was risking one in the back, but they had to take the chance.

As Amber had hoped, Finn's break to the front of the plane had confused Prado. He'd glanced toward the cockpit door, and in that instant, she dove, sliding the rest of the way to him on her belly and catching him by the ankles.

Fate was on her side, because they hit an air pocket, and the plane dropped, the motion sending Prado sprawling. The gun flew from his hand, clattering across the metal flooring to balance precariously in front of the open door, nothing but sky beyond.

Amber threw herself forward as the wind ripped around them, icy cold. She slammed her hands on his chest and straddled him, the boots she'd found in the utility room gripping the floor and providing some traction.

"Get off me, you bitch!"

"Not a chance!" She grabbed hold of his arm and twisted until he screamed in agony and rolled over. She held him that way, face-down with his arm behind his back, as she reached for a cargo strap that was secured to the floor by Velcro.

She ripped the strap free, then twisted it around his arm. But before she could secure his other arm, the plane lurched sideways, throwing her balance off.

Prado didn't waste any time. He swung his leg

back and over, tossing her onto the ground. Then he scrambled to his feet and stumbled to the open door. Two parachutes were strapped behind a bungee cord. He grabbed them, tossing one out into the sky and holding tight to the remaining chute. "See you in hell," Prado said, not even bothering to put it on as he leapt from the plane.

Shit. Amber rushed to the open door, the wind stinging her face. Below her, Prado seemed to float in midair, the clouds and ocean beneath him, as he struggled to don the chute.

Finn burst through the cockpit door.

"What the hell did you do?" she yelled.

"I didn't touch a thing," he shouted over the din. "He preprogrammed some maneuvers, and I can't get access. Not before we crash, anyway. Plus, he dumped the fuel."

Amber realized the plane was now on a slow descent.

"We're going to crash and there's nothing I can do about it."

"Come here," Amber said, even as she yanked another cargo strap loose. "And hurry."

Finn was at her side in an instant.

"Behind me," she said, her voice almost swallowed up in the wind. "Grab my waist." He did, and she looped the thick cargo strap around them like a giant belt, then pulled it tight and secured the buckle. She could barely breathe, but she didn't want to lose the man.

"What are you—"

"Just cross your arms over my chest, grab your wrists, and *don't let go.*"

She didn't even give him time to answer. She couldn't. Precious seconds were ticking by . . . and Prado was getting farther and farther away.

She heard Finn's sharp intake of air as she jumped, but to his credit, he did exactly what she'd told him, holding tight around her chest. He even did more, seeming to instinctively know how to help her by keeping his legs in line with her and not fighting her movements. A good thing, too. She'd never jumped without a chute before, and she sure as hell had never done it with a man strapped to her back. If they survived this, she was definitely putting in for hazard pay.

Below them, Prado had struggled into the chute and was in the typical boxman position. Good. That meant he knew what he was doing. If she was lucky, he was going to stay in free fall for a while . . . and that gave Amber just the edge she needed.

She aimed her face down, legs straight back, getting into the most aerodynamic position possible. They were moving faster than Prado now, gaining with every second of the fall. Her eyes stung as the wind bit into them, and blinking offered no relief. The discomfort wasn't a concern, though. Landing with a splat was about as uncomfortable as you can get, and she didn't intend to let that happen.

Closer . . . closer . . .

Almost there . . .

And then they were in position, about thirty feet above Prado and a little to the right. She used her arm as a rudder, guiding them to the left. Maneuvering was tricky with Finn's extra weight, but she managed to finesse it until they ended up in Prado's burble.

Once she was in that pocket of dead air, it was easy. Without the resistance, they literally fell on top of him. The element of surprise is a wonderful thing, and in midair, it's hard not to be surprised when someone falls on your back. One solid punch to the temple, and Prado was out like a light.

Amber flattened out, Finn still on her back, and her right hand grasping the strap of Prado's harness.

"How are we going to get the chute?" Finn shouted, his mouth right at her ear.

A good question. Even if she took the chute off Prado, it wouldn't fit around both of them. And Amber had no interest in loosening the strap that bound them together. It would be altogether too easy to lose Finn to the deep blue sea.

"We're not," she finally shouted, not certain he could hear her over the din.

Having made the decision, she realized it was the only possible one she could have made, and she tugged Prado toward her, looping her arms through the straps of his chute. Once her arms were secure, she clamped her legs around his thighs and hooked her ankles together. She gestured for Finn to do the same.

Behind her, she felt Finn nod as he released her chest and instead hugged the straps. At the same time, his legs curved around, also enveloping Prado.

She twisted, managing to get her mouth near his ear. "Have you ever skydived before?" she yelled.

He nodded.

Considering how unobtrusively he'd clung to her back, the answer didn't surprise her. But this was going to be different. She took a deep breath as the wind screamed past her ears, and the deep blue of the ocean was fast rising up to meet them. The jolt of the chute opening was going to practically rip their arms out. *"Don't* let go," she shouted. "For any reason."

"Right." The wind and his reply echoed in her ears.

She nodded, then let go of her hold on Prado's harness just long enough to release the pilot chute. "Here we go," she said, and as she spoke, the main chute deployed, jerking them upward as the canopy caught the wind. Pain shot through her body, her arms and shoulder joints bursting into red hot flames.

But that was a small price to pay for being alive.

Eighteen

Finn prayed.

As they'd been hurtling through the atmosphere toward Prado, he hadn't had time to form coherent thoughts, his head too filled with visions of a violent and messy death.

Now, he was making up for lost time. And, though he hesitated to be too optimistic, he was beginning to think his prayers were going to be answered.

Below them, the deep blue of the ocean was broken by a lush island and, in the distance, a shore. Dozens of small boats were anchored off the island, bobbing peacefully. The aerial view was tranquil, belying the circumstances that had led Finn to such a perspective.

"Beautiful, isn't it," Amber said. He clung to Amber's back, her body heat filtering through him, a counterpoint to the chill of the thin air.

Finn grinned. She had a way of reading his thoughts. "One of the perks of your job?" he asked. "Getting a new perspective on the world?"

"Absolutely," Amber said, her voice filled with such awe that he knew she meant it. Now that the chute had slowed their descent, he could hear her much better.

"So where are we?" he asked. "Catalina?"

"I think so," she said. "Yeah. Definitely. There's the casino."

Finn looked down from the dizzying height that was rapidly decreasing. Sure enough, he could make out the familiar round structure on the far side of the island.

"We need to try and get to that side of the island," Amber said. "The backside is basically wilderness, and unless we get lucky and hitch a ride with a dive boat, we'll have a daylong walk ahead of us." As she spoke, she tugged on the chute's cords, expertly steering them.

"I guess there's no chance of getting across the channel to Los Angeles," he said.

"No way," she said. "We're descending too fast. We'd come down miles from either shore and end up shark bait."

"So how *do* we plan to get from Catalina to Los Angeles?"

"One step at a time," Amber said.

"Check his pockets," Finn said.

Amber nodded and scrounged, her delighted "aha" letting Finn know she'd found something. He couldn't see what she was doing, but from her movements, he guessed she was tucking it into her coveralls.

Prado groaned, his eyes still closed as he shook his head.

"Welcome back to the living," Amber said. And then she let go of the straps and unhooked her legs from around his body. "Let go," she ordered Finn.

"But—"

"Just do it," she said.

He did. And they plunged the remaining distance to the ocean below.

The cold water of the Pacific sucked them in, and Finn struggled with the belt that kept him attached to Amber. Her hands closed over his, pushing him away gently as she released the buckle. As soon as they were separated, he kicked to the surface, breaking through just as she did.

He gasped for air, coughing up the salt water he'd swallowed during their unexpected dive. Above them, Prado still glided on an air current. A glint of sunlight against metal caught Finn's eye, and he realized the man had pulled out a gun, probably from an ankle holster that had been out of Amber's reach.

With a determined jerk, Finn grabbed Amber's hand, diving back beneath the water's surface just as the bullet whizzed by.

Amber whipped around, giving Finn a thumbs-up sign as she dove deeper. He followed, feeling absurdly proud for the kudo.

They stayed under the water until Finn had almost reached his level of endurance. Then Amber surfaced, Finn right beside her. They broke the water, and Finn gasped for breath. "You said you wanted adventure," she said. But her smile was weak, her face a little too pale.

"Are you okay? Did he get you?" He reached out for her, but she kicked away, avoiding his touch. Finn frowned, more disturbed than he should have been by her distance.

"Come on," she said. She kicked toward the shore, and he followed in silence, first checking the skies for any signs of Prado. The thug, however, was long gone, his chute disappearing over the hills on the south end of the island.

Colorful boats bobbed in the water in the distance, but the area where they'd landed was empty, several hundred yards away from a cordoned off swimming area. They headed toward the beach, and as soon as their feet could touch ground, they half-stumbled, half-swam for the shore.

He crawled out of the water and onto the sand, breathing deep. "Where to?" he asked, even as he silently prayed for just a moment's rest.

"This looks good to me," Amber said, as she collapsed into the sand, her face to the afternoon sun.

Finn joined her, the cool, wet sand against his body remarkably relieving. And as he lay there, staring at the cloudless sky, he reached out and found her fingers.

And, to his infinite relief, she didn't pull away.

She needed to move, needed to get to the mainland and contact Brandon. Needed to set in motion the wheels that would ultimately stop Drake and his insane plan.

But she couldn't. Couldn't move, could barely even breathe. Exhaustion and the brittle heat of fever had taken her and she could only lie there, breathing in the salty sea air and letting the sun's warmth beat against her body, tackling the fever's residual chill. She hoped she'd made the right decision by not trying to take Prado out before dropping into the ocean. But the truth was, the man was small potatoes. And considering her weakened state—not to mention the man who'd been strapped to her back—she needed to stay focused on stopping Drake, and not on risking her ass taking out an underling.

Now she simply lay there, soaking in the sun's soothing rays, her heart pounding and her head clouding. Finn's hand held hers tight, and as much as she wanted to pull it away, she couldn't. It would take so little effort, and she had strength enough. But she wanted the support. Needed it, and she was too sick to fight a longing that she knew she would ultimately regret.

And so she held on, and when he squeezed her fingers, his grip tentative yet supportive, she squeezed back. And then, because she couldn't stand it any more, she let the void take her and plunged into sweet, safe blackness.

"Amber. Amber, wake up." Finn's voice. And his hand on her shoulder.

She blinked, barely able to see through the haze that filled her head. Fingers of pain radiated from her shoulders, and she trembled from chills even as her body heated to temperatures found only in hell. "How long?" she asked, forcing the question out. "How long was I out?"

She turned her head, fighting pain and nausea, and realized they were no longer on a beach, but were instead on a hard metal bench. "And where the hell are we?"

"Long Beach," Finn said.

Of all the answers he could have given, that one hadn't even been on her radar. "How?" she asked, trying to make sense of events. She couldn't. She knew only that her body had broken down. She'd fought the fever and infection as long as possible and as soon as the adrenaline rush had faded, illness had taken hold. "When?"

"Just now. On the ferry. I found a couple of hundred in Prado's wallet, and I carried you. Most everyone on the ferry thinks a bottle of tequila got the better of you." He shrugged, then ran a hand through his hair, his eyes bloodshot. Lines etched his face, both exhaustion and concern. And that one gesture spoke volumes. The man was bone weary and in way over his head. But he'd taken care of her.

"I—"

"Don't even say it," he said. "I didn't know what else to do. You needed some rest, but we needed to move, so a hotel wasn't an option. What you *really* need is a hospital, but I figured you'd have my head if I took you to one."

"You're right about that." She managed a weak smile. "Cold," she said. "So cold."

"I know." He gathered her closer, his arms around her chest. "I don't have any blankets. But the sun's warm, and our clothes are dry, and I'm not going to let go of you."

"Thanks," she said, hoping that got the message across because it was the best she could do.

His eyes searched hers, and then he nodded, apparently satisfied. "You're welcome. But we need to get out of here, and since I don't know where else to go, I'm going to take you to a hotel and call a friend of mine who's a doctor."

"No," she said, fighting to get the word out past her parched lips and swollen tongue. "There's someone better to call. . . ."

"The plane went down, sir. It's a heap of twisted metal by now, and them two along with it."

Drake kept his eyes down, concentrating on the paper he was folding. The origami kept him sane. And it kept Beltzer alive. Because if Drake's hands weren't otherwise occupied, he doubted he could have resisted the urge to pull his sidearm and pop the son of a bitch.

Beltzer was lucky.

Drake crimped the paper, creating the chicken's beak. As much as Beltzer tried his patience, the truth was that Drake had a soft spot for the idiot. The man could be dim at times, but he was loyal to a fault. And with Drake that counted. A lot.

"Have we heard from Prado?" Drake asked, when Beltzer finally quit rambling.

"No, sir."

"No, sir," Drake repeated. "And what were Prado's orders?"

"To get rid of Teague and the girl. Crash the plane, dump them in the ocean, and signal for a rescue copter for himself." He paused. "Sir."

Drake crossed his arms, waiting.

Beltzer looked down, then side to side. "Sir?"

"We haven't heard from Prado, you imbecile," Drake said, his words measured. "And until we do, we cannot assume that the mission is complete." He waved a hand toward the door. "Take a team, find my man, and get confirmation that Ms. Robinson and Mr. Teague are dead."

"Yes, sir," he said, then turned to head out the door.

"And, Beltzer," Drake added, "don't come back without answers."

"Holy shit," Brandon said, the second he saw Amber lying limp in Finn's arms. Teague was holding her in a bridal carry, and Amber had one weak arm thrown around the man's shoulder. Brandon slammed the Buick into park and jumped out, racing around the front of the car to take her from Teague, who looked about to collapse himself.

"Kline?" Finn asked, before he relinquished Amber.

"Who the hell else?" Brandon answered. "Let me get her in the backseat."

"Watch her shoulder," Teague said.

Brandon nodded, noticing that the back of her coveralls was stained a brownish red. He closed his eyes and allowed himself one silent curse before hustling her into the car. He kept an aid kit under the driver's seat, and he dug out a vial of penicillin and jammed a hefty dose into her thigh. She was feverish, dehydrated, and in desperate need of an IV, but that was going to have to wait. "Get in," he said to Teague, who'd been watching the whole procedure with an unreadable expression.

Finn didn't hesitate, just slid into the passenger side and waited for Brandon to get the car moving. "How much do you know?" he asked.

"Not a damn thing," Brandon said. "Except that you called my cell phone and told me to get my ass down to Long Beach to give you two a lift. And you told me not to call in any other help from the Unit." He paused, looking Teague in the eye. "I took one hell of a chance, Teague," he said. "For all I know, you sliced her shoulder yourself, and you're looking to weasel your way into our organization."

To his credit, Teague didn't start protesting his innocence. Instead, he just looked over his shoulder to Amber, curled up in the fetal position on the Buick's backseat. "Just doing what the lady asked," he said. "She only wanted you."

Brandon nodded, willing, for the moment, to believe Finn. "Why?"

"She didn't say," Finn said. "But I'm assuming she thinks there's a mole in your group."

Brandon already knew that, but he was surprised that Amber or Finn knew as well. "Why the hell do you think that?"

"A guess," Finn said with a shrug. "But a reasonable one. On the plane, they had no idea who she was. The next day, suddenly Drake not only knows she's an operative, but knows the agency she's with and her name." He met Brandon's eyes. "I figure somebody must have clued him in."

Brandon nodded, tending to agree but ever cautious. "Could be he sent her picture and prints to one of his sources. She's crossed paths with CIA, NSC, MI5, Mossad, DGXE, and countless other agencies. Anybody could have snitched on her."

"All right," Finn said, twisting around to look at her. "So maybe there's not a mole. But there's still a risk." He turned in his seat, and Brandon saw real concern on his face. "I may be new here, but I'm not blind. Amber knows her stuff, and she thinks you need to avoid the Unit. If you're going to go against her wishes . . ."

Brandon laughed. "You'll what? All I have to do is press the horn and you'll get plugged in the gut by the gun wired to the glove box. Believe me, Teague, you're not calling the shots here."

"That's a state of affairs I'm getting used to." Finn leaned back against the upholstery and looked straight ahead, his eyes not even dipping down to check out the glove box. "But I still want an answer to my question."

Brandon paused. He wasn't about to go to the Unit, but he still wasn't certain if he trusted this guy. Amber had, though. She'd trusted him with her life. And if Finn *had* been the one to gouge her shoulder, the odds were he wouldn't have stood by her. "No," he finally said. "I've got someplace else in mind."

"Where?"

Brandon licked his lips. "You'll see." He shot Finn a look. "And we've got at least two hours of driving ahead of us. Use that time to tell me what's been going on." He paused, turning to look at his companion. "And, Finn," he added, "tell me everything."

Nineteen

Despite Brandon's insistence on knowing every little detail, Finn edited the story a bit, just to keep it from getting an NC-17 rating. He wasn't stupid—he knew damn well that sex had been part of Amber's mission all along, and Brandon was probably well aware of her assignment. But that didn't change the basic fact—telling Brandon would require Finn to admit just how hard and how fast he'd fallen for Amber. And just how much her deception hurt.

Everything else, though, he told in meticulous detail. Brandon interrupted twice, to clarify minor points, but for the most part he stayed silent, his eyes on the road, his jaw firm. By the time Finn finished the tale, they were high in the San Bernardino Mountains, well past Lake Arrowhead and on the Rim of the World Drive heading toward Big Bear.

"She jumped out of a plane with you strapped to her back?" Brandon laughed. "Damn, the woman's good."

Finn swallowed, Brandon's unabashed praise reminding him that he was way, way out of his league. When they were on the island, he hadn't felt like he was in over his head. Or, more precisely, he'd been so far in over his head that he hadn't had time to think about it. He'd just done what he needed to do to survive.

Now, though . . .

Now he was alone with Brandon, a guy who held the very job Finn had always fantasized about. And damned if Finn wasn't reverting back to his freshman days, wanting to look cool in front of the seniors. He'd done damn good on the island; he knew that. But he couldn't tell that to Brandon without sounding like an asshole.

There was more, too, but Finn hated to admit it, even to himself. *Amber*. He'd fallen hard for her. Passion forged by fire, intense and undeniably strong. But he didn't know if Amber felt the same way, or, if she did, if she'd ever admit it.

Finn blew out a slow breath, then turned to look at her. Her breathing was regular and her color seemed better. That, at least, was good.

"Four days," Brandon said, clearly still musing about all that Finn had said. "And then he blows the mosque."

"That's about the sum of it," Finn said.

Brandon shook his head. "The goddamn Hollywood sign. The FBI's been busting their ass looking for domestic terrorists, and you tell me it came from Prometheus. I guess Drake was right.

No one at the Unit has a clue the thing was even fired. Shit."

Finn didn't comment, but Brandon didn't seem to notice. He just tapped the brakes, closing his eyes. All in all, he slowed for less than thirty seconds, but to Finn it seemed forever.

Finally he looked up, his eyes meeting Finn's before shifting to the backseat. "Does she have a plan?"

Finn shook his head. "I don't know."

Brandon's jaw shifted. "Twelve hours. I need her awake and coherent and ready to give me a debriefing by dawn tomorrow." He tapped his fingers on the steering wheel. "And if she's not, I'm going to call the shots myself."

Finn didn't argue. He didn't know what to say, and no matter what he did say, Brandon would do whatever the hell he wanted. So instead, Finn just sat back and hoped like hell an IV, some drugs, and a good night's sleep would get Amber back in shape.

"Don't worry," Brandon said. "I know Amber. She'll be back in form in no time. Hell, less than twelve hours ago, she was tossing you out of airplanes."

Finn reached into the backseat to stroke her cheek. "True enough. I just wonder if she didn't blow her wad surviving to Long Beach. Her shoulder's a mess and she's burning up. She's been drugged, beat up, handcuffed, almost drowned, and shot at. Do you really think twelve hours will do it?"

Brandon's eyes were deadly serious. "It's going to have to." He tapped a stick of gum out of a pack on the dash, then offered one to Finn. "Juicy Fruit?"

"No thanks."

Brandon tucked the stick into his own mouth.

"Gave up smoking," he said. Then he grinned. "That shit can kill you."

The sun was descending through the tall fir trees, casting long shadows on the narrow, winding roads. Brandon had turned off the main road, taking a small, poorly paved route up into an undeveloped part of the mountain. At first, they'd passed a few other houses, mostly small A-frames, but now Finn saw nothing except the crush of trees against the road.

He considered asking again where they were going, but ruled it out. He'd find out soon enough.

A few more twists and turns, and Brandon maneuvered the Buick onto a dirt road. He turned to Finn, nodding toward the lightly traveled road in front of them. "Amber's idea of paradise," he said. "My idea of hell."

Finn didn't understand what Brandon meant until they passed a clump of trees and he saw the house—a charming blue A-frame surrounded on three sides by tall pines. Brandon maneuvered the car to a small parking area at the side, revealing a multileveled redwood deck instead of a backyard.

The house butted up against a steep descent, and the deck hung out over the edge of the mountain, providing what had to be a stunning view of the valley below.

"Wow," Finn said.

Brandon shrugged. "The view's spectacular," he conceded. "But I'm a city guy, myself."

"So why are we here? Whose house is this?"

Brandon glanced into the backseat at Amber. "Hers, of course," he said.

* * *

Amber woke with a start, sitting bolt upright and breathing hard, every muscle on alert. Then she recognized the familiar sounds and textures of the room and she relaxed. *Her hideaway.*

Her shoulder ached, her sheets were soaking wet, and she had no memory of how the hell she'd gotten here. But even so, things were definitely looking up.

She tried to move, to get off the bed, but she couldn't. Her legs were crushed to the bed like dead weight. And for a split second, the fear sliced through her again. Then she heard the shallow breathing and realized—Brinkley had fallen asleep on her legs, a hundred or so pounds of solid Black Lab sitting like a sentry to watch over his injured mistress.

She tugged harder, and Brinkley rolled sideways, lost in doggie heaven. Amber stifled a smile, reaching out to stroke his belly. *Some watchdog!*

Brinkley stayed still, but she heard a low chuckle from the far side of the room. Once again she was on alert, her hand sliding under her pillow for the gun she kept there. She trained the weapon toward the source of the noise. "Who's there?" Her voice was thin and weak, her throat dry and swollen.

"It's me."

All tension faded from her body, replaced by relief and a disconcerting flood of desire. *Finn.*

He turned on the lamp next to his chair, casting his face in shadows. Concern had etched lines in his forehead, and his eyes were tired and bloodshot. She knew instinctively that she was the cause of his worry, and she waited for the familiar flash of irritation. She didn't need someone worrying about her, didn't want that kind of attachment. But the irritation never came. Instead, she simply felt relief that he was okay, too.

"How are you feeling?" he asked.

She lifted the arm into which someone had stuck an IV. "A bit like Frankenstein."

He chuckled. "I'm not surprised."

"Mrs. Digby?" she asked, assuming her so-called housekeeper had hooked her up.

He blinked, clearly not understanding the question.

"The IV," she clarified. "Who put it in?"

"Brandon," he said. "I would have preferred a doctor to look at you, but it didn't seem like a good idea under the circumstances. And Brandon said you had everything you needed here." His eyes met hers, and she saw the question underneath. "He seemed to know what he was doing."

She nodded. The house was her retreat for both her physical and mental well-being. "I keep the place well stocked," she said simply. "You never know when you'll have one of those pesky medical emergencies where it's just not practical to involve a hospital." She would have preferred Mrs. Digby's care over Brandon's, but so long as she survived, she couldn't really complain.

She looked at the IV bag. "Antibiotics?"

Finn nodded. "Big time. And saline, I think. Your shoulder was a mess, and you were dehydrated on top of that." He stood up, coming over to sit on the edge of the bed by Brinkley. He gave the dog a quick scratch behind the ears, then took her hand. "How do you feel now?"

"Stiff," she said. "My head's filled with cotton, I've lost a lot of strength, and my throat is parched. But I think I'll survive."

His mouth twitched. "Glad to hear it."

"Where's Brandon?"

"Getting some sleep, I assume." His eyes met hers. "You woke up with two hours to spare."

She shook her head, not understanding.

"Sun up," he said. "Brandon was giving you just until dawn. If you were still out then, he was going to take things into his own hands. Including contacting the Unit if that's what it took."

"Shit." She couldn't blame Brandon, but it irked her that he didn't trust her judgment.

"That was my reaction, too. But we do have to do something. If you were still down for the count, that wouldn't leave him with a whole lot of options."

She put her hand over her mouth to hide her grin.

His eyes narrowed to a squint. "What?"

"You," she said. "Talking the talk and walking the walk."

"Yeah, well, when in Rome . . ."

"And you love it," she said. She could see it in his eyes. Behind the concern, behind the exhaustion, she saw a reflection of herself. He might have been scared stiff when they'd jumped out of that plane, but he'd do it again in a minute if that's what it took.

"I do," he said. "Hell, I almost wish I didn't."

She didn't have to ask what he meant. The past few days had been an aberration in his life. A life he'd be going back to soon enough. The thought depressed her, and she told herself it was simply because if they'd got him when he was younger, he could have been a damn good agent. But it was more than that, and she knew it. She just didn't want to think about it right then.

A soft knock sounded at the door, followed by the creak of hinges. Brandon stepped in without comment and walked straight to Amber's bed, his face all hard lines and angles.

Something had happened, and she sat up more, wincing slightly at the pressure she put on her shoulder. "What?"

"A school bus," he said. "In Israel. Blown to bits." Amber's stomach twisted as Brandon continued, turning slightly to bring Finn into the conversation. "The Israeli prime minister has already issued a statement promising retaliation."

"Well, that's it, then," Finn said. "That Saudi prince is going to blow up the mosque and blame the Israelis."

Amber nodded, meeting Brandon's eyes. "He's right."

"I know."

"Are we screwed?" Brandon asked. "Now that you two escaped, Drake's going to want to get the show on the road. The mosque is still standing now, but—"

"No." Amber shook her head, cutting him off. "If he didn't blow it already, we're fine. The satellite moved out of range at midnight."

Finn nodded. "She's right."

Brandon looked dubious, but Amber broke in before he could dissent. "Drake explained the possible firing dates to Mujabi. Trust me. We're cool."

"What if he shifts the satellite's orbit?"

Amber frowned. That was out of her expertise.

"Doubtful," Finn said. "That's the kind of thing that would likely show up to the folks at the Unit, even if he does it when they're not running a sim. Plus, it takes time to retask a satellite. Diana might have the know-how, but I bet they don't risk it. They know they can fire it unnoticed. Why change the orbit and risk compromising their whole setup?"

Brandon's jaw set into a hard line. "All right," he said. "Let's hope you're right."

"So the question is, what do we do?" Amber looked at both men, unconsciously including Finn in the planning. "How do we stop this?"

"Drake said they got in through the back door," Finn said. "If we can find the programmer ourselves, maybe we can do an override and close the door."

"I found him," Brandon said.

"Who?" Amber asked.

"He was right under our noses the whole time. Bernie Waterman."

Amber couldn't have been more surprised if he'd slapped her. "But Waterman's a clerk. He does data entry."

"Someone must have known he'd attract attention and reclassified him."

"Let's go get him," Finn said.

"He's gone," Brandon said. "And his apartment has been ransacked."

Amber nodded, remembering Diana's comment on the plane about their so-called cargo. "They've got him on the island."

"So we go back," Finn said.

Amber shook her head. "Look, Finn. I can tell you're going to be useful in helping us plan this operation, but there's no way I'm knowingly taking a civilian back to that island."

Finn opened his mouth, presumably to argue, but Brandon spoke up first.

"Let's just blow the fucking thing out of the water."

"And sacrifice Waterman?" Finn asked.

"Collateral damage," Brandon said.

Finn didn't look pleased, but neither did he argue.

Amber licked her lips, considering the possible scenarios. "We can't do it," she said. "Not without help. You and I don't have access to the weapons, and we don't have the authority to scramble fighters." She ran a hand through her hair. "I'd wanted to keep a lid on this. There's a leak in the Unit," she added, directing the comment to Brandon.

"I know," Brandon said. "So we'll go through James. He's back, you know. And worried about you."

She nodded. James understood discretion. If they moved fast, they could blow the island out of the water before sunrise. And even if someone other than James got wind of their plans, the mole wouldn't have time to warn Drake—not without revealing himself. "So we take care of Drake, take a deep breath, and then figure out who the son of a bitch is who's leaking Unit secrets."

"Exactly," Brandon agreed.

"Okay." She picked up the phone and dialed the Unit's access number. "Go secure," she said when the operator answered.

She heard the familiar click, and then the computer generated voice, "Identify."

"Two seven niner dash niner."

"Password?"

"Tribeca."

"Invalid." The line went dead.

"What the fuck?" Amber stared at the phone, shook her head, and tried again.

Still invalid.

She licked her lips, a cold chill settling in her bones as she was struck with the direness of the situation. "I've been disavowed," she said, her eyes meeting Brandon's.

"Bullshit," Brandon said.

"Your mole," Finn said.

Brandon ignored him, but Amber silently agreed with Finn. She passed Brandon the phone. "You're going to have to pull this one off," she said.

He nodded, then dialed and went through the same process. Then he paled, and she knew the second he heard the flat voice speak that one, telling word—"Invalid."

Brandon slammed the phone down. "Shit."

"So what does this mean?" Finn asked.

"It means we're shit out of luck," Brandon said, pacing the room.

Finn stood up. "There must be some way to get help. Another agency. Hell, the White House."

Amber licked her lips. "*Disavowed*, Finn. Brandon and I are traitors and liars now. No one's going to believe us. Hell, if we went in, they'd probably arrest us. Or worse."

"Then I'll go," he said.

She and Brandon exchanged glances.

"What?" Finn asked.

"You were with me," Amber said. "Congratulations. You never even made it into the CIA and yet for all practical purposes, you've been disavowed, too."

"You don't know that."

"Not for certain, no. But call it an educated guess."

Finn's glance cut to Brandon. "You agree?"

"I'm afraid so. We're on our own now."

"On our own?" Finn asked. "You mean shit out of luck."

"No," Amber said. "I'm not letting Drake get away with this. All I mean is that we're going to have to do this the hard way. No outside help. None." She took a deep breath. "We've got time," she said. "We go in, we stop the satellite at the source."

"Looks like we don't have a choice," Brandon said. He stalked to the door, his vile mood practically dripping off him. She understood completely. *Disavowed.* The Unit was her life. And now, in the blink of an eye, her net had been pulled out from under her.

"Get some rest," Brandon said. "We'll regroup at oh eight hundred." He turned to leave, stopping at the door to look back at Finn. "Go back to your room, Finn. The lady needs her rest."

"No," Amber said, facing Finn. "Stay. I need to talk to you." The words were out before she had a chance to think, but she knew it was the right thing to do. They needed to clear the air.

Brandon raised an eyebrow, but he didn't say anything. And as soon as the door shut, Finn returned to his chair, his arms crossed over his chest. "Are you okay?" he asked.

She nodded. "Sure," she lied. "All part of the wonderful world of espionage."

"Find the mole," he said, "and you'll be reinstated."

She couldn't help her smile. "Thanks," she said. "I appreciate your concern. But right now I need to worry about Drake."

"One battle at a time," he said.

"Exactly." She licked her lips, realizing that the conversation had shifted subtly. There was one other battle she had to face. It was the reason she'd asked him to stay, but now it seemed almost more difficult than returning to the island. She drew a deep breath and jumped in. "Everything I told you about myself was true," she said. "I just left a few things out."

"Misrepresentation by omission," he said. "It's still fraud."

"Don't play lawyer with me, Teague. I'm as well trained as you are. And it's only fraud if there's a duty to speak. Believe me. Duty required silence."

"At first," he said conceded. "Maybe. But later?" He ran a hand through his hair. "Jesus, Amber, I was as deep into all of this as you were, risking my butt right alongside yours. You should have told me in my cell, and you damn well know it."

"There wasn't any need," she said. "Telling you would have been pointless."

He moved to sit on the edge of the bed then, taking her face in the palms of his hands. "Pointless? Is that really all I was to you? Someone you confided in on a need-to-know basis and someone you fucked on a need-to-fuck basis? Because, god-damn it, you mean a hell of a lot more to me than that."

She flinched. She didn't want to mean anything to him. So long as she'd simply been having a good time in his arms, she could wash away whatever feelings she had for him.

And she *did* have feelings. As much as she wanted to avoid it, he'd snuck into her heart. His humor, his resourcefulness, his reluctance to take the backseat. She admired and respected him.

Hell, she was falling in love with him.

So, yes, she definitely had feelings for the man. And her only hope was to ignore them. To not let them grow into something wild and dangerous. To beat them back into one of the dark, hidden chambers of her soul. That was her plan, at any rate. But if her feelings were reciprocated . . .

She shook her head, not wanting to think about that. And then she took a deep breath. She was ana-lyzing too much. "It was the circumstances, Finn," she said, speaking gently. "There's nothing real between us and there never will be. We were tossed in a cell together with the sure knowledge that tor-ture or death was facing us. That's not real. That's adrenaline." She spoke to convince herself as much as him.

"There was no adrenaline on the cliff," he said. "There was just you and me and this thing that's between us."

"Thing?" she repeated. "That *thing* was certain sex. You knew damn well you were going to get laid."

"Yes," he said, his voice hard. "I'm well aware

that I was the subject of your mission. But you have to admit there was more to it than that."

"I don't have to admit anything," Amber said.

From his grin, she could tell he knew she was avoiding the unspoken question. "We're good together, Amber. I knew it on the cliff, and I think we proved it on the island."

"You didn't even know me on the cliff."

"So I've been told," he said, his voice cold.

"I'm supposed to break an oath because you say we feel some connection?" She ran a hand through her hair in frustration. "It doesn't work that way, Finn, and it never will."

Any other man and she would have told him to just get the hell out of the room. But she wasn't saying that to Finn. She didn't want to hurt him any more than was necessary, because the frustrating truth was that she did want him. In some other life, she wanted him with all her heart and soul.

But not this life.

James's voice seemed to echo in her ear, reminding her of the duties she'd undertaken and the oaths she'd sworn. *"Your loyalty is to your country, your team, and to this Unit. Everything else is extraneous. Everyone else is expendable."*

And he was right. She'd given the Unit her life, and she'd never once regretted it. Not once, that is, until now. When Phineus Teague had stumbled into her life, and she'd started to wonder what exactly she might be missing.

"Amber." He took her hand, his touch a plea, but she couldn't answer. Couldn't even try.

"Just go," she said. "Go, and let me sleep."

For a moment she thought he would argue, but

in the end his concern for her health won out. "This isn't over," he said.

She nodded, knowing what he said was true. But even though it might not be over, and even though a part of her wanted to curl up with Finn and never let go, she knew what the end would be.

This was the life she'd chosen, and it was the life she loved. For now, and for always.

Twenty

May I help you?"

The harsh female voice seemed to come out of nowhere, and Finn almost dropped the carafe of orange juice he was liberating from the refrigerator. He turned to face a tall woman with silver gray hair pulled into a tight knot at the nape of her neck. She wore a business suit, carried a clipboard, and looked like she belonged in a boarding school whipping obstinate teenagers into shape.

Finn put the carafe back and offered his hand. "Mrs. Digby?"

She looked him up and down, then sniffed. "There is no need to rummage through the kitchen," she said. "Go. Sit. I'll bring you breakfast momentarily."

"I really just need a gla—"

"Go. Sit."

Finn went into the dining room and sat. Less than five minutes later, Mrs. Digby appeared bearing a tray with scrambled eggs, bacon, toast, and a tall glass of orange juice. She slid it onto the table in front of him, then turned back toward the kitchen without a word.

"Wait," he called, not completely sure what prompted him to speak.

She turned, her brow riding high above the bifocals she wore. "Do you need ketchup, Mr. Teague?"

He frowned, then shook his head. "No. No the meal is fine. Great. What I need is information." He gestured to the chair opposite him. "I don't suppose you'd join me?"

For a moment he thought she'd turn him down, but then she nodded briskly. "You have questions, of course," she said, taking a seat. "I don't know that I'm authorized to answer them, but you may ask."

"Thank you," he said. He found himself sitting straighter than normal, the woman's oh-so-proper demeanor making him feel like a knight at court. "Have you spoken with Amber this morning?"

"Of course," she said. "She and Mr. Kline are discussing their options." She looked down her nose at him. "I presume that if they wanted you to have access to any of the details of their conversation, they would have invited you to participate. I won't, of course, divulge anything they discussed in my presence."

"Right," Finn said. "I was just making conversation. What I really want to know about is Amber. Have you known her long?"

Mrs. Digby blinked, then took off her glasses and set them on the table. "Yes," she said, her voice somehow warmer. "I've known her since she was thirteen."

Finn leaned forward, his elbows on the table, his breakfast forgotten. If what Amber had said was true, she was recruited by the Unit when she was thirteen. "What was she like? How did you know her?"

"She was hell on wheels, that girl," Mrs. Digby said, the corners of her eyes crinkling. "And a cocky little twit, too."

"How—"

"I trained her, Mr. Teague. I was the Unit's first female operative, and I was responsible for, shall we say, softening some of Amber's rougher edges."

"She mentioned someone named James."

Mrs. Digby nodded. "James Monahan. Second-in-command of the Unit. For a few more weeks, anyway." Finn must have looked confused, because she added, "He's retiring, you see."

"But who is he? I mean, to Amber."

"Her boss and her mentor. I may have helped her along the way, but he was like family." A thin smile graced her lips. "A family proficient in the use of small weapons and trained to assassinate dissident leaders, of course."

"Right," Finn said, not entirely sure what he should say to something like that. "Has Amber—"

"Certainly."

"Right." He supposed he should have expected the answer, but with Amber he never quite knew what to expect. He took a sip of coffee, then decided to start at the beginning. "She told me James got her out of some trouble with the law. But she didn't tell me what."

"A number of things. But I believe the specific charge against her when the Unit brought her in was murder."

Finn frowned. "She killed someone? At thirteen?"

"Felony murder," Mrs. Digby clarified. "She didn't pull the trigger." Finn nodded, remembering the doctrine from law school, as Mrs. Digby continued. "She and two men—boys, really—set out to rob a liquor store. They had plastic guns—thought they were being smart and avoiding a weapons charge—but the clerk didn't know the guns were plastic. He pulled a rifle out from behind the counter and shot one of the boys. Killed him instantly. Amber, of course, was charged along with the other boy."

Finn licked his lips.

"That's the woman you've fallen for, Mr. Teague. Does that change your assessment of her, knowing all this?"

"No," Finn said automatically. "But how—"

"I have eyes, young man."

Apparently so. Finn just nodded, wanting to know more—hell, wanting to know everything—but not knowing what to ask next. Finally, he concentrated on Mrs. Digby herself. "If you were an operative, why are you here? Serving breakfast, I mean?" He held up his hands, realizing how that sounded. "I don't mean to be rude, but it just seems odd."

"I worked as an operative for ten full years," she said. "And then I met another Unit agent. He became something of a distraction to me, as I did to him."

Finn shook his head. "I'm sorry. I don't understand."

"Field operatives in the Unit cannot be involved in a relationship. Any relationship."

"Why not?"

"A number of reasons. A love interest can provide an unneeded distraction. Or a vulnerable spot, a weak point upon which the enemy can apply pressure. Also," she added with a smile, "agents are sometimes required to use *all* the means at their disposal to discern important information."

"Yes," Finn said dryly. "I'm aware of that."

"Spouses tend to react negatively toward their mate sleeping with another simply to gain information."

"Can't argue with that," Finn said. "So you were kicked out of the Unit?"

"Out of the Unit, no. Out of the field, yes. Patrick and I were both assigned to the D.C. Bureau. After he died, I was assigned as Amber's liaison officer. When I retired, I came to live here. I take care of her house while she's away. Which, as you might imagine, is quite often."

Finn glanced around the dining room. Like the rest of the house, it was sparse, but still homey. "Amber didn't strike me as the domestic type."

Mrs. Digby raised an eyebrow. "What makes you think she is?"

"Well . . ." Finn trailed off, suddenly uncertain. "This house, I guess."

"Mmm." Mrs. Digby got up and disappeared into the kitchen, returning moments later with the coffee pot. "She didn't buy this house so she could escape to some bit of domestic bliss," the woman said. "She bought it so that she would never have to leave."

"I don't get it."

"Her work is very trying. As a result, the Unit imposes mandatory vacation time. Amber comes here."

"Because . . ." Finn said, prompting.

"The house is quite well equipped," Mrs. Digby said. "She can access the Unit computers, download the language-learning software, monitor ongoing missions, do any number of tasks. During her last sabbatical, she taught herself Japanese. And, of course, there is no other house around for miles, so the woods provide a good area for honing survival skills, not to mention target practice. And, of course, I work with her on her martial arts skills."

Finn kept his face impassive, but in truth, he was impressed. Never in his life had a job stirred such devotion in him. This one, though . . . Well, he could both understand and empathize with Amber's commitment. A spark of envy flared in his gut and he tamped it down. He'd made his choices, however much he regretted them. And this peek into a life he coveted was just that—a peek. But while he was here, he intended to make the most of it. Soon enough he'd return to the real world.

Assuming, that is, he survived the week.

A buzzer sounded in the kitchen, and Mrs. Digby rose. "It's been lovely chatting with you, Mr. Teague, but I need to go upstairs and see what Amber and Mr. Kline need." She nodded toward his plate. "Do eat. I'd hate for your food to get cold."

Finn didn't care about his food. Instead, he tilted his head back to gaze at the ceiling. He wanted in that room. Wanted to know what Amber and Brandon were planning. "Do you think she'll tell me?" he asked.

Mrs. Digby just shook her head. "Amber prefers to work alone."

"She's working with Brandon," Finn said, hoping he sounded curious rather than jealous.

"Out of necessity. Besides, she's known him since she was thirteen. They can practically read each other's thoughts." She aimed a hard look at him. "Brandon's not a distraction."

"And I am," Finn said.

Mrs. Digby nodded. "Yes, Mr. Teague. I believe you are."

"How's my houseguest?" Amber asked, the moment Mrs. Digby stepped into the room.

"Curious," Mrs. Digby said. She crossed to the bed to check Amber's IV, then gently pushed her forward and pulled aside the tank top Amber was wearing to inspect the wound. "The stitches are sloppy, but the wound looks much better."

"I was in a rush," Brandon said. But the expression he turned on Amber was apologetic. "Sorry, kid. I should have waited for Digby here."

"I picked an inconvenient time to run into town," Mrs. Digby said, an apology in her voice.

"We've got better things to worry about than my scars," Amber said. "Brandon and I are going to launch an operation. Try to destroy their connection to the satellite. If we're lucky, we'll even get Waterman out alive. I don't want Finn running loose while we do that. Are you okay keeping an eye on him?"

"I don't see why that would be a problem," Mrs. Digby said.

"Good." Amber knew Finn was resourceful, but

she had no doubt that Mrs. Digby would make good her word. "We leave tomorrow."

"Anything else?"

Amber shook her head. "Let Finn know I'll be down soon. Brandon and I are almost done here."

Mrs. Digby aimed a stern look over her glasses, her gaze aimed first at Amber, and then at the bed. "Down?"

Amber stiffened, feeling a bit like a reprimanded child. "I don't need the IV anymore, Delia," she said. "Don't be a mother."

Mrs. Digby didn't answer, but Amber was certain she saw a flicker of amusement cross the woman's face as she headed toward the door.

"You need rest," Brandon said, the moment the door closed behind Mrs. Digby. "Let Teague entertain himself while you get some more sleep."

A finger of irritation trailed up her spine. "I've already got Mrs. Digby fussing over me," she said. "I don't need you, too."

"You need to be worrying about two things," Brandon said. "Getting back on that island and getting well. Finn shouldn't even be on your radar."

"He's not," she lied.

"Bullshit. I was here last night. The air between you two practically crackled."

Amber opened her mouth to argue, but no argument came out. Brandon knew her too well, and she respected him too much to lie. "The truth?" she said. "There's something about that man. Something that gets me. Right in the gut, you know?"

"No," Brandon said. "I don't know." He looked her in the eye, his expression serious. "Are you in love with him?"

"No, of course not," Amber said, the lie coming automatically to her lips. "It's just that there's something about him. . . ." She trailed off, unable to find a common point of reference. Brandon had repeatedly told her he'd never been in love, never even come close, and she had no reason to doubt him. So how did she explain the way Finn made her feel?

Brandon just shook his head, like a disappointed older brother. "You couldn't do it," he said. "Walk away from field op status. Not in a million years."

"That's not even on my radar," she said, and that was the God's honest truth. "And even if I were in love with him," she said, stumbling over the word, "I know better than to think he feels the same way. He's just thrill-seeking anyway. I'm the embodiment of everything he wants to be. He wants to *be* me, not have me."

Brandon just crossed his arms and shook his head.

"What?"

"You're talking like a woman scorned," he said.

"Fuck you," she retorted.

Brandon laughed. "That's better. That's the Amber I know and love."

She sighed, a long slow exhale. "Don't worry about me. I'll admit to wanting the man in my bed, but that's all I want." She met his eyes, determined to convince him—and herself. "Really."

"The last thing you need is to be burning off energy between the sheets," he said. "We're heading for the island tomorrow morning. I want you sharp."

"I can take care of myself," she said.

"That explains why I had to stitch up your shoulder," he said, but there was no real recrimination. He knew damn well that she had pushed past the pain to get off the island. "Speaking of," he continued, "Finn said you were drugged. Narcrylotine?"

She nodded. "I think so. That explains why the infection set in so quickly." An unintended side effect of the drug was a temporary suppression of a person's immune system.

"Under the conditions you were subjected to, it might have anyway, but yeah," Brandon agreed.

"Well, sleep and drugs have done wonders. I feel human again. Stiff, but human."

"Are you sure you're up to going back to the island?"

"Of course," she said. That wasn't even an issue. "But I've been thinking. What if we fail?" She met his eyes, saw the familiar defiance there.

"We won't."

"Come on, Brandon. There's too much riding on this. We have to at least consider the possibility of failure."

He blew out a noisy breath. "Fine. We get to the island and we each take a bullet in the back. World War Three starts and we don't give a fuck because we're dead."

"I have an idea about backup," she said, ignoring him. "If you and I fail, someone's going to have to blow the island."

"We went through this last night," he said. "*All alone*, remember? *Disavowed*, remember?"

"I haven't forgotten," she said.

Brandon's brow furrowed. "Are you thinking of somehow using Prometheus itself?"

Amber licked her lips. In fact, she had considered that. If Prometheus could blow up the mosque, it could also blow up the island. "Even if we could find someone at ZAEL who'll overlook our new status, I'm not certain that they'll still have control. Drake's back door may lock them out."

"Good point," Brandon said. "But we're out of options."

Amber pressed her lips together. "James."

Brandon crossed his arms over his chest. "Amber . . ."

"We're going to have to get James involved," she said. It was bad form—very bad form—to go to James and beg for help considering they'd been disavowed. Hell, if Schnell or his superiors found out that they'd contacted James, they'd be putting him at risk for the same fate. But this went beyond work. This was *James*, and she knew that even now he had to be working to get them both reinstated.

For a moment, she thought Brandon would balk. But then he nodded, the gesture slow and thoughtful. "You're right. We need paramilitary backup. Without James, it's impossible."

She ran a hand through her hair. "Damn, but this sucks. Two weeks before his retirement, and we're going to go tell him the Unit's got a mole."

"It's worse than that," Brandon said. "I think it's Schnell."

Amber exhaled slowly and then nodded. She'd seen that coming.

"I might be wrong," Brandon said. "Any number of operatives could have identified you."

"Identified me, yes," Amber agreed. "But disavowed me?" She shook her head. "Besides, Drake knew when ZAEL ran its test programs. That's how he's able to fire the weapon without detection. And that kind of information is classified."

"And only a few of the higher-ups would have access," Brandon said, thinking aloud.

"Exactly." She wasn't entirely certain Schnell was the mole, but she was damn sure not going to trust him.

"There's more," Brandon added. "I talked to Alcott this morning."

Amber winced. "Not from my phones, I hope." The odds that her lines were tapped were significant.

"Not even on my cell," Brandon said. "I went to the market about dawn and called from the pay phone."

Amber flashed an apologetic smile. She should have known better than to doubt Brandon.

"Whoever reassigned Waterman left an electronic fingerprint. It's part of the training system, so the information tech guys can go in and see which of their operators has screwed-up input. Al just traced the fingerprint back to Schnell's computer."

Amber shook her head. "It just doesn't make any sense. If he was with Drake, why assign me to watch Diana?"

"I think it's exactly what you originally thought," Brandon said. "Nails and pedicures. Drake was going to blow the satellite by himself. Schnell assigned you as an alibi, someone he could point to and say, 'See, I had an agent on it the whole time.' But then Finn came along—"

"And they had to figure out what he knew."

"And they got you, too."

She exhaled, focusing only on the job. Pushing personalities and loyalties from her mind. "Then we're settled, right? We go in, and if we haven't reported back a successful mission on time, James will arrange to have the island destroyed."

"That's it, then. Assuming James agrees." He stood up. "I'm going into town to call him," he said. He paused at the door. "We leave for the island tomorrow afternoon and attack during the night," he said. "Get some rest."

"What the hell else would I do?" she retorted. But as soon as he was gone, she tossed the sheet aside, unhooked the IV bag, and padded downstairs.

"I hope you're finding the accommodations hospitable," Amber said as she walked into the dining room.

Finn put down his coffee, taking a long, hard look at her. Her color was better and her eyes were bright. Her arm was bandaged and bruised from the IV, but that was the only clue that twenty-four hours earlier she'd been seriously under the weather. "The accommodations are exceptional," he said. "This is a great house."

"Thanks. I bought it the first time I visited California. I fell in love with the mountains."

"It's rather secluded," he said.

"All the more reason," Amber answered.

Finn nodded, not surprised with her response. Especially after his talk with Digby, it didn't take a Ph.D. to realize that the woman was a loner. He just wanted her to be alone with him.

Mrs. Digby stepped into the room, an apron tied around her waist and a pistol in her hand. She popped the clip, slipped the gun into the pocket of the apron, and started sliding bullets into the magazine. "Supply kits for you and Mr. Kline?" she asked.

"That's right," Amber said. "And would you join me in the study for a minute? There are a few things we need to discuss."

"Of course," Mrs. Digby answered, then headed toward the far wall lined with a china cabinet. Finn watched as she moved a vase aside to reveal a keypad. Her fingers tapped an entry code, and the entire china cabinet rotated inward.

"Clever," he said.

Amber shrugged, following Mrs. Digby into the room. "I made some refinements."

He stood up to follow, but Amber held out a hand. "Wait here, okay? I'll be back soon."

"Wait? If you two are talking about tomorrow, I want to be in on it."

She shook her head. "Need-to-know basis only. You're not going. You don't need to know." She slipped in the room and the door shut behind her.

Finn pounded his fist on the table. Like hell he wasn't going. He wasn't about to come this far only to get shafted at the end. And if he had to tail Amber all the way to the island, that's what he intended to do.

He had a feeling, though, that persuasion might work just as well. It was, at least, worth a shot.

Knowing she was going to be pissed, he went to the china cabinet and pushed the vase aside. The keypad stared back at him. A standard keypad, typical of what was on the right-hand side of just about any keyboard on any computer. A keypad he knew well.

He closed his eyes, playing back like a video the way Mrs. Digby had tapped the pad. Played it once, then again, and again. His fingers moved as he concentrated, mimicking her pattern, and he opened his eyes long enough to place his hand over the keys, then closed them and moved in that mechanical rhythm.

Nothing happened.

Shit. Okay. No problem. Probably just off a bit. He took a deep breath, closed his eyes, and tried again. A click, and then the mechanical grind of the door creaking open. Thirty seconds later, he was in. *Damn, he was good.*

The cabinet opened onto a short hallway, at the far end of which, Finn could see another door. He sighed, his euphoria dissolving with the realization that the odds were good he was going to have to get through another security system. And he wouldn't have Mrs. Digby's nimble fingers to guide him.

He lucked out, though. The door was cracked open, a sliver of light cutting across the hall. He took a deep breath and pushed it open, and both women turned to stare at him.

"How the hell did you get in here?" Amber asked.

"Same way you two did," he said. "The pass code." He looked from Amber to Mrs. Digby and back again. "What? You're not happy to see me?"

Amber ignored him, turning instead to Mrs. Digby. "Escort Mr. Teague back to the kitchen, please."

Mrs. Digby headed toward the door, nodding at Finn as she passed. "Come along, please."

"Goddamn it, Amber. Hear me out."

"Mrs. Digby." Amber's voice held both exasperation and a command. Finn held his breath, then watched as her shoulders sagged. "Fine," she said. "He stays." She met his eyes. "You can stay. But that doesn't mean you're coming with us."

"Can I at least plead my case?"

He heard Amber's sigh, imagined her steeling herself for the argument he intended to win. After the briefest of hesitation, she nodded. "You've got one minute."

So much for small talk. "Let me see if I've got a handle on your plan," he said. "You and Brandon are going to sneak onto the island, break into the operations center, and put Drake and the bitch out of commission."

"You managed to hit the high points, yes."

"Then what?" he said.

"Excuse me?"

He moved toward her, not stopping until he was standing close enough to feel her breath on his face. Her proximity fired his senses, tightened his neurons. Put him on edge.

Good. Maybe he put her on edge, too. He hoped so. He wanted an honest answer, one she hadn't mulled over and flowcharted and pondered all possible outcomes.

"It's a simple question," he said. "What next? You take control of the satellite, right? Stop it from destroying the mosque? All's well that ends well?"

"Not a bad plan," she said. Her breath hitched, but her eyes were clear and determined. "Wish I'd thought of it."

He grinned. "Doesn't matter who thought of it. The question is, can you do it?"

"I can do a lot of things," she said. "I thought you'd figured that out."

"But can you break into a computer system?"

For the first time since he'd met her, doubt flickered across her face.

"I *can*," he said. "And even more, you know I can."

"I don't need to," she said. "I'm going to blow up the satellite dish."

"What if he's got more than one?" Finn asked.

"We only saw one. And satellite photos confirm that."

"The others could be hidden," Finn said. "And even if there is only one, what if you fail? Plan to blow up the dish, sure. But you need to disable the satellite at the source, too. And I can do that for you."

"The gentleman has a point," Mrs. Digby said, and Finn stifled the urge to kiss her. "I read his dossier. According to the FBI, he's quite adept at maneuvering through even the most secure system."

Amber crossed her arms over her chest. "Maybe so," she said. "But I'll have Bernie to help me," she said.

"Bernie might already be dead," Finn said. He hated giving voice to the possibility, but he had to make her see. She needed him.

She didn't answer, and he pressed his advantage. "Amber, you know I'm right."

"Why?" she said. "This isn't some video game, and it sure as hell isn't fantasy. It's real life, and you might not make it out of there. You could end up hurt. Or dead." She drew in a deep breath and squared her shoulders. "Go home, Finn. Your life may not be exciting, but at least you know it'll be there tomorrow."

"Amber . . ."

"No." She licked her lips. "I don't want you getting hurt, okay? I can't say it any plainer than that."

"Hurt?" Finn shook his head. "Oh, babe, who cares about getting hurt. Unless you get in and stop Drake, that Saudi dude's going to start World War Three. *That* will hurt." He met her eyes. "You need me, Amber."

"No," she said, punctuating the word with a firm shake of her head. "*I* don't." She closed her eyes, exhaling loudly. "But maybe the mission does."

"Then I can come?"

"Looks like I don't have much of a choice."

Finn restrained the urge to punch a victorious fist into the air, doubting that Amber would appreciate the gesture. Besides, while he may have won the battle, he still had to win the war. And he didn't mean the one brewing in the Middle East.

Amber thought she didn't need him. But Finn had a different take on that. They'd save the world. And then he'd get to work on saving the girl.

Twenty-one

Brandon maneuvered the Buick over the curving mountain road with ease, taking the twists and turns at a speed well above the posted thirty miles per hour. He was as worried as Amber about the potential interception of calls from her house or from either of their cell phones, so he didn't mind making the trip. He just wanted to be done and back to the cabin.

He planned to stop at the pay phone near the market in Running Springs, but if he found a phone earlier, that was fine with him. Because of the frequent inclement weather and the possibility of travelers getting stranded, the powers-that-be had installed a few pay phones along the main roads, and Brandon was more than willing to make use of the first one he noticed.

Ostensibly, he wanted to get the message delivered and get back to plan the assault on the island with Amber. In truth, he had an ulterior motive—he'd seen the way she and Finn looked at each other.

He didn't like it.

Not that Brandon had any illusions about having Amber—or any woman—for himself. But he didn't want the Unit to lose a damn good agent to some bullshit notion of a happily ever after. Amber wouldn't be happy shoved behind a desk in a dark basement. And that was true no matter how good in bed Mr. Phineus Teague happened to be.

He rounded a curve at a precarious seventy-three miles per hour, feeling rather giddy when the passenger-side wheels lifted off the pavement. A turnaround came into view, and he noticed the yellow telephone. *Perfect*.

He pulled into the gravel half-moon area that marked the turnaround—a place where slower traffic on the two-lane mountain road could move out of the way of impatient travelers—and twisted the key. He was out of the car and at the phone before the engine quit sputtering.

Brandon dialed, tapping his foot impatiently while he waited for his calling card information to go through.

"James Monahan," came the voice on the other end of the line.

"It's Brandon," he said, thankful he'd reached his mentor. "It's important."

And as he started to give James the rundown of the last couple of days, a shiny black Suburban rounded the corner, pausing at the crest of the hill just above Brandon.

The driver rolled down his window, screwed a silencer on the Glock he always kept in the car, then checked his rearview mirror. All clear. Just then, Brandon turned, his eyes widening with recognition as he saw the car. The driver aimed and fired, hitting Brandon dead center in the chest.

A kill shot, and the agent went down. Without smiling, the driver rolled the window back up, slipped the gun into the glove box, and continued down the road.

Mrs. Digby's bedside manner didn't allow for quibbling, which meant that Finn had the morning to himself while Amber succumbed to strict orders to relax. Since Mrs. Digby was in Amber's hidden study doing God knows what, Finn decided to use the free time productively.

He decided to snoop.

Not so much out of nosiness, but out of self-preservation. Amber seemed confident enough in her ability to get them onto the island, so Finn had to assume that even without Unit 7's blessing, she had access to weapons, transportation, and other stuff like that.

But Finn didn't intend to rely on assumptions. Not when his ass—and Amber's—were on the line.

So he went poking around the house looking for ingredients, containers, components—anything and everything from which he could make a bomb, a noisemaker, *something* to give them the advantage on the island.

He didn't find much. Certainly nothing prefab. If Amber had grenade launchers, flame throwers, or night-vision goggles lurking about, they were hidden behind the china cabinet or in some other secret room he'd yet to discover.

As he expected, the kitchen and the bathroom proved to be the most promising sources for supplies. Apparently Mrs. Digby had a membership to a Sam's Club, because all the basic staples—sugar, salt, dried pasta, beans, even a container of saltpeter—were bought in bulk and stored neatly on shelves in the walk-in pantry.

In a cabinet next to the oven he found Tupperware in a variety of shapes and sizes. The space under the bathroom sink, as he expected, yielded Drano, Ajax, bleach, and a box of wooden matches. The box gave him an idea, and he headed back to the pantry. Sure enough, twenty-four boxes of Strike Anywhere matches were lined up on the bottom shelf, just waiting for Finn to put them to good use.

Unfortunately, though, every idea he had for something that went boom required some ingredient that he couldn't locate. Frustrating. Dozens of pieces, but no way to complete an entire puzzle. If only he had a good solid length of pipe. Or a tennis ball, even.

He frowned, his eyes drifting to the bowl of dog food in the utility room that opened off the kitchen. If he was lucky, Brinkley would prove himself useful.

Finn headed out the side door into the cleared area next to the kitchen. He assumed Brinkley had a dog house and, sure enough, a miniature log cabin designed especially for the four-legged mountain resident was tucked in next to the house between a woodpile and a compost heap. Brinkley wasn't anywhere to be found, so Finn got down on his hands and knees and peered into the dog house. Nothing.

He sat back, balancing on his heels as he let his gaze drift over the yard. If he were a dog, he'd have chew toys, bones, balls, and big pieces of rope to tug on. Finn was only interested in the balls. And it was a long shot, too. Tennis was hardly the sport of choice for a woman like Amber. She was more the rock climbing/skydiving/rappelling down a cliff face type.

Even so, dogs liked tennis balls, and Amber liked Brinkley. So Finn figured it was worth the search. Fifteen minutes later, his persistence was rewarded, and he crawled out from under the front porch with two grungy, bald tennis balls.

Perfect.

Brinkley's barks drifted up from outside, squeezing through the fuzz in Amber's brain. She stretched and yawned and glanced at the clock—already four. She'd slept for hours, and felt another step closer to being human.

With a groan, she hauled herself out of bed, then pulled on jeans and a T-shirt and headed downstairs. She was somewhat surprised that Brandon hadn't poked his head in to update her on James, but knowing him, he was planning the assault and letting her sleep in.

All the more reason to head downstairs; Amber hated being left out of anything.

She found Finn on the porch, a tennis ball in his lap, Brinkley bouncing around Finn's chair like he was hyped up on speed. Amber laughed, shaking her head. "You're tormenting him," she said. She picked up the second ball, the one on the table next to Finn, planning to toss it into the side yard. But just as she grabbed it up, Finn caught her hand, his fingers closing gently over the ball.

"Probably best not to do that," he said.

She frowned, then peered more closely at the ball. A small hole had been cut through the rubber, and she squinted, realizing that it was chock full of match heads. She looked at Finn, her brows drawn together.

He shrugged. "I couldn't find Mrs. Digby, and I wasn't certain how well stocked you were. So Brinkley volunteered to let me turn his toys into bombs."

She licked her lips, the gesture designed to hide her amusement. "He volunteered, huh?"

Finn nodded gravely. "Absolutely." He glanced at the ball in his lap. "I'm working on the second one now. And I found some saltpeter in your pantry, so I made a couple of smoke bombs, too." He nodded toward the kitchen. "They're cooling in the fridge."

"Yummy," she said.

"Yeah, well, I figured the matches sticking out of them will keep you and Mrs. Digby from mistaking them for tiny popsicles."

"I'm impressed," she said. And, in truth, she was. Although her training had included the basic chemistry of explosives, she'd never had a need to cook her own supplies. It impressed her that not only did Finn have the skill, but that he'd taken the initiative. "What did Brandon say about all this?"

"Nothing," Finn said. "I haven't seen him." He looked at her face. "I take it that's not good?"

She shook her head. "I don't know." She headed

for the railing and looked down at the valley spread out below, as if Brandon would somehow emerge from the treetops. Brinkley padded over, then stood up on his hind legs, his fuzzy paws on the redwood rail as she idly scratched behind his ears.

Finn followed, swinging his arm around her shoulder. She pulled away, disconcerted by how right it felt to be in Finn's arms.

"Amber?" He turned to face her, disappointment simmering in his eyes.

"James may have called him in to debrief the air support guys. He's probably just in Los Angeles." She glanced at her watch. "I'll give him three more hours and then call."

She looked up at Finn, saw that his brow was creased, then remembered that he hadn't been privy to her and Brandon's plans. "If we're unsuccessful," she said, "James is going to arrange to bomb the island. At least, that's our plan." She cocked her head, meeting his eyes. "We may not get off in time. Are you sure you want to go along?"

"I'm sure."

She met his eyes, undone by the intensity of desire reflected there—both for her and for joining the mission. She shook her head. "Finn—"

He pressed a fingertip to her lips, silencing her, then slid his hand around to cup her neck. His lips met hers before she had time to think, to react. The frantic call of reason, telling her to back off, to escape, was lost in a haze of pleasure that filled her senses, conquering the last bits of the pain that still lingered in her body.

"Amber," he murmured, breaking the kiss and brushing his lips over her hair.

The sound of her name rang in her ears, his voice, so filled with want, with need.

For her.

She put her hands against his chest and pushed away, breaking not only the connection, but the magic. She watched his face, her own sadness growing as his features hardened. "I'm sorry," she said, wanting to be the first one to speak. "I can't do this. We want different things."

"I want you. You want me."

She shook her head. "No."

"Yes," he said. "And don't tell me that nothing can come of it, because that's not the point. Not yet." He ran a hand through his hair, and she could see the frustration building. "Tell me, then. Tell me straight out that you *don't* want me. Tell me that, and you'll never hear another word from me about it again."

She pressed her lips together, wishing she could say exactly that. It would be so simple. One little lie and her problem would be solved. She'd lied to him before; hell, she lied almost every day of her professional life.

But the words just wouldn't come.

"You see?" he said. "I was right."

She quirked an eyebrow, then sat down on the deck, her feet tucked under her. Brinkley trotted over and laid his head on her thigh, silently demanding that she pet him. She complied, burying her fingers in his scraggly fur. "You two are a lot alike," she said, lifting her head just long enough to meet Finn's eyes.

"Yeah," he said, kneeling down to pet the dog as well. "We both slobber all over you."

She laughed. "That, too," she said. She bent closer to Brinkley, receiving his sloppy dog kiss. "What I meant is that you both wandered into my life. I kept him. But I can't keep you. The Unit—"

"Doesn't allow it. I know. Mrs. Digby told me. But there has to be some way we can make this work."

"Why? You don't always get what you want in life, Finn. Believe me. Sometimes you have to make hard choices."

"Amber, I—"

"How?" she interrupted. "Just tell me how we can make it work." She didn't look at him, afraid that her eyes would reflect too much hope. Because right then she wanted him to have the answer. Because she sure as hell didn't.

He stayed silent.

She knew she'd made her point, but she drove it home anyway. "Suppose you were me," she said. "Would you just walk away from the Unit?" She met his eyes. "Would you?"

He didn't answer. Instead, he stood back up, propping his arms on the porch railing as he looked out over the valley.

"I didn't think so." Amber climbed to her feet, a weariness in her bones that had nothing to do with her illness. She brushed a light kiss against his cheek, fighting the urge to cling to him, holding tight throughout the night. Instead, she moved back toward the house. "Get some sleep. We've got a big day tomorrow."

She didn't turn back to look at him, afraid that her eyes would betray her. Instead, she walked straight into the house and into her study, locking the passage behind her.

* * *

He needed to rest, he knew that, but sleep didn't
come easy. Instead, Finn tossed in the bed, as if his
body was searching for some perfect position from
which he could slide into slumber, and yet never
managing to find it.

Amber's words filtered through his mind, tormenting him. Not only because he wanted her with
such a palpable, physical need, but because she was
absolutely right. There was no way. Not unless she
gave up her dream or deceived the Unit entirely.
And considering they were talking about an intelligence agency, that type of deception didn't seem too
likely.

How could he ask her to give up the very dream
he coveted? Especially when he couldn't answer the
question posed to him: *Would he turn them down
and walk away?*

He didn't know. He honestly didn't. He'd decided
against applying to the FBI because of his mother,
and he'd regretted the decision for most of his life.
Could he walk away from the Unit for Amber? He
liked to think that he could; liked to think that he
was the type of man who would value relationships
over career. But it was easy to make those decisions
in bed in the dark.

The real test would come only when he was
asked to join. And that wasn't a test with which he
was ever likely to be faced.

Frustrated, he forced himself to lay perfectly still
on his back, his eyes closed. The sounds of Amber's
house settled around him. The gentle scrape of the
pine boughs against the wooden frame of the
house. The whoosh of plumbing. The soft thud of

footsteps on the stairs. The creak of hinges on his door.

He sat up, squinting into the darkness. "Amber?"

No answer, but the soft pad of footsteps sounded on the wooden floor. Finn's heart picked up tempo, and he slid his hand under his pillow, frustrated when he didn't discover a gun. Didn't Amber know she should keep all her beds stocked with weapons?

"It's me," she said, barely a shadow framed in the window.

Finn relaxed back into the pillows. "This probably isn't the best of circumstances to sneak up on somebody."

"Sorry." Her weight settled on the bed, then the covers shifted as she got in, curling her body next to his. "Can I make it up to you?"

His body caught fire, burning with the heat of desire. A heat he had no intention of cooling. "What are you doing here?" he asked, unable to keep the harsh tone out of his voice.

She shifted away, moving to sit up and turn on the small reading light next to the bed. The light filtered from behind, illuminating her hair like an angel. Finn had to smile. Amber was a lot of things, but an angel, she wasn't.

"You're angry," she said simply. "I'm sorry."

He closed his eyes, feeling like an ass. "Yes. But not at you. I had no right to make demands on you. I just want—"

He broke off. The truth was, he wanted everything. The life he'd tasted, and this woman who'd come to mean more to him in such a short time than he could have possibly imagined. *He loved her.* Oh, God, he really loved her, and the realization hit him with stunning clarity. He loved her, and he couldn't have her. No matter how much he wanted her.

"I know," she said, stroking his cheek. "I want, too."

He breathed in deep, wondering if that could really be true, afraid to hope. "What? What do you want?"

"You," she said simply. "And the whole picture. A life I can't really have." She propped herself up on one elbow. "What do you think? Can you ever be truly happy if you don't have everything you want?"

He laughed. "I sure hope so," he said, then frowned at her. "Have you gotten everything you wanted before now?"

"I don't know," she said. "I never really thought about it."

"And now? What do you want now?"

She kissed her fingertips, then pressed her fingers against his lips. "I told you," she said. "I want everything. But barring that, I want you. Inside me. Now."

His body heated and hardened. He wanted her, too. Lord, how he wanted to sink inside this woman and lose himself. But that would be like tasting forbidden fruit, enticing a craving he'd never, ever be able to completely satisfy.

He kissed the top of her head, pulling her down beside him. "Oh, babe. I want that, too."

"But . . ."

"But I can't."

"You're not that kind of guy?" The words were spoken with a tease, but he answered them seriously.

"I used to be," he said. "Consider me reformed."

"Yeah," she said, the word barely a sigh. "Me, too. At least a little." She rolled over, facing him, her eyes gentle but serious. "You were right. About the first time. About us."

He nodded, not wanting to interrupt.

"I mean, I wanted you. Believe me. But it was also my job. Do you know I've never had sex—ever—without it being either a lark or part of a bigger picture? "

He turned to face her but didn't say a word.

"I was thirteen when James recruited me," she said. "And before then, I'd been a bad girl in all sorts of ways, but I was still a virgin. Sex for me became a tool of my trade. Enjoyable, sure. But always for some purpose. Power. Information. Stress relief. Something. It was never . . . personal."

He squeezed her hand, afraid that if he spoke, she'd clam up, quit confiding in him.

"With you . . . now . . ." She trailed off, then shrugged. "I don't do fear," she said. "And I'm not scared of going back to the island tomorrow. But you, Finn. You scare the hell out of me. Because with you, it is. It is personal."

Finn closed his eyes and pulled her closer. What could he say? Because the truth was, she scared the hell out of him, too.

Twenty-two

"Any luck?" Amber padded into the study in bare feet, her jeans frayed around her ankles and Finn's T-shirt thrown on for warmth.

Mrs. Digby looked up, noted the shirt, and turned back to the computer monitor. "Nothing." A pause, then, "I recommend a V-neck for a woman of your figure. Much more flattering than a crew."

Amber stifled a grin. She and Finn hadn't done any more than sleep in each other's arms. But still, Mrs. Digby's words were a solid opening, and she took it. "Did you ever regret your decision?"

Mrs. Digby didn't even pretend to misunderstand. "Never," she said. She maneuvered the mouse, the computer screen reflecting back on her face in the dim light of the room. She clicked the mouse, typed something, then turned to face Amber. "But we're different people, you and I."

Amber nodded in understanding. No easy answers. This one, she had to figure out all on her own. Somehow, the prospect seemed daunting. An odd reaction, she supposed, for a woman who'd spent her entire life essentially alone.

Mrs. Digby tapped out a few more strokes on the keyboard, then turned again to Amber, a bemused expression on her face. "You're lucky I'm retired," she said. "They'd fire me for this."

Amber grimaced, then crossed the room, coming up behind the other woman, who was deep into Unit 7's e-mail system. Amber had discovered James's administrative password years ago, but she'd never before used it. Now, however, she had Mrs. Digby searching for e-mails on the network that mentioned Drake or Prometheus.

"Anything?"

"I'm afraid not." Her expression turned concerned. "Did Brandon contact you yet?"

Amber shook her head, a crush of fear pressing against her chest. Brandon had never in his life failed to check in. But he had now. And Amber had been around the block enough to know what that meant. She closed her eyes, fighting a wave of grief.

Mrs. Digby pushed her glasses in place, all business. "I think it's safe to assume that Brandon isn't coming back." She spoke the words matter-of-factly, but Amber could hear the undertone of sadness.

Amber nodded, closing the pain off to some dark part of herself to deal with later. After the mission was over, she'd grieve for her friend. Right now, she had no time.

"Should we go after him?" Finn's voice.

Amber whirled. "Dammit, Finn. I thought you were asleep."

"I woke up." He moved toward her, jeans slung low on his hips, his chest bare since she was wearing his shirt. "I heard. I'm sorry." He took her hand and gave it a gentle squeeze. "He might not be dead. We can try to track him down."

"Thank you." She stroked his cheek, genuinely moved by his concern. "But we can't. We don't have time. We have to go forward with the mission."

"Do we change the plan?"

She shook her head. "No." She looked up at him, stifling the urge to insist he stay behind. This one was going to be dangerous, and losing both Finn and Brandon was more than she could bear. But he was right. She did need him. Unfortunately for her, she needed him in more ways than one.

Amber turned back to the computer, fearful she was making a mistake by taking Finn along, but at the same time sure that she wasn't. That, somehow, was even scarier. Finn kept creeping into her life, and now into her job. And when this was all over, she only hoped she had the strength to show him to the exit.

Numbers and letters scrolled across the monitor, and she blinked, forcing herself to focus on the problem at hand. She could deal with Finn after they got back. *If* they made it back.

She'd undertaken a lot of risky missions over the course of her career, but this was the first one that truly bordered on suicidal. With the mole, however, she didn't see any other option.

She turned to Mrs. Digby. "I need to get in touch

with James. I have no way of knowing if Brandon got through to him to arrange our backup."

"James might *be* the mole," Finn pointed out. "Or . . ." he trailed off.

"Brandon might." Amber finished the thought for him, her voice flat. "I know. But I don't think so."

Logically, she knew he was right, but she simply couldn't believe it. Emotion wasn't a good enough reason, though, and so she recited the facts. "All the evidence seems to lead back to Schnell. He reclassified Bernie, he was in the military with Drake. It's pathetic, but that's how the chips are stacking up."

Finn's expression remained dubious, but he moved on to other subjects. "The island's two hundred miles off the Pacific coast, and we're up in the mountains. How are we getting there?"

Amber looked at Mrs. Digby. Her expression was not encouraging. "I've had very little luck so far," the woman said. "I'll keep trying, but I'm afraid most of my usual channels are compromised."

"Tom," Finn said.

Amber raised an eyebrow. "You want to fly to the island in a biplane?"

"A chopper," he said. "His works just fine."

"Does it have enough range to get us there and get him back to the mainland?"

"Back?"

She met his eyes, sure she knew what he was thinking. "We find our own way off," she said. "If we don't make it, I'm not going to be responsible for Tom getting plugged by the bomb, too."

"Right," he said. "Of course." He nodded. "The range is good. He'll get back to the mainland with fuel to spare."

Amber met Mrs. Digby's eyes. The older woman shrugged.

"He'll, uh, want to know what's up," Finn said. "Other than that, I'm sure he'll do the run for free."

"What's up?" she repeated. "And you expect me to tell him?"

"Well, hell, sweetheart. We're already dealing with a mole. What's one stunt pilot in San Diego knowing the true story going to hurt?"

She glared at him, but the truth was, he had a point. She was just about to say so when Mrs. Digby spoke first.

"Amber." Her voice was harsh, a demand, and Amber forgot all about Tom as she peered over the other woman's shoulder.

She drew in a quick breath, her muddled mind processing what she was seeing on the monitor—someone had breached security. Someone uninvited was in her house.

She turned to Finn. "Stay here," she said. "And whatever you do, don't leave this room."

Amber crept up the stairs to her bedroom, hoping that she'd open the door to find Brandon, but somehow knowing that wasn't going to happen. She'd brought her gun, and now she held it at the ready.

She'd left the door open upon leaving, but now it was closed, and she eyed it suspiciously. The mole? Drake? Who the hell had found her hideaway?

In a quick move, she reached out and twisted the knob, pushing the door open just enough for the latch to disengage. She stepped back, gun aimed at the portal, and waited for someone to approach.

Nothing.

Here we go. With the tip of the barrel, she nudged the door open, letting the gun enter first, the rest of her body following. She switched the light on, then arced the gun in a covering pattern.

James was sitting in her armchair, his expression both amused and proud.

With a sigh of both relief and irritation, she lowered the gun. "Goddamn it," she said, but she wasn't really angry. On the contrary, she wanted to lay all her problems out at his feet and have him tell her they'd get through this, just like they had every other seemingly impossible mission. She drew in a breath. "What are you doing hiding out up here?"

"We need to talk," he said. "I couldn't call ahead."

She nodded in understanding. Considering her status, her phones were likely tapped. And if James were seen with her, his reputation would be shot, too.

"Did you come to commiserate with me?"

"There's a mole in Unit 7," he said, not answering her question.

Amber frowned as she moved to the foot of her bed. "I know."

A look of concern and then suspicion crossed his face. She held up her hands, unable to believe what she knew he was thinking. "For God's sake, James, it isn't me," she protested. But even in the protest, she felt a bit of relief, and she realized that—just a little—she'd wondered if it was him. Even the shadow of that thought seemed disloyal, and she hated herself for it.

His expression immediately shifted to contrite. "I know. I know, of course I know." He ran a hand through his hair, looking more frazzled than she'd ever seen him. "But Brandon . . ." He tilted his head up as he trailed off, the overhead light deepening the shadows under his eyes. He looked exhausted, and more than ready for his looming retirement. "Someone took him out. While he was on the phone." He closed his eyes as if to blot out a memory. "Talking to me."

Amber shook her head slowly, trying to process his words, trying to stay in professional mode. "Tell me."

He rubbed his temples. "That's all I know. He'd barely started talking when—" He cut himself off, pain flashing in his eyes. "What is going on? First you two are disavowed, and now Brandon's . . . dead. What do you know, and why does someone want you dead?"

Amber swallowed, her thoughts absurdly drifting to Finn. Her world was crashing down around her ears, and more than anything, she wanted him there with her, his presence a rock in the sudden storm. She shook her head, irritated by her own foolishness. The Unit's demise was a problem—a big one—but she could worry about that after she pulled Drake's plug. "Drake Mackenzie is about to start a war in the Middle East," she said, then gave him the rundown on what she and Finn had learned on the island. "Whatever's wrong in the Unit can wait. I have to stop this."

The lines creasing James's face deepened. "Shit. No wonder they want you dead." His frown tightened. "Do you know who? Have you discovered the mole?"

Amber closed her eyes. "Not for certain," she

said. She looked at James, about to indict his friend. "But everything points to Schnell."

James flinched. After a moment, he nodded slowly. "Well, that makes it trickier, doesn't it?"

"Trickier?"

"I can't just go through the Unit to authorize military deployment and blow the island."

"No. You can't."

"I have other contacts. Give me a few hours."

She shook her head. "No. I have to go. Make your calls, yes. But only as a contingency in case I fail."

"Amber, that's a suicide mission."

"Hear me out," she said, pacing the room. "If you call on your resources, you'll be aligned with me, and I'm disavowed. Not a good position for you, and I don't want you taking the risk unless it's truly necessary. I want you as backup in case I can't disable Drake's satellite connection. Not before."

He shook his head. "I'll still have to be ready. I'm going to have to call in some favors either way."

She nodded. "I know. I'm just hoping you'll stay under the radar if you never have to follow through." She took a deep breath. "There's another reason I have to go—I have to clear my name. If I can prevent this, I'll be reinstated."

He shook his head, his usually unreadable face sad.

"James, you know I'm right." She pressed her lips together. "The Unit is my life. Hell, you know that better than anyone. I have to go."

He was quiet another minute, and she feared he was going to argue. But then he got up, crossed the room, and stood right in front of her. "You don't deserve this, Amber."

She managed a watery smile, even as he pressed his palms to either side of her face and then brushed a kiss across her forehead. Amber blinked, unfamiliar tears welling in her eyes as she leaned up against him, this man who'd been like a father to her. The one man in the world she knew she could always turn to.

"Do you have weapons? Transportation?"

"Already on it," Amber answered. She didn't have much in the way of weapons at the house, but she had basic firearms and explosives. "I've got enough to get us in and blow up the dish."

She stepped back, standing up straight. The time for sentimentality was over.

"And this Teague fellow?"

Amber frowned. "What about him?"

"What agency is he with? Has he notified *his* superior?"

She almost laughed. "He's a civilian."

"A civilian," James repeated, his voice flat. "Is he here?"

"Yes."

His brow furrowed. "Is he going with you?"

She conjured a laugh. "Of course not." She'd never lied to James before, and she didn't intend to do it again. But Finn defied explanation. She'd satisfied herself that she was doing the right thing by taking him along. She wasn't about to waste time satisfying James as well. "Digby will babysit him while I'm gone. That's one of her many talents."

"Good. Tell her to keep him away from the telephone. There's still the possibility he's working with Drake and Schnell. I don't want him alerting them to your arrival on the island."

"They must already know," she said.

"Yes, but not when or how. I want you to retain some modicum of surprise."

She nodded, standing up, ready to get back to it. "Fair enough." She headed to her bed and ripped the copyright page out of the book on her night-stand. In the white space, she scribbled the island's coordinates. "Your men will need this."

He glanced at it, then pocketed the note. "Amber," he said, taking her hand.

"I know."

He closed his eyes, exhaling through his nose. "Just be careful. I've lost Brandon. I don't want to lose you, too."

They spent another hour discussing the details, and after James left, Amber sat on her bed, hugging her knees to her chest and thinking of Brandon. *Dead.* She'd never imagined this moment; couldn't imagine it now. What she *could* imagine was making Drake pay. And Schnell. She'd avenge Brandon. No matter what, she'd do that.

She drew a deep breath, shoving thoughts of retribution from her mind. She didn't have time to think about it. She had a mission to plan. They were leaving tomorrow, timing their arrival at the island with the onset of night. Anything to give them more cover. Once on the island, they had three hours to get in and disable the satellite. It came into firing range at oh-two-hundred hours. If they hadn't taken control by midnight, James would send the missiles flying.

Amber didn't intend to fail.

And so the day was filled with plans and with

rest. With making sure all the details were in order and her body was as healthy as she could make it.

Finn was busy preparing, too, happily hacking into various government agencies from the computer in her study, trying to find keys and clues that would help him crack the system on the island. If anyone at those agencies discovered his forays into their cyber world and traced it back to her computer, Amber was going to have some serious explaining to do.

As night fell and she headed back upstairs, thoughts of Brandon and Schnell edged into her mind. The anger was still there, coupled with a deep sadness. The Unit was changing. Shifting into something she didn't know, and she was losing her anchor on the world.

She paused outside her bedroom, her hand hesitating over the doorknob. She was being foolish, and she knew it, and she tried to force herself to go on in. To get sleep. To rest. To prepare.

But alone simply wasn't where she wanted to be.

The doorknob rested cool in her palm, but still she couldn't seem to turn it. Instead, she paused, looking back over her shoulder to Finn's room, just a few steps away. Light shone from under the door. He was still awake, and yet she hesitated.

The night before, they'd held each other, but they hadn't made love. Neither one had wanted to cross that line, starting something that could never be finished.

Now she wanted to go to him again, but still she hesitated, craving intimacy, even as much as she wanted to run from it.

She was still standing there, undecided, when his

door opened and Finn emerged wearing a pair of Brandon's old sweatpants and holding a toothbrush. He paused when he saw her, his expression shifting to concerned. "Amber? Are you all right?"

"I'm fine." She licked her lips, then shoved her hands deep into the pockets of her jeans. "No, I'm not fine. I was standing here trying to decide if I should knock on your door."

"Yes," he said. "If that's the question, the answer is always yes."

She followed him, feeling slightly pathetic for wanting his company, and at the same time absurdly grateful that he was there.

"Something's happened," he said, moving to sit on the bed.

"Yes and no," she said. She sat down beside him, sliding her bare feet under the covers and leaning back against the headboard.

"More yes, or more no?"

She smiled. She'd been certain that he'd be able to lighten her mood, and so far, she was right. "Nothing's happened as to the mission. We're on target in that regard." She turned to him. "Learn anything interesting today?"

He shrugged. "Some. I've got some clues about the system. And I think Waterman put in more than one back door. The only question is how to access it."

"That's good, though, right? Then even if Drake's closed one door, we can still get in."

Finn nodded. "Assuming I can get inside. I learned a lot of stuff about Bernie by poking around in his personal area on the ZAEL mainframe. I have no idea if any of it will help. Stuff about his family and classes he's taken and books he's read. We'll see." He frowned. "And there was one particularly odd e-mail."

She frowned. "What?"

"A draft Bernie was going to send to some-one named Armstrong. Something about taking Prometheus to the moon."

She shrugged. "Probably some sort of code for the fact that it's a space-based weapon's system."

"That makes sense." Finn took her hand. "I'm sorry. I got sidetracked. You're upset about Brandon."

She nodded. She'd told him what James had reported about the phone call. "That's part of it. The rest . . . I think it's you."

"Me?"

"Yeah." She paused, trying to figure out how to put the swell of raw emotion into words. "I've always considered the Unit my family. But it's not. No matter how many lies I told myself, no matter what I clung to, from the moment my mom gave me up, I was really and truly alone."

"Oh, babe." He put an arm around her, pulling her close.

She shook her head, trying out a small smile. "Don't worry about me. Just late-night ruminations before a mission."

"It's more than that," Finn said. "And I can't help but worry about you." He reached out and stroked her cheek, the unexpected touch flooding her senses. "Why are you here? An ear? Or more?"

"More," she confessed. She took a deep breath. "Is it wrong of me to come to you? To want to just lose myself in this?" She took his hand, her fingers intertwining with his. "I want you to make love to me."

"Amber, I—"

"Just hear me out," she said. "I want to make love because *I* want to make love. Not because it's the job. We might never leave that island, Finn, so do we really want to worry about what will happen in that magical land of ever after? I don't. I want you. I want you now and, if always turns out to be the span of just two days, I want you for always."

"And if always turns out to be longer?"

But that one she couldn't answer. Because despite everything, the Unit was still the life she knew.

Finn shook his head. "Don't bother answering," he said. "I get the drift."

"Finn . . ." She closed her fingers over his wrist.

His body tensed, his fingertips dancing so softly over her skin that she barely even registered his touch. "I shouldn't."

"But you're going to."

"Yeah," he said, then brushed his lips across hers. "I am."

Finn knew Amber was tired and upset; and he knew only that he wanted to make it better. It thrilled him—no, *touched* him—that she'd come to him for consolation. But he couldn't tell her that, couldn't tell her how much it meant to him that she'd revealed a vulnerable side.

He simply let his body talk for him, every stroke and caress a promise that he would never, ever hurt her. There was more, too, as much as he was ashamed to admit it. Tonight, she needed him.

Tomorrow, though . . . well, tomorrow was Amber's show. He'd pulled off successful missions in his fantasies, but Finn wasn't naïve enough to think that he was really qualified for this mission. The best he could hope for was not to hinder Amber, and maybe to help just a little.

And so he made love to her confidently, passionately. As if by taking her to heights to which she'd never ventured, he could somehow make up for any inadequacies he might bring to their mission tomorrow.

Twenty-three

Finn checked the helicopter's bearing, satisfied they were on course.

"You wanna cut that out?" Tom said. "I'll get you there." His grin was wide and eager. Finn's hunch that Tom would make the trip gratis—so long as he got the full story—had been right on the money.

Finn sighed. Tom sure as hell didn't need Finn's help to pilot the whirlybird. And Finn still wasn't at all certain that Amber needed his help to stop Drake.

Tom shot him a look. "What's on your mind, kid?"

"Not much," Finn said. "Just that I'm a fraud who ought to be home answering interrogatories, not skimming the ocean in a G model Bell."

"Bullshit." Tom tossed him a set of headphones, slipping his own back up and over his ears. Finn did the same, allowing them to talk to each other through the headset rather than trying to yell over the din of the rotors and the wind. "You know how to fly a plane, you know how to make a bomb. You ski, you dive, and you're healthy as a horse. What the hell more do you need? An on-line diploma from www.be-a-spy.com?" Chuckling, Tom shook his head, clearly amused with himself. Finn just rolled his eyes.

"I'm serious," Tom continued. "You don't think I'd risk my own neck flying you two out here if I thought you'd end up dead?"

"No," Finn said, managing a grin. "But I never said you were smart."

Tom laughed, his voice booming through the headset. "Quit fretting. You've got more important things to worry about than whether or not you should be here. You *are* here. Now just get in there and do it."

Finn nodded. That was sage advice. "Well then, get us there, already. This downtime isn't good for my disposition. I think too much."

"Always a dangerous thing." Tom checked the controls. "Not too much longer. I'm going to drop down, bring you in at just a few feet above the water. Just in case your friend's got radar."

"More than likely, he's got sentries posted."

"Can't shield us from those," Tom said. "But the sun's just about down. By the time we get to the island, you should have some cover of night. On top of that, well, I guess we'll just have to hope they're nearsighted." He motioned Finn out of the cockpit. "Get back there and get your gear on."

Finn tossed his headphones into the copilot's

seat, then complied. They were descending quickly, and his stomach lurched. *Great*. What a time to get motion sickness.

Amber squatted near the door wearing a one-piece Speedo. "You look a little green."

"I'm fine." He peeled off his jeans, revealing his own bathing suit. Their clothes were packed into airtight bags. Hopefully they'd have time to change once they reached the island. Finn didn't relish the idea of disarming the satellite in a tiny little Lycra bathing suit.

"Yes," she said, her gaze drifting down to his crotch as a smile played across her face. "I'd have to say you're very fine indeed."

He chuckled, his mood dissipating some. "No time for that," he said, sitting on the floor as he tugged on his wet suit.

"Too bad," she countered, her eyes bright. She was in her element, all right. She looked on-fire. Alive. And he wished they *did* have time. For all he knew, they might not be leaving the island. Last night might well have been the last time.

No. He couldn't think like that. They would leave. They'd leave together. He could do this. His doubts were just nerves. *He could do this*.

She met his eyes. "I only work with the best, Finn," she said, then stood up and gave the zipper on her wet suit a tug.

He couldn't help but smile as he finished putting on his own gear. The woman had a way of reading his mind. "Are you sure, then, that you want to be working with me?"

"You're here, aren't you?" She slipped her arms into the BC, then fastened the vest around her waist, adjusting it so the tank sat properly on her back. When he didn't answer, she turned and gave him another look. "And don't pull that bullshit about how you forced your way into this party. Believe me. If I didn't want you here, you wouldn't be here."

She lowered her mask over her eyes, then put the regulator in her mouth, silently signaling that their conversation was at an end. She'd said what she had to say; Finn would either believe it or he wouldn't.

Finn decided to believe it.

She clamped her hand over her face, using her palm to hold the regulator in place while her fingers kept her mask on. Then she took one giant step out the helicopter's door, splashing down into the ocean below. She went under, bobbed back up, and flashed him an okay sign.

Now or never. This was it. This was the real deal. No fantasies. No daydreaming. No Agent Python calling the shots. Just him and Amber, out to save the world.

He chuckled to himself. When you put it like that, what the hell was there to be nervous about?

The ocean floor sloped up to the island, and they stayed low. The surge was strong, pushing and pulling, and inching them toward the beach. She spotted a craggy outcropping of underwater rock up ahead and let the ocean's power take her there, her gloved fingers grasping the barnacled surface. Finn followed suit, maneuvering himself so that he faced her. They were both still under the water, hopefully still unseen. An efficient sentry might notice their exhaust bubbles or the greenish glow of their light sticks. It was a chance they had to take.

She pointed to Finn, then held out a hand, signaling for him to stay put. She pointed to herself and then the surface. Then she pointed to him and flashed an open hand three times.

He flashed the okay sign, and she nodded, hoping that he meant it. They'd discussed the plan on the plane, and she had no specific reason to doubt that he'd understood. But still she was nervous. She'd knowingly brought a civilian on a mission. At the time it had seemed prudent. Now, she hoped her decision wouldn't turn out to be fatal. For him, or for her.

With Finn stationed firmly by the rock, she tugged on the release valve of her BC, letting the air out of the inflatable vest. Then she slipped it off, along with the air tank that was attached to it. Fortunately, the tank was made of steel. An aluminum tank, once low on air, was likely to float to the surface.

She jammed the whole contraption against the rock, the regulator still in her mouth as she took her last tug of air from the tank. Then she released the mouthpiece and replaced it with her snorkel. Keeping her eyes on Finn, she ascended the few feet to the surface, working hard to keep her body underwater even as the tip of her snorkel emerged so that she could breathe.

Just below her, Finn whipped off a crisp little salute. She grinned—as much as she could without swallowing water—and gave him a thumbs-up sign.

Time to go. Hopefully Finn understood the mission. Wait fifteen minutes, and then follow. Amber was heading toward the satellite dish they'd seen on the bunker by the landing strip. Finn was heading into the building. One way or another, they'd keep Prometheus from firing. Either Finn would disarm the system at the computer, or Amber would blow up the dish.

She checked her watch. Five after nine. Less than four hours before the satellite came into range. And three hours before James's Black Ops contacts took out the island all together.

That left them almost sixty minutes to get in position, do their jobs, disarm the satellite, and contact James to call off the missile and come deliver them off the island. Fortunately, Amber worked best under pressure.

She smiled to herself. In that case, this was going to be her best mission ever.

The sun was beginning to set, casting long shadows across the beach. She dropped her weight belt and pulled off her fins, holding on to them so they wouldn't wash up to shore and give her away. With a practiced eye, she scanned the area. There was no cover, and that meant that she had to get from the beach to the rocky outcropping by virtue of pure good fortune. No sentries, no glimmers of light suggesting binoculars reflecting the fading sunlight. No whispers.

Time to haul ass.

With the surge pushing her forward, she emerged onto the beach, climbing immediately to her feet and running like hell. She scrambled over the rocks and crouched down, taking a moment to assess her progress. So far, so good. Her gaze drifted to the water. She thought she could make out the very tip of Finn's snorkel, but she wasn't certain. A good sign. He was well hidden. Hopefully he'd blend in as unobtrusively once he actually entered Drake's complex.

She needed to head up the stone steps to the plateau. It was risky, but that was faster than climbing the rock face. Decided, she shoved her fins under some sand, burying them, then covering them with loose rocks. Then she unfastened her dive knife and peeled off the wet suit. That left her clad in a wet bathing suit, which she also peeled off. A black Lycra cat suit, shoes, her gun, the C-4, and a lightweight backpack were in the watertight bag she'd hooked onto her utility belt. She dressed, then slipped on a shoulder holster and slid the gun home. Next, she strapped the dive knife back to her calf. The explosives she moved to the backpack, then donned it, too.

Once she was suited up and her leftover belongings buried in the sand, she took off for the dish. A nearly full moon hung in the sky, hidden behind a thick covering of clouds that left the island cast in a murky gray that seemed more impenetrable than full darkness.

She got to the airstrip without event, then checked her watch. Fifteen minutes. Finn should just be emerging from the water. She grimaced, fighting the urge to go back and make sure he was okay. She'd made the decision to bring him. Now she had to trust him.

The dish was huge, looming on the far side of the airfield. Stark white, it seemed to gather and reflect back all of the ambient light, giving it the appearance of a small moon hovering somewhere above the island.

An expensive, powerful piece of equipment, it was almost a shame to destroy it. Almost.

She raced across the open airfield, reaching the building on which the dish sat forty-five seconds later. It had taken her a total of nineteen minutes to emerge from the water, gather her gear, and get to the dish. And in all that time she hadn't seen any sign of a sentry, a guard, or even one of Drake's computer geeks outside smoking a cigarette.

She had a bad feeling.

The dish wasn't designed to be accessed by anyone who happened to be walking by. So there was no ladder, stairs, or other easy access from the supporting base structure to the actual dish component that captured and relayed signals. Fortunately, the designer had considered the possibility of maintenance and repair, and a series of foot and handholds were built into the metal structure of the base, leading up to a trapdoor in the dish itself.

Ideally, Amber would make her way through the trapdoor, then plant the C-4 in the center of the dish. A nice, neat bit of sabotage.

Today, however, Amber wasn't interested in neat. She climbed up to the roof of the building and stayed low as she got close to the base of the dish. She'd brought two pounds of C-4 and eight detonators, and she proceeded to pack the explosive around the base. Once they were in place, she'd set the timer on the primary detonator, which would relay the signal to the other seven. She'd run like hell, and in six minutes, the structure wouldn't be good for anything more than toasting marshmallows and making s'mores.

As soon as she put the last brick of C-4 into place, she reached into her backpack for the primary detonator.

"I wouldn't do that if I were you." The voice was hard, cold, and all too familiar.

Amber closed her eyes, calculating the odds of success if she set the detonator for five seconds, jammed it home, and went up in a ball of smoke with the dish.

It wouldn't be a personal best, but she would prevent a war.

Unfortunately, though (or fortunately, she supposed, if she wanted to be selfish about it), there was no way she could get the timer on the device set. Not before Beltzer blew her brains out. Dying in the course of her job to prevent a war she could handle. Dying because she did something stupid . . . that just wasn't her speed.

"Drop it," he said.

She did. And even as the detonator clattered on the warm asphalt, she wondered if Finn had made it into the complex. Because right then, Finn was their best hope.

Finn was absolutely certain he was capable of hacking into the computer system and shutting down the satellite. Whether or not his certainty was justified remained to be seen. Because while he was confident in his abilities once he infiltrated the control room, the initial problem of how the hell to get inside the complex left him baffled.

He'd made it to the complex entrance easily enough, but the building was equipped with one of those damn touch pads. If he had a few hours, he could probably hot-wire the thing. But he had no idea how much time he had before a sentry patrol came marching by. If Mackenzie was smart, Finn imagined he had a sentry patrol at least every fifteen minutes. Since Drake was practically a genius, Finn was betting on ten. Or less.

Which meant he had no time to screw around. *Damn.*

He ran his hands through his hair, considering his options. The best plan was to backtrack to the airstrip, find the grating they'd emerged from during their escape, and go back in that way. If worse came to worse, he could even navigate the air vent again, though he didn't relish the possibility.

He glanced at his watch. Time was ticking away. *Shit.*

He hugged the building, easing through the darkness toward the corner, knowing that once he rounded the side, the strip would come into view. He'd have to make a break across the open to the grating, but if he was lucky, he could get there in under a minute. If he was even luckier, no one would see him doing it.

He was just about to ease into the open when he heard the squawk of a radio. He pressed himself against the wall, trying to lose himself in the shadows.

"Garner, get your ass over here," Beltzer's voice boomed through the static.

"What's up?" Garner answered, his voice loud and all too close. Finn said a silent thank-you to Beltzer. If he'd buzzed a second later, Finn would have walked around the corner and right into Garner's line of sight.

"Got the bitch," he said. He might as well have kicked Finn in the gut, and he bit down on the inside of his cheek.

"Hot damn," Garner said.

"Take another pair of eyes and walk the perimeter," Beltzer said. "See if she brought any friends along with her."

"Negative," Garner said. "Mackenzie said she came alone."

Finn blinked, troubled by that statement, but too tense to sort it out at the moment.

"That's a good bit of news," the voice said. "In that case, get down here and back me up. I got her cuffed, but the bitch is tricky."

"Where are you?"

"Dish One. On the platform."

"Stupid twit. Guess her boss didn't tell her Mackenzie's running six dishes on the island. She could blow that one and he wouldn't even give a damn."

"No shit," Beltzer said. "Now get the fuck over here."

"On my way."

Footsteps sounded on the pavement, and Finn followed, taking care to move in silence. As soon as he rounded the corner, he could see the dish illuminated by the moon, a beacon against the black horizon.

He would have preferred the cloak of blackness provided by a moonless night, but he was hardly in a position to rearrange the universe. He'd settle for rearranging Garner's face.

The way Finn figured it, he had two options—he could follow Garner and then tackle both men, or he could tackle Garner now and approach Beltzer wearing Garner's hat and jacket. The second option was risky—they were in the open and Beltzer might be watching for Garner's approach—but the risk was worth it.

He took a deep breath, pulling the Walther from the holster Amber had given him. He'd told her he had experience with a gun, and that wasn't a lie. But his experience had been on a firing range. He'd never pulled a gun on a person before.

He would tonight, though. And he'd fire it, too. If that's what it took to save Amber, if that's what it took to prevent a war, he'd fire it without hesitation.

Twenty-four

$\mathcal{D}$iana paced in front of the console, her body a mass of energy. She watched the clock, wishing she could will time to move faster. She wanted this over and done. She wanted off the island. Drake swore they were safe, that his partner had taken care of everything.

Well, maybe he had and maybe he hadn't. But until Prometheus fired and they got the hell off the island, Diana wasn't about to relax.

And she needed some R and R. A beach, some tequila, and a copy of Hawking's *The Universe in a Nutshell*. Heaven. And she couldn't get there soon enough.

"Calm down, baby," Drake said, closing his hand over the microphone of his headset.

She flashed him a look of pure irritation, then

checked her watch. It was running one minute faster than the atomic clock on the wall.

"What's the word on Robinson?" she asked. "Anything?"

"Beltzer's taking her to a cell right now." He held his hands out wide. "We're home free, baby. Just like I told you."

The metal door feeding into the main corridor slid open, and Diana heard herself breathe out, a little "oh" escaping her lips as she recognized the figure in the doorway—one of Unit 7's bigwigs . . . and one of Drake's oldest enemies.

She wasn't armed, but Drake kept a pistol on the console, and she lunged for it. Drake's hand closed over hers. "Sweetheart," he said, "I want you to meet my partner."

"Hands up," Finn said, pressing the gun against the back of Garner's head. He stiffened, every muscle ready to spring should Garner make a stupid move.

Garner didn't. Instead, he lifted his hands above his head, a slow, calculated movement designed to show Finn just how cooperative he was being.

"Good boy," Finn said, keeping the gun on him with one hand as he frisked Garner with the other. He plucked Garner's gun out of his holster under his jacket, then slipped it into the waistband of his jeans. Finn didn't find any other weapons. He did, however, find handcuffs.

Handy.

He cuffed Garner's hands behind his back, then ordered the man onto the ground. He removed Garner's boots, then tied his ankles together with one of his laces. He held onto the second lace as he ordered Garner onto his belly.

The guard complied without question. Apparently the man wasn't as stupid as he looked.

Finn used the second lace to tie Garner's ankles to the handcuffs, securing the man's limbs behind his back. He stuffed Garner's sock into his mouth, and left him trussed up like a pig ready for roasting.

As he ran toward the dish he shoved Garner's baseball style cap onto his head and pulled on the battered leather jacket, then reached into his back pocket for a book of matches. Even with the moon, the night was dark, the cloud cover blocking the light and casting the world in dirty gray cotton.

With luck, the combination of Garner's clothes and the dim light would provide enough of a disguise.

Without luck, he was screwed.

"Move," Beltzer said. He jammed the barrel of his rifle into Amber's back, urging her toward the stairs. They were on the utility building above which the dish sat, and she was moving as slowly as possible. She had only been able to hear Beltzer's side of the radioed conversation, but he hadn't mentioned Finn. Hopefully, Finn hadn't been caught. More hopefully, he'd made it into the complex. If she could keep Beltzer and his buddy busy, that was two less thugs Finn had to deal with.

Footsteps sounded on the metal stairs below them, and she looked down. Leather jacket and baseball cap. Garner, she presumed.

"Get the fuck up here," Beltzer said. "The bitch

has lead feet. I swear, if Drake didn't want her alive, I'd just pop her right here."

Garner just grunted and kept plodding up the stairs, his head down so he could watch his feet, a gun in one hand, the other hand behind his back.

Amber squinted. There was something familiar about that gun. . . .

As he reached the platform, Amber realized, and the flood of relief that crashed over her was just as strong and palpable as the spurt of anger following on its heels. Neither emotion had time to register, though. There was only time to act.

The second Finn's boots hit the platform, he threw the tennis ball bomb off the platform. It exploded on impact, popping and zinging and completely distracting Beltzer. Amber took advantage of the lug's disorientation to back away. At the same time, Finn lashed out, kicking up and ramming Beltzer in the gut. Beltzer fell on his ass, his gun rattling across the metal grating on which he walked. His face contorted with pain, but he moved almost immediately to get up. No way, José. Amber rammed her foot down, slamming her heel into his nuts.

Beltzer howled in pain, and even Finn's face twisted into an unpleasant grimace.

There were definite advantages to being female.

Her hands were still cuffed behind her, but she dropped to the ground, pulling her knees up until she was in a fetal position. She eased her butt through the circle of her arms, wiggling until her bound hands were in front of her. The whole process took about ten seconds, and Finn kept his gun trained on Beltzer the entire time.

She reached back, clicking open the barrette that held her hair in a ponytail. The clasp was a cuff key, and she was free in no time.

She regarded Beltzer, twisting the barrette between her fingers before pulling her hair back up and away from her face. "Where's Garner?" she asked, keeping her eyes on Beltzer but talking to Finn as the wind did its job of clearing away the smoke.

"Trussed up like a turkey on the airstrip," he said.

"Alive?"

"Yes."

She turned to him, making an effort to keep her face impassive. "And what are *you* doing here?"

"Looks like I'm saving your butt," he said.

She tamped down a wave of anger, reminding herself that he was a civilian. "This isn't the time for chivalry," she said. "You need to be in that complex. We don't have much time."

"No shit," he said. "Let's get moving."

She nodded. They could argue if they survived. She took the gun from his hand and aimed it at Beltzer's head. "Nice knowing you," she said. "I'm sure you understand that I don't want any loose ends."

"Wait." Finn's hand came down on her wrist. "I've got an idea."

As it turned out, his idea was a good one. The security at the complex was intense, impenetrable without the appropriate key to get past the security system. Beltzer's hand did the trick just fine.

The door slid open and they entered with care, keeping Beltzer in front of them as a human shield.

The precaution was unnecessary; the corridor was deserted.

"I should just shoot you now," Amber said to Beltzer. But she didn't. They might need him again. Or at least his palm print. And for all she knew, a cold, dead hand wouldn't work.

"Here," Finn said. She turned and saw him point to a utility closet. Perfect.

Five minutes later, Beltzer was tied up and gagged, shoved in next to a row of metal shelving lined with rags and cleaning products. Amber pressed the hypodermic into his thigh. "Sweet dreams," she said, pulling the door closed with a click.

After that, she turned to Finn and took a deep breath. "That was a good move with the bomb," she said. "I'm sorry." They weren't words that came easy, but she meant them, and it was important that he know that.

A shadow crossed his face, his expression wary. "For what?"

"For chewing you out earlier. I told you that you needed to be inside the complex—"

"—but I couldn't get inside the complex," he finished.

"Exactly." She licked her lips. "Of course, you could have just used Garner's hand. You didn't have to keep schlepping across the airfield."

"Let's just stick to thank you, okay?"

She felt a smile tug at her mouth. "Fair enough."

He took her hand, and she squeezed back, comforted by the press of his skin against hers. "When I heard they'd caught you, my heart about stopped," he said, his voice a low whisper as they maneuvered their way down the corridor.

She didn't say anything, but the truth was that the wash of relief she'd felt when she'd seen him on the stairs was more than the relief of being rescued. It had been like a cry of joy at seeing him again. A feeling as if the whole world had opened just a little bit more because this man she loved was safe.

Which made it all the more difficult to know that she couldn't be with him. Not really. And certainly not forever. She would never leave the Unit. And when this was all over, she intended to see about bringing Finn in as an agent. If she couldn't be with the man she loved, she could at least help him get the career he wanted.

And from what she'd seen so far, with a little more training, he could be one of the best.

They'd reached an intersection, and Finn tugged her back, his hand automatically going across her chest to keep her pressed flat against the wall. Footsteps sounded in the distance, and she held her breath. Two people. Possibly three, coming toward them down an intersecting corridor.

She inched backward, ready to flee back the way they came if necessary. They didn't want a confrontation. The longer they went undetected, the better.

The footsteps receded, and she exhaled. A long, slow sigh of relief. "Come on," she said.

He tugged her back. "Wait."

Amber looked back over her shoulder in confusion, silently demanding an explanation.

"I haven't told you everything yet," he said.

Something in his voice made her pause, giving him her full attention. "What?"

"Could you hear Garner?" he said. "Over the walkie-talkie, I mean."

She scowled, trying to figure what this could be leading up to, and slowly shook her head. "No. Beltzer was wearing an earpiece."

Finn nodded, his expression unreadable.

"Finn?"

"I could hear him," he said. "I'm an idiot. I should have made the connection earlier." He took her hand. "Amber, they not only knew you were coming, they were certain you were coming alone."

She swallowed, the impact of his words hitting her with exactly the force she knew he'd anticipated.

"James," he said gently.

She closed her eyes, as if that could blot out the truth. As if by not looking she could somehow avoid the stench of betrayal that colored her life. It was becoming a theme. Her father. Her mother. James.

She shuddered, the implications overwhelming. He'd sent her to die. And Brandon. Had he killed Brandon? Just for being in the way?

"Amber?"

Finn's voice was gentle, but she recoiled, pulling back into herself.

"That's not all," Finn said.

She took a deep breath, then lifted her chin to meet his eyes. "What else? Did he kill my dog on the way out of the house?"

"Paramilitary support," he said. "They're not—"

She held up a hand to quiet him, irritated with herself for focusing so much on James's betrayal that she missed the more important ramifications. "Of course," she said. "We're it. If we fail, no one's going to target the island. If we fail, Prometheus is going to fire and we just might walk off this island and into a war."

"We're not going to fail," Finn said, his voice tight and determined.

It was the determination that centered her. Screw James. He was nothing. Right now, she had more important things to worry about. "No," she agreed. "We're not."

"So what now?" Finn asked.

"Now we go kick some terrorist butt."

Twenty-five

Drake watched as Monahan peered over Diana's shoulder at the terminal, his temper bubbling just beneath the surface.

"Excellent," Monahan said. "I see Waterman cooperated."

"With the right persuasion," Drake said. "Yes." He couldn't stand it anymore, and moved forward, cupping his hand against the small of Diana's back. She leaned against him, and he relaxed just slightly.

"Timing?"

"The satellite will be in range in two hours," Diana said. "I've preprogrammed the system and put it in fail-safe mode. It's firing the moment it comes into range unless I tell it otherwise."

Monahan nodded, then leaned over the console, staring at the rows of numbers and codes flashing across the monitor. "I would have preferred to fire the day she and Teague escaped. There's still time," he said. "Time for something to go wrong."

"That was a holy day," Drake said.

Monahan raised an eyebrow, fixing him with a dark look. "The bastard's blowing up a mosque."

"To further his cause," Drake said. "He wouldn't do it on a holy day." He kept his voice level. He'd gotten a lot of use out of Monahan. Not, he thought, enough to justify taking his friend's crap. But he might need Monahan again. Until the man was officially retired from Unit 7, he still had his uses. "Nothing will go wrong," he added.

"The money?" Monahan said.

"The balance will hit my account as soon as Mujabi confirms the mosque's destruction. You'll get your share soon enough."

"Half," Monahan said.

Drake forced a smile. "Yes," he said. "I know."

"And where is our little computer geek?" Monahan asked.

Drake glanced at Diana. "He had a rather bad night, I'm afraid."

Monahan closed his eyes, taking a deep breath. "You promised me you wouldn't kill him."

Drake had to laugh. "Turning sentimental on me, old man? We don't need him anymore. Diana's in, she's taken control. He's useless. As they say in the business, collateral damage."

"Shit."

Drake laughed. "I swear, there are times when I wonder how you had the balls to turn on your two young protégés."

"I do what's necessary." He licked his lips. "Of course, I would have preferred a different outcome," he admitted. "Neither one was supposed to be in Los Angeles during this project. Amber's assignment to watch Diana was without my authorization."

Drake laughed. "You just keep getting screwed. Schnell's assigning your people all over the god-damn globe, and you're getting pushed into forced retirement with a piss-poor pension plan."

Monahan's smile registered about thirty-two degrees Fahrenheit. "That's why I decided to create my own retirement plan."

Drake just shook his head. "All those years," he said. "You and I could have been working together all along."

"No," Monahan said. "I'm not like you."

Drake looked him up and down, then nodded. The man standing before him was a selfish coward, utterly lacking in loyalty, and willing to sacrifice his friends just to make his own life more comfortable. "No," Drake said. "You're right. We're not alike at all."

Amber held out a hand, stopping Finn as she poked her head into the corridor to make sure the way was clear. He pressed himself back against the wall, his heart pounding in his ears.

"Okay, partner," she said. "What now?"

The import of the question wasn't lost on Finn. Somewhere along the line, they'd become equals. But he wasn't about to dwell on the victory. There wasn't time. "I'm going to see about grabbing one of those lab coats and joining the other rats in the control room. If I'm lucky, I can access the controls through any terminal. If I'm even luckier, they won't realize what I'm doing."

"Good," she said. "I'm going back to the dish."

Finn shook his head, then repeated what he'd heard Garner explain to Beltzer.

She shook her head. "Six dishes. Shit." She met his eyes. "Then you really are up at bat, sweetheart. We've got to do everything we can to make sure you take control. In the meantime, I'll see about rescuing Bernie. If anyone can help you, he can."

He nodded. "Once I get in and find a terminal, it'll take me a few minutes to patch into the system. If we're lucky, they won't notice me nosing around. I'll just be another guy in a lab coat."

"But?"

"But I can't just turn the thing off or set it for some other coordinates. As soon as the plan goes awry, they'll know, and they'll blow my head off. We don't have any backup. We have to kill all their options from the get-go."

"Self-destruct," she said.

He nodded. "As soon as I set it for self-destruct, everyone in that room is going to know. It's going to show up on that giant television screen and Diana's monitor and everywhere else. I don't know if there's an instantaneous destruct button or a countdown. If there's a countdown, there's time for Diana to blow me away and reset the commands."

"Unless she's otherwise occupied," Amber put in.

"Exactly."

"So you need a distraction."

"That I do."

She grinned, and he wondered if she was thinking about a Mrs. Digby type of distraction. "I can do that," she said. She glanced at her watch. "Eighty-four minutes to range. Hopefully, it won't take me long to find Bernie." She squinted, eyeing him carefully. "Is that enough time to get in?"

"It better be," he said.

She nodded, a silent show of both support and agreement, and then started to turn away. He pulled her back, needing to feel her against him one last time. His lips pressed against hers, then lingered in a sweet kiss that built to an explosive frenzy with each passing moment.

As they broke the kiss, her breathing was uneven, her eyes bright—adrenaline mixed with a hint of sex. "If that was your 'in case we don't see each other again' kiss, I'm going to be sorely disappointed."

"No way, babe," he said. "Previews of coming attractions."

She kissed her palm, then pressed it over his lips. "Good man. Now go kick butt."

"Sixty-five minutes," Diana said.

Drake watched as the screen on the far wall displayed the countdown. Soon . . . soon . . .

His hands practically itched, and he rubbed his thumbs over the pads of his fingertips. A red light on the console squawked, indicating an incoming call, and he waved a hand, gesturing for one of his technicians to answer it. The man did, his face turning visibly paler as he signaled for Diana to pick up.

"What?" she snapped, her voice reflecting Drake's own irritation. This was not a time for interruptions. Not at all. A second passed, and then her face went totally flat. And as it did, a sick sensation rose in Drake's stomach, and he knew that

James had been right—there was still time for something to go wrong.

"What?" he barked.

Diana licked her lips, replacing the handset. "No one's heard from Beltzer, and they can't raise him on the radio."

"She's in the complex," Monahan said.

Drake turned on him, barely able to contain his fury. "She's your goddamn loose cannon. Go take care of this. And you," he said, pointing to Diana. "Close the control center doors after him. So long as we're locked in here, she's not getting in. Not through solid steel, and certainly not in sixty-five minutes."

The doors clanged shut with solid determination, the sound echoing through the domelike room. Finn kept his head down and his hands in the pockets of his lab coat, trying to look blasé yet productive as he ambled toward an unoccupied terminal.

The other lab coats essentially ignored him, and Finn considered that a stroke of luck. He wasn't certain if they were all busy working hard, or if they were just so scared of Drake that they were afraid to look up from their appointed tasks. Not that the reason mattered. Finn was just grateful he could blend into the background.

Considering Drake had sealed the doors, Finn had no idea how Amber intended to cause the appointed distraction. But he'd leave that up to her. If her assignment was to distract, Finn knew damn well that's what she'd do.

Besides, there was no sense worrying about what

Amber was going to do when he hadn't yet even figured out what *he* was going to do.

First things first.

It took a bit of maneuvering, but he got logged
into the compound's network. As he'd hoped,
Prometheus's operational controls were on the network—a nice little benefit that allowed whoever
was programming the thing to move from terminal
to terminal, just in case they were being pursued.
Of course, that added bit of convenience for the bad
guys was also a perk for the good guys. And in less
than five minutes, Finn had found his way to
Prometheus's front door.

So far, at least, he was right on schedule.

Too bad he hadn't yet gotten to the tricky part.

He started with the basics, trying every gamer's
back door he knew. It wasn't uncommon for game
programmers to put in sort of a "master key,"
thereby letting programmers across the globe get
into the meat of the game. But none of the codes he
ran through worked. Okay. On to other options. In
addition to the information he'd collected poking
around on Bernie's computer, he'd also asked Digby
to make him a file on Bernie, and he'd memorized
the key information. Now he tried variations on
Bernie's name, birth date, mother's birth date, and
other assorted factors. No luck there, either, but
even with a computer, it would take him days to run
all the combinations. And Finn didn't have days. He
wished he had the software he'd developed, but it
was at home and useless to him.

Think, dammit. Think!

There had to be something. Some tidbit that held
the key.

Finn shook his head, trying to focus. One by one, he mentally ran down every item he knew about Bernie, but nothing stood out. Nothing until he got to that odd e-mail about the moon. Could that be it?

He played the moon landing in his head, the famous words so familiar—*Houston, the Eagle has landed.* And then Neil Armstrong had opened the hatch, climbed down the ladder, and been the first man to walk on the moon. *One small step for man, one giant leap for mankind.* Beautiful. And utterly unhelpful.

Armstrong. That was who the draft e-mail was addressed to. Finn had assumed Bernie intended to send the e-mail. But maybe not. Maybe that was just Bernie's way of remembering his codes. Hide them in plain sight.

He stared at the monitor, gnawing on the end of a pencil as he typed in moon, and Apollo and Armstrong. Nothing.

The Eagle has landed. . . .

Finn squinted. What was the story about Prometheus? He stole fire, sure. That explained why the Unit had named a laser after the god. But there was something else.

And then he remembered—Prometheus had been doomed to eternity. Every day, an eagle pecked out his liver, and every day his liver was renewed to start the process all over again.

That had to be it.

He typed in *Eagle,* then *Apollo Eagle,* then *Eagle 11,* all to no avail. He typed in a few more random words related to the moon mission, including the absurd *Eleven Leaping Eagles.* He was all set to try *Eagle-eye Armstrong* when he realized he was in—*Eleven*

Leaping Eagles had done the trick. What do you know?

Bless Bernie. The man *was* a genius. And Finn wasn't too shabby himself.

Now all Finn had to do was find the self-destruct. He glanced at his watch; time was getting away. He had to move fast, or else this whole trip was going to be for nothing.

He took another quick glance around the room. As far as he could tell, he was still unnoticed. That wasn't likely to last for long, and he hoped Amber got going with the distraction. As soon as Finn figured out how to convince the satellite to commit suicide, they were going to need it.

He entered a few more codes, poking around in the inner workings of the program. It was a Unix system, one he knew well, but damned if he could figure out how to conjure a self-destruct. The satellite seemed determined not to commit hari-kari.

And that's when he realized—someone else had been in here before him. Fiddling around just like he was. *Diana.* And she'd basically locked the system down.

He couldn't operate the self-destruct.

He couldn't shut the system down.

He couldn't even change the time at which the satellite was scheduled to fire.

Fail-safe.

Diana Traynor knew her stuff. And Finn was all out of options.

Unless . . .

There was still one possibility left. It was extreme, but if he was lucky it was something Diana had overlooked.

Once again, Finn maneuvered through the system like a thief in the night. And, sure enough, his theory panned out. He might not be able to stop the satellite from firing, but he could change its target. And Finn knew one set of coordinates in all the world—the island.

He took a deep breath, realizing he might be signing his and Amber's death warrant. But what other choice did he have? He couldn't let Drake go through with blowing up the mosque. And if he shifted the coordinates just slightly—hopefully pointing the laser at the sea—that would leave open the possibility that Diana would get back into the system and simply fire again.

No, this was the only way. And with slightly trembling fingers, he started to type in the new targeting coordinates, hoping all the while that he and Amber could get the hell off the island before the damn thing blew.

Twenty-six

*D*ead.

Amber scowled at the locked control center doors, the vision of Bernie's cold, lifeless form still playing in her mind. She should have known, should have expected it, but still it was a shock.

And now she feared for the man behind these doors. Would Finn end up dead, too? Would they both?

She shook her head, banishing such thoughts. She had to focus on this problem. On these solid steel doors with the unpickable lock. And the clock was ticking.

To her right, the touch pad glowed its dim electric glow, as if taunting her with its power. She studied the door, frustrated. She knew only one way in. *Beltzer.* She was going to have to go back for the little worm.

She hugged the wall as she maneuvered back to the intersecting corridor. She took a deep breath, then eased around the corner, leading with her gun.

And that's when it happened—a powerful thrust slamming down hard against her wrist with a force and precision powerful enough to rip a howl from her throat and send her gun flying from her fingers to clatter across the concrete floor. Amber hit the deck, instinctively knowing that if the first attack was meant to disarm, the second would be to kill.

As soon as she hit ground, she rolled, ending up in a crouch, her dive knife poised and ready. She hauled back, prepared to launch it at her attacker, to spear his throat and get on with her mission. But in the keen acuity of sense brought on by fear and adrenaline, her brain signaled recognition. At the same moment, he spoke, his voice stilling her hand.

"Amber, it's you. Thank God I found you."

"James," she said, her voice flat. She kept the knife raised, a fact that wasn't lost on the man.

"Amber, it's me." He held a gun loose in one hand. "I know you wanted to work alone. But it's too dangerous. I came after you. I came to help you." He paused, his eyes cutting to her hand. "Put the knife down."

She pressed her lips together, the full impact of his betrayal finally hitting her. She'd trusted this man, believed in the life he'd given her. And he'd thrown it all away. She didn't lower the knife; she didn't move a muscle. "Why?" she asked, a thousand questions echoing in that one word.

To his credit, he didn't even pretend to misunderstand. An expression of pure misery settled on his face, and his shoulders sagged as if in defeat. His fingers, however, tightened around the gun. "I didn't intend for you to get hurt. You or Brandon."

"Brandon," she repeated, feeling sick. "You . . . ?"

"It had to be done." His free hand clenched into a fist. "Goddamn Schnell. If only he'd kept you overseas . . ."

"Then what?" she asked, forcing the words out past the lump in her throat. "It would have made it easier on your conscience? Your betrayal would have been that much easier to justify?"

"They're forcing me out, Amber. I've given the Unit my life and they're kicking me out." His face contorted, sadness mixed with an unfamiliar rage. "I should be leading the Unit, not answering to Schnell."

Her own rage bubbled to the surface. "You're pathetic," she whispered, forcing the words out. "Everything you've ever told me about honor and sacrifice and being part of a team"—she shook her head—"it was all a lie. You just wanted power. And you'll take it however you can get it. Even if it means hurting the people you love."

"I never meant to hurt you," he said. He reached out, and she automatically took a step back. He stiffened, as if her movement had inflicted physical pain. "Come with me. We're a team, you and I."

She shook her head, his words filling her with disgust. "I work alone." Her eyes welled, and she blinked back tears. She never cried, and she didn't intend to start now.

Alone. Her whole career, she'd thought she had James. The Unit. She'd been alone, and yet she'd had her team. Now, she had nothing.

Except Finn. She still had Finn. And somehow,

instinctively, she knew that where everything with James had been illusion, Finn's love was real. And permanent. And not laced with ulterior motives.

Her eyes met his, and she saw the shadow reflected there.

"I'm sorry," he said. His finger moved, almost imperceptibly, and she knew he wasn't apologizing for his past mistakes, but for the gun he was about to fire.

She lashed out, her knife catching him in the wrist, slicing deep. He fired as she dove to the ground, the bullet barely missing her.

She leaped forward, kicking him in the chest and knocking him backward. He'd grabbed his wrist with his left hand to staunch the blood, and now he was scrambling on the floor, his knees slipping in the bright red fluid as he scrabbled for the gun.

She kicked it clear, recovering her knife and pressing the blade across his neck. "You should have killed me when you had the chance," she said. "When I first turned the corner."

"No," he said. "I should have killed myself." He closed his eyes. "Do it fast."

The muscles in her arm tightened and then went slack. Her face was wet, and she realized she was crying. Fucking hell. She urged him up, the blade of the knife flat under his chin. "Up," she said. "And move."

"Am—"

"Shut up, James. We have nothing to say to each other." She led him down the corridor, pausing only long enough to retrieve both their guns. She shoved hers in her shoulder holster, then sheathed her knife, keeping his gun trained at his back. She used the opportunity to pat him down, liberating the knife strapped just above his ankle in the process.

"Now walk," she said. He did, and she led him down the corridor to the control room doors. "Open it."

He shook his head. The color had drained from his face, leaving him pale and hollow, his face a mix of angles and shadows. In contrast to the gray of his face, his arm was bright red. The blood from his wrist had stained his shirt and his other hand where he clutched it, trying to staunch the flow of blood. Amber opened her waist pack and pulled out a length of rubber tubing.

"Open the door," she said, "and the tourniquet is yours."

He paused, his face a mass of indecision. And for a moment, Amber actually believed that he would decline. That he would summon the courage to let his own life flow away rather than betray his new friends, and by so doing, somehow redeem the faith she'd had in him.

Instead, he pressed his palm against the touch pad, opening the door for her. Not to assist her mission, but to further his own.

She tossed him the tourniquet. If she never saw him again, it would be too soon.

Blackness everywhere. All around him blackness, and the dull throbbing of red-hot pain in his head and chest.

The suit. Linus's suit had saved him. But saved him from what? From whom?

And then he remembered, and the memory jolted

him awake. *James*. Oh, Jesus in heaven, James had turned traitor.

With a groan, Brandon opened his eyes and tried to sit up. He was a little unstable, but he made it. He was still on the road, the stars winking above him, and he had to figure some way back to Amber's house. She'd be on the island now. Walking into a trap.

He had to help her. Had to get to her.

And with every muscle in his body aching, he climbed to his feet and headed for his car, abandoned still at the side of the road.

With any luck, Digby could get him onto that island. With a little more luck, he'd get there in time.

They were running out of time. And, still, no Amber.

Finn swallowed. He had to assume she wasn't coming, and he railed against the unfairness of finding love only to have it slip through his fingers. Love wasn't his problem. Not now. Possibly not ever again. This satellite was. And without Amber there to provide a distraction, everyone in the chamber was going to notice when he entered the change in coordinates.

Even if he encrypted a password—and hoped Diana couldn't break it in only a few minutes—he was still a dead man. Without Amber's cover, Drake would pick him off like a duck at a shooting range. And then Drake and Diana would waltz out the door to their plane. Their equipment would be destroyed, but they would not. And Finn would lie dead on the floor.

He clutched the edge of the keyboard, wishing

there was another option, but seeing only that one possible path. If he was going to die anyway, he might as well wait to engage the change in coordinates at the last possible moment. So that no one—not him, not Drake, not Diana—made it off the island.

And so he sat, his eyes glued to the monitor, trying to look unobtrusive, as precious seconds ticked down. And he wondered if that was how soldiers felt, in those last moments before fate found them, calling itself duty, and asked them to die for God and country.

Was it wrong to be scared when faced with such a noble task?

Finn shook his head, frustrated with himself. He'd known from the outset that he might not be returning. His only regret—well, the only regret worth counting—was that he hadn't seen Amber one last time.

Ten minutes to range.

His stomach twisted, and he chanced a look around. The monitor displayed an image of old Jerusalem, the mosque prominent. Drake stood beneath it, a phone to his ear. Diana stood at the console nearest the podium, her eyes fixed on the computer screen. On either side of Finn were more lab rats, going about their business at terminals and monitoring equipment. He caught sight of the monitor next to him, and realized the guy was pulling weather and tourism information about Bali off the Internet. Drake and company's next stop, Finn assumed.

With studied casualness, he entered the island's coordinates onto his own terminal. He didn't send the coordinates to the system, though. Just stood there waiting, his finger poised over the Enter key, as he waited for that nebulous point of no return.

A shriek of metal grating against metal rang out from the far side of the room, and Finn whirled around, fearing that Beltzer had gotten free and was coming to warn Drake.

Instead, he saw Amber. Her face was hard—sadness mixed with anger—and she held a gun on a man he'd never seen before.

He glanced at the projection screen. *Eight minutes.*

The doors were open, his distraction had arrived. *Now.* He had to do it now if they had any hope of getting off the island.

"I will kill him." Amber's voice carried from the doorway. "Shut down Prometheus, or I'll splatter him all over this room."

It was a bluff, of course. Finn knew perfectly well that Amber didn't believe Drake would comply. But it bought them time, kept their eyes on her rather than on the projection screen.

He pressed ENTER, and on the screen, the coordinates shifted, rattling through an array of numbers like a slot machine before it came up all cherries.

"You'd never hurt him," Diana was saying. "Your precious Mr. Monahan."

Amber's eyes darted to his, her chin lifting just the slightest. A signal. Any second now, they were going to run.

"Is that a bluff you're willing to call?" she said.

And unreadable expression flickered across Diana's face, and in the same instance, Drake whipped out a gun, aiming it straight at Amber's head. "Shoot the bastard," he said. "I'll just keep his half of the money, and you'll be dead, too."

Finn inched his hand toward the folds of his lab coat, seeking the gun that was tucked in a holster at his side.

"Don't even think about moving." *Garner.* The familiar voice came from right behind Finn, even as the cold end of a gun barrel pressed at the back of his neck. "You want to tell me what you're doing at this computer?"

"Not really," Finn said.

The man walloped him on the back of the head with the butt of the gun. Finn saw red, his knees buckling, but he didn't go down.

"Aw shit," Garner said. And then, "He did something," he yelled. "Teague got in the goddamn system and fucked something up."

If any good came from being caught, it was the fact that both Drake and Diana turned at the sound of Garner's voice. And as they did, Amber fired, hitting Garner in the shoulder and spinning him backward to crash against the terminal. Finn didn't waste any time; he ran toward Amber as fast as he could, pushing aside the lab-coated peons who stepped into his path, urged along by Diana's shouted orders: "Stop him. *Stop him!*"

"Did you encrypt it?" Amber yelled, loud enough for Drake and Diana and the rest of the free world to hear.

"Hell yes," he said. "Multiple levels. They're never getting through." In truth, he'd only had time to do one layer of encryption. Diana could probably be through in five minutes. Hopefully, though, she wouldn't try.

A needle of fire stabbed his arm, and Finn realized he'd been shot. He stumbled, but didn't stop, just kept pumping his legs, determined to get to Amber.

"I'll kill you, Mackenzie. Fire again, and I swear I'll blow your head off." Amber's voice carried over the din in the room, not loud but sharp enough to cut through the noise. Finn knew without looking what was happening. Drake was poised to take him out. And the only thing that stood between him and death was Amber.

He kept running.

"Drake!" Diana's piercing scream reverberated through the room. "Forget them and get the hell over here. We've got bigger problems."

Finn knew he shouldn't, but he couldn't help himself. He turned and saw Diana frantically entering code at the keyboard, Drake racing up behind her. Time to add a distraction of his own. He reared back and threw the second tennis ball, sending it smashing through a computer monitor, the explosion setting off a flurry of sparks and sputters in that corner of the room, which drew the attention of the remaining lab rats.

Not that they were home free. Garner had gotten into the act, but by the time he got off the first shot, Amber was grabbing Finn's arm and pulling him forward. James reached for her, but Amber pulled back. James lunged, desperation on his face, and then surprise as a bullet meant for Amber caught him in the back. "I'm sorry," he whispered, and Finn watched as a single tear slid down Amber's cheek.

He grabbed her by the elbow and pulled. "Six minutes," Finn gasped. "The island's going to blow."

Amber didn't waste time asking why Finn had arranged for their impending demise. "Stairs," she said, racing in that direction. "The chopper's our only chance."

"Can you redirect it?" Drake asked, fearing he knew the answer already.

Diana shook her head. "In six minutes? I doubt it."

A surge of rage burst through Drake, and he stepped back, aiming his gun at the monitor. He fired, the bullet punching through glass and tubes, transistors and resistors. Unlike in the movies, there was no explosion, and even in his fury, he felt a little stupid.

Behind him, Garner and some of the control center operators were on Teague and Robinson's tail. But they didn't know the truth. It didn't matter if they caught the agents or not. Soon they'd all be dust.

"The chopper," Drake said. "And give the evacuation signal."

Diana complied, and immediately the complex filled with a periodic loud squawk interspersed with a piercing red light. Diana and Drake headed to the theater chairs, the same ones that had sent Teague and Robinson to the flood chamber. Now, the floor tiles rose, taking them to the helipad atop the control room.

His staff, Drake knew, would be scrambling for the ten speedboats anchored in the basement of the building. The door to the sea—which looked like nothing more than the cliff face—would open with the evacuation signal to allow them to speed to safety. The coast guard might pick them up—and he didn't envy their task of explaining their predicament—but it was no longer his problem.

He and Diana were heading for Bali. And since he sincerely doubted that James would make it out of the building in his condition, Drake would make a point of reacquiring his partner's half of Mujabi's down payment.

Of course, in light of recent developments, Mujabi would probably ask that the funds be returned. But returning money wasn't something that Drake did. Ever. And since Drake was now officially a fugitive, he intended to remain a very well-financed one.

"Time?"

"Four minutes, thirty seconds," Finn answered. He and Amber were pounding up the metal stairs that led to the helipad on the roof. Finn was right at her heels and they were racing against time to reach the chopper.

They rounded the last turn of the stairs and found themselves facing a steel door with a metal bar across it. The sign on the door made perfectly clear that it was only to be opened in emergencies, and an alarm would sound.

Amber burst through, quite certain this qualified.

They were on the roof. Almost home free.

Her elation, however, was short-lived. In front of them, the blades of the chopper were spinning, and Drake was in the pilot's chair. Beside him, Diana was strapping herself in.

Amber came to a dead stop and aimed, Drake's head in her sight. She fired.

And nothing happened. The gun clicked uselessly, the chamber empty.

"Shit." She reached behind her for James's gun, but the copter was already rising. And that's when she realized that Finn had pulled out a lighter and was about to toss something. He heaved, and the burning mass of what looked like solid plastic flew from his hand, landing in the cockpit.

A smoke bomb.

Dense white smoke filled the cockpit, and the helicopter twisted as Drake fought for control.

"Fire," Finn yelled.

She did. Aiming at where Drake's head had to be. Had she hit him?

She fired again. And again. And again, emptying the chamber into the smoke-filled cockpit. Nothing. And the helicopter rose into the sky.

She felt ill. The nausea of failure. And then the copter swooped back, out of control. She hit the deck, Finn beside her, the blades barely missing them as the copter spun out of control, racing over the helipad and the building to crash on asphalt below.

"They're dead," Finn said.

She nodded. "We will be too unless we get the hell out of here." And dying wasn't an option. Not now. Not when her entire future with Finn loomed open before her. There had to be another way.

Her heart pounded in her chest as her gaze swept the helipad. Behind them lay the way they came. There were escape routes, of that she was sure. Otherwise the evac siren was pointless. But there was no time to find those routes.

In front of her lay thirty or so feet of concrete and then the sheer drop-off they'd seen from the lagoon. Fifty or so feet to the Pacific, the ocean's depth unknown. She closed her eyes. "Time?"

"Two minutes, twelve seconds."

She licked her lips. They were all out of options.

"We're going to have to jump," she said.

The corner of Finn's mouth lifted, the gesture almost imperceptible. "Babe," he said. "We've already done that. You're gonna have to get some new material."

She wanted to laugh, but instead she kissed him. Just once on the cheek for luck. And then they jumped.

They broke the surface, the blast of water knocking all reason from Amber. Finn was already at her side, and together they surfaced and started kicking like mad out to sea.

"Three," Finn said. "Two . . . one."

Amber dove, pulling Finn down with her even as Prometheus did its work on the island. When they surfaced, only a pile of rubble remained where the complex once stood. "The fire is spreading over the island," she said. "We'll need to go to the lagoon. We can't stay out here."

Finn started kicking in that direction. "What do we do then?" he asked.

"We wait," she said. If he expected a better answer, she didn't have it. They could try raising Tom on the radio, but their equipment was likely ruined in the sea. With luck, the coast guard would see the fire and come looking. With even more luck, Diana was wrong about Prometheus, and even now Schnell was sending agents to investigate the location to which Prometheus had directed his rage.

They reached the lagoon and let the surf do its

job, taking their weight and tossing them up onto the beach. Around them, the trees and flora burned, but in this sandy alcove, they were safe. A reddish glow covered their bodies, and smoke swirled around them. And despite the horror of the situation, it seemed like something beautiful.

Finn took her hand. "I'm sorry about James."

Amber nodded, closing her eyes. "Thank you." She squeezed back. "But you don't have to worry about me. I'm strong enough."

"I know. But that doesn't mean it doesn't hurt."

She blinked, and a single tear streamed down her cheek. "It does hurt. In the space of a few days, I lost Brandon and James." She grimaced. "I'd lost James a long time ago," she amended. "I just didn't know it." She met his gaze. "All I have now is you," she said.

"No," he said. "All we have now is each other."

Finn lowered his lips to Amber's, tasting heaven, and wondering how long it would last. He had her now. But he knew it wouldn't last. She'd be reinstated and he'd . . . what? Go back to being a lawyer? Pine over this woman, this life?

It was a fate he couldn't accept, and he pushed the thoughts out of his head, instead concentrating on the pure, sweet heaven of her touch. Raw emotion crashed through his brain like a windstorm, wild and frantic, and he clung to her, wanting to never let go. But knowing that in the end he'd have to.

"Finn?" Her voice held more than passion. Instead it was sharp, alert.

He opened his eyes. That wind wasn't in his

head. That sound was out there . . . and getting closer.

Amber climbed into a crouch, her gun aimed at the sky. Finn had no idea if a gun would still function after their dive into the sea, much less if it would be any protection against the helicopter. He hoped so, on both accounts.

The helicopter appeared over the burning complex, its spotlight sweeping the ground. There was nowhere to run, and it would be on top of them any moment.

"Into the water," Amber called.

He nodded and they started racing for the lagoon.

The spotlight caught them less than a foot out. Finn stiffened, sure that this was the end.

The crackle of an amplifier sounded, the noise rising above the roar of the fire, and then, "Rebecca. It's Han."

Amber's shoulders sagged in relief, and she turned around, looking up at the helicopter with her hands shielding her eyes from the light. Finn had no idea what the hell was going on.

"Brandon," she whispered. "Brandon's alive, and he's in Tom's helicopter." She turned to him, her smile bright. "Looks like we found a ride home."

The chairs in the waiting room to Schnell's private office lacked both style and comfort. Not that Amber minded. Her thoughts were too full of the mission and the debriefing to worry about creature comforts.

"You'll be an active agent again soon," Finn said, looking as uncomfortable as the chair. Amber hid a smile, knowing it must be intimidating as hell to meet a man like Schnell. "Hell, they'll probably give you a medal."

"A medal, maybe," she said. "Reinstatement, though . . ." She trailed off, shaking her head. "No."

Finn's brow creased. "What the hell are you talking about?"

"My life," she said. She'd been thinking a lot over the past few hours. "I'm retiring. I can't go back. Not after what's happened. I need to move forward. I need to rely on my own resources for a while."

"You're giving up the work?"

She shook her head. "Not the work. Just the employer."

"And the employer's rules," he said. She heard the hope in his voice, and it just about broke her heart.

She nodded. "Yes."

His brow furrowed. "What? What aren't you telling me? That there's nothing between us? That we're not even going to try?"

She closed her eyes, not wanting this moment. Part of her wished she'd never met him, and part of her knew that not knowing him would have left a little hole in her gut.

"We can't try, Finn." She swallowed. "The rules won't apply to me any longer, but they will apply to you."

Silence hung between them, and then he spoke, his words measured as if he wasn't entirely sure he could believe the subtext of their conversation. "As far as I know, my firm allows relationships."

"Your not a lawyer, Finn. You have the degree, but it's not in your blood. You belong with the Unit.

You kicked butt in there. The CIA was foolish to turn you down."

"Yeah," he said dryly. "I'll write them a letter."

"Don't bother," she said. "I'll do it for you."

She saw the light in his eyes and couldn't suppress her grin. "I asked Schnell to get you in the Unit, and I'm pretty sure he will. You'll have to go through training, of course, but—"

"Why?"

"Because this is who you are, Finn." She blinked, and a tear slid down her cheek. Damn, but she was a mess today. "I love you," she added. "And this is the only gift I have to give."

She loved him. She really loved him.

Finn repeated the words over and over, turning them in his mind, caressing them, wondering at them. She really loved him.

And yet, if he joined the Unit, there was no way they could be together. It was an unsolvable riddle. He wanted both lives. But how the hell could he put them together?

"It'll be a long road," Schnell was saying. Amber had already been debriefed, and she'd given Finn a quick kiss as she'd left the waiting room. Finn had taken a deep breath and followed the receptionist into the leader's office. "But from what Amber says and from what I've seen, you'll be a real asset."

"Thank you, sir. I appreciate that."

Schnell flipped through a file on his desk. "I have a group of agents beginning training in London on Friday. We can have you on a plane tomorrow."

Finn swallowed. "I, uh, have obligations. Debts . . ."

"Yes. They've been taken care of."

Finn blinked. "Excuse me?"

Again, Schnell opened the file. "Student loans, yes?" Finn nodded, silent. "They were paid off this morning. Our way of saying thank-you."

"Oh." He wasn't sure what else to say.

Schnell passed him a folder. Finn opened it. An airline ticket from Los Angeles to Heathrow. "I assume you have a passport?"

Finn nodded.

"Excellent. Then that's it. We'll talk again in London." The older man paused, looking at him over metal half-glasses. "Unless there's something else?"

Finn hesitated only a moment, and then he stood up. "No, sir. This is amazing. Thank you. Thank you very much."

"Don't thank me," Schnell said. "Just do your job. And do it well."

"Go get it, boy! Go on!" Amber laughed as Brinkley bounded after the tennis ball. She hadn't laughed in over twenty-four hours, and the noise sounded awkward to her ears.

Above her, a commercial jet swooshed by, heading east with its belly full of passengers. She swallowed, then sighed. Finn probably wasn't on that plane. But he was on a plane somewhere. Heading to London. Heading out of her life.

She'd taken a risk, and she'd paid the price. She'd wanted him to turn down the job, to stay with her. But it wasn't something she could ask him to do. What was that saying? If you love something, set it free? Well, she had. And he'd left.

She closed her eyes and counted to ten, telling herself that she'd made the right decision, no matter how much it hurt.

Behind her, she heard the unmistakable sound of tires crunching gravel. *Brandon.* She checked her watch. He was early. Not that she minded. Unlike any other moment in her life that she could remember, right then she craved company.

With Brinkley at her heels, she turned and walked to the front of the house. As they neared the corner, Brinkley started barking, bounding forward and then turning back as if to ask why she wasn't hurrying.

"I'm coming," she said, shaking her head in amusement. Brinkley had never been that excited about Brandon before.

But when she turned the corner, her heart started thudding wildly, as if she'd not only hurried, but had sprinted around the house. *Finn.* Crouched next to his beat-up Mustang, his fingers buried in Brinkley's fur.

"I— Aren't you supposed to be on a plane?"

"I said no." He stood up, looking rugged and sexy in an open flannel shirt over a white T-shirt.

She blinked, sure she'd misunderstood. "What?"

"You heard me."

She had heard him, but she wasn't sure if he'd really spoken the words or if it was just wishful thinking on her part. "You said no?"

He nodded.

"Why?" The word was almost a whisper, and she held her breath, knowing just how much was at stake with his answer.

"I love you, Amber." She saw him draw a deep

breath. "And I can't love you the way I want to if I'm in the Unit. You of all people should know that."

She couldn't help her smile. "You love me."

"Hell yes. I don't want the job," he said. "I want you." He took a deep breath, then moved closer, taking both of her hands in his own. *"I want you."* His mouth quirked into an ironic grin. "Even if it means keeping a job that I hate."

She licked her lips. "What if I told you that you didn't have to keep that job?"

His eyes narrowed. "What are you talking about?"

"Forget the Unit," she said. "Work for me." She raised both eyebrows, punctuating the point. "I promise I won't have any rules against fraternization."

Finn could only blink. "What are you talking about?"

"Freelance," she said. "The downside is there's no government sponsorship. No expensive gadgets ours for the taking. No support network. The upside is we work where we want and when we want. And the pay's a hell of a lot better. Interested?"

He was staring at her. "Interested? You know I am. But why the hell didn't you tell me sooner?"

There was anger in his voice, but mostly curiosity. She licked her lips, wanting him to understand why she'd walked away. "I needed to be sure," she said. "Hell, I needed *you* to be sure."

He shook his head, clearly not following.

"Don't you see? I didn't want you to wake up ten years from now wondering *what if*. Because if you did, I was going to be the one you looked at. The one who held you back."

"My choice," he said.

"Of course. But emotions don't work that way. I'd be the bad guy, and you'd start to resent me." This time she reached for his hand. "But now . . ."

"Now you know," he said. "We both do."

"So tell me, Mr. Teague. Are you in the market for a new job?"

"Oh yeah," he said, gathering her into his arms, where she belonged. "So long as you come with it, I'm very, very interested." He lowered his lips to hers, sealing their new pact with a kiss. It was heaven to kiss him. Pure, sweet heaven, and a rush of emotion crashed through her brain, wild and frantic.

She never even heard the man's approaching footsteps. Not until his gun was aimed at her back.

"Don't even think about moving," the voice said.

"Prado," Finn whispered. His head was up now, and he was facing behind her, looking at the man.

Amber started to turn.

"Oh, I don't think so. You just stay where you are. You two cost me a lot of money. I think you owe me."

"You can have whatever you want," Finn said. As he spoke, he stepped back from her, just slightly, the move almost imperceptible.

"Thanks," Prado said. "Considering I want you both dead, that's very generous."

Finn licked his lips. "Maybe we can work something out."

"Not damn likely," Prado said. "Now move away from the bitch," he said.

Amber couldn't see what was happening behind her, but she did see Finn's hand snake under the open shirt. And she saw the glint of a gun.

"I love you," she whispered.

His smile was his only response. And in one smooth motion she twisted to the left. He fired through his shirt, and Prado went down. The man didn't even have a chance.

Amber leaned against him, her palms flat against his chest. "Good shot."

"I'm glad you think so," he said, pulling her close. "That's one of my many, many talents." He met her eyes, and she saw the heat—and the love—reflected there. This was a man she could joke with and make love with. A man who'd watch her back. A man who'd never, ever let her go.

She lifted herself up onto her toes and gave him a quick kiss. "You know something, Mr. Teague? I think we're going to make one hell of a team."

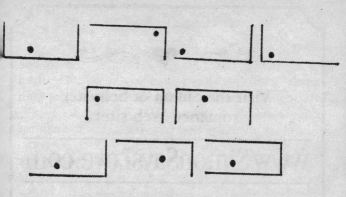

**Visit the Simon & Schuster
romance Web site:**

---

www.SimonSaysLove.com

**and sign up for our
romance e-mail updates!**

Keep up on the latest
new romance releases,
author appearances, news, chats,
special offers, and more!
We'll deliver the information
right to your inbox—if it's new,
you'll know about it.